The Constitution of India

Bare Act with Short Notes for Students

Third Edition

The Constitution of India

Bare Act with Short Notes for Students

Third Edition

A R Khan *Ph.D*

Title : The Constitution of India (Bare Act with Short Notes for Students)

Language : English

Author's Name : A R Khan

Typeset & Published by :

Career Launcher Infrastructure (P) Ltd.

A-45, Mohan Cooperative Industrial Area, Near Mohan Estate Metro Station, New Delhi - 110044

Marketed by :

G.K. Publications (P) Ltd.

Plot No. 9A, Sector-27A, Mathura Road, Faridabad, Haryana-121003

ISBN : **978-93-94168-36-7**

Printer's Details : Printed in India, New Delhi.

Preface to the Third Edition

The *third edition of *The Constitution of India : Bare Act with Short Notes for Students* is updated with **two Appendices** that further enhances the relevance of this book.

Appendix I

(a) Update on interpretations of Article 21.

(b) An update on Article 370 regarding Jammu and Kashmir (abrogated in August 2019)

(c) An update on Amendments in the First & Fourth Schedule

(d) An update on the Union Territories of India

Appendix II

It is a compilation of some key amendments done in our Constitution so far.

With these updates the book maintains its relevance in the present times.

We are hopeful that these updates would enhance the value of the book among the aspirants of various competitive examinations, especially the UPSC and state civil services examinations.

We wish all readers/aspirants the best in their endeavours.

The Publishers

**For a detailed insight on what this book is about please refer to Preface to*

Preface to the Second Edition

The Constitution of India is referred to as a lawyer's paradise for the kind of terminology adopted by the framers of our Constitution.

It was not an easy task to have a single Constitution for the country as diverse as India. In the process of accommodating all the complexities of governance, the framers of the Constitution adopted technical terms. These terms have their exclusive connotation and denotation. To be able to understand the Constitution in true perspective, it is important to understand its terms.

This updated new edition aims to present a simplified version of the elephantine Constitution of the largest democracy in the world.

The Constitution is the most sacred law of our country. It touches all of us, in all walks of life. It is therefore expected that all the aspiring Civil Servants understand the intricacies of the Constitution.

Students appearing for various competitive examinations usually have a common paper of General Studies/General Knowledge. Competitive examinations expect students to know the working of the Indian political system. The political system is based on the structure defined by the Indian Constitution. It is therefore, essential to know the Indian Constitution to understand the political system of India.

During the course of teaching General Studies in the last two decades, I have encountered many [illegible] ough, there are many books on the [illegible] such books assume students to [illegible] to start understanding Indian

the Second Edition.

[illegible] ution. One might ask, why one [illegible] keeping in mind students who may not have formally studied the Indian Constitution beyond their school level. The notes given in this book are simple and short. Students are advised to use the index to make multiple cross references and understand the articles in a holistic manner.

I would like to express a deep sense of gratitude to clique KSG and students who have been my motivation all along. This book is dedicated to them. My love goes to Heira and Humd, my emotional driving force. I must also thank V Biju Kumar and Abhishek Sharma of Access Publishing for their patience and for being able to bear with my request of all kinds to make this book more useful for the competitive examinations.

A R Khan

CONTENTS

THE CONSTITUTION OF INDIA

PREAMBLE

WE, THE PEOPLE OF INDIA, having solemnly resolved to constitute India into a [1][SOVEREIGN SOCIALIST SECULAR DEMOCRATIC REPUBLIC] and to secure to all its citizens:

JUSTICE, social, economic and political;

LIBERTY of thought, expression, belief, faith and worship;

EQUALITY of status and of opportunity;

and to promote among them all

FRATERNITY assuring the dignity of the individual and the [2][unity and integrity of the Nation];
IN OUR CONSTITUENT ASSEMBLY this twenty-sixth day of November, 1949, do HEREBY ADOPT, ENACT AND GIVE TO OURSELVES THIS CONSTITUTION.

Notes on Preamble

Analysis

The Preamble embodies the fundamental values and the philosophy on which the Indian Constitution is based. The aims and objectives of the Constitution are amply reflected in the Preamble. The preamble to our constitution makes a solemn resolve to constitute India into a "Sovereign Socialist Secular Democratic Republic" securing for all its citizens justice, liberty and equality, promoting among them fraternity. The noble ideal of justice is further defined in terms of social, economic and political justice. Similarly, liberty finds its realization in liberty of thought, expression, belief, faith and worship and equality, which means equality of status and of opportunity.

In fact, justice, liberty and equality are the basic traits of a democratic order and therefore their inclusion in Preamble to the Indian Constitution elucidates the concept of a democratic republic. Thus, the preamble serves two purposes. First, it declares in unequivocal terms that the people of India are the source of all authority under the Constitution and that sovereignty resides with the people. Obviously, Indian polity is democratic with fundamental rights and freedom guaranteed to the people. Secondly, the Preamble states the objectives (e.g. justice, liberty, equality and fraternity) which the Constitution seeks to establish and promote.

In this connection two recent judgements of the Supreme Court deserve mention. It is well accepted by thinkers, philosophers and academicians that if JUSTICE, LIBERTY, EQUALITY and FRATERNITY, including social, economic and political justice, the golden goals set out in the Preamble of the Constitution, are to be achieved, the Indian polity has to be educated and educated with excellence; *P.A. Inamdar v. State of Maharashtra*, (2005) 6SCC 537.

In the constitutional set up every citizen is under a duty to abide by the Constitution and respect its ideals and institutions; Official Liquidator v. Dayanand, (2008) 10 SCC 1.

Judicial decisions

The debate on whether the Preamble is a part of the Constitution or not started with the case of *Gopalan v. State of Madras, 1950*. In this case, the Supreme Court ruled that Preamble is not enforceable in a Court of law. In the Berubari case (1960), the Supreme Court observed that

1 Subs. by the Constitution (Forty-second Amendment) Act, 1976, sec.2(a), for "SOVEREIGN DEMOCRATIC REPUBLIC" (w.e.f. 3-1-1977).

2 Subs. by the Constitution (Forty-second Amendment) Act, 1976, sec.2(b), for "unity of the Nation" (w.e.f. 3-1-1977).

the Preamble was the basis for understanding the minds of the framers of the Constitution. The Preamble helps in the legal interpretation of the Constitution where language or word is found to be ambiguous. Nevertheless, Justice Gajendragadkar opined that the Preamble was not a part of the Constitution.

Decisive shift

In "Sajjan Singh Vs. State of Rajasthan" Justice Madholkar highlighted the importance of the Preamble by observing that the Preamble had the stamp of "deep deliberation", that it was "marked by precision" and "the framers of the Constitution attached special significance to it". The Preamble was "an epitome" of the basic features of the Constitution and those basic features were deduced from the concepts enshrined in the Preamble. In another landmark Judgment "*Golak Nath v. State of Punjab*, Justice Hidayatullah observed that "the Preamble provides the basic principle on which the government is to function". The Preamble is the very "soul of the Constitution–eternal and unalterable."

Thus, in the cases mentioned above, there was a clear departure from the earlier stand of the Supreme Court in the Berubari case. The case established in no uncertain terms that the preamble is very much a part of the Constitution.

Basic structure of Constitution

In *Keshavnand Bharti v. State of Kerala, (AIR 1973 SC 1461)*, the Supreme Court held that the Preamble was a part of the Constitution and it was of extreme importance. "The constitution should be read and interpreted in the light of the noble vision expressed in the Preamble. Amendment to any of the provisions of the constitution could be made under Article 368 only within the broad contours of the preamble. In the words of the learned Court, "The edifice of our constitution is based upon the basic elements mentioned in the Preamble". If any of these elements are removed, the structure will not survive and it will not be the same Constitution or it cannot maintain its identity.

Thus, it has been conclusively established that no amendment under Article 368 can be made to alter the basic features or elements of the Constitution as contained in the Preamble. This was reiterated in three other judgments of the Supreme Court viz.:

(*i*) *Indira Gandhi v. Raj Narain AiR 1975 SC 2299*
(*ii*) *Minerva Mills Ltd. v. Union of India, AIR 1980 SC 1789* (*Majority*)
(*iii*) *S.R. Bommai v. Union of India, JT (1994) 2 SC 215*

Secularism

Pluralism is the quintessence of Indian culture and religious tolerance is the hallmark of Indian secularism. Here, it is widely believed that all religions are good and efficacious pathways to the perfection of God realization;

Valsamma Paul v. Cochin University, AIR 1996 SC 1011, paragraph 25.

Idealism: socialism

The ideal of socialism finds an important place in our Constitution. The word, 'socialist' (read with articles 14 and 16), made it easier for the Courts to deduce a fundamental right to equal pay for equal work. This again (if we read it with Article 14) enables the Court to declare a statute void, which fails to achieve the socialist goals. The relevant decisions in this regard are:

(*i*) *Excel Wear v. Union of India, AIR 1979 SC 25, paragraph 24.*
(*ii*) *Atam Prakash v. State of Haryana, AIR 1986 SC 859, paragraph 5.*
(*iii*) *Randhir v. Union of India, AIR 1982 SC 879, paragraph 8.*
(*iv*) *Nakara v. Union of India, AIR 1983 SC 130, paragraphs 33-34.*

Interpretation of the Preamble

In *Bharti Chandra Bhavan v. State of Mysore (AIR 1970 SC 2042, paragraph 13),* the Supreme Court observed that the Preamble may be of substantial help in determining the ambit of Directive Principles and Fundamental Rights. Two decisions may be cited in this context.

(*i*) *Keshavanand Bharti v. State of Kerala, AIR 1973 SC 1461*

(*ii*) *Dharwad District P.W.D. Leterate Daily wage Employees Association v. State of Karnataka (1990) 2 SCC 396, paragraphs 14-27.*

Social justice

The rights to social and economic justice as envisaged in the Preamble and enumerated in Fundamental Rights and Directive Principles vide articles 14, 15(4), 16 (4) 38, 39 and 46 are meant for making the life of the poor, disadvantaged and disabled citizens of the society, meaningful. The concept of social justice has enabled the Courts to uphold legislation –

a. to remove economic inequalities

b. to protect the interest of the weaker sections of the society.

Undermentioned decisions are relevant on this point:

(I) *Lingappa v. State of Maharashtra, AIR 1985 SC 389, paragraphs 14, 16, 18 and 20*

(II) *Nakara v. Union of India, AIR 1983 SC 130, paragraphs 33-34.*

(III) *Sadhuram v. Polin, AIR 1984 SC 1471, paragraphs 29, 70, 73.*

Res extra commercium

The doctrine of *res extra commercium* cannot be extended to prohibit employment of women in Hotels and Bars serving liquor; *Anuj Garg v. Hotel Association of India*, AIR 2008 SC 663.

PART - I

THE UNION AND ITS TERRITORY

1. Name and territory of the Union -

(1) India, that is Bharat, shall be a Union of States.

[1][(2) The States and the territories thereof shall be as specified in the First Schedule.]

(3) The territory of India shall comprise–

(a) the territories of the States;

[2][(b) the Union territories specified in the First Schedule; and.]

(c) such other territories as may be acquired.

Notes on Article 1

The Union of India is a federal one, with a clear-cut distribution of powers between centre and the units. An independent and impartial judiciary ensures that the above scheme should remain intact. Although there has been considerable controversy over the nature of Indian federalism and some commentators have dubbed it "quasi federal", a thorough analysis would show that the Indian constitution is basically a federal one; special reference of 1956, AIR 1965 SC 745, 762.

1 Subs. by the Constitution (Seventh Amendment) Act, 1956, sec.2, for clause (1)(a). (w.e.f. 1-11-1956)

2 Subs. by the Constitution (Seventh Amendment) Act, 1956, sec.2(1)(b), for sub-clause (b). (w.e.f. 1-11-1956)

Territory of India

The expression "territory of India", wherever used, suggests the territory which comes within the ambit of Art. 1(3). See the undermentioned decisions:

(*i*) *Thakur Amar Singh V. State of Rajasthan,* AIR 1955 SC 504.

(*ii*) *N. Masthan Sahib V. Chief Commissioner, Pondicherry,* AIR 1962 SC 797, 803.

Action subsequent to acquisition

Foreign territories acceding to India on acquisition may (i) either be admitted into the Union, or (ii) constituted into new States under article 2, or (iii) merged into an existing State under article 3(a) or 3(b), or (iv) formed into a union territory. Of course, a foreign territory would not come under article 1(3)(c) until it is legally transferred to India, as such to constitute its "acquisition" in international law. The undermentioned decisions are the pointers:

(*i*) *Harivansh V. State of Maharashtra,* (1971) 2 SCC 54, 56.

(*ii*) *Masthan Sahib V. Chief Commissioner, Pondicherry,* AIR 1962 SC 797.

(*iii*) *Amar Singh V. State of Rajasthan,* AIR 1955 SC 504.

2. **Admission or establishment of new States:** Parliament may by law admit into the Union, or establish, new States on such terms and conditions as it thinks fit.

[1][2A. **Sikkim to be associated with the Union-** *[Rep. by the Constitution (Thirty sixth Amendment), Act, 1975, sec. 5(a) (w.e.f. 26-4-1975).]*

3. **Formation of new States and alteration of areas, boundaries or names of existing States**. Parliament may by law-

(a) form a new State by separation of territory from any State or by uniting two or more States or parts of States or by uniting any territory to a part of any State;

(b) increase the area of any State;

(c) diminish the area of any State;

(d) alter the boundary of any State;

(e) alter the name of any State:

[2][Provided that no Bill for the purpose shall be introduced in either House of Parliament except on the recommendation of the President and unless, where the proposal contained in the Bill affects the area, boundaries or name of any of the States[3]***, the Bill has been referred by the President to the Legislature of that State for expressing its views thereon within such period as may be specified in the reference or within such further period as the President may allow and the period so specified or allowed has expired.]

[4][Explanation I : In this article, in clauses (a) to (e) , "State" includes a Union territory, but in the provision, "State" does not include a Union Territory.

Explanation II: The power conferred on Parliament by clause (a) includes the power to form a new State or Union territory by uniting a part of any State or Union territory to any other State or Union territory.]

---

1 Ins. by the Constitution (Thirty-fifth Amendment) Act, 1974, sec.2 (w.e.f. 1.3.1975).

2 Subs. by the Constitution (Fifth Amendment) Act, 1955, sec.2, for the proviso(w.e.f. 24.12.1955).

3 The words and letters "specified in Part A and Part B of the First Schedule" omitted by the Constitution (Seventh Amendment) Act, 1956, sec.29 and Sch(w.e.f. 1.11.1956).

4 Ins. by the Constitution (Eighteenth Amendment) Act, 1966, Sec.2.

Notes on Article 3

Effects of re-organisation of territory under existing laws

A re-organisation of territory of a state under Article 3 is not affected by the principles relating to a change of sovereignty in international law. On the re-organisation of territories, the existing laws as well as administrative order remains in force unless they are modified, changed or repudiated.

Reference of Bills: No fresh reference is required every time an amendment to the Bill is moved and accepted according to the rules of procedure in parliament if the original bill is referred to the state or states. In Babulal v. State of Bombay AIR 1960 SC 51, it was held that the parliament is not bound to accept or act upon the views of the state legislatures.

4. Laws made under articles 2 and 3 to provide for the amendment of the First and the Fourth Schedules and supplemental, incidental and consequential matters.

(1) Any law referred to in article 2 or article 3 shall contain such provisions for the amendment of the First Schedule and the Fourth Schedule as may be necessary to give effect to the provisions of the law and may also contain such supplemental, incidental and consequential provisions (including provisions as to representation in Parliament and in the Legislature or Legislatures of the State or States affected by such law) as Parliament may deem necessary.

(2) No such law as aforesaid shall be deemed to be an amendment of this Constitution for the purposes of article 368.

Note on Article 4

Legislative power of state:- State cannot claim to have legislative powers over waters in question; Mullaperiyar Environmental protection forum vs union of India, AIR 2006.

Levy of Penalty :- State has power to levy Penalty; State of Bihar v. Industrial corporation Pvt. Ltd. AIR 2004.

PART II

CITIZENSHIP

5. **Citizenship at the commencement of the Constitution-** At the commencement of this Constitution, every person who has his domicile in the territory of India and

(a) who was born in the territory of India; or

(b) either of whose parents was born in the territory of India; or

(c) who has been ordinarily resident in the territory of India for not less than five years immediately preceding such commencement, shall be a citizen of India.

Notes on Article 5

Every Person

The expression "every person" also includes-

(a) a prisoner;

(b) a member of the armed forces (but subject to article 33)

See the following judgement of the Supreme court:

(i) State of Maharashtra v. Prabhakar, AIR 1966 SC 424, 426.

(ii) Sunil Batra v. Delhi Admn., AIR 1978 SC 1675.

(iii) Lt. Col. Prithvi Pal Singh Bedi v. Union of India, AIR 1982 SC 1813, paragraph 45.

One Domicile

The Indian Constitution provides for only one domicile viz, the domicile of the country and there is no separate domicile for a state; *Pradeep v. Union of India,* AIR 1984 SC 1420,

In Chandigarh Housing Board v. Gurmit Singh (2002) 2 SCC 29, the meaning of domicile was given and was held that it means a person must be having permanent home in Chandigarh or he being there for years with the intention to live permanently or indefinitely.

6. Rights of citizenship of certain persons who have migrated to India from Pakistan.- Notwithstanding anything in article, 5, a person who has migrated to the territory of India from the territory now included in Pakistan shall be deemed to be a citizen of India at the commencement of this Constitution if–

(a) he or either of his parents or any of his grand-parents was born in India as defined in the Government of India Act, 1935 (as originally enacted); and

(b) (i) in the case where such person has so migrated before the nineteenth day of July, 1948, he has been ordinarily resident in the territory of India since the date of his migration, or

(ii) in the case where such person has so migrated on or after the nineteenth day of July, 1948, he has been registered as a citizen of India by an officer appointed in that behalf by the Government; of the Dominion of India on an application made by him therefore to such officer before the commencement of this Constitution in the form and manner prescribed by that Government:

Provided that no person shall be so registered unless he has been resident in the territory of India for at least six months immediately preceding the date of his application.

7. **Rights of citizenship of certain migrants to Pakistan** -Notwithstanding anything in articles 5 and 6, a person who has after the first day of March, 1947, migrated from the territory of India to the territory now included in Pakistan, shall not be deemed to be a citizen of India:

Provided that nothing in this article shall apply to a person who, after having so migrated to the territory now included in Pakistan, has returned to the territory of India under a permit for resettlement or permanent return issued by or under the authority of any law and every such person shall for the purposes of clause (b) of article 6 be deemed to have migrated to the territory of India after the nineteenth day of July, 1948.

8. Rights of citizenship of certain persons of Indian origin residing outside India.-Notwithstanding anything in article 5, any person who or either of whose parents or any of whose grand-parents was born in India as defined in the Government of India Act, 1935 (as originally enacted), and who is ordinarily residing in any country outside India as so defined shall be deemed to be a citizen of India if he has been registered as a citizen of India by the diplomatic or consular representative of India in the country where he is for the time being residing on an application made by him therefore to such diplomatic or consular representative, whether before or after the commencement of this Constitution, in the form and manner prescribed by the Government of the Dominion of India or the Government of India.

9. Persons voluntarily acquiring citizenship of a foreign State not to be citizens.-No person shall be a citizen of India by virtue of article 5, or be deemed to be a citizen of India by virtue of article 6 or article 8, if he has voluntarily acquired the citizenship of any foreign State.

Notes on Article 9

Section 9(2) of the citizenship Act, 1955 gives the central government exclusive jurisdiction to decide the question whether a person, who was a citizen of India, has lost that citizenship by acquiring the citizenship of a foreign state. No court can decide such matter. A state government can determine the question only when the function is delegated by the central government under Article 258.

Obtaining Passport

Mere obtaining passport, by a person from a foreign country would not suffice to sustain an order for deportation or prosecution, unless there has been a decision of the Central Government under section 9(2), Citizenship Act, 1955. The inquiry by the Central Government under this section is quasi-judicial. We may enumerate these decisions.

(i) *Govt. of Andhra Pradesh v. Syed Md., AIR 1962 SC 1778; State of U.P. v. Roshan, (1969) 2 SCWR 232, 233.*

(ii) *State of U.P. v. Rahimatullah, AIR 1971 SC 1382.*

(iii) *Ayub Khan v. Commissioner of Police (1965) 2 SCR 884; Moinuddin v. Govt of India, (1967) 2 SCR 401.*

10. Continuance of the rights of citizenship-Every person who is or is deemed to be a citizen of India under any of the foregoing provisions of this Part shall, subject to the provisions of any law that may be made by Parliament, continue to be such Citizen.

11. Parliament to regulate the right of citizenship by law.-Nothing in the foregoing provisions of this Part shall derogate from the power of Parliament to make any provision with respect to the acquisition and termination of citizenship and all other matters relating to citizenship.

PART III

FUNDAMENTAL RIGHTS

General

12. Definition- In this part, unless the context otherwise requires, "the State" includes the Government and Parliament of India and the Government and the Legislature of each of the States and all local or other authorities within the territory of India or under the control of the Government of India.

Notes on Article 12

Local authorities : writ

A local authority harbouring a legal grievance is in a position to take out a writ. Thus, on the petition of a local authority a writ was issued against a public utility concern for its failure to fulfil statutory obligation to supply power to the local authority, a consumer; *Corporation of city of Nagpur v. N.E.L. & P.Co.,* AIR 1958Bom 498.

State

The definition of "State" is not limited to the Government and the Legislature only rather it extends to any action-administrative (whether statutory or non-statutory), judicial or quasi-judicial, which may come within the fold of 'state action' and said action goes to violate a fundamental right. See the decisions below:

(i) *Ramana v. International Airport Authority of India,* AIR 1979 SC 1628, 1638, paragraphs 14-16; *State of Punjab v. Raja Ram,* AIR 1981 SC 1694, paragraph 5.

(ii) *Gulam v. State of Uttar Pradesh,* AIR 1981 SC 2198, paragraph 23.

(iii) *Som Prakash v. Union of India,* AIR 1981 SC 212, paragraphs 34, 37.

Even actions of a broadly private body may come within the ambit of "State action"; *Mahabir Auto Stores v. Indian Oil Corporation, (*1990*)* 3 SCC 752.

Other authorities

Judicial decisions have widened the scope of the expression "other authorities" in article 12. The concept of "instrumentality or agency" of the state has evolved. A "department of the government" is a major component of this concept. The concept embraces every public authority weilding statutory powers, every authority created by Legislature and even a non-statutory authority exercising public functions.

Undermentioned decisions may be cited in this connection:

(i) *Som Prakash v. Union of India,* AIR 1981 SC 212;

(ii) *State of Punjab v. Raja Ram,* (1981) 2 SCC 66, paragraphs 9-10.

(iii) *Umesh Chandra v. V.N. Singh,* AIR 1967 Pat 3, 9 (FB).

Board of Control for Cricket in India (BCCI)

BCCI is not financially, functionally or administratively dominated by Government nor it is under control of Government, therefore not a State; *Zee Telefilms Ltd. V. Union of India*, AIR 2005 SC 2677.

State — meaning of

Assam Small Scale Industries Development Corporation Ltd. is a statutory body and so is a 'State' within the meaning of Article 12 of Constitution of India; *Assam Small Scale Ind. Dev. Corporation Ltd. v. J. D. Pharmaceuticals*, AIR 2006 SC 131.

The Central Coal Fields Ltd. falls within the definition of State; *Mohan Mahto v. Central Coal Fields Ltd.* (2007) 8 SCC 549

13. Laws inconsistent with or in derogation of the fundamental rights.

(1) All laws in force in the territory of India immediately before the commencement of this Constitution, in so far as they are inconsistent with the provisions of this Part, shall, to the extent of such inconsistency, be void.

(2) The State shall not make any law which takes away or abridges the rights conferred by this Part and any law made in contravention of this clause shall, to the extent of the contravention, be void.

(3) In this article, unless the context otherwise requires,

(a) "law" includes any Ordinance, order, by-law, rule, regulation, notification, custom or usage having in the territory of India the force of law;

(b) "laws in force" includes laws passed or made by a Legislature or other competent authority in the territory of India before the commencement of this Constitution and not previously repealed, notwithstanding that any such law or any part thereof may not be then in operation either at all or in particular areas.

[1][(4) Nothing in this article shall apply to any amendment of this Constitution made under article 368.]

Notes on Article 13

Article 13 makes the chapter of "Fundamental Rights" sacrosanct and thus secures the **paramountcy** of the Constitution in this regard. This serves as a bulwark against the executive and legislative excesses. Clearly the main object of this article is to act as limitations upon the powers of the executive and legislature. The judiciary has been given an exalted position. If the Parliament enacts a law transgressing any of the limitations, the Supreme Court and the High Courts are competent to declare that law unconstitutional or void. The important point to be

[1] Ins. by the Constitution (Twenty-fourth Amendment) Act, 1971, sec.2 (w.e.f 5–11-1971)

noted here is that fundamental rights as such, though not immune from constitutional amendment, may, in some cases, form part of the "theory of basic features" enunciated in certain decisions of the Supreme Court. Important decisions of the Supreme Court on this subject may be listed as under:

(i) *Golak Nath v. State of Punjab,* AIR 1967 SC 1643.

(ii) *Keshavanada Bharati v. State of Kerala,* AIR 1973 SC 1461, which, while upholding the validity of the Constitution (24th Amendment) inserting article 13(4), laid down the theory that there were certain basic features which couldn't be amended under the constituent power of the Parliament.

(iii) *Minerva Mills Ltd. v. Union of India,* AIR 1980 SC 1789 - The 42nd Amendment sought to restore the unlimited constituent power of the Parliament to amend the constitution. This was invalidated by the Supreme Court in the above case, adhering to the docrtine of "basic features". The Supreme Court, further, pronounced that a constitutional amendment which relates to a basic feature (e.g. total exclusion of judicial review) would be void.

Right to Equality

14. Equality before law.- The State shall not deny to any person equality before the law or the equal protection of the laws within the territory of India.

Notes on Article 14

Meaning and exceptions

The first expression 'equality before the law' is somewhat a negative concept and has been taken from the Irish Constitution and is of English origin. The concept implies absence of any special privilege on the grounds of birth, creed or the like in favour of any individual. Every person is subject to the jurisdiction of ordinary courts and no person is above law. The latter expression "equal protection of laws" is a positive concept taken from the American Constitution and implies the right to equality of treatment in equal circumstances. However, the Indian constitution recognizes certain exceptions to the above rule of 'equality before the law' and "the equal protection of laws". Thus the constitution does give certain privileges to the President, the Governor and members of Parliament and State Legislatures.

The President or the Governor of a state shall not be answerable to any court for the exercise of his powers and duties of his office. Similarly no civil or criminal proceeding shall be instituted against the President or the Governor in any court during his term of office.

Similarly, there are some provisions in the statutory framework of India which introduce or maintain a certain amount of inequality between Government officers and ordinary citizens. For a suit against the Govt. or a Government officer, a two months' notice is ordinarily required under Section 80 of the Code of Civil Procedure 1908. Likewise, no criminal proceeding can be initiated against a public servant without previous sanction of the Central Government or the State Government (as the case may be) under section 197 of the Code of Criminal Procedure, 1973.

The second concept "equal protection of the Laws" means "that among equals the law should be equal and equally administered, that like should be treated alike. But here is an exception. Equal protection requires positive action by the State towards unequals by providing facilities and opportunities. The case below illustrates this:

Panchayat Varga Shramajivi Samudaik Sahakari Khedut Cooperative Society v. Haribhai Mevabhai, AIR 1996 SC 2578.

Elaboration

"Equal Protection of Laws" means the right to equal treatment in similar circumstances both in the privileges conferred and in the liabilities imposed by the laws. None should be favoured and none should be discriminated against in circumstances that do not admit of any reasonable justification for a different treatment.

Thus, if there is some reasonable basis for classification, the legislature is empowered to make provisions for a different treatment with a section of the society. In the case of *Anukul Chandra Pradhan v. Union of India*, 1997, the Supreme Court upheld the competence of the legislature to exercise discretion and make classification. The legislature has the final authority to identify the people to be given protection and to decide the basis for such protection.

Courts in India have upheld legislations containing seemingly discriminatory provisions where the discrimination is based on a reasonable basis (protective discrimination). "Reasonable" means that a classification must not be arbitrary but must be rational. The classical test as judicially enunciated in 1952 requires the fulfilment of two conditions, namely:

1. that the classification must be founded on an intelligible differentia which distinguishes those that are grouped together from others; and
2. that differentia must have a rational relation to the object sought to be achieved by the law. Judicial decisions highlighting the important propositions on the subject may be listed as under:
   - *i.* *Chiranjitlal v. Union of India*, (1950) SCR 869.
   - *ii.* *State of West Bengal v. Anwar Ali*, (1952) SCR 284.
   - *iii.* *Yusuf V. State of Bombay,* AIR 1954 SC 321.
   - *iv.* *Chitralekha v. State of Mysore*, AIR 1964 SC 1823, 1827.
   - *v.* *Atam Prakash v. State of Haryana* AIR 1986 SC 859.

Reasonableness

An important outcome of the "Right to Equality" is the element of reasonableness. Any classification which is unreasonable i.e. without any sufficient reason, is open to challenge and to this extent the policy of legislation is subject to judicial review. This aspect is reflected in the following decisions:

- *i.* *Northern India Caterers v. State of Punjab,* AIR 1967 SC 1581.
- *ii.* *N.M.C.S. Mills v. Ahemdabad Municipality,* AIR 1967 SC 1801, 1810.
- *iii.* *Nagpur Improvement Trust v. Luther,* AIR 1973 SC 689, 694.

Arbitrary action and discretion

Legislations which empower the executive to select cases for special treatment without indicating the rationale of the policy may be annulled as violative of equality. Following decisions may be cited in this connection:

- *i.* *State of Bengal v. Anwar Ali*, (1952) SCR 284.
- *ii.* *Meenakshi Mills v. Vishwanath,* AIR 1955 SC 13.
- *iii.* *Avinder v. State of Punjab,* AIR 1979 SC 321, paragraph 9.
- *iv.* *Ajit Singh v. State of Punjab,* AIR 1967 SC 885, 886.

The law provides for special treatment to Government or other public bodies was held not to be discriminatory; but from that it does not follow that every law which gives differential treatment to Govt. or other public bodies is necessarily immune from challenge on the ground of discrimination; *Maganlal Changalal (P.) Ltd. V. Municipal Corpn. Of Greater Bombay,* (1974) 2SCC 402: AIR 1974 SC 2009: (1975) 1 SCR I.

Backward Areas

Discrimination protecting persons residing in backward areas is permissible as in "*M.P. Oil Extraction v. State of Madhya Pradesh,* (1997) 7 SCC 592".

Ban on Sex Selection

A prospective mother who does not want to bear a child of a particular sex cannot be equated with a mother who wants to terminate the pregnancy not because of the sex of the child but because of other circumstances laid down under the Medical Termination of Pregnancy Act; *Vijay Sharma v. Union of India*, AIR 2008 Bom 29.

Board of Control for Cricket in India (BCCI)

BCCI enjoys monopoly status as regards to the regulation of the sport of cricket in India. It exercises enormous public functions, hence is bound to follow doctrine of fairness and good faith in all its activities; *Board of Control of Cricket, India v. Netaji Cricket Club,* AIR 2005 SC 592.

Defection

Defection-Para 2(2) of Tenth Schedule prohibiting independent candidates from joining any political party after his election as an independent candidate is not discriminatory; *Imkong Imchen V. Union of India*, AIR 2006 Gua 1

Cable T.V. and Doordarshan

Legislation taxing the cable television cannot be questioned merely on the ground that similar tax is not levied on Doordarshan. Doordarshan is not run for commercial purposes and revenue accruing from advertisements is meant for defraying expenses;

A. Suresh v. State of Tamil Nadu, AIR 1997 SC 1889.

Doctrine of natural justice

Article 14 of the constitution may be seen as the biggest effort in bringing about justice in the Indian society. Here it may be noted that the Preamble to the constitution speaks of equality of status and of opportunity. This Article seems to be enriching and expanding this objective. However, no conscious effort has been made to define the doctrine of natural justice in a specific manner. Compliance of the doctrine depends heavily upon the facts and circumstances of each case. For a proper understanding, the totality of the situation should be taken into consideration. If we examine such totality, we find that the executive action suffers from the vice of non-compliance of the doctrine. In that event law courts should set right the wrong inflicted upon the concerned person and this is what our judiciary is doing. In fact, the doctrine is now being perceived as synonym of fairness in the concept of justice and stands as the most accepted methodology of governmental action;

Kumaon Mandal Vikas Nigam Ltd. V. Girija Shankar Pant, AIR 2001 SC 24.

The concept of equality and equal protection of laws in its proper spectrum encompasses social and economic justice in a political democracy like ours.

Dalmia Cement (Bharat) Ltd. V. Union of India (1996) 10 SCC 104. See also notes on "Preamble".

Equality: The equality clause under Article 14 guarantees equality before law or equal protection of laws within the territory of India. However differential treatment can be made if classification is a reasonable one and is based on intelligible differentia having nexus with the object sought to be achieved.

Concept of equality cannot be pressed to commit another wrong; *Kastha Niwarak G.S.S. Maryadit, Indore v. President, Indore Development Authority,* AIR 2006 SC 1142

Equals and unequal: It has been held that equal treatment of unequal will bring inequality and unequal treatment of unequal will bring equality. In St. Stephens College v. University of Delhi (1992) 1 SCC 558, the apex court held that unequal are not only permitted to be treated unequally but also they have to be so treated. On the same ground 'creamy layer' in the Backward class is treated on par with the forward class to avoid the violation of Article 14, 16(1) and 16(14).

The superiors of disabled employees are duty bound to follow law and it is not open to them to allow their bias to defeat their lawful rights.

What the law permits to them is no charity or largesse but their right as equal citizens of the country; *Bhagwan Dass v. Punjab State Electricity Board*, AIR 2008 SC 990.

Equal pay for equal work

The doctrine of equal pay for equal work postulates equal pay for equal work for those who are equally placed in all respects, *Uttar Pradesh Sugar Corpn. Ltd. v. Sant Raj Singh,* AIR 2006 SC 2296.

Illegal action

Equality clause cannot be applied to legitimize an illegal action; *Ekta Shakti Foundation v. Govt. of NCT of Delhi*, AIR 2006 SC 2609.

Illegalities cannot be perpetuated

Where unauthorized construction by appellant in violation of building by-laws and terms and conditions in lease deed prejudicially affecting proper planning of industrial area, he cannot claim that benefit extended to others though illegally should be extended to him. Articles 14 provides for positive equality and not negative equality; *Vishal Properties Pvt. Ltd. v. State of Uttar Pradesh*, AIR 2008 SC 183.

Mala fide

Action taken by State in undue haste may be held to be *mala fide*; *Inderpreet Singh Kahlon v. State of Punjab*, AIR 2006 SC 2571.

Reasonable restriction

A limited power of exemption from the operation of noise rules granted by the Central Government in exercise of its statutory powers is not unreasonable. The power to grant exemption is a reasonable restriction placed in public interest; *Forum, Prevention of Enun. & Sound Pollution v. Union of India*, AIR 2006 SC 348.

Right to have reasoned order

The Courts though are not liable to furnish the information like public bodies are still expected to reveal reasons in order; *Kasim Maraikkayar v. Haji Kathija Beevi Trust, Nagapattinam*, AIR 2008 Mad 91.

Scope

Article 14 has a positive concept. No body can claim equality in illegality; *Uttar Pradesh State Sugar Corpn. Ltd. v. Sant Raj Singh*, AIR 2006 SC 2296

Power granted by a provision may be abused and cannot merely be ground to declare provision unconstitutional; *Ahmed Noormohammed Bhatti v. State of Gujarat*, AIR 2005 SC 2115

State Policy

Issuance of notification/circulars giving concessions to entrepreneurs for rapid industrialization cannot be said to be against provisions of law; *Parenteral Drugs India Ltd. v. State of Himachal Pradesh*, AIR 2008 (NOC 380 (HP).

Limitations: Judicial decisions recognize the need of consideration of reality to have certain limitations while interpreting Article 14. Article 14 has two parts. The first part carries the negative concept while the second part has the positive concept. **Dices** thinks the first part as a second corollary of rule of law and denies any special privilege, but certain privileges to the president, the governor, members of the parliament and state legislatures are given by the constitution.

15. Prohibition of discrimination on grounds of religion, race, caste, sex or place of birth.

(1) The State shall not discriminate against any citizen on grounds only of religion, race, caste, sex, place of birth or any of them.

(2) No citizen shall, on grounds only of religion, race, sex, place of birth or any of them, be subject to any disability, liability, restriction or condition with regard to-

(a) access to shops, public restaurants, hotels and places of public entertainment; or

(b) the use of wells, tanks, bathing ghats, roads and places of public resort maintained wholly or partly out of State funds or dedicated to the use of general public.

(3) Nothing in this article shall prevent the State from making any special provision for women and children.

[1][(4) Nothing in this article or in clause (2) of article 29 shall prevent the State from making any special provision for the advancement of any socially and educationally backward classes of citizens or for the Scheduled Castes and the Scheduled Tribes.]

[2](5) Nothing in this article or in sub – clause (g) of clause (1) of article 19 shall prevent the state from making any special provision, by law, for the advancement of any socially and eductionally backward classes of citizens or for the Scheduled Castes or the Scheduled Tribes in so far as such special provisions relate to their admission to educational institutions including private educational institutions whether aided or unaided by the state, other than the minority educational institutions referred to in clause (1) of article 30.

Notes on Article 15

Relationship with Article 14

The Principle of equality laid down in Article 14 has its manifestation in Article 15 and some of the succeeding articles. Article 15 deals with particular aspects of the principle of equality in greater detail but it should be noted at the very outset that Article 15 is available to citizens only, while article 14 extends to all. Secondly, Article 15(1) and (2) prohibits discrimination on the grounds of religion, race, sex, place of birth or any of them. Article 14 advocates the absence of discrimination in general. Thirdly, there is a faint reference of protective discrimination in Article 14, while Article 15 permits the state to make special provisions for women and children. The Article further empowers the state to make special provisions for the following:

a. Socially and educationally backward classes of people

b. Scheduled Castes, and

c. Scheduled Tribes.

Discrimination

The crucial word here in this Article is 'discrimination' which in common parlance means 'making an adverse distinction with regard to, or 'distinguishing unfavourably from others; *Kathi Rani Rawat v. State of Saurashtra* (1952) SCR 435, 442. Another crucial word is 'only'. If the discrimination is based on some rational factors, it would be valid.

1 Added by the Constitution (First Amendment) Act, 1951, sec. 2 (w.e.f. 18.6.1951)

2 Inserted by the constitution (Ninety – third Amendment) Act 2005 sec. 2 (w.e.f. 20.1.2006).

Discrimination on grounds of sex

The exclusion of women not exclusively based on sex but taking into consideration peculiar nature of duties to be performed by electricity workers is not violative of Article 15 of Constitution; *Kerala State Electricity Board, Thiruvanathapuram v. Siniya Mol C.S.*, AIR 2008 (NOC) 730 (Ker).

Reservation

Children born out of inter-caste marriage, in which either father or mother belongs to SC/ST category can claim reservation benefits only on proof that he is subjected to some handicap and disadvantages having been born as member of SC/ST; *M.C. Valsala v. State of Kerala*, AIR 2006 Ker 1.

Scheduled Caste – Acquiring of Scheduled Caste status

A person by reason of marriage alone cannot *ipso facto* become a member of Scheduled Caste or Scheduled Tribe; *Meera Kanwaria v. Sunita*, AIR 2006 SC 597.

Women

Clause (3) of Article 15 providing for special provision for women and children has been widely resorted to and the courts have upheld the validity of reservation of certain posts and seats for women. The undermentioned decisions may be seen in this context:

i. *Giridhar v. State*, AIR 1953, MB 147. (Section 354, Indian Penal Code)

ii. *Yusuf v. State of Bombay*, AIR 1954, SC 321, 322 (Section 497, Indian Penal Code).

iii. *Choki v. State of Rajasthan*, AIR 1957 Raj. 10 (Bail).

Women: Reservation: Reservation of 50% of posts in favour of female candidates not arbitrary; Rajesh Kumar Gupta v. state of Uttar Pradesh 2005

Women and Sexual Harassment: Sexual harassment of working women accounts to violation of the rights guaranteed by article 14, 15, 23 (equality and diginity), the court issued detailed directions on the subject, Vishakha v state of Rajasthan 1997.

Reservation of 50% of posts in favour of female candidates not arbitrary; *Rajesh Kumar Gupta v. State of Uttar Pradesh*, AIR 2005 SC 2540.

Backward Class

Article 15(4) appears to be a blanket provision protecting any kind of discriminatory provisions for the benefit of the classes placed under the weaker sections of the society but if discriminatory provisions lack any rationale, they are bound to be declared unreasonable by the courts. This is here that the right to equality under Art. 14 would prevail over the special provision under Article 15(4). Hence, reservation above 50% of available seats may not be upheld. The following decisions are pointers in this context:

(i) *State of Uttar Pradesh v. Balram*, AIR 1972, SC 1375, 1395.

(ii) *Rajendran v. Union of India*, AIR 1968 SC 507.

(iii) *Balaji v. State of Mysore,* AIR 1963, SC 649, 662.

(iv) *Anil v. Dean, Govt. Medical College,* Nagpur, AIR 1985 Bom. 153, paragraph 6.

In making reservation by executive order under Article 15(4), the state has to ensure that it is not unduly wide. Apart from Scheduled Castes and Scheduled Tribes, there is the category of "socially and educationally backward classes" of citizens. Under Article 46, (a directive principle of state policy) it is the obligation of the state to promote with special care the educational and economic interests of "the weaker sections of the people" and in particular of Scheduled Castes and the Scheduled Tribes". Article 335 provides in similar fashion that the claims of the members

and posts in connection with the affairs of the Union or of a State: but this Article does not mention backward classes. The Supreme Court has held "the maintenance of efficiency in the administration" as a limitation on Article 16(4) which speaks of reservation of appointment of posts in favour of any Backward class citizens, which in the opinion of the state, is not adequately represented in the services under the state. This article is to be construed in the background of Article 335 as mentioned above. Undermentioned decisions are reflective of the above aspect:

(i) *K.C. Vasanth Kumar v. State of Karnataka,* AIR 1985, SC 1495.

(ii) *CAG V. Jagannathan,* AIR 1987 SC 537 paragraphs 21-22 and 30-31.

(iii) *Deepak v. State of Bihar*, AIR 1982 Pat. 126 paragraph 12.

(*iv*) State of Kerala v. N.M. Thomas, AIR 1976 SC 490.

Discrimination: Discrimination means making an 'adverse distinction with regard to' or distinguishing unfavorably from others. The discrimination would be valid if it is based on some ground not connected with religion but based on some other rational factor.

Article 15 forbids the discrimination based on religion. The right conferred by clause (1) of Article 15 is personal. Therefore a statute, which restricts the right of a class of citizens, does not attract the provision of clause (12) of Article 15.

Gay Sex: Suresh Kumar Kaushal v Naz foundation Dec: 13 Supreme Court ruled that sect. 377 of IPC does not suffer from the vice of unconstitutionality and earlier declaration of Divison Bench of High Court is legally unsustainable.

Reservation on the basis of domicile: On comparing Article 15(1) and Article 16(2), it appears that Article 15(1) refers to 'place of birth' alone while Article 16(2) refers to 'domicile', 'residence' and place of birth. Therefore it can be said that the expression 'place of birth' is not synonymous to the expression 'domicile'. Thus the reservation on the basis of domicile may be given in terms of Article 15(1) of the constitution.

Constitutional 93rd Amendment 2005: Act of 2005 introducing article 15 (5) does not interfere with the executive power of the state and is not invalid for not following procedure under article 368; Ashok Kumar Thakur v. Union of India, 2008, K.G Balakrishan, CJI.

16. Equality of opportunity in matters of public employment.-

(1) There shall be equality of opportunity for all citizens in matters relating to employment or appointment to any office under the State.

(2) No citizen shall, on grounds only of religion, race, caste, sex, descent, place of birth, residence or any of them, be ineligible for, or discriminated against in respect of, any employment or office under the State.

(3) Nothing in this article shall prevent Parliament from making any law prescribing, in regard to a class or classes of employment or appointment to an office [1][under the Government of, or any local or other authority within, a State or Union territory, any requirement as to residence within that State or Union territory] prior to such employment or appointment.

(4) Nothing in this article shall prevent the State from making any provision for the reservation of appointments or posts in favour of any backward class of citizens which, in the opinion of the State, is not adequately represented in the services under the State.

[2][(4A) Nothing in this article shall prevent the State from making any provision for reservation in matters of promotion, with consequential seniority to any class or classes of

1 Subs. by the Constitution (Seventh Amendment) Act, 1956, sec. 29 and Sch., for "under any State specified in the First Schedule or any local or other authority within its territory, any requirement as to residence within that State" (w.e.f. 1.11.1956). Subs. by the Constitution (Eighty-fifth Amendment) Act, 2001, sec. 2, for "in matters of promotion to any class" (w.e.f. 17.6.1995).

2 Ins. by the Constitution (Seventy-seventh Amendment) Act, 1995.

posts in the services under the State in favour of Scheduled Castes, and the Scheduled Tribes which in the opinion of the State are not adequately represented in the services under the State.]

[1][(4B) Nothing in this article shall prevent the State from considering any unfilled vacancies of a year which are reserved for being filled up in that year in accordance with any provision for reservation made under clause (4) or clause (4A) as a separate class of vacancies to be filled up in any succeeding year or years and such class of vacancies shall not be considered together with the vacancies of the year in which they are being filled up for determining the ceiling of fifty per cent reservation on total number of vacancies of that year.]

(5) Nothing in this article shall affect the operation of any law which provides that the incumbent of an office in connection with the affairs of any religious or denominational institution or any member of the governing body thereof shall be a person professing a particular religion or belonging to a particular denomination.

Notes on Article 16

Object

Articles 14 to 16 taken together enshrine the principle of equality and absence of discrimination. They are closely entertwined and should not be studied in isolation. Thus, Article 16 is to be read alongwith Articles 14 and 15. Like Article 15, Article 16 is also available to citizens only. Whereas Article 14 lays bare the principle of equality, Article 16 extends this principle to matters of public employment or appointment to any office under the State.

Certain exceptions to the right provided in clauses (1) and (2) of article 16, emanate from clauses (3), (4) and (5) of the article. They may be summed up as (a) requirement of residence within a state for particular classes of employement if sanctioned by parliamentary legislation, (b) provisions for the reservation of posts for backward class of citizens not adequately represented in the services under the state, and (c) prescription of professing a particular religion or belonging to a particular denomination if the office is concerned with a religious or denominational institution.

In case of this right, the courts have maintained that the general right enshrined in clauses (1) and (2) should be construed liberally and the exceptions in clauses (3), (4) and (5) may be construed strictly. We may cite the following decisions:

(i) *General Manager V. Rangachari,* AIR 1962 SC 36, 41.

(ii) *Rajendran v. Union of India,* AIR 1968 SC 507.

Employment

The words "employment or appointment" are comprehensive enough to include tenure, duration, emoluments, duties and obligations. Further, these words suggest nature of appointment, initial appointment, salary, increments, revision of pay, promotion, gratuity, leave, pension and age of superannuation. Decisions in this connection are:

i. *Sukhmandan v. State of Bihar*, AIR 1967 Pat. 617.

ii. *Champaklal v. Union of India*, AIR 1964 SC 1854.

iii. *Union of India v. Kashikar,* AIR 1986 SC 431, Paragraph 8.

Constitution (Seventy-Seventh Amendment) Act, 1995

The Scheduled Castes and Scheduled Tribes had been availing themselves the facility of reservation in promotion. On 16th November, 1992, the Supreme Court in the case of *Indra*

1 Ins. By the Constitution (Seventy-seventh Amendment) Act, 1995, sec.2 (w.e.f. 17-6-1995).

Sawhney v. Union of India, ruled that the reservation of posts under Article 16(4) of the constitution is confined to initial appointment only and so cannot be extended to reservation in promotion. This ruling of the Supreme Court was considered detrimental to the interests of Scheduled Castes and Scheduled Tribes. The Government was of the view that the representation of the SCs and STs in services had not yet reached the required level so it decided to continue the policy of reservation in promotion for the Scheduled Castes and Scheduled Tribes by amending Article 16 and inserting a new clause (4A). The constitution (seventy-seventh Amendment) Act. 1995 is an effort to achieve the aforesaid object.

Safeguards

Article 16(4), as the courts have consistently insisted, must be read with Article 335 which directs that while taking into consideration the claims of Scheduled Castes and Scheduled Tribes in matters of employment, the state should bear in mind that the claims should be consistent with the maintenance of efficiency of administration. It is to be noted here that Articles 16, 46 and 335 have much in common and so Article 16 should be read alongwith Articles 46, and 335. Important decisions in this regard are:

i. *Devadasan v. Union of India*, AIR 1985 SC 983, paragraph I.

ii. *Balaji v. State of Mysore,* AIR 1963 SC 649, 664.

iii. *Comptroller and Auditor General v. Jagannathan*, AIR 1987 SC 537.

Under article 16(2), discrimination against a citizen is prohibited on the ground of:

(*i*) religion (*ii*) race (*iii*) caste

(*iv*) sex (*v*) descent (*vi*) place of birth and

(*vii*) residence

The court has held that the general right conferred by the first two clauses of Article 16 should be interpreted liberally while the exceptions may be interpreted strictly. However the provision of clause (4) bears a double character. As a result, considerable controversy and uncertainty exists as to the quantum of reservation. It is considered that reservation in excess of 50% may override the general right to equality and prima facie, regarded as discriminatory.

17. Abolition of Untouchability.- "Untouchability" is abolished and its practice in any form is forbidden. The enforcement of any disability arising out of "Untouchability" shall be an offence punishable in accordance with law.

18. Abolition of titles-

(1) No title, not being a military or academic distinction, shall be conferred by the State.

(2) No citizen of India shall accept any title from any foreign State.

(3) No person who is not a citizen of India shall, while he holds any office of profit or trust under the State, accept without the consent of the President any title from any foreign State.

(4) No person holding any office of profit or trust under the State shall, without the consent of the President, accept any present, emolument or office of any kind from or under any foreign State.

(5) The National Awards such as Bharat Ratna, Padma Vibhushan, Padma Bhushan, and Padma Shri are not title under article 18(1). In union of India v. Bijan Ghosh, AIR 1997 SC 3019, it was held that where an award is not yet formally conferred and the government communiqué in respect of that is cancelled on account of sentiments expressed by family members of the proposed deceased recipient-1 writ would not be issued for the formal annulment of conferment of national award.

Right to Freedom

19. **Protection of certain rights regarding freedom of speech, etc.-**

(1) All citizens shall have the right -

(a) to freedom of speech and expression.

(b) to assemble peaceably and without arms;

(c) to form associations or unions [or co-operative societies][1];

(d) to move freely throughout the territory of India;

(e) to reside and settle in any part of the territory of India; [2][and][3][***]

(g) to practice any profession, or to carry on any occupation, trade or business.

[4][(2) Nothing in sub-clause (a) of clause (1) shall affect the operation of any existing law, or prevent the State from making any law, in so far as such law imposes reasonable restrictions on the exercise of the right conferred by the said sub-clause in the interests of [5][the sovereignty and integrity of India,] the security of the State, friendly relations with Foreign States, public order, decency or morality, or in relation to contempt of court, defamation or incitement to an offence.]

(3) Nothing in sub-clause (b) of the said clause shall affect the operation of any existing law in so far as it imposes, or prevents the State from making any law imposing, in the interests of [5][the sovereignty and integrity of India or] public order, reasonable restrictions on the exercise of the right conferred by the said sub-clause.

(4) Nothing in sub-clause (c) of the said clause shall affect the operation of any existing law in so far as it imposes, or prevents the State from making any law imposing, in the interests of the [5][the sovereignty and integrity of India or] public order or morality, reasonable restrictions on the exercise of the right conferred by the said sub-clause.

(5) Nothing in [6][sub-clause (d) and (e) of the said clause shall affect the operation of any existing law in so far as it imposes, or prevent the State from making any law imposing, reasonable restrictions on the exercise of any of the rights conferred by the said sub-clauses either in the interests of the general public or for the protection of the interests of any Scheduled Tribe.

(6) Nothing in sub-clause (g) of the said clause shall affect the operation of any existing law in so far as it imposes, or prevent the State from making any law imposing, in the interests of the general public, reasonable restrictions on the exercise of the right conferred by the said sub-clause, and, in particular, [7][nothing in the said-clause shall affect the operation of any existing law in so far as it relates to or prevent the State from making any law relating to,-

(*i*) the professional or technical qualifications necessary for practising any profession or carrying on any occupation, trade or business, or

(*ii*) the carrying on by the State, or by a corporation owned or controlled by the State, of any trade, business, industry or service, whether to the exclusion, complete or partial, of citizens or otherwise.]

---

1 Ins. by the Constitution (Ninety-seventh Amendment) Act, 2011, sec. 2 (w.e.f. 15-2-2012).

2 Ins. by the Constitution (Forty-fourth Amendment) Act, 1978, sec. 2(a)(*i*) (w.e.f. 20-6-1979).

3 Sub-clause (f) omitted by the Constitution (Forty-fourth Amendment) Act, 1978, sec. 2(a)(*ii*) (w.e.f. 20-6-1979).

4 Subs. by the Constitution (First Amendment) Act, 1951. sec. 3(a), for clause (2) (with retrospective effect).

5 Ins. by the Constitution (Sixteenth Amendment) Act, 1963, sec. 2(a).

6 Subs. by the Constitution (Forty-fourth Amendment) Act, 1978, sec. 2(b), for sub-clauses (d), (e) and (f) (w.e.f. 20-6-1979).

7 Subs. by the Constitution (First Amendment) Act, 1951, sec. 3(b), for certain words. (w.e.f. 18-6-1957).

Notes on Article 19

Under Article 19 certain positive rights are conferred by our constitution to promote the ideal of liberty as contained in the Preamble. Six freedoms under this Article form the core of Chapter on Fundamental Rights. Availability of these rights is reflective of the genuineness of our democracy.

However, no modern state can guarantee absolute individual rights. The guarantee of each of the rights under this Article is limited by the Constitution itself by conferring upon the "State" a power to impose reasonable restrictions on the enjoyment of those rights in the larger interests of the community. The Indian constitution has not followed the philosophy of '*Laisseze Faire*' enumerating uncontrolled individual rights. It has rather sought to ensure that where collective interests are involved, individual liberty must yield to the common good. Thus, the constitution has specified the permissible limitations in clauses (2) to (6) of Article 19 itself. The Indian Constitution attempts to strike a balance between individual liberty and social control. The case below is a pointer in this direction:

Gopalan v. State of Madras, (1950) SCR 88, 253-54.

Relationship with Articles 21 and 22

Article 19 is a bulwark against State action encroaching upon the most basic rights of man. In the past there was a controversy whether the operation of this article is ruled out where articles 21 and 22 apply, the current trend is not to regard these articles mutually exclusive. For example, a person whose freedom of movement is done away with by imprisonment or detention does not thereby lose his freedom of expression so long as it is exercised within the valid conditions relating to the detention. Hence, a detenu cannot be barred from sending outside the jail for publication matter which contains nothing prejudicial to the grounds for which he had been detained. See the undermentioned decisions:

i. *State of Maharashtra v. Prabhakar*, AIR 1966 SC 424.

ii. *Khan v. State of Maharashtra*, AIR 1967 Bom. 254.

iii. *Narayan v. State of Kerala*, AIR 1973 Ker. 97,

iv. *Minerva Mills Ltd. V. Union of India*, AIR 1980 SC 1789.

Right of Minority to Administer Educational institution

Right of Minority to administer educational institution is not infringed by making Tamil as compulsory subject in school syllabi. It does not restrict minority students to learn his mother tongue as well. K. R Ramaswamy v state AIR 2008.

State Acts: Educational Institution

The State Acts strike a balance between autonomy of institutions and measures to be taken to prevent commercialisation of education; Tamil Nadu Nursery, Matriculation and Higher Secondary Schools Association, Chennai v. state of Tamil Nadu, AIR 2010.

Burden of Proof

If a law *prima facie* violates a right guaranteed by any clause of the article, it is incumbent upon the state to show how the law or any state action falls within the permissible limits enumerated in clauses (2) to (6) of the article. Relevant decisions in this regard are:

(i) *Vrijlal v. State of Madhya Pradesh,* AIR 1970 SC 129.

(ii) *Sagir Ahmed v. State of Uttar Pradesh,* AIR 1954 SC 728.

Reasonable restrictions

Directive Principles are also relevant considerations in deciding reasonableness of restrictions imposed on Fundamental Rights; *State of Gujarat v. Mirzapur Moti Kureshi Kasab Jamat*, AIR 2006 SC 212.

The test of reasonableness

The classic test of reasonableness of a restriction imposed by the state is whether the law strikes a proper balance between the rights of the individual and those of the society. The court must take into consideration the following things:

a. nature of the right infringed,

b. underlying purpose of the restriction imposed,

c. evil sought to be remedied by the law, its extent and urgency,

d. how far the restriction is or is not proportionate to the evil and

e. prevailing conditions at the time e.g. social values obtaining at the time.

Important decisions of the Supreme Court in this regard are as under:

(i) *Chintaman Rao v. State of Madhya Pradesh,* (1950) SCR 759.

(ii) *Khare v. State of Delhi,* (1950); SCR 519.

(iii) *Qureshi v. State of Bihar,* (1959) SCR 629.

(iv) *Luxmi v. State of Uttar Pradesh,* AIR 1981 SC 873.

The Supreme Court has dealt with the question of reasonableness on several occasions and has laid down several tests and guidelines. Two important tests to be borne in mind are the directive principles of state policy and the reconciliation between individual liberty and social control.

(i) *Keshavananda Bharti v. State of Kerala,* AIR 1973 SC 1461,

(ii) *State of Kerala v. N.M. Thomas,* AIR 1976 SC 490.

(iii) *Fatehchand Himatlal v. State of Maharashtra,* AIR 1977 SC 1825.

Freedom of Assembly

The freedom of assembly can be restricted on various grounds as mentioned in Article 19(3). These restrictions may be for maintaining sovereignty and integrity of India and public order, including the maintenance of traffic in the area concerned. Moreover, this freedom can only be exercised on public land but in normal times, these restrictions cannot take the form of absolute prohibition.

Freedom of Association

The right to freedom of association encompasses a variety of rights and the associations or the unions in the form of political parties are the instrumentalities through which the wishes of the people are articulated in a democracy. These rights are also subject to reasonable restrictions in the interest of sovereignty and integrity of India, public order and morality. Decisions in consonance with this right are:

(i) *Kulkarni v. State of Bombay,* AIR 1954 SC 73.

(ii) *O.K. Ghosh v. Joseph,* AIR 1963 SC 812, 815.

(iii) *DAV College v. State of Punjab,* (1971) 2 SCC 269, 281.

(iv) *Delhi Police Sangh v. Union of India,* AIR 1987 SC 379.

Co-operative Societies Act, 1965 (U.P.)

Though article 19(1)(c) guaranteed freedom to form an association the freedom is subject to certain permissible restrictions imposed by law. Provisions of the U.P. Co-operative Societies Act, 1965 do not infringe on this freedom. Court cannot interfere with policy of the Government, *State of Uttar Pradesh v. C.O.D. Chheoke Employees Co-operative Housing Society Ltd.*, AIR 1997 SC 1413 paragraph 16: (1997) 3 SCC 681: 1997 All LJ576.

By-laws under co-operative societies is a contract. This freedom of contract cannot be curtailed by relaxing on fundamental rights; *Zoroqstrian Co-operative Housing Society Ltd. v. District Registrar*, Co-operative Societies (Urban), AIR 2005 SC 2306.

Freedom of Movement

The freedom of movement under Article 19(4) has much in common with the right to personal liberty guaranteed under Article 21. Orders of externment and internment infringe this right unless they fall within the category of reasonable restrictions. While judicial decisions have limited this right to physical movement, it may get protection under Article 21. If we read the right with the right to personal liberty, we find their contours much along the same lines.

The people living in hilly areas have a right to be provided access to the roads for the proper exercise of their right to life. A blanket ban on the freedom of movement is *prima facie* suspect. Relevant decisions in this regard may be listed as under:

(i) *Kharak Singh v. State of Uttar Pradesh,* AIR 1953 SC 1295, 1303.

(ii) *Govind v. State of Madhya Pradesh,* AIR 1975 SC 1378.

(iii) *Malak v. State of Punjab,* AIR 1981, SC 760, paragraphs 7, 9, 10.

(iv) *Maneka Gandhi v. Union of India,* AIR 1978 SC 597, paragraph 54.

Freedom of profession etc.

Liberally interpreted, Article 19(1) gives unbridled freedom of profession, trade or business to the citizens. Conversely speaking, citizens' right to business does not stem from the grant by the state. However, a reasonable restriction in the interest of general public may be imposed on carrying on a particular business at any place or at any time. Yet a citizen cannot be compelled to do a particular business. Some cases may be listed as under:

(i) *Ibrahim v. Regional Transport Authority,* (1953) SCR, 290, 299. (reasonable restrictions for public convenience).

(ii) *Hari Shankar v. Deputy Commissioner,* AIR 1975 SC 1121. (absolute prohibition in harmful trades).

(iii) *Lakhanlal v. State of Orissa,* AIR 1977 SC 722 (dangerous trade).

(iv) *Pyare Lal v. Delhi Municipality,* AIR 1968 SC 133, 138. (business on the streets).

Freedom of residence

Freedom to reside and settle in any part of India guaranteed by clause (e) of Article 19(1) can be restricted in the interest of the general public or for the protection of the interests of Scheduled Tribes. In India the state of Jammu and Kashmir and some areas of Assam, Mizoram and Meghayala have been given special status and settlement of outsiders there are legally prohibited. Besides certain areas may be banned for certain kinds of people such as prostitutes. Following decisions buttress the above propositions:

(i) *State of Madhya Pradesh v. Bharat,* AIR 1967 SC 1170, 1172.

(ii) *Kharak Singh v. State of Uttar Pradesh,* AIR 1953 SC 1295, 1303.

(iii) *Ebrahim v. State of Bombay,* (1954) SCR 923, 950 (passport).

(iv) *State of Uttar Pradesh v. Kaushaliya,* AIR 1964 SC 416, 423 (prostitutes).

Freedom of speech and expression – press

Freedom of speech and expression guaranteed in Article 19 (a) gives Indian citizens precious rights to express themselves, rightly called the watchdog of democracy. Subject to reasonable restrictions, this right connotes the freedom to write and publish what the writer considers proper. The freedom of the press emanates from this right only. Disseminating information, educating the people and highlighting the loopholes of the government by the press, keep the administration on its toes. The government cannot remain oblivious of the problems of the people except at its own peril. Any atempt at the curtailment of this freedom raises a hue and cry. However, sensational journalism may be prohibited by law. The law requires the press to remain within certain limits. The right to privacy and to reputation and the law of contempt of court serve as limits on the freedom of the press. Following decisions are relevant to the freedom of press:

(i) *Virendra v. State of Punjab,* AIR 1958 SC 986.

(ii) *Express Newspapers v. Union of India,* AIR 1958 SC 578.

(iii) *Bennett Coleman v. Union of India,* AIR 1973 SC 106.

(iv) *Prabha v. Union of India,* AIR 1982 SC 6.

(v) *Express Newspapers v. Union of India,* AIR 1986 SC 872.

Right to Know

The freedom of speech and expression under Article 19 has given birth to another right i.e. the right to know about the activities of the state, instrumentalities, the departments and agencies of the state. The freedom of speech is contingent upon the freedom of right to know. No doubt the state can and should impose restrictions on this right if it affects the national security or nation's integrity. The privilege of secrecy is an old weapon not to be used in present day world. Now every citizen has a right to know how the government is running its affairs and why it withholds some information on any matter;

L.K. Koolwal v. State of Rajasthan, AIR 1988 Raj.2.

In another case it was held that citizens have a right to know about the affairs of the govt. But this right is not absolute. Secrecy can be legitimately claimed in respect of transactions with imminent repercussions on public security.

Dinesh Trivedi v. Union of India, (1997) 4 SCC 306 (case relating to Vohra Committee Report).

Right to carry on business: In Maharashtra Ekta Hawkers Union v. Municipal Corporation greater Mumbai AIR 2004 SC 416, it was held that Article 19(1) (g) gives the right to a hawker. But the right to the hawker is subject to reasonable restrictions under article 19(6). It was also held that there is no fundamental right under Article 21 to carry on hawking business. There is also no right to do hawking at any particular place; *Maharashtra Ekta Hawkers Union v. Municipal Corporation Greater Mumbai,* AIR 2004 SC 416; (2004) 625

Right to carry profession: In Inspector General of Registrations and Stamps, Hyderabad v. Andhra Pradesh state Document writer's Association AIR 2003 AP 193 it was held that there exist no contract between document writers and the state as per which they can carry on their profession within the compound of the sub-registrars office, then the right of ownership exercised by the state prohibiting the document writers to carry on their profession within the sub-registrars office is not violative of Article 19(1)(g) of the constitution.

20. **Protection in respect of conviction for offences-**

(1) No person shall be convicted of any offence except for violation of a law in force at the time of the commission of the act charged as an offence, nor be subjected to a penalty greater than that which might have been inflicted under the law in force at the time of the commission of the offence.

(2) No person shall be prosecuted and punished for the same offence more than once.

(3) No person accused of any offence shall be compelled to be a witness against himself.

Notes on Article 20

The rights under Article 20 of the constitution are in the nature of prohibitions which are directly relevant to the criminal process. While clause (1) deals with the substantive law of criminal liability and penalty, clauses (2) and (3) deal mainly with the stage of procedure. In the jurisprudence of constitutional law, article 20(1) provides a prohibition against retrospective criminal legislation commonly known as "*expost facto* legislation", Article 20(2) incorporates a prohibition against 'double jeopardy' or punishment for the same offence more than once. Article 20(3) provides protection against 'testimonial compulsion' i.e. compulsion to give self-incriminating evidence. This article is also applicable to a corporation which, like persons, is accused, prosecuted, convicted or punished for an offence;

Sharma v. Satish, (1954), SCR 1077.

Applicability: Article 20(2) is applicable only when there is a second prosecution and punishment for the same offence for which the accused has been prosecuted and punished previously. If the ingredients of two offences are different then a subsequent trial or prosecution and punishment are not barred.

Clash between fundamental rights: In case of clash between two fundamental rights, only that right would be enforced through the process of court which would advance the public morality or public interest.

Commencement of protection

The protection or the immunity available to the accused commences as soon as a formal accusation is made either before or during prosecution. The process of lodging of a first information report, the filing of a complaint in court or the issue of a show cause notice under a special criminal statute are sufficient grounds for invoking Article 20. But there must be a proceeding contemplating action against a particular person. Important relevant cases are:

(i) *Dastgir v. State of Madras,* AIR 1960 SC 756, 761.

(ii) *State of Bombay v. Kathi Kalu,* AIR 1961 SC 1808, 1816.

(iii) *R.K. Dalmia v. Delhi Adm.,* AIR 1962 SC 1821, 1870.

(iv) *Joseph v. Narayana,* AIR 1964 SC 1552, 1556.

(v) *Veera Ibrahim v. State of Maharashtra,* AIR 1976 SC 1167.

Double jeopardy

Article 20(2) provides immunity from "double jeopardy" (an American term for double prosecution), which bars prosecution and punishment after an earlier punishment for the same offence. 'Offence' here means an offence as defined in General Clauses Act, 1897 and incorporated in the constitution vide Article 367. The offence must be the same, that is to say, it must possess the same ingredients in all respects. If any law provides for double punishment, such law would be declared void. The Article, however, does not give immunity from any other separate and distinct proceeding which may be initiated. The object of the article is to ensure fair trial and mitigate the possibility of harassment which may be caused to a person by successive criminal proceedings for the same offence.

Some of the important decisions on Article 20(2) are as follows:

(i) *Makbool v. State of Bombay* (1953) SCR 730.

(ii) *Kalawati v. State of H.P.* (1953) SCR 546.

(iii) *Narayanlal v.* Mistri, *AIR 1961 SC 29.*

(iv) *Assistant Customs Collector v. Melwani,* AIR 1970 SC 962.

Testimonial compulsion for the accused.

Article 20(3) protects a person against compulsion "to be a witness" against himself. This is available to a person 'accused of an offence.' Two important cases in this regard may be listed:

(i) *Narayanlal v. Maneck,* AIR 1961 SC 29, 38-39.

(ii) *Chaurasia v. State of Maharashtra,* AIR 1988 SC 938, 947.

To be a Witness:

Taking specimen fingerprints and handwritings from accused is not hit by Article 20(3) as being "witness against himself"; *State through SPE and CBI, A.P. v. M. Krishna Mohan,* AIR 2008 SC 368.

21. Protection of life and personal liberty- No person shall be deprived of his life or personal liberty except according to procedure established by law.

Notes on Article 21

Right to life and personal liberty guaranteed under Article 21 is the most precious of all rights provided in our constitution. This article ensures that the executive shall not be entitled to interfere with the liberty of citizens unless it is armed with some provision of law to justify its action. No man can be subjected to physical coercion that lacks any legal justification. In the case of *"Ram Narain v. State of Bombay,"* (1952) SCR 652, the court observed that when the state or any of its agents deprives an individual of his personal liberty, such action can be justified only if there is a law to support such action and the procedures prescribed by such law have been strictly and scrupulously observed.

It is to be noted here that there can be no absolute freedom of the individual. There are laws to regulate the rights in the collective interests or in the interest of the security of the state itself. This is the logic adopted by our Constitution which provides that life and personal liberty are subject to the "procedure established by law". The Supreme Court through its pronouncements has, however, held that 'the procedure' inherently means a procedure which is reasonable, fair and just. Article 21, thus, has been turned into a safeguard against arbitrary legislation.

We just may see the journey of right to "life and personal liberty" from being a vulnerable right "to one of a safeguard against arbitrary legislation". Before the historic decision of the Supreme Court in *Maneka v. Union of India* case in 1978, there was a widely held view that there was no guarantee in our constitution against arbitrary legislation encroaching upon personal liberty. The validity of a law depriving a person's personal liberty could not be challenged in a court of law on the ground that the law is unreasonable, unfair or unjust. In *Gopalan v. State of Madras,* the majority view in the Supreme Court propounded the view that Indian Constitution embodied the British concept of personal liberty by adopting the expression "procedure established by law" in preference to that of American "due process". The Supreme Court thus, accepted the supremacy of the legislature thereby throwing the most vital right to life and personal liberty at its mercy.

However, the above position was overturned in the case *Maneka v. Union of India,* 1978 in which the Supreme Court observed that a law seeking to deprive a person of his personal liberty must prescribe a procedure for such deprivation and that the procedure must not be arbitrary, unfair and unreasonable. The court further observed that such law shall be invalid it if violates the principles of natural justice. This historic case laid down that Articles 19 and 21 have much in common. The expression of personal liberty in Art. 21 is of the widest amplitude encompassing a variety of rights some of which have been put under Article 19 and given additional protection. Naturally there is bound to be some overlapping between Art. 19 and Art. 21.

procedure in the context of Article 21 have come up before the court. The stream is endless and the case law can only be surveyed and examined in a fullfledged commentary. By way of illustration, some important propositions laid down in that case are mentioned in the paragraphs below. For convenience of reference, important topics to which the cases relate have been arranged alphabetically, as far as possible, in the following paragraphs:

Atomic energy

Under Article 21 and 32, the court has given directions that the Gamma Chambers housed in Jawaharlal Nehru University, New Delhi, be sent to Bhabha Atomic Research Centre, Bombay, for recharging;

M.C. Mehta v. Union of India AIR 1987 SC 1086.

Bail

Pre-trial release on personal bond (i.e. without surety) should be allowed where the person to be released on bail is indigent and there is no substantial risk of his absconding;

Hussainara v. Home Secretary, State of Bihar, AIR 1979 SC 1360.

Child offenders

Child offenders are entitled to speedy trial;

Sheela Barse v. Union of India, AIR 1986 SC 1773, paragraph 12.

Compensation

Compensation was awarded to dependents of persons (of backward classes) killed or injured in firing; *People's Union for Democratic Rights v. State of Bihar,* AIR 1987 SC 355, (1987) Cr.LJ 528: (1987) 1 SCC 265.

Cruel punishment

A punishment which is too cruel or torturesome is unconstitutional;

Inderjeet v. State of U.P., AIR 1979 SC 1867.

Death sentence

Compulsory death sentence for murder committed by a life convict undergoing imprisonment is unconstitutional;

Mithu v. State of Punjab, AIR 1983 SC 473, paragraphs 23-25.

Delay in execution

Unjustifiable delay in the execution of death sentence infringes Article 21; *Sher Singh v. State of Punjab,* AIR 1983 SC 465, paragraphs 13, 16 and 19.

Shatrughan Chauhan v Union of India, AIR 1998 SC 2026 Supreme Court on January 21, 2014 commuted death sentences of 15 death convicts to life sentence.

Environment : hazardous chemicals

The Supreme Court in *M.C. Mehta v. Union of India,* (1987) Supp. SCC 131: AIR 1987 SC 1086 observed that life, public health and ecology have precedence over unemployment and loss of revenue and gave certain directions to the government regarding hazardous chemicals.

In another case, the Supreme Court ruled that right to pollution free air falls within Article 21; *Subhash v. State of Bihar,* AIR 191 SC 420, paragraph 7.

Insane

Imprisonment of a person declared insane is unconstitutional;

Veena v. State of Bihar, AIR 1983 SC 339.

Medical Test

The Court has the power to order a person to undergo medical test and such an order would not be in violation of the right of personal liberty under Article 21 of the Constitution; *Shaik Fakhruddin v. Shaik Mohammed Hasan*, AIR 2006 AP 48.

Euthanasia

Aruna Ramchandra Shanbaug v. UOI March 2011 SC allowed Passive Euthanasia of withdrawing life support to patients in permanently vegetative state (PVS).

Legal aid

The Supreme Court seems to be implementing Art. 39(A) in observing that an accused person, if he is too poor to afford counsel is entitled to free legal aid. But this will be applicable only when the charge is an offence punishable with imprisonment. Further, counsel for the accused must be given sufficient time and facility to prepare for the defence. Violation of these safeguards of fair trial would invalidate trial and conviction, even if the accused does not ask for legal aid. The cases below can be seen in this connection:

(i) *Hussainara v. State of Bihar,* AIR 1979 SC 1369, 1377.

(ii) *Khatri v. State of Bihar,* AIR 1981 SC 928.

(iii) *State of Maharashtra v. Champalal,* AIR 1981 SC 1675.

Passport

A citizen's passport cannot be impounded for an indefinite period of time;

Maneka Gandhi v. Union of India, AIR 1978 SC 597, paragraphs 68, 84, 135, 143.

Preventive detention

The Maharashtra Govt. ordered preventive detention immediately after revoking the earlier order on the report of the Advisory Board. It failed to defend its action in the court. Its action was held violating Articles 21 and 22 of the constitution in the circumstances obtaining:

Mohd. Ibrahim Md. Sasin v. State of Maharashtra (1987) Supp. SCC

Prisoners: handcuff

In *Sunil v. State of M.P.,* (1990) 2 SC 409, the Supreme Court observed that handcuffing should be resorted in only extraordinary circumstances.

Prisoners : torture

The courts in India have taken strong notice of the acts which constitute human degradation. Thus, undertrial or convicted prisoner cannot be subjected to a physical or mental restraint—

i. which is not warranted by the punishment awarded by court, or

ii. which is in excess of the requirements of prisoners' discipline, or

iii. which constitutes human degradation.

See the decisions below:

(i) *Sunil Batra v. Delhi Administration,* AIR 1978 SC 1675.

(ii) *Sita Ram v. State of Uttar Pradesh,* AIR 1979 SC 745.

(iii) *Javed v. State of Maharashtra,* AIR 1985 SC 231, paragraph 4.

(iv) *Sher Singh v. State of Punjab,* AIR 1983 SC 465.

Illegal encroachment

An encroacher has no right whatsoever to put forth a claim that he has the protection of Article 21 of the Constitution; *Ranital Chowk Vyapari Sangh, Jabalpur v. State of Madhya Pradesh,* AIR 2006 NOC 299 (MP).

Privacy

Right to privacy forms the part of Art. 21;

Govind v. State of Madhya Pradesh, AIR 1975 SC 1378.

The act of recording conversation of his wife by husband without her knowledge would amount to infringement of her right to privacy; *Rayala M. Bhubhaneswari v. Nagapharnender Rayala*, AIR 2008 AP 98.

Right to privacy vis-à-vis freedom of press is available as long as privacy is maintained by parties; *Managing Director v. V. Muthulakshmi*, AIR 2008 (NOC) 381 (Mad.).

Speedy trial

A procedural law may be declared void if it does not provide for speedy trial. See the cases below:

(*i*) *Sher Singh v. State of Punjab*, AIR 1983 SC 465 (Delay in execution).

(*ii*) *Hussainara v. Home Secretary,* Bihar AIR 1979 SC 1360.

Speedy Justice

In the matter of denial of speedy justice, the court expressed the concern at delay in disposal of cases. The concerned authorities were directed to do the needful in the matter urgently before the situation goes totally out of control; *Moses Wilson v. Kasturiba*, AIR 2008 SC 379.

Right to appeal

The right of appeal from a judgment of conviction as under section 374 of Cr. P.C. is a fundamental right. It is obvious. Neither can be inferred with or impaired nor can it be subjected to any condition; *Dilip S. Dahanekar v. Kotak Mahindra Co. Ltd.* (2007) 6 SCC 528.

Right to livelihood or work

Article 21 cannot be stretched so far as to mean that everyone must be given a job. Article 41 has been deliberately kept by the Founding Fathers in the directive principles chapter and hence made unenforceable; *Indian Drugs & Pharmaceuticals Ltd. v. Workmen*, (2007) 1 SCC 408.

Right to Life and Liberty

Right to electricity is also right to life and liberty in terms of Article 21 because no one in the modern days can survive without electricity; *Molay Kumar Acharya v. Chairman-cum-Managing Director, W.B. State Electricity Distribution Co. Ltd.*, AIR 2008 Cal 47.

Third Gender

National Legal Services Authority v Union of India and others, April 2014, SC. ruled that transgender persons have a right to be legally recognised according to their self identified gender including third gender.

Right to work

Right to work can be considered as fundamental right only in case where legislative guarantee is given the form of legislation; *State of Maharashtra v. Sau Shobha Vitthal Kolte*, AIR 2006 Bom 44.

Right to life: various rights included

The Supreme Court in *P. Nalla Thampi v. Union of India,* AIR 1985 SC 1133, observed that the right to life embodies "the finer graces of human civilization." Thus, the apex court made this fundamental right a repository of various human rights. The cases mentioned above are reflective of this interpretation of the Supreme Court. However, two more rights can be added to that list:

(*i*) Right to live with human dignity; *Francis Coralite Mulin v. Administrator*, Union Territory of Delhi, AIR 1981 SC 746.

(*ii*) Free education upto 14 eyars of age. *J.P. Unnikrishnan v. State of Andhra Pradesh,* AIR 1993 SC 2178.

(iii) **Donation of Organ**– Donation of organ by husband to his ailing father cannot be objected by wife on ground of violation of her fundamental right to life, *Sumakiran Mallena v. Secretary, Medical and Health Secretariat Building, Saifabad,* AIR 2008 (NOC) 374 AP.

The right to life and personal liberty has been liberally interpreted by the Supreme Court and the High Courts. These interpretations have been very helpful in implementing the directive principles of state policy. The relationship of article 21 with articles 19, 22 and 32 is an established fact. Hence, article 21 should be read alongwith Articles 19, 22 and 32 and also with directive principles in Articles 39(A), 41, 47 and 48(A).

Notes–Right to Education includes right to safe education. Avinash Mehrotra vs Union of India (2009)

[1]**[21A. Right to education**.- The State shall provide free and compulsory education to all children of the age of six to fourteen years in such manner as the State may, by law, determine.]

[2]22. **Protection against arrest and detention in certain cases.-**

(1) No person who is arrested shall be detained in custody without being informed, as soon as may be, of the grounds for such arrest nor shall he be denied the right to consult, and to be defended by, a legal practitioner of his choice.

(2) Every person who is arrested and detained in custody shall be produced before the nearest magistrate within a period of twenty-four-hours of such arrest excluding the time necessary for the journey from the place of arrest to the court of the magistrate and no such person shall be detained in custody beyond the said period without the authority of a magistrate.

(3) Nothing in clauses (1) and (2) shall apply -

(a) to any person who for the time being is an enemy alien; or

(b) to any person who is arrested or detained under any law providing for preventive detention.

(4) No law providing for preventive detention shall authorise the detention of a person for a longer period than three months unless-

(a) an Advisory Board consisting of persons who are, or have been, or are qualified to be appointed as, Judges of a High Court, has reported before the expiration of the said period of three months that there is in its opinion sufficient cause for such detention:

Provided that nothing in this sub-clause shall authorise the detention of any person beyond the maximum period prescribed by any law made by Parliament under sub-clause (b) of clause (7); or

(b) such person is detained in accordance with the provisions of any law made by Parliament under sub-clauses (a) and (b) of clause(7).

(5) When any person is detained in pursuance of an order made under any law providing for preventive detention, the authority making the order shall, as soon as may be, communicate to such person the grounds on which the order has been made and shall afford him the earliest opportunity of making a representation against the order.

(6) Nothing in clause (5) shall require the authority making any such order as is referred to in that clause to disclose facts which such authority considers to be against the public interest to disclose.

(7) Parliament may by law prescribe-

(a) the circumstances under which, and the class or classes of cases in which, a person may be detained for a period longer than three months under any law providing for preventive detention without obtaining the opinion of an Advisory Board in accordance with the provisions of sub-clause (a) of clause (4);

---

1 Ins. by the Constitution (Eighty-sixth Amendment) Act, 2002 sec. 2 (w.e.f. 1.4.2010).

2 On the enforcement of sec. 3 of the Constitution (Forty-fourth Amendment) Act, 1978, article 22 shall stand amended as directed in sec.3 of that Act. For the text of sec.3 of that Act, see Appendix.

(b) the maximum period for which any person may in any class or classes of cases be detained under any law providing for preventive detention; and

(c) the procedure to be followed by an Advisory Board in an inquiry under sub-clause (a) of clause (4).

Notes on Article 22

Analysis

Article 22 of the Constitution of India provides procedural safeguards against arbitrary arrest and detention. This Article has two parts. Clauses (1) and (2) apply to persons arrested or detained for illegal action committed by them. This is called punitive detention. Clauses (3) to (7) apply to those persons arrested or detained under preventive detention law. Detention here takes place on the apprehension that the person in question is going to do something wrong, an act which is prejudicial to the security of the State, maintenance of public order and supply and services essential to the community, defence, foreign affairs or security of India. Obviously, the object of this provision is to prevent a person from doing a wrongful act by detaining him.

Safeguards

A person arrested or detained must be informed of the grounds of his arrest. The Supreme Court has, in its rulings, made it mandatory;

(*i*) *Gopalan Vs. State of Madras (1950) SCR 88*

(*ii*) *Hansmukh Vs. State of Gujarat, AIR 1981 SC 28.*

Similarly, the Supreme Court has also made it mandatory that a person arrested or detained has right to consult and to be defended by a legal practitioner of his choice and that the person must be produced before the nearest Magistrate within 24 hours. Relevant cases in this regard are as follows:

(*i*) State of M.P. Vs. Shobharam, AIR 1968 SC 1910.

(*ii*) State of U.P. Vs. Abdul Samad, AIR 1962 SC 1506.

Besides, the Supreme Court has made it clear that arrest under the order of the Court, deportation of an alien and arrest on a civil cause are not matters falling under rule Article 22(1) and 22(2);

State of U.P. Vs. Abdul Samad, AIR 1962 SC 1506

State of Punjab Vs. Ajaib Singh, (1953) SCR 2564

Preventive Detention

Detention without trial is an extraordinary instrument to suppress apprehended breach of public order, public safety, security of State and the like. The provisions of the Constitution on preventive detention are not self-executory rather require a law to be made by the Parliament in conformity with the conditions laid down in Article 22. In other words, the Legislature can enact a law providing for preventive detention, laying down the circumstances, the classes of cases, maximum period of detention, establishing an Advisory Board and its procedure. However, these ostensibly sweeping provisions of preventive detention are subject to certain safeguards.

Thus, the detention of a person cannot exceed three months unless an Advisory Board finds sufficient cause for detention beyond this limit. In any case, the law has to specify the maximum permissible period of such detention. In each case, the grounds of detention shall be communicated to the detenu who will be provided opportunity to make representation before the competent authority. These safeguards are the fundamental rights upon the violation of which the individuals are entitled to approach the Supreme Court and the High Courts.

Courts have taken strong exceptions to the laws of detention without trial. Except in the *bonafide* cases of preventive detention, the Courts have nullified orders for the same in a number of cases e.g. in proceedings for '*habeas corpus*'. The court strikes down a law, which is unreasonable or unjust. Similarly, if the order of arrest and detention suffers from an infirmity, the detenu may be ordered forthwith to be released by the Court. We can see two important decisions in this connection:

(*i*) *Gopalan Vs. State of Madras (1950) SCR 88.*

(*ii*) *A.D.M. Vs. Shukla. AIR 1996, SC 1207.*

Safeguards to be observed in preventive detention have now taken roots. Clauses (3) to (7) of Article 22 must now be read alongwith numerous judicial decisions on these clauses and on preventive detention laws, as also with the case laws on Article 21.

Right Against Exploitation

23. Prohibition of traffic in human beings and forced labour.-

(1) Traffic in human beings and beggar and other similar forms of forced labour are prohibited and any contravention of this provision shall be an offence punishable in accordance with law.

(2) Nothing in this article shall prevent the State from imposing compulsory service for public purposes, and in imposing such service the State shall not make any discrimination on grounds only of religion, race, caste or class or any of them.

Notes on Article 23

As an adjunct to the guarantee of personal liberty under Article 21, Article 23 seeks to provide protection against exploitation of the weaker sections of the society by unscrupulous individuals or even by the state. Exploitation through traffic in human beings, beggar, forced labour militates against human dignity, which is a fundamental value enshrined in the Preamble to the Indian Constitution. Traffic in human beings is meant to be a prohibition against slavery and traffic in women stands for immoral or other purposes, e.g. prostitution. The relevant decisions in this regard are:

(*i*) *Sanjit Vs. State of Rajasthan, AIR 1953 SC 328, Paragraph 4*

(*ii*) *People's Union Vs. Union of India, AIR 1982 SC 1473 Paragraph 14-15*

Similarly, "beggar and forced labour" is construed to be a prohibition against forced labour of any kind. Under the old Zamindari system, the landlords used to compel their tenants to render free service. This was known as begar. The idea here is that the State or any person cannot compel another person to work against his will. A labour is legally entitled not to work in a particular situation or to receive a negotiated remuneration for it. The Courts have observed in various judgments that even if some remuneration is paid, the labour may be a forced one;

People's Union v. Union of India, AIR 1982 SC 1473

The Parliament through Bonded Labour System (Abolition) Act, 1976, has abolished forced labour thereby doing away with the exploitation of the weaker sections of the society.

Children of Prostitutes

The Supreme Court held that segregating children of prostitutes by locating separate schools and providing separate hostels, would not be in the interest of such children and of society at large, and that the children should not be deprived of their mothers' care and be allowed to mingle with others and become a part of the society.

Gaurav Jain v. Union of India, AIR 1990 SC 292.

Legislation relevant to Article 23: Article 23(1) envisages legislation for the enforcement of constitutional prohibition. For example, section 374 of Indian penal code, specific legislation regarding immoral traffic in women and girls and regarding bonded labour.

24. Prohibition of employment of children in factories, etc.- No child below the age of fourteen years shall be employed to work in any factory or mine or engaged in any other hazardous employment.

Notes on Article 24

The important thing to be noted here is that the prohibition imposed by this article is absolute. While interpreting this article the Supreme Court has issued elaborate guidelines on child labour. Children should not be engaged in hazardous employment and that positive steps should be taken for the welfare of such children. The Court has also given directions with regards to education, health and nutrition of child labour. Relevant decisions on this article are:

(i) *M.C. Mehta Vs. State of Tamil Nadu, AIR 1997 SC 699.*

(ii) *Bandhua Mukti Morcha Vs. Union of India, AIR 1997 SC 2218.*

Right to Freedom of Religion

25. Freedom of conscience and free profession, practice and propagation of religion-

(1) Subject to public order, morality and health and to the other provisions of this Part, all persons are equally entitled to freedom of conscience and the right to freely profess, practise and propagate religion.

(2) Nothing in this article shall affect the operation of any existing law or prevent the State from making any law-

(a) regulating or restricting any economic, financial, political or other secular activity which may be associated with religious practice;

(b) providing for social welfare and reform or the throwing open of Hindu religious institutions of a public character to all classes and sections of Hindus.

Explanation I: The wearing and carrying of Kirpans shall be deemed to be included in the profession of the Sikh religion.

Explanation II: In sub-clause (b) of clause (2), the reference to Hindus shall be construed as including a reference to persons professing the Sikh, Jaina or Buddhist religion, and the reference to Hindu religious institutions shall be construed accordingly.

Notes on Article 25

Scope & object

The ideal of secularism as enshrined in the preamble finds its fullest realization in Article 25 which guarantees right to freedom of religion to individuals. The article ensures equality of all religions, thereby establishing India as a secular State. A secular state observes an attitude of neutrality and impartiality towards all religions i.e. there is no state religion and there is equal respect for and protection of all religions. Further, this state is founded on the idea that the State regulates the relations between man and man and not the relation between man and God, which is primarily a matter of 'individual conscience'. Thus Article 25 provides that all persons are equally entitled to freedom of conscience and the right to freely profess, practise and propagate religion. However, the right to religion is subject to some reasonable restrictions in the forms of public order, morality and health. The practice of religious freedom by individuals is the main object of this article. The act of "practice" in its purest form connotes religious worship, ritual and observation. "Propagation likewise is concerned mainly with the right to communicate beliefs to another person or to expound the tenets of one's religion, but as the Supreme Court has held, the right to propagate does not include any right to forcible conversions as they may disturb public order;

Stainslaus v. State of Madhya Pradesh, AIR 1977 SC 908.

Use of loudspeaker

As the right to religion is subject to public order, no prayers should be performed by disturbing the peace of others. Prayers through voice-amplifiers or beating of drums may adversely affect the rights of others including that of being not disturbed in their activities. The undermentioned decision supports the above proposition.

Church of God (Full Gospell) in India v. K.K. R. Majestic Colony Welfare Association, AIR 2000 SC 2773.

Regulation by the State

Article 25, clause (2)(a) gives power to the State to regulate or restrict secular activities associated with religious practice. These regulations should be primarily concerned with the secular aspects of religious practice. As per judicial pronouncement in *Ratilal v. State of Bombay 1954 SCR 1055*, regulations by the state should not interfere with the essentials of religion. This view has been followed in all later cases and still holds good. The above classification is not easy to apply. The dividing line between the two sets of religious practice may be blurred and it is for the court to determine. We may cite two cases in this connection.

In Anand Margi case, the right to perform tandava dance with lethal weapons and human skulls in a public procession was held not to be an essential religious practice and the subsequent banning of the procession in the interest of 'public order and morality' was considered to be a reasonable restriction.

Jagdishwaranand v. Police Commissioner, AIR 1984 SC 51.

Similarly, cow slaughter on the occasion of 'baqrid' was declared a non–essential practice of Islam and could therefore be prohibited by law in the interest of public order.

Mohd. Hanif Qureshi v. State of Bihar, AIR 1958 SC 731.

Secular activities associated with religious practice have been interpreted to mean non-essential aspects or peripheral aspects of religion e.g. matters of secular administration of religious properties. As the various clauses of Article 25 are interconnected, it is advisable to study the following cases to have a proper understanding of this right.

(*i*) *Ratil v. State of Bombay (1954) SCR 1055 (Legislation on public trusts)*

(*ii*) *Ramjilal v. State of Uttar Pradesh, AIR 1957 SC 620 (Section 153 A of the I.P.C.)*

(*iii*) *Saifuddin v. State of Bombay, AIR 1962, SC 853, 863 (Excommunication).*

(*iv*) *Commissioner, Hindu Religious Endowent v. Lakshmindra, (1954) SCR 105 (Religious Trust).*

(*v*) *Satinslaus v. State of Madhya Pradesh, AIR 1977 SC 908 (Freedom of conscience).*

(*vi*) *Ramanuja v. State of Tamil Nadu, AIR 1972 SC 1586 (Scrutiny of essentials of religion).*

(*vii*) *Moti Das v. Sahi AIR 1959 SC 942, 949 (Administration of religious endowment).*

(*viii*) *Venkataramana v.State of Madras, AIR 1958 SC 255 267(Religious practices)*

(*ix*) *Durgah Committee v. Hussain, AIR 1961 SC 1402 1415 (Judicial Scrutiny).*

Narendra Vs. State of Gujarat, AIR 1974 SC 2092, paragraph 25.

Restriction that can be imposed under Article 25(1) of the constitution are:

(*i*) public order

(*ii*) morality

(*iii*) health

(*iv*) other provisions of this part which includes article25(2)(b) itself.

Use of loudspeakers: If the use of loud speaker adversely affect the rights of others, it cannot be permitted as no religion prescribes that prayers should be performed by disturbing the peace of others.

Religious Freedom

Where temples and other religious institutions of Hindus are affected by frequent communal violence, the State is duty-bound to maintain public order; *Shyamal Ranjan Mukherjee v. Nirmal Ranjan Mukherjee*, AIR 2008 (NOC) 568 (All).

26. **Freedom to manage religious affairs**- Subject to public order, morality and health, every religious denomination or any section thereof shall have the right-

(a) to establish and maintain institutions for religious and charitable purposes;

(b) to manage its own affairs in matters of religion;

(c) to own and acquire movable and immovable property; and

(d) to administer such property in accordance with law.

Notes on Article 26

Article 26 springs from Article 25 and bestows a fundamental right on all religious denominations to establish and maintain institutions for religious and charitable purposes, to manage their own affairs in matters of religion and to acquire and administer property. The qualifying clause here is that the administration of property has to be according to law. As in the case of article 25, the rights under this article are also not absolute and are subject to public order, morality and health but article 26 is not subject to other fundamental rights under Part III.

Administration of property of religious endowments (institutions)

As is inherent in the article itself, the State can regulate the administration of property of religious institutions by law. But it has been judicially established that the right of administration of property cannot be taken away altogether See the decisions below:

(*i*) *Ratilal v. State of Bombay, (1954) SCR 1055.*

(*ii*) *Ramanuja v. State of Tamil Nadu, AIR 1961 SC 1402.*

(*iii*) *Ram v. State of Punjab AIR 1981 SC 1576.*

(*iv*) *Azeez v. Union of India, AIR 1968 SC 662.*

Implementation of Directive Principles

In the context of administration of property of religious institutions, the Courts have also taken into account the Directive Principles of State Policy (particularly article 37). The Courts have observed that the property of a religious institution can be acquired under Article 31A (i) for effecting agrarian reform. However, the core of the religious institutions should not be interfered with;

Narendra v. State of Gujarat, AIR 1974 SC 2098.

As under Article 25, under article 26 also, the Courts have made a distinction between essential and non-essential aspects of religion. The fact is that both articles have much in common. These articles together appear to define the separate spheres and roles of the State and religion with both being free to carry on their secular and religious activities without interference from each other.

27. Freedom as to payment of taxes for promotion of any particular religion- No person shall be compelled to pay any taxes, the proceeds of which are specifically appropriated in payment of expenses for the promotion or maintenance of any particular religion or religious denomination.

28. Freedom as to attendance at religious instruction or religious worship in certain educational institutions -

(1) No religious instruction shall be provided in any educational institution wholly maintained out of State funds.

(2) Nothing in clause (1) shall apply to an educational institution which is administered by the State but has been established under any endowment or trust which requires that religious instructions shall be imparted in such institution.

(3) No person attending any educational institution recognized by the State or receiving aid out of State funds shall be required to take part in any religious instruction that may be imparted in such institution or to attend any religious worship that may be conducted in such institution or in any premises attached thereto unless such person or, if such person is a minor, his guardian has given his consent thereto.

Cultural and Educational Rights

29. Protection of interests of minorities-

(1) Any section of the citizens residing in the territory of India or any part thereof having a distinct language, script or culture of its own shall have the right to conserve the same.

(2) No citizen shall be denied admission into any educational institution maintained by the State or receiving aid out of State funds on grounds only of religion, race, caste, language or any of them.

Notes on Article 29

Although generally Article 29(1) is assumed to relate to minorities, its scope does not indicate so. It guarantees to every section of citizens resident in the territory of India and 'having a distinct language, script or culture' the right to conserve the same. Thus, it may be interpreted to include 'the majority' as well as was pointed out in the case;

Ahmedabad St. Xavier's College Society v. State of Gujarat, AIR 1974 SC 1389.

Article 29(2) should be read and interpreted subject to Article 15(4) (as inserted in 1951) providing for special provision for backward classes, thus overriding the earlier decision in *State of Madras v. Champakam Dorairajan, (1951), SCR 525.*

Minorities:

Although the marginal heading of the article uses the term 'minorities' it has found no place in the text of the article. The original proposal of the Advisory committee in the Constituent Assembly recommended the following:

Minorities in every unit shall be "protected in respect of their language, script and culture and no laws or regulations may be enacted that may operate oppressively or prejudicially in this respect".

[B. Siva Rao "Selected Documents" (1957) Vol. 2, Page 281].

But after the clause was taken up for consideration by the Drafting Committee on Ist November, 1947, it emerged with the substitute "section of citizens" *[B. Siva Rao, Select Documents, (1957) vol. 3 pages 525-26, clause 23,* Draft Constitution]. However, it was explained that the intention has always been there to use 'minority' in a wider sense.

30. Right of minorities to establish and administer educational institutions-

(1) All minorities, whether based on religion or language, shall have the right to establish and administer educational institutions of their choice.

[1][(IA) In making any law providing for the compulsory acquisition of any property of an educational institution established and administered by a minority, referred to in clause (1), the State shall ensure that the amount fixed by or determined under such law for the acquisition of such property is such as would not restrict or abrogate the right guaranteed under that clause.]

(2) The State shall not, in granting aid to educational institutions, discriminate against any educational institution on the ground that it is under the management of a minority, whether based on religion or language.

Notes on Article 30

Scope

Article 30 is strictly in the nature of a minority right which intends to protect the rights of minorities whether based on religion or language. Its ambit is wider than Article 29, which is confined to the conservation of language, script or culture. Article 30 confers two precious rights-(i) right to establish an institution and (ii) right to administer it. The right to conservation of language, script or culture is implied therein.

This was pointed out by Justice Mathew in *'Ahmedabad St Xaviers College Society v. State of Gujarat, AIR 1974 SC 1389.*

The first right i.e. the right to establish an institution means the right to create an institution of the choice of a minority, while latter (the right to administer) means that the management of the affairs of the institution must not be subject to external control so that the founders can manage it (the institution) according to their ideas of how best the interest of the community in general and the institution in particular will be served;

Md. Joyanal Abedin v. State, AIR 1990 Cal. 193, 201, 202 paragraphs 12 and 13.

Autonomy of a minority institution cannot be completely taken away as it will defeat the very purpose of this right;

St. Stephen's College v. University of Delhi (1992) SCC 558.

Condition as to admission fees: So long as minority institutions are unaided by the state, the state cannot impose any restriction on the right of the minorities to administer educational institution except to the limited extent that regulations can be made for educational excellence.

Minorities: There is no definition of 'minority' in the constitution. Neither Motilal Nehru Report nor Sapru Report defined minority. The term minority has been defined by the UN sub-commission on prevention of discrimination and protection of minorities as (a) the term minority includes only those non-document groups in a population which possess and wish to preserve stable ethnic, religious or linguistic traditions or characteristics markedly different from those of the rest of the population (b) such minorities should include a number of persons sufficient to preserve such tradition or characteristics and (c) such minorities must be loyal to the state of which they are nationals.

Though the constitution has not defined the expression minority by its literal meaning can be given as a non-dominant group. It is a relative term.

Right: not absolute (regulatory laws)

The right provided under Article 30 is not absolute. It is subject to regulatory power of the State. Legislation in the interests of social welfare, industrial relations, public order, morality etc. does not constitute infringement of Art. 30 so long as it does not deprive the minority of its right to manage the institution. A law enacted to safeguard the service interests of teachers and regulate their conditions of service in the matter of dismissal, removal or reduction in rank in no way violates Article 30. The undermentioned decisions support the propositions stated above:

(*i*) *Kerala Education Bill (in re) AIR, 1958 SC 956.*

---

1 Ins. by the Constitution (Forty-fourth Amendment) Act, 1978, sec. 4 (w.e.f. 20-6-1979)

Requirements of regulation

A regulation by the state should not interfere with the core of Article 30 and hence should satisfy the following requirements:

i. It must be reasonable.

ii. It must touch upon the educational character of the institution.

iii. It must be conducive to the interest of the Institution *Sidhrajbhai v. State of Gujarat, AIR 1963 SC 540.*

iv. It must not annihilate the right itself.

1. Sate of Kerala v. Mother Provincial, AIR 1970 SC 2079.

2. St. John's T.T. Institute (for women) Madurai v. State of Tamil Nadu, AIR 1994 SC 43, paragraph 6.

[1]31. **Compulsory Acquisition of Property**- *[Rep. by the Constitution (Forty-fourth Amendment) Act, 1978, sec. 6 (w.e.f. 20-6-1979)].*

[2]*[Saving of Certain Laws]*

[3][31A. **Saving of laws providing for acquisition of estates, etc.** - [4][(1) Notwithstanding anything contained in article 13, no law providing for-

(a) the acquisition by the State of any estate or of any rights therein or the extinguishment or modification of any such rights, or

(b) the taking over of the management of any property by the State for a limited period either in public interest or in order to secure the proper management of the property, or

(c) the amalgamation of two or more corporations either in public interest or in order to secure proper management of any of the corporations, or

(d) the extinguishment or modification of any rights of managing agents, secretaries and treasurers, managing directors, directors, or managers of corporations, or of any voting rights of shareholders thereof, or

(e) the extinguishment or modification of any rights accruing by virtue of any agreement, lease or licence for the purpose of searching for, or winning any mineral or mineral oil or the premature termination or cancellation of any such agreement, lease or licence, shall be deemed to be void on the ground that it is inconsistent with or takes away or abridges any of the rights conferred by [5][article 14 or article 19].

[Provided that where such law, is a law made by the Legislature of a State, the provisions of this article shall not apply thereto unless such law, having been reserved for the consideration of the President, has received his assent:]

[6][Provided further that where any law makes any provision for the acquisition by the State of any estate and where any land comprises therein is held by a person under his personal cultivation, it shall not be lawful for the State to acquire any portion of such land as is within the ceiling limit applicable to him under any law for the time being in force or any building or structure standing thereon or appurtenant thereto, unless the law relating to the acquisition of such land, building or structure, provides for payment of compensation at a rate which shall not be less than the market value thereof.]

1 Article 31 was earlier amended by the Constitution (Fourth Amendment) Act, 1955, sec. 2 (w.e.f. 27-4-1955) and by the Constitution (Twenty-fifth Amendment) Act, 1971, sec. 2 (w.e.f. 20-4-1972)

2 Ins. by the Constitution (Forty-second Amendment) Act, 1976, sec.3 (w.e.f. 3-1-1977).

3 Ins. by the Constitution (First Amendment) Act, 1951, sec.4 (with retrospective effect).

4 Subs. by the Constitution (Fourth Amendment) Act, 1955. sec.3(a), for clause (1) (with retrospective effect).

5 Subs. by the Constitution (Forty-fourth Amendment) Act, 1978, sec.7, for "article 14, article 19 or article 31" (w.e.f. 20-6-1979).

6 Ins. by the Constitution (Seventeenth Amendment) Act, 1964, sec.2 (w.e.f. 20.6.1964).

(2) In this article:

[1][(a) the expression 'estate' shall, in relation to any local area, have the same meaning as that expression or its local equivalent has in the existing law relating to land tenures in force in that area and shall also include:

(i) *any jagir, inam or muafi* or other similar grant and in the State of [2][Tamil nadu] and Kerala, any *janmam* right;

(ii) any land held under *ryotwari* settlement;

(iii) any land held or let for purposes of agriculture or for purposes ancillary thereto, including waste land, forest land, land for pasture or sites of buildings and other structures occupied by cultivators of land, agricultural labourers and village artisans;]

(b) the expression 'right', in relation to an estate, shall include any rights vesting in a proprietor, sub-proprietor, under-proprietor, tenure-holder, [3]*[raiyat, under-raiyat]* or other intermediary and any rights or privileges in respect of land revenue.]

[4][31B. **Validation of certain Acts and Regulations** - Without prejudice to the generality of the provisions contained in article 31A. none of the Acts and Regulations specified in the Ninth Schedule nor any of the provisions thereof shall be deemed to be void, or ever to have become void, on the ground that such Act, Regulation or provision is inconsistent with, or takes away or abridges any of the rights conferred by any provisions of this Part, and notwithstanding any judgment, decree or order of any court or tribunal to the contrary, each of the said Acts and Regulations shall, subject to the power of any competent Legislature to repeal or amend it, continue in force.]

[5][31C. **Saving of laws giving effect to certain Directive Principles** - Notwithstanding anything contained in article 13, no law giving effect to the policy of the State towards securing [6][all or any of the principles laid down in Part IV] shall be deemed to be void on the ground that it is inconsistent with, or takes away or abridges any of the rights conferred by [7][article 14 or article 19]; [8]*[and no law containing a declaration that it is for giving effect to such policy shall be called in question in any court on the ground that it does not give effect to such policy]:*

Provided that where such law is made by the Legislature of a State, the provisions of this article shall not apply thereto unless such law, having been reserved for the consideration of the President, has received his assent.]

[9][31D. **Saving of laws in respect of anti-national activities.** - *[Rep. by the Constitutions (Forty - third Amendment) Act, 1977, sec. 2 (w.e.f. 13-4 -1978)].*

---

1 Subs. by the Constitution (Seventeenth Amendment) Act,1964, sec. 2, for sub clause (a) (with retrospective effect).

2 Subs. by the Madras State (Alteration of Name) Act, 1968 (53 of 1968), sec.4, for "Madras " (w.e.f. 14-1-1969).

3 Ins. by the Constitution (Fourth Amendment) Act, 1955, sec.3 (with retrospective effect).

4 Ins. by the Constitution (First Amendment) Act, 1951, sec.5 (w.e.f. 18.6.1951).

5 Ins. by the Constitution (Twenty-fifth Amendment) Act, 1971, sec.3. (w.e.f. 20-4-1972).

6 Subs. by the Constitution (Forty-second Amendment) Act, 1976, sec.4, for "the principles specified in clause(b) or clause(c) or article 39" (w.e.f. 3-1-1977); See Minerva Mills Ltd. v. Union of India, AIR 1980 SC 1787: (1981) Uchatam Nyayalaya Nirnaya Patrika 146; and Sanjeev Coke Manufacturing Co. V. Bharat Coking Coal Ltd., AIR 1983 SC 239.

7 Subs. by the Constitution (Forty-fourth Amendment) Act, 1978, sec.8, for "article 14, article 19 or article 31" (w.e.f. 20-6-1979).

8 In Keshavananda Bharati v. The State of Kerala (1973) Supp SCR 1, Supreme Court held the provision in italics to be invalid.

9 Ins. by the Constitution (Forty-second Amendment) Act, 1976, sec.5. (w.e.f. 3-1-1977).

Notes on Article 31(A), 31(B) and 31(C)

The inclusion of these articles in the Constitution was aimed at mitigating the glaring economic inequalities and thereby making India a welfare state, a State capable of delivering socio-economic justice. These provisions have given substance to otherwise non-fundamental rights included in our Constitution as Directive Principles of State Policy. Provisions of Article 31(A) added by the Constitution 1 First amendment) Act, 1951 are intended to save certain laws providing for acquisition cf estates, take over of corporation etc. from being questioned and invalidated on the ground of inconsistency with articles 14 and 19. The object of this acquisition and take over is to enable the Government to effect agrarian reforms which were so urgently needed to protect the interests of the tenants as well as to improve the agricultural wealth of the country. Article 31(B) validates certain acts and regulations specified in the 9th Schedule, which have been saved against the challenge on the ground of inconsistency with any of the fundamental rights. Finally, Article 31(C) inserted by the Constitution (Twenty fourth Amendment) Act, 1971, gives protection to certain laws giving effect to Directive Principles in article 39(b) and (c) and saves them from being questioned and invalidated on the grounds of contravention of articles 14 and 19. By the Forty second Amendment Act, 1976, this protection was further extended to legislation implementing any of the Directive Principles.

Here a brief survey of the Supreme Court's decisions concerning the above provisions may be taken up. Dwelling upon article 31(B), the Supreme Court in *Keshvanand Bharati Vs. State of Kerala, 1973*, held that despite inclusion in the Ninth Schedule, a law is open to challenge on the ground of being violative of the basic features of the Constitution and that the power of judicial review to question whether a law is in pursuance of Directive Principles cannot be taken away. This decision also crippled the effectiveness of Article 31(C) which provides as under:

"and no law containing a declaration that it is for giving effect to such policy shall be called in question in any court on the ground that it does not give effect to such policy."

The Supreme Court in the above case itself struck down this portion as unconstitutional on the same ground as noted above. The Forty second Amendment Act, giving protection to legislation for implementing any of the Directive Principles was challenged in the Supreme Court. The Supreme Court in the *Minerva Mills v. Union of India (AIR 1980 SC 1789)* held this extension of protection to be unconstitutional on the ground that such an omnibus withdrawal of legislation from judicial review would undermine the basic structure of the constitution. Relevant decisions of the Supreme Court can be cited as under

(i) *Srinivasa v. State of Karnataka, AIR 1987 SC 1518.*

(ii) *Minera Mills v. Union of India, AIR 1986 SC 2030*

(iii) *Sanjiv Coke v. Bharat Coking, AIR 1983 SC 239*

(iv) *Waman Rao v. Union of India, AIR 1981 SC 271*

What follows is that the power of judicial review is a basic feature of our Constitution which cannot be dispensed with by any Constitutional amendment. The Court can look into any particular law purporting to give effect to any Directive Principle and can question its constitutionality if it finds that the nexus between the law and the Directive Principle to be implemented is illusory or colourable or whether the law has "direct and reasonable" nexus with the directive principle in Article 39 (b) or 39(c);

(i) *Bim Singhji v. Union of India, AIR 1981 SC 234, Paragraph 2*

(ii) *State of Maharashtra v Basantibai (1986) 2 SCC 516, Paragraph 13.*

Right to Constitutional Remedies

32. Remedies for enforcement of rights conferred by this Part -

(1) The right to move the Supreme Court by appropriate proceedings for the enforcement of the rights conferred by this Part is guaranteed.

(2) The Supreme Court shall have power to issue directions or orders or writs, including writs in the nature of *habeas corpus*, *mandamus*, prohibition, *quo warranto* and *certiorari*, whichever may be appropriate, for the enforcement of any of the rights conferred by this Part.

(3) Without prejudice to the powers conferred on the Supreme Court by clauses (1) and (2), Parliament may by law empower any other court to exercise within the local limits of its jurisdiction all or any of the powers exercisable by the Supreme Court under clause (2).

(4) The right guaranteed by this article shall not be suspended except as otherwise provided for by this Constitution.

Notes on Article 32

Scope

Article 32 is the cornerstone of the entire edifice established by the Constitution. Mere declarations of Fundamental Rights would be a meaningless exercise if there are no adequate safeguards or means to make them effective. The reality of the availability of such rights is tested only in Courts. Art. 32 of the Constitution is there a "Constitutional remedy" for the enforcement of Fundamental Rights in Part III. This remedial right is itself a fundamental right guaranteeing the enjoyment of Fundamental Rights and working as a bulwark against draconian executive order and legislative enactments. Acticle 32 supplements the general provision in Article 13 that any act of the executive or Legislature which goes to abridge any rights in Part III, shall be declared void by the Courts. This article goes a step further and empowers the Supreme Court to issue writs in the forms of '*habeas corpus*, *mandamus*, *quo warranto*, prohibition, *certiorari*" so that it may enforce Fundamental Rights against any authority in the state at the instance of an individual whose right has been infringed.

Only fundamental rights in Part-III can be enforced under Article Three important cases illustrating this position about the scope of Art. 32 may be seen as follows:

(*i*) *Haji Esmail v. Competent Officer,* AIR 1967 SC 1244.

(*ii*) *Kuraikose v. State of Kerala,* AIR 1977 SC 1509.

(*iii*) *Indian Express Newspapers v. Union of India,* (1986) 1 SCC 633, paragraphs 200 and 207.

Supreme Court and High Court: concurrent jurisdiction.

The Supreme Court under Article 32 and the High Courts under 226 can issue writs for the enforcement of Fundamental Rights. An aggrieved party is free to approach either of the two courts. In fact this had been the earlier judicial approach;

M.K. Gopalan v. State of M.P. (1955) 1 SCR 168, 174.

Now, some judicial decisions have concluded that since the remedy under Article 32(1) is itself a Fundamental Right the Supreme Court is expected to grant relief for violation of substantive fundamental right:

(*i*) *Kochunni v. State of Madras,* AIR 1959 SC 725, 729.

(*ii*) *Tata Iron and Steel Co. v. Sarkar,* AIR 1961 SC 65.

(*iii*) *Bishan Das v. State of Punjab,* AIR 1961 SC 1570.

(*iv*) *Kharak Singh v. State of M.P.,* AIR 1963 SC 1295.

There have been historic decisions holding article 32 to be a basic feature of the constitution; *Fertilizer Corporation of India v. Union of India,* AIR 1981 SC 344, paragraph 11.

Further, judicial review under Articles 32 and 226 forms one of the basic features of the constitution beyond the pale of amendability;

Kihota v. Zachilhu, AIR 1993 SC 412, paragraphs 26, 85 and 107.

The Supreme Court in two of its decisions in 1987 observed that where relief through High Court is available under article 226, the party should first approach the High Court.

(*i*) *P.N. Kumar v. Municipal Corporation of Delhi,* (1987) 4 SCC 609, 610, 611.

(*ii*) *Kanubhai Brahmbhatt v. State of Gujarat,* AIR 1987 SC 1159.

Certiorari

(a) The writ of '*certiorari*' may be issued where the law which forms the basis of decision is void; *Himmat Lal v. State of M.P.,* AIR 1954 SC 403.

(b) The decision itself infringes a fundamental right; or

(c) The decision violates the law or is in excess of jurisdiction; *Ranjit Singh v. Territory of Chandigarh,* AIR 1991 SC 2296.

(d) The decision is against the canons of natural justice, malafide, perverse or based on non-applicability of avenue.

Mere misapplication of law is not a sufficient ground for invoking *certiorari.*

Detention

Regarding preventive decision, the main ground of interference by the Supreme Court is breach of Article 22(5); *Gracy v. State of Kerala,* AIR 1991 SC 1090, paragraphs 9-10.

Court may pass the order of release of a detenue if he is not provided opportunity to appear before the board within the period prescribed; *State of Punjab v. Sukhpal Singh,* AIR 1990 SC 231.

Court may order the release of a detenue if Government approval is not obtained within the statutory period; *Kiran Dasha v. Govt. of A.P.,* (1990) 1 SCC 328.

Undue delay in passing detention order may entail release of the detenu; *Anand Prakash v. State of Uttar Pradesh,* AIR 1990 SC 516.

Liability

The court has evolved a new basis of liability in public law (as distinguished from private law) where violation of fundamental rights is involved;

Nilabati Behara v. State of Orissa, (1993) 2 SCC 746, paragraphs 10, 11, 19 and 26.

In the above case the Supreme Court carried out its duty of enforcing fundamental rights under articles 14 & 21 and thus made the guaranteed remedies effective.

Liability of officers

It is now an established fact that the bureaucracy is also accountable for the acts done illegally thus inviting interference by the Courts; *State of Bihar v. Subhash Singh,* AIR 1997 SC 1390, paragraph 3.

Mandamus

Mandamus under Article 32 is issued where a fundamental right is violated by a statute, statutory order or by an executive order. Following cases in this connection may be cited:

(*i*) *Prabodh v. State of Uttar Pradesh,* AIR 1985 SC 167, paragraph 38 and 50;

(*ii*) *Abdul Hakim v. State of Bihar* (1961) SCR 610.

Public Interest Litigation

The phenomenon of public interest litigation in the last two decades has added a new dimension to the fundamental rights. It has made the people of India more aware of their rights. This concept was propounded by the Supreme Court in its historic judgment in the "Transfer of Judges Case." It is no more necessary for the affected party to approach the Court for violation of Fundamental Rights. The seven Judge Constitution Bench of the Supreme Court held that any member of the public if not directly involved but having "sufficient interest" can approach the High Court under article 226 or in case of violation of Fundamental Rights the Supreme Court for redressal of the grievances of the persons who cannot move the Court because of their socially or economically disadvantaged position. In other words, public interest litigation is a proceeding in which an individual or group seeks relief in the interest of the general public. Now the Court can be approached even through a letter by a public spirited individual who espouses the cause of large number of people suffering under some legal wrong or injury.

S.P. Gupta v. India, AIR 1982 SC 149.

After this judgment, a spate of such public interest litigations have come up before the Supreme Court and High Courts and the aggrieved persons have got justice without physically approaching the Courts. This concept has enriched the law and modified the traditional doctrine of *locus standi*. It has further devised new remedies and procedures against the violation of Fundamental Rights. Of the numerous decisions in this context, some important ones may be cited to illustrate the basic and important features:

(*i*) *S.P. Gupta v. Union of India, AIR 1982 SC 149, 194 (scope and basic approach).*

(*ii*) *Ratlam Municipality v. Virdichand, AIR 1980 SC 1622 (general)*

(*iii*) *D.C. Wadhwa v. State of Bihar, AIR 1987 SC 579, paragraph 38 (locus standi)*

(*iv*) *Fetiliser Corporation v. Union of India, AIR 1981 SC 344 (locus standi)*

(*v*) *People's Union for Democratic Rights v. Union of India, AIR 1982 SC 1473 (general)*

A public interest litigation may be transferred to appropriate High Court; *Kasturi v. State of U.P. (1990) Supp. SCC 784.*

Threatened

An imminent threat of infringement of a Fundamental Right is enough to justify issue of writ; *Simranjit v. Union of India,* (1993) 1 UJSC 32, paragraph 7.

Service matters

Where the petitioner's Fundamental Right is infringed by legislation or rules, the Court can interfere even if it is a matter concerning service; *F.C.I. Workers v. F.C.I., AIR 1990 SC 2178.*

Similarly, the Court can interfere in a situation where fundamental rights of a public sector employee are infringed; *Bhagwati v. S.M.D.C. (1990) 1 SCJ 433, paragraph 6.*

Denial of equal pay for equal work becomes irrational classification within the meaning of article 14; *Grih Kalyan v. Union of India, (1991) 1 SC 619, paragraph 6.*

Sovereign Power of Legislature

Court cannot direct legislature to make particular enactment; *Suresh Seth v. Commissioner, Indore Municipal Corporation,* AIR 2006 SC 767.

Writ Petition

The writ petition under Article 32 against the contravention of Article 351 is not maintained; *Ashirwad films v. Union of India,* (2007) 6 SCC 624

Commissioner

Another case of guaranteeing the fundamental rights is that the Court may appoint a person to act as a Commissioner to inquire into allegations made against govt. officers for breach of fundamental rights; *Delhi Judicial Service Association v. State of Gujarat, (1991) 4 SCC 406.*

Estoppel against Petitioner

A petitioner who has voluntarily accepted benefit under a statute cannot question its validity later on; *Pramod v. Medical Council (1991) 1 UJSC 400*

Estoppel against the State

In *T.N. Sangam v. Union of India, AIR 1990 SC 1317, paragraph 6*, the Supreme Court held that where a State party supports a petition on the merits, it cannot be allowed to raise a technical plea after a long lapse of time.

The remedial right under Article 32 has rightly been dubbed as "the soul of the Constitution". The Supreme Court in its numerous decisions has upheld the primacy and inviolability of fundament rights. It has dubbed Part III as one of the basic structures of the Constitution which are beyond the pale of amendability. The interpretations of various rights in Part III particularly articles 20, 21 and 22 by the Supreme Court have given birth to a large number of new rights. Thus, the doctrine of implied rights has unofficially heralded in India. For a proper understanding of the remedies available to people, article 32 should be read alongwith article 226 which empowers the High Court to give directions and issue writs in all cases of breach of any right.

PIL: Public Interest Litigation cannot be entertained where stand taken was contrary to stand taken by those who are affected by any action; Rameshwar Prasad v. Union of India, AIR 2006

[1]32A. **Constitutional validity of State laws not to be considered in proceedings under article 32** - *[Rep. by the Constitution (Forty-third Amendment) Act, 1977. sec. 3 (w.e.f. 13-4-1978)].*

[2][33. **Power of Parliament to modify the rights conferred by this Part in their application to forces, etc.** - Parliament may, by law, determine to what extent any of the rights conferred by this Part shall, in their application to-

(a) the members of the Armed Forces; or

(b) the members of the Forces charged with the maintenance of public order; or

(c) persons employed in any bureau or other organization established by the State for purposes of intelligence or counter intelligence; or

(d) persons employed in, or in connection with the telecommunication systems set up for the purposes of any Force, bureau or organization referred to in clauses (a) to (c).

be restricted or abrogated so as to ensure the proper discharge of their duties and the maintenance of discipline among them.

34. **Restrictions on rights conferred by this Part while martial law is in force in any area.** - Notwithstanding anything in the foregoing provisions of this Part, Parliament may by law indemnify any person in the service of the Union or of a State or any other person in respect of any act done by him in connection with the maintenance or restoration of order in any area within the territory of India where martial law was in force or validate any sentence, passed punishment inflicted, forfeiture ordered or other act done under martial law in such area.

---

1 Ins. by the Constitution (Forty-second Amendment) Act, 1976, sec. 6 (w.e.f. 1-2-1977).

2 Subs. by the Constitution (Fiftieth Amendment) Act, 1984, sec. 2 for article 33 (w.e.f. 11-9-1984).

35. **Legislation to give effect to the provisions of this part:** Notwithstanding anything in this Constitution,-

(a) Parliament shall have, and the Legislature of a State shall not have, power to make laws-

(i) with respect to any of the matters which under clause (3) of article 16, clause (3) of article 32, article 33 and article 34 may be provided for by law made by parliament; and

(ii) for prescribing punishment for those acts which are declared to be offences under this Part; and Parliament shall, as soon as may be after the commencement of this Constitution, make laws for prescribing punishment for the acts referred to in sub-clause (ii);

(b) any law in force immediately before the commencement of this Constitution in the territory of India with respect to any of the matters referred to in sub-clause (i) of clause (a) or providing for punishment for any act referred to in sub-clause (ii) of that clause shall, subject to the terms thereof and to any adaptations and modifications that may be made therein under article 372, continue in force until altered or repealed or amended by Parliament.

***Explanation*:** In this article, the expression 'law in force' has the same meaning as in article 372.

PART IV

DIRECTIVE PRINCIPLES OF STATE POLICY

36. **Definition:** In this Part, unless the context otherwise requires, 'the State' has the same meaning as in Part III.

Notes on Article 36

A state authority exercises statutory control over the functions of a statue but it is another thing to say thereby an agency is created which would be separate in entity over which the state exercises control. Agency of a state would ordinarily mean an instrumentality of a state. A statutory authority does not answer the description of an agency under the control of the state;

Deewan Singh v. Rajendra Pd. Ardevi AIR 2007.

37. **Application of the principles contained in this Part**: The provisions contained in this Part shall not be enforceable by any court, but the principles therein laid down are nevertheless fundamental in the governance of the country and it shall be the duty of the State to apply these principles in making laws.

Notes on Article 37

Directive principles constitute the non-justiciable portion of the Indian constitution and yet, they are fundamental in the governance of the country. It shall be the duty of the state to apply these principles both in the matter of administration as well as in the making of laws. Directive principles have been taken from the constitution of Eire and aim at the establishment of the economic and social democracy which is pledged for in the Preamble. These principles may be described as forerunners of the "UN Convention" on "Right to Development" as an inalienable human right:

Air India Statutory Corporation v. United Labour Union, AIR 1997

Effect : The negative aspect

The establishment of a welfare state is the main objective of Directive Principles; *Keshavanand Bharti v. State of Kerala* (1973) 4 SCC 225, paragraphs 134, 139. However, the directives do not confer any justiciable rights and their breach does not invalidate a law, nor does it entitle a citizen to seek mandatory relief in case of its violation by the state. Undermentioned decisions support the above propositions:

(*i*) *Deep Chand v. State of Uttar Pradesh,* AIR 1959 SC 648.

(*ii*) *State of Madras v. Champakam Dorairajan* AIR 1951 SC 525.

(*iii*) *Naserwanji v. State of Bombay*, AIR 1951 Bom. 216.

Effect : Positive aspect

The Directive Principles, as the decisions of the Supreme Court show, have a positive aspect. Thus, the directives are supposed to supplement fundamental rights in achieving the goal of a welfare state. Parliament can amend fundamental rights for implementing the directives, so long as the amendment does not infringe upon the basic features. Constitutional provisions may be construed in the light of Directive Principles. Undermentioned decisions may be cited to illustrate the above propositions:

(*i*) *Chandra Bhavan v. State of Madras* AIR 1970 SC 2042, Paragraph 13.

(*ii*) *State of Kerala v. N.M. Thomas*, AIR 1976 SC 496.

(*iii*) *Lingappa v. State of Maharashtra,* AIR 1985 SC 389.

(*iv*) *Mukesh v. State of Madhya Pradesh,* AIR 1985, SC 537.

(*v*) *Laxmi Kant v. Union of India*, AIR 1987 SC 2

38. State to secure a social order for the promotion of welfare of the people- [1][(1) The State shall strive to promote the welfare of the people by securing and protecting as effectively as it may a social order in which justice, social, economic and political shall inform all the institutions of the national life.

[2][(2)] The State shall, in particular, strive to minimize the inequalities in income, and endeavour to eliminate inequalities in status, facilities and opportunities, not only amongst individuals but also amongst group of people residing in different areas or engaged in different vocations.

39. **Certain principles of policy to be followed by the State.** - The State shall, in particular, direct its policy towards securing-

(a) that the citizens, men and women equally, have the right to an adequate means of livelihood.

(b) that the ownership and control of the material resources of the community are so distributed as best to subserve the common good;

(c) that the operation of the economic system does not result in the concentration of wealth and means of production to the common detriment;

(d) that there is equal pay for equal work for both men and women;

(e) that the health and strength of workers, men and women, and the tender age of children are not abused and that citizens are not forced by economic necessity to enter vocations unsuited to their age or strength.

[3](f) that children are given opportunities and facilities to develop in a healthy manner and in conditions of freedom and dignity and that childhood and youth are protected against exploitation and against moral and material abandonment.

---

1 Article 38 renumbered as clause (1) thereof by the Constituion (Forty-fourth Amendment) Act, 1978, sec.9 (w.e.f. 20-6-1979).

2 Ins. by the Constitution (Forty-fourth Amendment) Act, 1978, sec.9. (w.e.f. 20-6-1979).

3 Subs. by the Constitution (Forty-second Amendment) Act, 1976, sec.7, for clause (f) (w.e.f. 3-1-1977).

Notes on Article 39

Object

This article clearly spells out the real intentions of the framers of the constitution to realize the goal of a welfare state. The undermentioned decisions are points in that direction:

(*i*) *Srinivasa v. State of Karnataka* AIR 1987 SC 1518.

(*ii*) *Keshavanand Bharti v. State of Kerala* (1973) 4 SC 228.

Declaration in law

It is now an established fact that a law was enacted vide constitution 42nd Amendment Act, 1976 for giving effect to the directive principles of State Policy in Article 39(b) and 39(c), and it was made totally immune from unconstitutionality on the ground of contravention of the fundamental rights conferred by Art. 14 and 19. (44th Amendent Act, 1976) [read it alongwith Article 31(c)].

Equal Pay for equal work

Denial of equal pay for equal work becomes irrational classification within the meaning of Article 14; *Grihakalyan v. Union of India* (1991) 1 SCC 619 paragraph 6.

Difference in duties justifies discrimination in pay; *Vasudevan v. Union of India,* AIR 1990 SC 2295, paragraphs 18-19.

Writ can be issued to enforce the principle of equal pay for equal work if Article 14 is infringed; S*tate of Haryana v Chiranjit Singh AIR 2006*

Person employed on contract cannot claim equal pay on the basis of equal pay for equal work; *State of Haryana v. Charanjit Singh*, AIR 2006 SC 161.

The doctrine of equally pay for equal work postulated equal pay for equal work for those who are equality placed in all respects, *Uttar Pradesh Sugar Corpn. Ltd. v. Sant Raj Singh*, AIR 2006 SC 2296.

[1][39A. **Equal justice and free legal aid**- The State shall secure that the operation of the legal system promotes justice, on a basis of equal opportunity, and shall, in particular, provide free legal aid, by suitable legislation or schemes or in any other way, to ensure that opportunities for securing justice are not denied to any citizen by reason of economic or other disabilities.]

40. **Organization of village panchayats**- The State shall take steps to organize village panchayats and endow them with such powers and authority as may be necessary to enable them to function as units of self-government.

Notes on Article 40

See the amending Act on Panchayats under Article 243.

41. **Right to work, to education and to public assistance in certain cases.**- The State shall, within the limits of its economic capacity and development, make effective provision for securing the right to work, to education and to public assistance in cases of unemployment, old age, sickness and disablement, and in other cases of undeserved want.

42. **Provision for just and humane conditions of work and maternity relief.**- The State shall make provision for securing just and humane conditions of work and for maternity relief.

43. **Living wage, etc., for workers** - The State shall endeavour to secure, by suitable legislation or economic organization or in any other way, to all workers, agricultural, industrial or otherwise, work, a living wage, conditions of work ensuring a decent standard of life and full enjoyment of leisure and social and cultural opportunities and in particular, the state shall endeavour to promote cottage industries on an individual or co-operative basis in rural areas.

---

1 Ins. by the Constitution (Forty-second Amendment) Act, 1976, sec. 8 (w.e.f. 3-1-1977)

[1][43A **Participation of workers in management of industries**— The State shall take steps, by suitable legislation or in any other way, to secure the participation of workers in the management of undertakings, establishments or other organisations engaged in any industry.]

[2]43B**Promotion of Co–operative societies** – The state shall endeavour to promote voluntary formation, autonomous functioning, democratic control and professional management of Co–operative societies.

44. Uniform civil code for the citizens- The State shall endeavour to secure for the citizens a uniform civil code throughout the territory of India.

Notes on Article 44

Uniform law for all persons professing different faiths is a highly desirable thing. But its enactment in a pluralist society like ours in one go may be counterproductive to the unity and integrity of the nation; *Pannalal Bansilal Patil v. State of Andhra Pradesh,* AIR 1996 SC 1023 paragraph 12.

Personal Law

The Supreme court has rejected attempts (through public interest litigation) to seek the issue of writs:

(a) praying for the introduction of uniform civil code, or

(b) declaring certain enactments concerning family law as unconstitutional.

Certain petitioners prayed thus:

(a) to declare Muslim Personal Law which permits polygamy as void, infringing Articles 14 and 15 of the constitution.

(b) to declare Muslim Personal Law which gives a Muslim male overwhelming superiority over his wife by enabling him to give unilateral talaq to her and without resort to judicial process of courts, as void, offending Articles 13, 14 and 15 of the constitution.

The Supreme Court ruled that the petitions mentioned above did not deserve disposal on merit as the issues involved were matters of policy with which the court had nothing to do.

[3][45. **Provision for early childhood care and education to children below the age of six years.**- The State shall endeavour to provide, early childhood care and education for all children until they complete the age of six years.

46. Promotion of educational and economic interests of Scheduled Castes, Schedule Tribes and other weaker sections.- The State shall promote with special care the educational and economic interests of the weaker sections of the people, and in particular, of the Scheduled Castes and the Scheduled Tribes, and shall protect them from social injustice and all forms of exploitation.

47. Duty of the State to raise the level of nutrition and the standard of living and to improve public health.- The State shall regard the raising of the level of nutrition and the standard of living to its people and the improvement of public health as among its primary duties and, in particular, the State shall endeavour to bring about prohibition of the consumption except for medicinal purposes of intoxicating drinks and of drugs which are injurious to health.

48. Organization of agriculture and animal husbandry.- The State shall endeavour to organize agriculture and animal husbandry on modern and scientific lines and shall, in particular take steps for preserving and improving the breeds, and prohibiting the slaughter of cows and calves and other milch and draught cattle.

---

1 Ins. by the Constitution (Forty-second Amendment) Act, 1976, sec. 9 (w.e.f. 3-1-1977).

2 Ins. by constitution (Ninety seventh amendment) Act 2011 sec. 3 (w.e.f. 15-2-2012).

3 Subs. by the Constitution (Eighty Sixth Amendment) Act 2002 for Art. 45. Provision for free and compulsory education for children.

[1][48A. **Protection and improvement of environment and safeguarding of forests and wild life.**- The State shall endeavour to protect and improve the environment and to safeguard the forests and wild life of the country.] Tarun Bharat Sangh, Alwar v Union of India (1992)

49. **Protection of monuments and places and objects of national importance.**- It shall be the obligation of the State to protect every monument or place or object of artistic or historic interest [2][declared by or under law made by Parliament] to be of national importance, from spoilation, disfigurement, destruction, removal, disposal or export, as the case may be.

50. **Separation of judiciary from executive.**- The State shall take steps to separate the judiciary from the executive in the public services of the State.

Court and Legislature

Court cannot direct legislature to enact particular kind of laws. The prohibition of slaughter of cows, buffaloes and horses cannot be imposed by court. It is a matter of policy of govt; Bal Ram Bali v. Union of India AIR 2007

Separation of Powers

The separation of power has to be viewed through prison of constitutionalism and for upholding goals of justice in its full magnitude; University of Kerala v. Council principals, colleges, Kerala AIR 2010.

51. **Promotion of international peace and security**- The State shall endeavour to -
    (a) promote international peace and security;
    (b) maintain just and honourable relations between nations;
    (c) foster respect for international law and treaty obligations in the dealings of organized people with one another; and
    (d) encourage settlement of international disputes by arbitration.

---

[3][PART IVA]

FUNDAMENTAL DUTIES

51A **Fundamental Duties:** It shall be the duty of every citizen of India,—

(a) to abide by the Constitution and respect its ideals and institutions, the National Flag and the National Anthem;

(b) to cherish and follow the noble ideals which inspired our national struggle for freedom;

(c) to uphold and protect the sovereignty, unity and integrity of India;

(d) to defend the country and render national service when called upon to do so;

(e) to promote harmony and the spirit of common brotherhood amongst all the people of India transcending religious, linguistic and regional or sectional diversities; to renounce practices derogatory to the dignity of women;

(f) to value and preserve the rich heritage of our composite culture;

(g) to protect and improve the natural environment including forests, lakes, rivers and wild life, and to have compassion for living creatures;

---

1 Article 48A was inserted by Constitution (Forty-second Amendment) Act, 1976, sec.10 (w.e.f. 3-1-1977).

2 Subs. by the Constitution (Seventh Amendment) Act, 1956, sec. 27, for 'declared by Parliament by law' (w.e.f. 1-11-1956)

3 Ins. by the Constitution (Forty-second Amendment) Act, 1976, sec. 11 (w.e.f. 3-1-1977).

(h) to develop the scientific temper, humanism and the spirit of inquiry and reform;

(i) to safeguard public property and to abjure violence;

(j) to strive towards excellence in all spheres of individual and collective activity; so that the nation constantly rises to higher levels of endeavour and achievement.

[1][(k) who is a parent or guardian to provide opportunities for education to his child or, as the case may be, ward between the age of six and fourteen years.]

Notes on Article 51A

Provisions as to fundamental duties are non-justiciable and thus cannot be enforced by writs. There is no provision for any sanction to prevent their violation. They can be promoted by constitutional methods only. But these duties can help clear ambiguities in statutes; See the below mentioned decisions:

(*i*) *Mumbai Kamgar Sabha v. Abdul Bhai*, AIR 1976 SC 1455.

(*ii*) *Surya v. Union of India*, AIR 1982 Raj. I.

PART V

THE UNION

CHAPTER 1 — THE EXECUTIVE

The President and Vice-President

52. **The President of India.**- There shall be a President of India.

53. **Executive power of the Union.**-

(1) The executive power of the Union shall be vested in the President and shall be exercised by him either directly or through officers subordinate to him in accordance with this Constitution.

(2) Without prejudice to the generality of the foregoing provisions, the supreme command of the Defence Forces of the Union shall be vested in the President and the exercise thereof shall be regulated by law.

(3) Nothing in this article shall-

(a) be deemed to transfer to the President any functions conferred by any existing law on the Government of any State or other authority; or

(b) prevent Parliament from conferring by law functions on authorities other than the President.

54. Election of President— The President shall be elected by the members of an electoral college consisting of—

(a) the elected members of both Houses of Parliament; and

(b) the elected members of the Legislative Assemblies of the States.

[2][*Explanation.*—In this article and in article 55, "State" includes the National Capital Territory of Delhi and the Union Territory of Pondicherry.]

55. **Manner of election of President.**

(1) As far as practicable, there shall be uniformity in the scale of representation of the different States at the election of the President.

1 Ins. by the Constutiton (Eighty-sixth Amendment) Act, 2002 sec. 4 (w.e.f. 1.4.2010).

2 Ins. by the Constitution (Seventieth Amendment) Act, 1992, sec. 2 (w.e.f. 1-6-1995)

(2) For the purpose of securing such uniformity among the States *inter se* as well as parity between the States as a whole and the Union, the number of votes which each elected member of Parliament and of the Legislative Assembly of each State is entitled to cast at such election shall be determined in the following manner:

(a) every elected member of the Legislative Assembly of a State shall have as many votes as there are multiples of one thousand in the quotient obtained by dividing the population of the State by the total number of the elected members of the Assembly;

(b) if, after taking the said multiples of one thousand, the remainder is not less than five hundred, then the vote of each member referred to in sub-clause (a) shall be further increased by one;

(c) each elected member of either House of Parliament shall have such number of votes as may be obtained by dividing the total number of votes assigned to the members of the Legislative Assemblies of the States under sub-clause (a) and (b) by the total number of the elected members of both Houses of Parliament, fractions exceeding one-half being counted as one and other fraction being disregarded.

(3) The election of the President shall be held in accordance with the system of proportional representation by means of the single transferable vote and the voting at each election shall be by secret ballot.

[1][*Explanation* — In this article, the expression 'population' means the population as ascertained at the last preceding census of which the relevant figures have been published:

Provided that the reference in this *Explanation* to the last preceding census of which the relevant figures have been published shall, until the relevant figures for the first census taken after the year [2][2026] have been published, be construed as a reference to the [3][2001] census.]

56. **Term of office of President.**

(1) The President shall hold office for a term of five years from the date on which he enters upon his office; Provided that-

(a) the president, may by writing under his hand addressed to the Vice-President, resign his office;

(b) the President may, for violation of the Constitution be removed from office by impeachment in the manner provided in article 61;

(c) the President shall, notwithstanding the expiration of his term, continue to hold office until his successor enters upon the office.

(2) Any resignation addressed to the Vice-President under clause (a) of the provision to clause (1) shall forthwith be communicated by him to the Speaker of the House of the People.

57. **Eligibility for re-election.**- (1) A person who holds, or who has held office as President shall, subject to the other provisions of this Constitution be eligible for re-election to the office.

---

1 Subs. by the Constitution (Forty-second) Amendment Act, 1976, sec. 12, for the Explanation (w.e.f. 3-1-1977).

2 Subs. by the Constitution (Eighty fourth Amendment) Act, 2001, sec.2, for "2000" (w.e.f. 21-2-2002).

3 Subs. by the Constitution (Eighty fourth Amendment) Act, 2001, sec.5 for "1971" (w.e.f. 21-2-2002) and again subs. by the Constitution (Eighty-seventh Amendment) Act, 2002, for '1991' (w.e.f. 22-6-2003).

58. **Qualifications for election as President-**

(1) No person shall be eligible for election as President of India, unless he —

(a) is a citizen of India.

(b) has completed the age of thirty five years, and

(c) is qualified for election as a member of the House of the People.

(2) A person shall not be eligible for election as President if he holds any office of profit under the Government of India or the Government of any State or under any local or other authority subject to the control of any of the said Governments.

Explanation—For the purposes of this article, a person shall not be deemed to hold any office of profit by reason only that he is the President or Vice-President of the Union or the Governor [1][***} of any State or is a Minister either for the Union or for any State.

59. **Conditions of President's office-**

(1) The President shall not be a member of either House of Parliament or of a House of the Legislature of any State, and if a member of either House of Parliament or of a House of Legislature of any State be elected President, he shall be deemed to have vacated his seat in that House on the date on which he enters upon his office as President.

(2) The President shall not hold any other office of profit.

(3) The President shall be entitled without payment of rent to the use of his official residences and shall be also entitled to such emoluments, allowances and privileges as may be determined by Parliament by law and, until provision in that behalf is so made, such emoluments, allowances and privileges as are specified in the Second Schedule.

(4) The emoluments and allowances of the President shall not be diminished during his term of office.

60. **Oath or affirmation by the President.**- Every President and every person acting as President or discharging the function of the President shall, before entering upon his office, make and subscribe in the presence of the Chief Justice of India, or in his absence, the senior-most Judge of the Supreme Court available, an oath or affirmation in the following form, that is to say-

"I,A.B. do swear in the name of God/solemly affirm that I will faithfully execute the office of President (or discharge the functions of the President) of India and will to the best of my ability preserve, protect and defend the Constitution and the law and that I will devote myself to the service and well-being of the people of India."

61. **Procedure for impeachment of the President-**

(1) When a President is to be impeached for violation of the Constitution, the charge shall be preferred by either House of Parliament.

(2) No such charge shall be preferred unless-

(a) the proposal to prefer such charge is contained in a resolution which has been moved after at least fourteen days' notice in writing signed by not less than one fourth of the total number of members of the House has been given of their intention to move the resolution, and

(b) Such resolution has been passed by a majority of not less than two-thirds of the total membership of the House.

(3) When a charge has been so preferred by either House of Parliament, the other House shall investigate the charge or cause the charge to be investigated and the President shall have the right to appear and to be represented at such investigation.

---

1 The words "or Rajpramukh or Uparajpramukh" omitted by the Constitution (Seventh Amendment) Act, 1956, sec. 29 and Sch (w.e.f. 1.11.1956).

(4) If as a result of the investigation a resolution is passed by a majority of not less than two-thirds of the total membership of the House by which the charge was investigated or caused to be investigated, declaring that the charge preferred against the President has been sustained such resolution shall have the effect of removing the President from his office as from the date on which the resolution is so passed.

62. **Time of holding election to fill vacancy in the office of President and the term of office of person elected to fill casual vacancy.**

(1) An election to fill a vacancy caused by the expiration of the term of office of the President shall be completed before the expiration of the term.

(2) An election to fill a vacancy in the office of President occurring by reason of his death, resignation or removal, or otherwise shall be held as soon as possible after, and in no case later than six months from, the date of occurrence of the vacancy; and the person elected to fill the vacancy shall, subject to the provisions of article 56, be entitled to hold office for the full term of five years from the date on which he enters upon his office.

63. **The Vice-President of India.**- There shall be a Vice-President of India.

64. **The Vice-President to be ex-officio Chairman of the Council of States.**- The Vice-President shall be *ex-offico* Chairman of the Council of States and shall not hold any other office of profit;

Provided that during any period when the Vice-President acts as President or discharge the functions of the President under article 65, he shall not perform the duties of the office of Chairman of the Council of States and shall not be entitled to any salary or allowance payable to the Chairman of the Council of States under Article 97.

65. **The Vice-President to act as President or to discharge his functions during casual vacancies in the office, or during the absence, of President.**-

(1) In the event of the occurrence of any vacancy in the office of the President by reason of his death, resignation or removal, or otherwise, the Vice-President shall act as President until the date on which a new President elected in accordance with the provisions of this Chapter to fill such vacancy enters upon his office.

(2) When the President is unable to discharge his functions owing to absence, illness or any other cause, the Vice-President shall discharge his functions until the date on which the President resumes his duties.

(3) The Vice-President shall, during and in respect of, the period while he is so acting as, or discharge the functions of President, have all the powers and immunities of the President and be entitled to such emoluments, allowances and privileges as may be determined by Parliament by law and until provision in that behalf is so made, such emoluments, allowances and privileges as are specified in the Second Schedule.

66. **Election of Vice-President.**

(1) The Vice-President shall be elected by the [1][members of an electoral college consisting of the members of both Houses of Parliament] in accordance with the system of proportional representation by means of the single transferable vote and the voting at such election shall be by secret ballot.

(2) The Vice-President shall not be a member of either House of Parliament or of a House of the Legislature of any State, and if a member of either House of Parliament or of a House of the Legislature of any State be elected Vice-President, he shall be deemed to have vacated his seat in that House on the date on which he enters upon his office as Vice-President.

---

1 Subs. by the Constitution (Eleventh Amendment) Act, 1961, sec.2, for "members of both Houses of Parliament assembled at a joint meeting".

(3) No person shall be eligible for election as Vice-President unless he-

(a) is a citizen of India;

(b) has completed the age of thirty-five years; and

(c) is qualified for election as a member of the Council of States.

(4) A person shall not be eligible for election as Vice-President if he holds any office of profit under the Government of India or the Government of any State or under any local or other authority subject to the control of any of the said Governments.

Explanation—For the purposes of this article, a person shall not be deemed to hold any office of profit by reason only that he is the President or Vice-President of the Union or the Governor [1][***} of any State or is a Minister either for the Union or for any State.

67. **Term of office of Vice-President**- The Vice-President shall hold office for a term of five years from the date on which he enters upon his office:

(a) a Vice- President may, by writing under his hand addressed to the President, resign his office;

(b) a Vice-President may be removed from his office by a resolution of the Council of States passed by a majority of all the then members of the Council and agreed to by the House of the People; but no resolution for the purpose of this clause shall be moved unless at least fourteen days notice has been given of the intention to move the resolution;

(c) a Vice-President shall, notwithstanding the expiration of his term, continue to hold office until his successor enters upon his office.

68. **Time of holding election to fill vacancy in the office of Vice-President and the term of office of person elected to fill casual vacancy.**

(1) An election to fill a vacancy caused by the expiration of the term of office of Vice-President shall be completed before the expiration of the term.

(2) An election to fill a vacancy in the office of Vice-President occurring by reason of his death, resignation or removal, or otherwise shall be held as soon as possible after the occurrence of the vacancy, and the person elected to fill the vacancy shall, subject to the provisions of article 67, be entitled to hold office for a full term of five years from the date on which he enters upon his office.

69. **Oath or affirmation by the Vice-President**- Every Vice-President shall, before entering upon his office, make and subscribe before the President, or some person appointed in that behalf by him, an oath or affirmation in the following form, that is to say-

"I, A.B., do $\frac{\text{swear in the name of God}}{\text{Solemnly affirm}}$ that I will bear true faith and allegiance to the Constitution of India as by law established and that I will faithfully discharge the duty upon which I am about to enter."

70. **Discharge of President's functions in other contingencies.**- Parliament may make such provision as it thinks fit for the discharge of the functions of the President in any contingency not provided for in this Chapter.

[2][71. **Matters relating to, or connected with, the election of a President or Vice President.**

(1) All doubts and disputes arising out of or in connection with the election of a President or Vice-President shall be inquired into and decided by the Supreme Court whose decision shall be final.

---

1 The words "or Rajpramukh or Uparajpramukh" omitted by the Constitution (Seventh Amendment) Act, 1956, sec. 29 and Sch (w.e.f. 1.11.1956).

2 Subs. by the Constitution (forty-fourth Amendment) Act, 1978, sec. 10, for article 71 (w.e.f. 20-6-1979). Earlier article 71 was amended by the Constitution (Eleventh Amendment) Act, 1961, sec. 3 (w.e.f. 19-12-1961) and was substituted by the Constitution (Thirty-ninth Amendment) Act, 1975, sec. 2 (w.e.f. 10-8-1975).

(2) If the election of a person as President or Vice-President is declared void by the Supreme Court, acts done by him in the exercise and performance of the powers and duties of the office of President or Vice-President, as the case may be on or before the date of the decision of the Supreme Court shall not be invalidated by reason of that declaration.

(3) Subject to the provisions of this Constitution, Parliament may by law regulate any matter relating to or connected with the election of the President or Vice-President.

(4) The election of a person as President or Vice-President shall not be called in question on the ground of the existence of any vacancy for whatever reason among the members of the electoral college electing him.

72. **Power of President to grant pardons, etc., and to suspend, remit or commute sentences in certain cases.**

(1) The President shall have the power to grant pardons, reprieves, respites or remissions of punishment or to suspend, remit or commute the sentence of any person convicted of any offence-

(a) in all cases where the punishment or sentence is by a Court Martial;

(b) in all cases where the punishment or sentence is for an offence against any law relating to a matter to which the executive power of the Union extends;

(c) in all cases where the sentence is a sentence of death.

(2) nothing in sub-clause (a) of clause (1) shall affect the power conferred by law on any officer of the Armed Forces of the Union to suspend, remit or commute a sentence passed by a Court-Martial.

(3) Nothing in sub-clause (c) of clause (1) shall affect the power to suspend, remit or commute a sentence of death exercisable by the Governor [1][***] of a State under any law for the time being in force.

Notes on Article 72

The sum and substance of a series of decisions of the Supreme Court (and of some High courts) is:

(a) The exercise of the power by the President under Article 72 is basically a matter to be disposed off in his discretion and the courts would not interfere with his actual decision on the merits.

(b) The President can go into the mertis of the case afresh and take a different view.

The above two principles were laid down in:

Kehar Singh v. Union of India, AIR 1989 SC 653.

(c) The court enjoys a very limited power of judicial review and can interfere only when the Presidential decision is wholly irrelevant to the object of Art. 72 or is irrational, arbitrary, discriminatory or malafide. *Manu Ram v. Union of India* AIR. 1980. SC 2147, Para 62.

(d) The President is not bound to hear a petitioner seeking clemency before he rejects the petition. The undermentioned decisions buttress the above propositions.

(*i*) *Nanavati v. State of Bombay,* AIR 1961 SC 122.

(*ii*) *Godse v. State of Maharashtra,* AIR 1961 SC 600.

(*iii*) *Sarat v. Khagendra*, AIR 1961 SC 334.

(*iv*) *Kuljit v. Lt. Governor*, AIR 1982 SC 774.

1 The words "or Rajpramukh" omitted by the Constitution (Seventh Amendment) Act, 1956, sec. 29 and Sch (w.e.f. 1.11.1956).

Remission of Sentence

The power of president and Governor of grant remission of sentence is absolute and unfettered; State of Haryana v Jagdish AIR 2010

73. **Extent of executive power of the Union-**

(1) Subject to the provisions of this Constitution, the executive power of the Union shall extend.

(a) to the matter with respect to which Parliament has power to make laws; and

(b) to the exercise of such rights, authority and jurisdiction as are exercisable by the Government of India by virtue of any treaty or agreement:

Provided that the executive power referred to in sub-clause (a) shall not, save as expressly provided in this Constitution or in any law made by Parliament, extend in any State [1][***] to matters with respect to which the Legislature of the State has also power to make laws.

(2) Until otherwise provided by Parliament, a State and any officer or authority of a State may, notwithstanding anything in this article, continue to exercise in matters with respect to which Parliament has power to make laws for that State such executive power or functions as the State or officer or authority thereof could exercise immediately before the commencement of this Constitution.

74. **Council of Ministers to aid and advise President-**

[2][(1) There shall be a Council of Ministers with the Prime Minister at the head to aid and advise the President who shall, in the exercise of his functions, act in accordance with such advice;]

[3][Provided that the President may require the Council of Ministers to reconsider such advice, either generally or otherwise, and the President shall act in accordance with the advice tendered after such reconsideration].

(2) The question whether any, and if so what, advice was tendered by Ministers to the President shall not be inquired into by any court.

Notes on Article 74

Advice of Cabinet

By the preamptory provisions of Article 74(1) as it stands now (i.e. after 42nd and 44th Amendment Acts), the President is bound to act in accordance with the advice tendered by the Cabinet. This view was judicially established in *Shamsher Singh v. State of Punjab,* AIR 1974 SC 2192.

Confidentiality of Cabinet Decision

See *S.P. Gupta v. Union of India,* AIR 1982 SC 149, Para 60-61, and *State of Rajasthan v. Union of India*, AIR 1977 SC 1361, Para 82-83. See also comments on Article 78.

Article 74(2) does not exclude scrutiny of advice tendered by the Council of Ministers to the President.

Power of President to Consult Supreme Court

The text of "123 Agreement" between India and United States of America on Nuclear Co-operation was released. The Court cannot assume power and jurisdiction to itself of issuing

---

1 The words and letters "specified in Part A or Part B of the First Schedule" omitted by the Constitution (Seventh Amendment) Act, 1956, sec. 29 and Sch.(w.e.f. 1.11.1956).

2 Subs. by the Constitution (Forty-second Amendment) Act, 1976, sec. 13, for clause (1) (w.e.f. 3-1-1977).

3 Ins. by the Constitution (Forty-fourth Amendment) Act, 1978, sec. 11 (w.e.f. 20-6-1979).

mandamus to Union to make reference to President of India to exercise power vested under provisions of Article 143. It is for President to determine whether and what questions should be referred under Article 143; *Sarvjeet Kumar v. Union of India*, AIR 2008 Del 37.

75. Other Provisions as to Ministers (1) The Prime Minister shall be appointed by the President and the other Ministers shall be appointed by the President on the advice of the Prime Minister.

Clause (1A) and (1B) have been inserted in the Constitution by (Ninety first Amendment) Act 2003.

[1]**Clause (1A)**: The total number of Ministers, including the prime minister in the council of Ministers shall not exceed fifteen per cent of the total number of members of the House of the people.

[1]**Clause (1B)**: A member of either house of parliament belonging to any political party who is not disqualified for being a member of that house under paragraph 2 of the Tenth Schedule shall also be disqualified to be appointed as a Minister under clause (1) for duration of the period commencing from the date of his disqualification till the date on which the term of his office as such member would expire or where he contests any election to either House of Parliament before the expiry of such period till the date on which he is declared elected, whichever is earlier.

(2) The Ministers shall hold office during the pleasure of the President.

(3) The Council of Ministers shall be collectively responsible to the House of the People.

(4) Before a Minister enters upon his office, the President shall administer to him the oaths of office and of secrecy according to the forms set out for the purpose in the Third Schedule.

(5) A Minister who for any period of six consecutive months is not a member of either House of Parliament shall at the expiration of that period cease to be a Minister.

(6) The salaries and allowances of Ministers shall be such as Parliament may from time to time by law determine and until Parliament so determines, shall be as specified in the Second Schedule.

The Attorney-General for India

76. **Attorney- General for India.-**

(1) The President shall appoint a person who is qualified to be appointed a Judge of the Supreme Court to be Attorney-General for India.

(2) It shall be the duty of the Attorney-General to give advice to the Government of India upon such legal matters, and to perform such other duties of a legal character, as may from time to time be referred or assigned to him by the President, and to discharge the functions conferred on him by or under the Constitution or any other law for the time being in force.

(3) In the performance of his duties the Attorney-General shall have right of audience in all courts in the territory of India.

(4) The Attorney-General shall hold office during the pleasure of the President, and shall receive such remuneration as the President may determine.

Conduct of Government Business

77. **Conduct of business of the Government of India.-**

(1) All executive action of the Government of India shall be expressed to be taken in the name of the President.

---

1 Ins. by the Constituton (Ninety First Amendment) Act, 2003, Sec. 2 (w.e.f. 1.1.2004)

(2) Orders and other instruments made and executed in the name of the President shall be authenticated in such manner as may be specified in rules[1] to be made by the President, and the validity of an order or instrument which is so authenticated shall not be called in question on the ground that it is not an order or instrument made or executed by the President.

(3) The President shall make rules for the more convenient transaction of the business of the Government of India, and for the allocation among Ministers of the said business.[2][* * *]

78. **Duties of Prime Minister as respects the furnishing of information to the President, etc.**- It shall be the duty of the Prime Minister-

(a) to communicate to the President all decisions of the Council of Ministers relating to the administration of the affairs of the Union and proposals for legislation.

(b) to furnish such information relating to the administration of the affairs of the Union and proposals for legislation as the President may call for; and

(c) if the President so requires, to submit for the consideration of the Council of Ministers any matter on which a decision has been taken by a Minister but which has not been considered by the Council.

Notes on Article 78

Cabinet Secrecy

Resolutions or other deliberations of the Cabinet and the advice tendered subsequently in the light of such deliberations are privileged from disclosure in the court but if the Government produces them without any objection, the court will be empowered to look into them. Following decisions may be cited:

(*i*) *State of Punjab v. Sodhi Sukhdev,* AIR 1961 SC 512, 5

(*ii*) *State of Madhya Pradesh v. Nandlal,* AIR 1987 SC 251.

CHAPTER II — PARLIAMENT

General

79. **Constitution of Parliament**- There shall be a Parliament for the Union which shall consist of the President and two Houses to be known respectively as the Council of States and the House of the People.

80. **Composition of the Council of States.**-

(1) [3][[4][* * *]The Council of States shall consist of-

(a) twelve members to be nominated by the President in accordance with the provisions of clause (3); and

(b) not more than two hundred and thirty-eight representatives of the States [5][and of the Union territories.]

---

1 See Notification No. S.O.2297, dated the 3rd November. 1958, Gazette of India, Extra., 1958, Pt. II, Sec. 3 (ii), p. 1315, as amended from time to time.

2 Clause (4) was ins. by the Constitution (Forty-second Amendment) Act, 1976, sec. 14 (w.e.f. 3-1-1977) and omitted by the constitution (Forty-fourth Amendment) Act, 1978, Sec, 12 (w.e.f. 20-6-1979)

3 Subs. by the Constitution (Thirty-fifth Amendment) Act, 1974, sec. 3, for "The Council of States" (w.e.f. 1-3-1975).

4 The words "Subject to the provisions of paragraph 4 of the Tenth Schedule" omitted by the Constitution (Thirty-sixth Amendment) Act, 1975, sec. 5 (w.e.f. 26-4-1975).

5 Added by the Constitution (Seventh Amendment) Act, 1956, sec. 3(1)(a) (w.e.f. 1-11-1956)

(2) The allocation of seats in the Council of States to be filled by representatives of the States [1][and of the Union territories] shall be in accordance with the provisions in that behalf contained in the Fourth Schedule.

(3) The members to be nominated by the President under sub-clause (a) of clause (1) shall consist of persons having special knowledge or practical experience in respect of such matters as the following, namely;-

- literature, science, art and social service.

(4) The representatives of each State [2][***] in the Council of States shall be elected by the elected members of the Legislative Assembly of the State in accordance with the system of proportional representation by means of the single transferable vote.

(5) The representatives of the [3][Union territories] in the Council of States shall be chosen in such manner as Parliament may by law prescribe.

[4][81 Composition of the House of the People.-

(1) [5][Subject to the provisions of article 331 [6][***], the House of the People shall consist of-

(a) not more than [7][five hundred and thirty members] chosen by direct election from territorial constituencies in the State, and

(b) not more than [8][twenty members] to represent the Union territories, chosen in such manner as Parliament may by law provide.

(2) For the purposes of sub-clause (a) of clause (1) -

(a) there shall be allotted to each State a number of seats in the House of the People in such manner that the ratio between that number and the population of the State is, so far as practicable, the same for all States; and

(b) each State shall be divided into territorial constituencies in such manner that the ratio between the population of each constituency and the number of seats allotted to it is, so far as practicable, the same throughout the State:

[9][Provided that the provisions of sub-clause (a) of this clause shall not be applicable for the purpose of allotment of seats in the House of the People to any State so long as the population of that State does not exceed six millions.]

(3) In this article, the expression 'population' means the population as ascertained at the last preceding census of which the relevant figures have been published.

---

1 Added by the Constitution (Seventh Amendment) Act, 1956, sec. 3(1)(a) (w.e.f. 1-11-1956).

2 The words and letters "specified in Part A or Part B of the First Schedule" omitted by Constitution (Seventh Amendment) Act, 1956, sec. 3(1)(c) (w.e.f. 1.11.1956) .

3 Subs. by the Constitution (Seventh Amendment) Act, 1956, sec. 3(1)(d), for "states specified in Part C of the First Schedule." (w.e.f. 1.11.1956)

4 Subs. by the Constitution (Seventh Amendment) Act, 1956, sec.4, for articles. 81 (w.e.f. 1.11.1956). Earlier article 81 was amended by the Constitution (Second Amendment Act, 1952, sec. 2 (w.e.f. 1.5.1953).

5 Subs. by the Constitution (Thirty-fifth Amendment) Act, 1974, sec. 4, for "Subject to the provisions of article 331" (w.e.f. 1-3-1975).

6 The words and figure "and paragraph 4 of the Tenth Schedule" omitted by the Constitution (Thirty-sixth Amendment) Act, 1975, sec. 5 (w.e.f 26-4-1975).

7 Subs. by the Goa, Daman and Diu Reorganisation Act, 1987 (18 of 1987), sec. 63 for "five hundred and twenty-five members" (w.e.f 30-5-1987). Earlier the words 'five hundred and twenty-five menbers' were substituted by the Constitution (Thirty-first Amendment) Act, 1973, sec. 2(a)(i), for the words "five hundred members" (w.e.f. 17.10.1973)

8 Subs. by the Constitution (Thirty-first Amendment) Act, 1973, sec. 2(a)(ii), for "twenty-five members" (w.e.f. 17.10.1973). Earlier the words "twenty-five members" were substituted by the Constitution (Fourteenth Amendment) Act, 1962, sec. 2, for the words "twenty members" (w.e.f. 28.12.1962)

9 Ins. by the Constitution (Thirty-first Amendment) Act, 1973, sec. 2(b) (w.e.f. 17.10.1973).

[1][Provided that the reference, in this clause to the last preceding census of which the relevant figures have been published shall, until the relevant figures for the first census taken after the year [2][2026] have been published [3][be construed,-

(i) for the purposes of sub-clause (a) of clause (2) and the provision to that clause, as a reference to the 1971 census; and

(ii) for the purposes of sub-clause (b) of clause (2) as a reference to the [4][2001] census.

82. [5][**Readjustment after each census.**- Upon the completion of each census, the allocation of seats in the House of the people to the State and the division of each State into territorial constituencies shall be readjusted by such authority and in such manner as Parliament may by law determine:

Provided that such readjustment shall not affect representation in the House of the People until the dissolution of the then existing House;

[6][Provided further that such readjustment shall take effect from such date as the President may, by order, specify and until such readjustment takes effect, any election to the House may be held on the basis of the territorial constituencies existing before such readjustment:

Provided also that until the relevant figures for the first census taken after the year 2026[7] have been published, it shall not be necessary to [8][readjust –

i. the allocation of seats in the House of the People to the States as readjusted on the basis of the 1971 census; and

ii. the division of each State into territorial constitutencies as may be readjusted on the basis of the [9](2001) census, under this article.]]

83. Duration of Houses of Parliament.-

(1) The Council of States shall not be subject to dissolution, but as nearly as possible one-third of the members thereof shall retire as soon as may be on the expiration of every second year in accordance with the provisions made in that behalf by Parliament by law.

(2) The House of the People, unless sooner dissolved, shall continue for [10][five years] from the date appointed for its first meeting and no longer and the expiration of the said period of [five years] shall operate as a dissolution of the House.

Provided that the said period may, while a Proclamation of Emergency is in operation, be extended by Parliament by law for a period not exceeding one year at a time and not extending in any case beyond a period of six months after the Proclamation has ceased to operate.

---

1 Ins. by the Constitution (Forty-second-Amendment) Act, 1976, sec. 15 (w.e.f. 3-1-1977).

2 Subs. by the Constitution (Eighty-fourth Amendment) Act, 2001, sec.3, for "2000" (w.e.f. 21-2-2002).

3 Subs. by the Constitution (Eighty-fourth Amendment) Act, 2001, sec. 3(ii) for "be construed as a reference to the 1971 census" (w.e.f. 21-2-2002).

4 Subs. by the Constitution (Eighty-seventh Amendment) Act, 2003 sec. 2, for '1991' (w.e.f. 22-6.2003).

5 Subs. by the Constitution (Seventh Amendment) Act, 1956, sec. 4, for Art. 82 (w.e.f. 1.11.1956).

6 Ins. by the Constitution (Forty-second Amendment) Act, 1976, sec. 16 (w.e.f. 3-1-1977).

7 Subs. by the Consititution (Eighty-fourth Amendment) Act, 2001, sec. 4, for "2000" (w.e.f. 21.02.2002)

8 Subs. by the Constitution (Eighty-fourth Amendment) Act, 2001, sec. 4, for certain words (w.e.f. 21.02.2002).

9 Subs. by the Constitution (Eighty-seventh Amendment) Act, 2003 sec. 3, for '1991' (w.e.f. 22.06.2003).

10 Subs. by Constitution (Forty-fourth Amendment) Act, 1978, sec. 13, for 'six years' (w.e.f. 20-6-1979). The word 'six years' were subs. for the original words 'five years' by the Constitution (Forty-second Amendment) Act, 1976, sec. 17(i) (w.e.f. 3-1-1977).

84. Qualification for membership of Parliament.- A Person shall not be qualified to be chosen to fill a seat in Parliament unless he-

[1][(a) is a citizen of India, and makes and subscribes before some person authorized in that behalf by the Election Commission an oath or affirmation according to the form set out for the purpose in the Third-Schedule;]

(b) is, in the case of a seat in the Council of States, not less than thirty years of age and, in the case of a seat in the House of the People, not less than twenty-five years of age; and

(c) possesses such other qualifications as may be prescribed in that behalf by or under any law made by Parliament.

[2][**85. Sessions of Parliament, prorogation and dissolution-**

(1) The President shall from time to time summon each House of Parliament to meet at such time and place as he thinks fit, but six months shall not intervene between its last sitting in one session and the date appointed for its first sitting in the next session.

(2) The President may from time to time-

(a) prorogue the Houses or either House;

(b) dissolve the House of the people.

Notes on Article 85

The undermentioned cases illustrate this:

(*i*) *Rao v. Indira,* AIR 1971 SC 1002.

(*ii*) *Indira v. Rajnarain,* AIR 1975 SC 2299.

86. Right of President to address and send messages to Houses-

(1) The President may address either House of Parliament or both Houses assembled together, and for that purpose require the attendance of members.

(2) The President may send messages to either House of Parliament, whether with respect to a Bill then pending in Parliament or otherwise, and a House to which any message is so sent shall with all convenient dispatch consider any matter required by the message to be taken into consideration.

87. Special address by the President.-

(1) At the commencement of [3][the first session after each general election to the House of the People and at the commencement of the first session of each year] the President shall address both Houses of Parliament assembled together and inform Parliament of the causes of its summons.

(2) Provision shall be made by the rules regulating the procedure of either House for the allotment of time for discussion of the matters referred to in such address [4][***].

88. Rights of Ministers and Attorney-General as respects Houses.- Every Minister and the Attorney-General of India shall have the right to speak in, and otherwise to take part in the proceedings of, either House, any joint sitting of the Houses, and any Committee of Parliament of which he may be named a member, but shall not by virtue of this article be entitled to vote.

---

1 Subs. by the Constitution (sixteenth Amendment) Act, 1963, sec. 3, for clause (a) (w.e.f. 5.10.1963).

2 Subs. by the Constitution (First Amendment) Act, 1951, sec. 6, for article, 85 (w.e.f. 18.6.1951).

3 Subs. by the Constitution (First Amendment) Act, 1951, sec.7, for 'every session' (w.e.f. 18.6.1951).

4 The words "and for the precedence of such discussion over other business of the House" omitted by the Constitution (First Amendment) Act, 1951, sec. 7(2) (w.e.f. 18.6.1951).

Officers of Parliament

89. The Chairman and Deputy Chairman of the Council of States.-

(1) The Vice-President of India shall be *ex-officio* Chairman of the Council of States.

(2) The Council of States shall, as soon as may be, choose a member of the Council to be Deputy Chairman thereof, and, so often as the office of Deputy Chairman becomes vacant, the Council shall choose another member to be Deputy Chairman thereof.

90. Vacation and resignation of, removal from, the office of Deputy Chairman.- A member holding office as Deputy Chairman of the Council of States-

(a) shall vacate his office if he ceases to be a member of the Council;

(b) may at any time, by writing under his hand addressed to the Chairman, resign his office; and

(c) may be removed from his office by a resolution of the Council passed by a majority of all the then members of the Council:

Provided that no resolution for the purpose of clause (c) shall be moved unless at least fourteen days notice has been given of the intention to move the resolution.

91. Power of the Deputy Chairman or other person to perform the duties of the office of, or to act as, Chairman.-

(1) While the office of Chairman is vacant, or during any period when the Vice-President is acting as, or discharging the functions of President, the duties of the office shall be performed by the Deputy Chairman, or, if the office of Deputy Chairman is also vacant, by such member of the Council of States as the President may appoint for the purpose.

(2) During the absence of the Chairman from any sitting of the Council of States the Deputy Chairman or, if he is also absent, such person as may be determined by the rules of procedure of the Council, or, if no such person is present, such other person as may be determined by the Council, shall act as Chairman.

92. The Chairman or the Deputy Chairman not to preside while a resolution for his removal from office is under consideration.-

(1) At any sitting of the Council of States, while any resolution for the removal of the Vice-President from his office is under consideration, the Chairman or while any resolution for the removal of the Deputy Chairman from his office is under consideration, the Deputy Chairman, shall not though he is present, preside, and the provisions of clause (2) of article 91 shall apply in relation to every such sitting as they apply in relation to a sitting from which the Chairman, or, as the case may be, the Deputy Chairman, is absent.

(2) The Chairman shall have the right to speak in, and otherwise to take part in the proceedings of the Council of States while any resolution for the removal of the Vice President from his office is under consideration in the Council, but, notwithstanding anything in article 100 shall not be entitled to vote at all on such resolution or on any other matter during such proceedings.

93. The Speaker and Deputy Speaker of the House of the People.- The House of the People shall, as soon as may be, choose two members of the House to be respectively Speaker and Deputy Speaker thereof and, so often as the office of Speaker or Deputy Speaker becomes vacant, the House shall choose another member to be Speaker or Deputy Speaker, as the case may be.

94. Vacation and resignation of, and removal from, the offices of Speaker and Deputy Speaker.- A member holding office as Speaker or Deputy Speaker of the House of the People-

(a) shall vacate his office if he ceases to be a member of the House of the People;

(b) may at any time, by writing under his hand addressed, if such member is the Speaker, to the Deputy Speaker and if such member is the Deputy Speaker, to the Speaker, resign his office; and

(c) may be removed from his office by a resolution of the House of the People passed by a majority of all the then members of the House;

provided that no resolution for the purpose of clause (c) shall be moved unless at least fourteen days notice has been given of the intention to move the resolution:

Provided further that, whenever the House of the People is dissolved, the Speaker shall not vacate his office until immediately before the first meeting of the House of the People after the dissolution.

95. Power of the Deputy Speaker or other person to perform the duties of the office of, or to act as, Speaker. -

(1) While the office of Speaker is vacant, the duties of the office shall be performed by the Deputy Speaker, or, if the office of Deputy Speaker is also vacant, by such member of the House of the People as the President may appoint for the purpose.

(2) During the absence of the Speaker from any sitting of the House of the People the Deputy Speaker, or, if he is also absent, such person as may be determined by the rules of procedure of the House, or, if no such person is present, such other person as may be determined by the House, shall act as Speaker.

96. The Speaker or the Deputy Speaker not to preside while a resolution for his removal from office is under consideration.-

(1) At any sitting of the House of the People, while any resolution for the removal of the Speaker from his office is under consideration, the Speaker or while any resolution, for the removal of the Deputy Speaker from his office is under consideration, the Deputy Speaker, shall not, though he is present, preside, and the provisions of clause (2) of article 95 shall apply in relation to every such sitting as they apply in relation to a sitting from which the Speaker, or, as the case may be, the Deputy Speaker, is absent.

(2) The Speaker shall have the right to speak in, and otherwise to take part in the proceedings of the House of the People while any resolution for his removal from office is under consideration in the House and shall, notwithstanding anything in article 100, be entitled to vote only in the first instance on such resolution or on any other matter during such proceedings but not in the case of an equality of votes.

97. Salaries and allowances of the Chairman and Deputy Chairman and the Speaker and Deputy Speaker.- There shall be paid to the Chairman and the Deputy Chairman of the Council of States, and to the Speaker and the Deputy Speaker of the House of the People, such salaries and allowances as may be respectively fixed by the Parliament by law and, until provision in that behalf is so made, such salaries and allowances as are specified in the Second Schedule.

98. Secretariat of Parliament.-

(1) Each House of Parliament shall have a separate secretarial staff:

Provided that nothing in this clause shall be construed as preventing the creation of posts common to both Houses of Parliament.

(2) Parliament may by law regulate the recruitment, and the conditions of service of persons appointed, to the secretarial staff of either House of Parliament.

(3) Until provision is made by Parliament under clause (2), the President may, after consultation with the Speaker of the House of the People or the Chairman of the Council of States, as the case may be, make rules regulating the recruitment, and the conditions of service of persons appointed, to the secretarial staff of the House of the People or the

Council of States, and any rules so made shall have effect subject to the provisions of any law made under the said clause.

Conduct of Business

99. Oath or affirmation by members.- Every member of either House of Parliament shall, before taking his seat, make and subscribe before the President, or some person appointed in that behalf by him, an oath or affirmation according to the form set out for the purpose in the Third Schedule.

100. Voting in Houses, Power of Houses to act notwithstanding vacancies and quorum.-

(1) Save as otherwise provided in this Constitution, all questions at any sitting of either House or joint sitting of the Houses shall be determined by a majority of votes of the members present and voting, other than the Speaker or person acting as Chairman or Speaker.

The Chairman or Speaker, or person acting as such, shall not vote in the first instance, but shall have and exercise a casting vote in the case of an equality of votes.

(2) Either House of Parliament shall have power to act notwithstanding any vacancy in the membership thereof, and any proceedings in Parliament shall be valid notwithstanding that it is discovered subsequently that some person who was not entitled so to do sat or voted or otherwise took part in the proceedings.

(3) Until Parliament by law otherwise provides, the quorum to constitute a meeting of either House of Parliament shall be one-tenth of the total number of members of the House.

(4) If at any time during a meeting of a House there is no quorum, it shall be the duty of the Chairman or Speaker, or person acting as such, either to adjourn the House or to suspend the meeting until there is a quorum.

Disqualifications of Members

101. Vacation of Seats-

(1) No person shall be a member of both Houses of Parliament and provision shall be made by Parliament by law for the vacation by a person who is chosen a member of both Houses, of his seat in one House or the other.

(2) No person shall be a member both of Parliament and of a House of the Legislature of a State [1][***] and if a person is chosen a member both of Parliament and of a House of the Legislature of [2][a State], then, at the expiration of such period as may be specified in rules[3] made by the President, that person's seat in Parliament shall become vacant, unless he has previously resigned his seat in the Legislature of the State.

(3) If a member of either House of Parliament-

(a) becomes subject to any of the disqualifications mentioned in [4][Clause (I) or clause (2) of article 102] or

[5][(b) resigns his seat by writing under his hand addressed to the Chairman or the Speaker as the case may be, and his resignation is accepted by the Chairman or the Speaker, as the case may be]

---

1 The words and letters "specified in Part A or Part B of the First Schedule" omitted by the Constitution (Seventh Amendment) Act, 1956, sec. 29 and Sch. (w.e.f. 1.11.1956)

2 Subs. by the Constitution (Seventh Amendment) Act, 1956, sec. 29 and Sch., for 'such a State' (w.e.f. 1.11.1956).

3 See the Prohibition of Simultaneous Membership Rules, 1950, published with the Ministry of Law Notification No. F.46/50-C, dated 26th January, 1950, Gazette of India, Extraordinary, p. 678.

4 Subs. by the Constitution (Fifty-second Amendment) Act, 1985, sec.2, for the words in brackets and figures 'clause (1) of article 102' (w.e.f 1-3-1985).

5 Subs. by the Constitution (Thirty-third Amendment) Act, 1974, sec.2, for sub-clause (b) (w.e.f. 19.5.1974).

his seat shall thereupon become vacant:

[1][Provided that in the case of any resignation referred to in sub-clause (b), if from information received or otherwise and after making such inquiry as he thinks fit, the Chairman or the Speaker, as the case may be, is satisfied that such resignation is not voluntary or genuine, he shall not accept such resignation.]

(4) If for a period of sixty days a member of either House of Parliament is without permission of the House absent from all meetings thereof, the House may declare his seat vacant:

Provided that in computing the said period of sixty days no account shall be taken of any period during which the House is prorogued or is adjourned for more than four consecutive days.

102. Disqualifications for membership-

(1) A person shall be disqualified for being chosen as, and for being, a member of either House of Parliament-

(a) if he holds any office of profit under the Government of India or the Government of any State, other than an office declared by Parliament by law not to disqualify its holder;

(b) if he is of unsound mind and stands so declared by a competent court;

(c) if he is an undischarged insolvent;

(d) if he is not a citizen of India, or has voluntarily acquired the citizenship of a foreign State, or is under any acknowledgment of allegiance or adherence to a foreign State;

(e) if he is so disqualified by or under any law made by Parliament.

[2][*Explanation* — For the purposes of this clause] a person shall not be deemed to hold an office of profit under the Government of India or the Government of any State by reason only that he is a Minister either for the Union or for such State.

[3][(2) A person shall be disqualified for being a member of either House of Parliament if he is so disqualified under the Tenth Schedule.]

Office of profit

If the 'pecuniary gain' is 'receivable' in connection with the office then it becomes an office of profit, irrespective of whether such pecuniary gain is actually received or not; *Jaya Bachchan v. Union of India*, AIR 2006 SC 2119

[4][103. Decision on questions as to disqualifications of members.-

(1) If any question arises as to whether a member of either House of Parliament has become subject to any of the disqualifications mentioned in clause (1) of article 102, the question shall be referred for the decision of the President and his decision shall be final.

(2) Before giving any decision on any such question, the President shall obtain the opinion of the Election Commission and shall act according to such opinion.

---

1 Ins. by the Constitution (Thirty-third Amendment) Act, 1974, sec. 2(2) (w.e.f. 19.5.1974).

2 Subs. by the Constitution (Fifty-second Amendment) Act, 1985, sec. 3. "for the purposes of this article" (w.e.f. 1-3-1985)

3 Ins. by the Constitution (Fifty-second Amendment) Act, 1985, sec. 3 (w.e.f 1-3-1985).

4 Article 103 has been successively subs. by the Constitution (Forty-second Amendment) Act 1976, sec.20 (w.e.f. 3-1-1977) and the Constitution (Forty-fourth Amendment) Act, 1978, sec. 14, to read as above (w.e.f 20-6-1979).

Office of profit

If the 'pecuniary gain' is 'receivable' in connection with the office then it becomes an office of profit, irrespective of whether such pecuniary gain is actually received or not; *Jaya Bachchan v. Union of India*, AIR 2006 SC 2119

104. Penalty for sitting and voting before making oath or affirmation under article 99 or when not qualified or when disqualified.- If a person sits or votes as a member of either House of Parliament before he has complied with the requirements of article 99, or when he knows that he is not qualified or that he is disqualified for membership thereof, or that he is prohibited from doing so by the provisions of any law made by Parliament, he shall be liable in respect of each day on which he so sits or votes to a penalty of five hundred rupees to be recovered as a debt due to the Union.

Powers, Privileges and Immunities of Parliament and its Members

105. Powers, privileges, etc., of the Houses of Parliament and of the members and committees thereof.-

(1) Subject to the provisions of this Constitution and to the rules and standing orders regulating the procedure of Parliament, there shall be freedom of speech in Parliament.

(2) No member of Parliament shall be liable to any proceedings in any court in respect of anything said or any vote given by him in Parliament or any committee thereof, and no person shall be so liable in respect of the publication by or under the authority of either House of Parliament of any report, paper, votes or proceedings.

(3) In other respects, the powers, privileges and immunities of each House of Parliament and of the members and the committees of each House, shall be such as may from time to time be defined by Parliament by law, and until so defined, [1][shall be those of that House and of its members and committees immediately before the coming into force of section 15 of the Constitution (Forty-fourth Amendment) Act, 1978].

(4) The provisions of clause (1), (2) and (3) shall apply in relation to persons who by virtue of this Constitution have the right to speak in, and otherwise to take part in the proceedings of, a House of Parliament or any Committee thereof as they apply in relation to members of Parliament.

106. Salaries and allowances of members.- Members of either House of Parliament shall be entitled to receive such salaries and allowances as may from time to time be determined by Parliament by law and, until provision in that respect is so made, allowances at such rates and upon such conditions as were immediately before the commencement of this Constitution applicable in the case of members of the Constituent Assembly of the Dominion of India.

Legislative Procedure

107. Provisions as to introduction and passing of Bills.-

(1) Subject to the provisions of articles 109 and 117 with respect to Money Bills and other Financial Bills, a Bill may originate in either House of Parliament.

(2) Subject to the provisions of articles 108 and 109, a Bill shall not be deemed to have been passed by the Houses of Parliament unless it has been agreed to by both Houses, either without amendment or with such amendments only as are agreed to by both Houses.

(3) A Bill pending in Parliament shall not lapse by reason of the prorogation of the Houses.

1 Subs. by the Constitution (Forty-fourth Amendment) Act, 1978, sec. 15, for certain words (w.e.f. 20-6-1979).

(4) A Bill pending in the Council of States which has not been passed by the House of the People shall not lapse on a dissolution of the House of People.

(5) A Bill which is pending in the House of the People, or which having been passed by the House of the People is pending in the Council of States, shall, subject to the provisions of article 108, lapse on a dissolution of the House of the People.

108. Joint Sitting of both Houses in certain cases.-

(1) If after a Bill has been passed by one House and transmitted to other House -

(a) the Bill is rejected by the other House; or

(b) the Houses have finally disagreed as to the amendments to be made in the Bill; or

(c) more than six months elapse from the date of the receipt of the Bill by the other House without the Bill being passed by it,

the President may, unless the Bill has lapsed by reason of a dissolution of the House of the People, notify to the Houses by message if they are sitting or by public notification if they are not sitting, his intention to summon them to meet in a joint sitting for the purpose of deliberating and voting on the Bill:

Provided that nothing in this clause shall apply to a Money Bill.

(2) In reckoning any such period of six months as is referred to in clause (1) no account shall be taken of any period during which the House referred to in sub-clause (c) of that clause is prorogued or adjourned for more than four consecutive days.

(3) Where the President has under clause (1) notified his intention of summoning the Houses to meet in a joint sitting, neither House shall proceed further with the Bill, but the President may at any time after the date of his notification summon the Houses to meet in a joint sitting for the purpose specified in the notification and, if he does so, the Houses shall meet accordingly.

(4) If at the joint sitting of the two Houses the Bill, with such amendments, if any, as are agreed to in joint sitting, is passed by a majority of the total number of members of both Houses present and voting, it shall be deemed for the purposes of this Constitution to have been passed by both Houses:

Provided that at a joint sitting-

(a) if the Bill having been passed by one House, has not been passed by the other House with amendments and returned to the House in which it originated, no amendment shall be proposed to the Bill other than such amendments (if any) as are made necessary by the delay in the passage of the Bill;

(b) if the Bill has been so passed and returned, only such amendments as aforesaid shall be proposed to the Bill and such other amendments as are relevant to the matters with respect to which the Houses have not agreed,

and the decision of the person presiding as to the amendments which are admissible under this clause shall be final.

(5) A joint sitting may be held under this article and a Bill passed thereat, notwithstanding that a dissolution of the House of People has intervened since the President notified his intention to summon the Houses to meet therein.

109. Special procedure in respect of Money Bills.-

(1) A Money Bill shall not be introduced in the Council of States.

(2) After a Money Bill has been passed by the House of the People it shall be transmitted to the Council of States for its recommendations and the Council of States shall within a period of fourteen days from the date of its receipt of the Bill, return the Bill to the House of the People with its recommendations and the House of People may thereupon either accept or reject all or any of the recommendations of the Council of States.

(3) If the House of the people accepts any of the recommendations of the Council of States, the Money Bill shall be deemed to have been passed by both Houses with the amendments recommended by the Council of States and accepted by the House of the People.

(4) If the House of the People does not accept any of the recommendations of the Council of States, the Money Bill shall be deemed to have been passed by both Houses in the form in which it was passed by the House of the People without any of the amendments recommended by the Council of States.

(5) If a Money Bill passed by the House of the People and transmitted to the Council of states for its recommendations is not returned to the House of the People within the said period of fourteen days, it shall be deemed to have been passed by both Houses at the expiration of the said period in the form in which it was passed by the House of the People.

110. Definition of 'Money Bills'.-

(1) For the purposes of this Chapter, a Bill shall be deemed to be a Money Bill if it contains only provisions dealing with all or any of the following matters, namely:-

- (a) the imposition, abolition, remission, alteration or regulation of any tax;
- (b) the regulation of the borrowing of money or the giving of any guarantee by the Government of India, or the amendment of the law with respect to any financial obligations undertaken or to be undertaken by the Government of India;
- (c) the custody of the Consolidated Fund or the Contingency Fund of India, the payment of moneys into or the withdrawal of moneys from any such fund;
- (d) the appropriation of moneys out of the Consolidated Fund of India;
- (e) the declaring of any expenditure to be expenditure charged on the Consolidated Fund of India or the increasing of the amount of any such expenditure.
- (f) the receipt of money on account of the Consolidated Fund of India or the public account of India or the custody or issue of such money or the audit of the accounts of the Union or of a State; or
- (g) any matter incidental to any of the matters specified in sub-clause (a) to (f).

(2) A Bill shall not be deemed to be a Money Bill by reason only that it provides for the imposition of fines or other pecuniary penalties, or for the demand or payment of fees for licences or fees for services rendered, or by reason that it provides for the imposition, abolition, remission, alteration or regulation of any tax by any local authority or body for local purposes.

(3) If any question arises whether a Bill is a Money Bill or not, the decision of the Speaker of the House of the People thereon shall be final.

(4) There shall be endorsed on every Money Bill when it is transmitted to the Council of States under article 109, and when it is presented to the President for assent under article 111, the certificate of the Speaker of the House of the People signed by him that it is a Money Bill.

111. Assent to Bills.- When a Bill has been passed by the Houses of Parliament, it shall be presented to the President, and the President shall declare either that he assents to the Bill, or that he withholds assent therefrom:

Provided that the President may as soon as possible after the presentation to him of a Bill for assent, return the Bill if it is not a Money Bill to the Houses with a message requesting that they will reconsider the Bill or any specified provisions thereof and, in particular, will consider the desirability of introducing any such amendments as he may recommend in his message, and when a Bill is so returned, the Houses shall reconsider the Bill accordingly, and if the Bill is passed again by the Houses with or without amendment and presented to the President for assent, the President shall not withhold assent therefrom.

Procedure in Financial Matters

112. Annual Financial Statement.-

(1) The President shall in respect of every financial year cause to be laid before both the Houses of Parliament a statement of the estimated receipts and expenditure of the Government of India for that year, in this Part referred to as the "annual financial statement".

(2) The estimates of expenditure embodied in the annual financial statement shall show separately-

(a) the sums required to meet expenditure described by this Constitution as expenditure charged upon the Consolidated Fund of India; and

(b) the sums required to meet other expenditure proposed to be made from the Consolidated Fund of India,

and shall distinguish expenditure on revenue account from other expenditure.

(3) The following expenditures shall be expenditure charged on the Consolidated Fund of India-

(a) the emoluments and allowances of the President and other expenditure relating to his office;

(b) the salaries and allowances of the Chairman and the Deputy Chairman of the Council of States and the Speaker and the Deputy Speaker of the House of the People;

(c) debt charges for which the Government of India is liable including interest, sinking fund charges and redemption charges, and other expenditure relating to the raising of loans and the service and redemption of debt;

(d) (*i*) the salaries, allowances and pensions payable to or in respect of Judges of the Supreme Court,

(*ii*) the pensions payable to or in respect of Judges of the Federal Court;

(*iii*) the pensions payable to or in respect of Judges of any High Court which exercises jurisdiction in relation to any area included in the territory of India or which at any time before the commencement of this Constitution exercised jurisdiction in relation to any area included in [1][a Governor's Province of the Dominion of India];

(e) the salary, allowances and pension payable to or in respect of the Comptroller and Auditor-General of India;

(f) any sums required to satisfy any judgement, decree or award of any court or arbitral tribunal;

(g) any other expenditure declared by this Constitution or by Parliament by law to be so charged.

113. Procedure in Parliament with respect to estimates.-

(1) So much of the estimates as relates to expenditure charged upon the Consolidated Fund of India shall not be submitted to the vote of Parliament, but nothing in this clause shall be construed as preventing the discussion in either House of Parliament of any of those estimates.

(2) So much of the said estimates as relates to other expenditure shall be submitted in the form of demands for grants to the House of the People, and the House of the People shall have power to assent, or to refuse, to assent, to any demand, or to assent to any demand subject to a reduction of the amount specified therein.

(3) No demand for a grant shall be made except on the recommendation of the President.

---

1 Subs. by the Constitution (Seventh Amendment) Act, 1956, sec. 29 and Sch., for "a Province corresponding to a State in Part A of the First Schedule". (w.e.f. 1-11-1956)

114. Appropriation Bills.-

(1) As soon as may be after the grants under article 113 have been made by the House of the People, there shall be introduced a Bill to provide for the appropriation out of the Consolidated Fund of India of all moneys required to meet-

(a) the grants so made by the House of the People; and

(b) the expenditure charged on the Consolidated Fund of India but not exceeding in any case the amount shown in the statement previously laid before Parliament.

(2) No amendment shall be proposed to any such Bill in either House of Parliament which will have the effect of varying the amount or altering the destination of any grant so made or of varying the amount of any expenditure charged on the Consolidated Fund of India, and the decision of the person presiding as to whether an amendment is inadmissible under this clause shall be final.

(3) Subject to the provisions of articles 115 and 116, no money shall be withdrawn from the Consolidated Fund of India except under appropriation made by law passed in accordance with the provisions of this article.

115. Supplementary, additional or excess grants.-

(1) The President shall -

(a) if the amount authorised by any law made in accordance with the provisions of article 114 to be expended for a particular service for the current financial year is found to be insufficient for the purposes of that year or when a need has arisen during the current financial year for supplementary or additional expenditure upon some new service not contemplated in the annual financial statement for that year, or

(b) if any money has been spent on any service during a financial year in excess of the amount granted for that service and for that year,

cause to be laid before both the Houses of Parliament another statement showing the estimated amount of the expenditure or cause to be presented to the House of the People a demand for such excess, as the case may be.

(2) The provisions of articles 112, 113 and 114 shall have effect in relation to any such statement and expenditure or demand and also to any law to be made authorizing the appropriation of moneys out of the Consolidated Fund of India to meet such expenditure or the grant in respect of such demand as they have effect in relation to the annual financial statement and the expenditure mentioned therein or to a demand for a grant and the law to be made for the authorization of appropriation of moneys out of the Consolidated Fund of India to meet such expenditure or grant.

116. Votes on account, votes of credit and exceptional grants.-

(1) Notwithstanding anything in the foregoing provisions of this Chapter, the House of the People shall have power-

(a) to make any grant in advance in respect of the estimated expenditure for a part of any financial year pending the completion of the procedure prescribed in article 113 for the voting of such grant and the passing of the law in accordance with the provisions of article 114 in relation to that expenditure;

(b) to make a grant for meeting an unexpected demand upon the resources of India when on account of the magnitude or the indefinite character of the service the demand cannot be stated with the details ordinarily given in an annual financial statement;

(c) to make an exceptional grant which forms no part of the current service of any financial year,

and Parliament shall have power to authorise by law the withdrawal of moneys from the Consolidated Fund of India for the purposes for which the said grants are made.

(2) The provisions of articles 113 and 114 shall have effect in relation to the making of any grant under clause (1) and to any law to be made under that clause as they have effect in relation to the making of a grant with regard to any expenditure mentioned in the annual financial statement and the law to be made for the authorization of appropriation of moneys out of the Consolidated Fund of India to meet such expenditure.

117. Special provisions as to financial Bills.-

(1) A Bill or amendment making provision for any of the matters specified in sub-clauses (a) to (f) of clause (1) of article 110-shall not be introduced or moved except on the recommendation of the President and a Bill making such provision shall not be introduced in the Council of States;

Provided that no recommendation shall be required under this clause for the moving of an amendment making provision for the reduction or abolition of any tax.

(2) A Bill or amendment shall not be deemed to make provision for any of the matters aforesaid by reason only that it provides for the imposition of fines or other pecuniary penalties, or for the demand or payment of fees for licences or fees for services rendered, or by reason that it provides for the imposition, abolition, remission, alteration or regulation of any tax by any local authority or body for local purposes.

(3) A Bill which, if enacted and brought into operation, would involve expenditure from the Consolidated Fund of India shall not be passed by either House of Parliament unless the President has recommended to that House the consideration of the Bill.

Procedure Generally

118. Rules of Procedure.-

(1) Each House of Parliament may make rules for regulating, subject to the provisions of this Constitution, its procedure[1][***] and the conduct of its business.

(2) Until rules are made under clause (1), the rules of procedure and standing orders in force immediately before the commencement of this Constitution with respect to the Legislature of the Dominion of India shall have effect in relation to Parliament subject to such modifications and adaptations as may be made therein by the Chairman of the Council of States or the Speaker of the House of the People, as the case may be.

(3) The President, after consultation with the Chairman of the Council of States and the Speaker of the House of the People, may make rules as to the procedure with respect to joint sittings of, and communications between, the two Houses.

(4) At a joint sitting of the two Houses the Speaker of the House of People, or in his absence such person as may be determined by rules of procedures made under clause (3), shall preside.

119. Regulation by law of procedure in Parliament in relation to financial business.- Parliament may, for the purpose of the timely completion of financial business, regulate by law the procedure of, and the conduct of business in, each House of Parliament in relation to any financial matter or to any Bill for the appropriation of moneys out of the Consolidated Fund of India, and, if and so far as any provision of any law so made is inconsistent with any rule made by a House of Parliament under clause (1) of article 118 or with any rule or standing order having effect in relation to Parliament under clause (2) of that article, such provision shall prevail.

120. Language to be used in Parliament.-

(1) Notwithstanding any thing in Part XVII, but subject to the provisions of article 348, business in Parliament shall be transacted in Hindi or in English:

---

1 The words "(including the quorum to constitute a meeting of the House)" omitted by the Constitution (Forty-fourth Amendment) Act, 1978, sec. 45. Earlier the words "(including the quorum to constitute a meeting of the House)" were inserted by the Constitution (Forty-second Amendment) Act, 1976, sec. 22 which had not been brought into force till then.

Provided that the Chairman of the Council of States or Speaker of the House of the People, or person acting as such, as the case may be, may permit any member who cannot adequately express himself in Hindi or in English to address the House in his mother-tongue.

(2) Unless Parliament by law otherwise provides, this article shall, after the expiration of a period of fifteen years from the commencement of this Constitution, have effect as if the words "or in English" were omitted therefrom.

121. Restriction on discussion in Parliament- No discussion shall take place in Parliament with respect to the conduct of any Judge of the Supreme Court or of a High Court in the discharge of his duties except upon a motion for presenting an address to the President praying for the removal of the Judge as hereinafter provided.

122. Courts not to inquire into proceedings of Parliament.-

(1) The validity of any proceedings in Parliament shall not be called in question on the ground of any alleged irregularity of procedure.

(2) No officer or member of Parliament in whom powers are vested by or under this Constitution for regulating procedure or the conduct of business, or for maintaining order, in Parliament shall be subject to the jurisdiction of any court in respect of the exercise by him of those powers.

CHAPTER III – LEGISLATIVE POWERS OF THE PRESIDENT

123. Power of President to promulgate Ordinances during recess of Parliament. -

(1) If at any time, except when both Houses of Parliament are in session, the President is satisfied that circumstances exist which render it necessary for him to take immediate action, he may promulgate such Ordinances as the circumstances appear to him to require.

(2) An Ordinance promulgated under this article shall have the same force and effect as an Act of parliament, but every such Ordinance-

(a) shall be laid before both Houses of Parliament and shall cease to operate at the expiration of six weeks from the reassembly of Parliament, or, if before the expiration of that period resolutions disapproving it are passed by both Houses, upon the passing of the second of those resolutions; and

(b) may be withdrawn at any time by the President.

Explanation-Where the Houses of Parliament are summoned to reassemble on different dates, the period of six weeks shall be reckoned from the later of those dates for the purposes of this clause.

(3) If and so far as an Ordinance under this article makes any provision which Parliament would not under this Constitution be competent to enact, it shall be void.[1][***]

Notes on Article 123

Scope

The object of this Article is to enable the President (an organ of Parliament) to promulgate Ordinances during the recess of the Parliament. The President becomes Parliament personified for all practical purposes. His satisfaction as to the existence of circumstances rendering it necessary to take immediate action, has to be on the advice of the cabinet. Undermentioned decisions illustrate these propositions:

(*i*) *Cooper v. Union of India,* AIR 1970 SC 564.

(*ii*) *A.K. Roy v. Union of India,* AIR 1982 SC 710.

(*vi*) *Satpal v. Lt. Governor,* AIR 1979 SC 1550.

1 Clause (4) was ins. by the Constitution (Thirty-eighth Amendment) Act, 1975, sec. 2 (restrospectively) and omitted by the Constitution (Forty-fourth Amendment) Act, 1978, sec. 16 (w.e.f. 20-6-1979).

CHAPTER IV — THE UNION JUDICIARY

124. Establishment and constitution of Supreme Court. -

(1) There shall be a Supreme Court of India consisting of a Chief Justice of India and, until Parliament by law prescribes a larger number, of not more than seven[1] other Judges.

(2) Every Judge of the Supreme Court shall be appointed by the President by warrant under his hand and seal after consultation with such of the Judges of the Supreme Court and of the High Courts in the States as the President may deem necessary for the purpose and shall hold office until he attains the age of sixty-five years;

Provided that in the case of appointment of a Judge other than the Chief Justice, the Chief Justice of India shall always be consulted:

Provided further that-

(a) a Judge may, by writing under his hand addressed to the President, resign his office;

(b) a Judge may be removed from his office in the manner provided in clause (4),

[2][2A)]. The age of a Judge of the Supreme Court shall be determined by such authority and in such manner as Parliament may by law provide].

(3) A person shall not be qualified for appointment as a Judge of the Supreme Court unless he is a citizen of India and-

(a) has been for at least five years a Judge of a High Court or of two or more such Courts in succession; or

(b) has been for at least ten years an advocate of a High Court or of two or more such Courts in succession; or

(c) is, in the opinion of the President, a distinguished jurist.

Explanation I. — In this clause "High Court" means a High Court which exercises, or which at anytime before the commencement of this Constitution exercised, jurisdiction in any part of the territory of India.

Explanation II.— In computing for the purpose of this clause the period during which a person has been an advocate, any period during which a person has held judicial office not inferior to that of a district Judge after he became an advocate shall be included.

(4) A Judge of the Supreme Court shall not be removed from his office except by an order of the President passed after an address by each House of Parliament supported by a majority of the total membership of that House and by a majority of not less than two thirds of the members of the House present and voting has been presented to the President in the same session for such removal on the ground of proved misbehaviour or incapacity.

(5) Parliament may by law regulate the procedure for the presentation of an address and for the investigation and proof of the misbehaviour or incapacity of a Judge under clause (4).

(6) Every person appointed to be a Judge of the Supreme Court shall, before he enters upon his office, make and subscribe before the President, or some person appointed in that behalf by him, an oath or affirmation according to the form set out for the purpose in the Third Schedule.

(7) No person who has held office as a Judge of the Supreme Court shall plead or act in any court or before any authority within the territory of India.

---

1 Now "thirty", *vide* the Supreme Court (Number of Judges) Amendment Act, 2008 (11 of 2009). Earlier it was "twenty-five", *vide* the Supreme Court (Number of Judges) Amendment Act, 1986 (22 of 1986).

2 Ins. by the Constitution (Fifteenth Amendment) Act, 1963, sec.2 (w.e.f. 5.10.1963).

Notes on Article 124

In re presidential reference AIR 1999 SC 1, the supreme court has held that recommendations made by the chief Justice of India were not binding on the Central Government if it does not comply with the norms and requirements of the consultation process. The following propositions were laid down when the president sought the court's opinion with respect to the appointment of Apex Court Judges and transfer of High court Judges:

(*i*) The chief justice of India should consult a collegium of four senior most judges of the Supreme Court in the appointment of the Apex court judges. The recommendation should not be sent to the Government if two judges give an adverse opinion.

(*ii*) The collegium should make the decision in consensus and no recommendation is to be made if the opinion of the collegium is not in conformity with that of the Chief Justice.

(*iii*) Apart from the collegium of four senior most judges, the Chief Justice of two high courts should be consulted by the Chief Justice of India in matter of the transfer of High Court Judges.

(*iv*) The Chief Justice of India was required to consult only two senior most judges of the supreme court in case of the appointment of high court judges.

(*v*) The sole opinion of the Chief Justice of India does not constitute the consultation process. It needs the consultation of plurality of judges.

(*vi*) The transfer of judges of the High Courts was judicially review able if it does not comply with the consultation process.

The views of the other judges consulted by the Chief Justice of India should be in writing and the same should be conveyed to the government.

Consultation

Consultation with the Chief Justice must be effective and implies exchange of views after examining the merits. But the concurrence of the Chief Justice is not mandatory. See the cases below:

(*i*) *S.P. Gupta v. Union of India,* AIR 1982 SC 149.

(*ii*) *Union of India v. Sankalchand Seth,* AIR 1977 SC 2328.

125. Salaries, etc., of Judges. -

[1][(1)1There shall be paid to the Judges of the Supreme Court such salaries, as may be determined by Parliament by law and, until provision in that behalf is so made, such salaries as are specified in the Second Schedule.]

(2) Every Judge shall be entitled to such privileges and allowances and to such rights in respect of leave of absence and pension as may from time to time be determined by or under law made by Parliament and, until so determined, to such privileges, allowances and rights as are specified in the Second Schedule:

Provided that neither the privileges nor the allowances of a Judge nor his rights in respect of leave of absence or pension shall be varied to his disadvantage after his appointment.

126. Appointment of acting Chief Justice.- When the office of Chief Justice of India is vacant or when the Chief Justice is, by reason of absence or otherwise, unable to perform the duties of his office, the duties of the office shall be performed by such one of the other Judges of the Court as the President may appoint for the purpose.

1 Subs. by the Constitution (Fifty-fourth Amendment) Act, 1986, sec.2, for clause (1) (w.e.f. 1-4-1986).

127. Appointment of *ad hoc* Judges. -

(1) If at any time there should not be a quorum of the Judges of the Supreme Court available to hold or continue any session of the Court, the Chief Justice of India may, with the previous consent of the President and after consultation with the Chief Justice of the High Court concerned, request in writing the attendance at the sittings of the Court, as an *ad hoc* Judge, for such period as may be necessary, of a Judge of a High Court duly qualified for appointment as a Judge of the Supreme Court to be designated by the Chief Justice of India.

(2) It shall be the duty of the Judge who has been so designated, in priority to other duties of his office to attend the sittings of the Supreme Court at the time and for the period for which his attendance is required, and while so attending he shall have all the jurisdiction, powers and privileges, and shall discharge the duties, of a Judge of the Supreme Court.

128. Attendance of retired Judges at sittings of the Supreme Court.- Notwithstanding anything in this Chapter, the Chief Justice of India may at any time, with the previous consent of the President, request any person who has held the office of a Judge of the Supreme Court or of the Federal Court [1][or who has held the office of a Judge of a High Court and is duly qualified for appointment as a Judge of the Supreme Court] to sit and act as a Judge of the Supreme Court, and every such person so requested shall, while so sitting and acting, be entitled to such allowances as the president may by order determine and have all the jurisdiction, powers and privileges of, but shall not otherwise be deemed to be, a Judge of that Court:

Provided that nothing in this article shall be deemed to require any such person as aforesaid to sit and act as a Judge of that Court unless he consents so to do.

129. Supreme Court to be a court of record. - The Supreme Court shall be a court of record and shall have all the powers of such a court including the power to punish for contempt of itself.

Notes on Article 129

Contempt of Supreme Court. - Supreme Court as a guardian of right to personal liberty, cannot do anything by which that right is taken away or obridged, especially when supreme court is acting suo moto as in proceedings for its own contempt, Leila David v. State of Maharashtra (2009) 4 SCC 578: AIR 2010

130. Seat of Supreme Court. - The Supreme Court shall sit in Delhi or in such other place or places, as the Chief Justice of India may, with the approval of the President, from time to time, appoint.

131. Original Jurisdiction of the Supreme Court. - Subject to the provisions of this Constitution, the Supreme Court shall, to the exclusion of any other court, have original jurisdiction in any dispute-

(a) between the Government of India and one or more States; or

(b) between the Government of India and any State or States on one side and one or more other States on the other; or

(c) between two or more States,

if and in so far as the dispute involves any question (whether of law or fact) on which the existence or extent of a legal right depends:

[2][Provided that the said jurisdiction shall not extend to a dispute arising out of any treaty, agreement, covenant, engagement, sanad or other similar instrument which, having been entered into or executed before the commencement of this Constitution, continues in operation after such commencement, or which provides that the said jurisdiction shall not extend to such a dispute.

---

1 Ins. by the Constitution (Fifteenth Amendment) Act, 1963, sec.3 (w.e.f. 5.10.1963).

2 Subs. by the Constitution (Seventh Amendment) Act, 1956, sec.5, for the proviso (w.e.f. 1.11.1956).

Notes on Article 131

In T.N. Cauvery Sangam v. Union of India (1990) 21 SCJ 547, it was held that in interstate water disputes, jurisdiction is excluded.

In interstate water disputes, original jurisdiction is excluded; *T.N. Cauvery Sangam v. Union of India,* (1990) 2 SCJ 547.

Dispute between two States

Article 131 will not be applicable where citizens or private bodies are parties either jointly or alternative with State; *Tashi Delek Gaming Solutions Ltd. v. State of Karnataka*; AIR 2006 SC 661.

[1]**131A. Exclusive jurisdiction of the Supreme Court in regard to questions as to the constitutional validity of Central Laws.** *[Rep. by the Constitution [Forty-third Amendment] Act, 1977, sec. 4 (w.e.f. 14-4-1978)].*

132. Appellate jurisdiction of the Supreme Court in appeals from High Courts in certain cases.-

(1) An appeal shall lie to the Supreme Court from any judgement, decree or final order of a High Court in the territory of India, whether in a civil, criminal or other proceeding, [2][if the High Court certifies under article 134A] that the case involves a substantial question of law as to the interpretation of this Constitution.[3][***]

(3) Where such a certificate is given, [4][***] any party in the case may appeal to the Supreme Court on the ground that any such question as aforesaid has been wrongly decided [5][***].

Explanation.—For the purposes of this article, the expression "final order" includes an order deciding an issue which, if decided in favour of the appellant, would be sufficient for the final disposal of the case.

Notes on Article 132

Under article 132, the appellate jurisdiction of the Supreme Court in constitutional cases has been spelt out. It must be read with Article 134A (inserted by the 44th Amendment Act, 1978) under which if a substantial question of interpretation of the constitution is involved, the High Court must grant a certificate to that effect.

133. Appellate jurisdiction of Supreme Court in appeals from High Courts in regard to civil matters.-

[6][(1) An appeal shall lie to the Supreme Court from any judgement, decree or final order in a civil proceeding of a High Court in the territory of India [7][if the High Court certifies under article 134A-]

(a) that the case involves a substantial question of law of general importance; and

(b) that in the opinion of the High Court the said question needs to be decided by the Supreme Court].

---

1 Ins. by the Constitution (Forty-second Amendment) Act, 1976, sec. 23 (w.e.f. 1-2-1977).

2 Subs. by the Constitution (Forty-fourth Amendment) Act, 1978, sec.17, for "if the High Court certifies" (w.e.f. 1-8-1979).

3 Clause (2) omitted by the Constitution (Forty-fourth Amendment) Act, 1978, sec. 17 (w.e.f. 1-8-1979).

4 The words "or such leave is granted," omitted by the Constitution (Forthy-fourth Amendment) Act, 1978, sec. 17(c) (w.e.f. 1-8-1979).

5 Certain words omitted by the Constitution (Forty-fourth Amendment) Act, 1978, sec. 17 (w.e.f. 1-8-1979).

6 Subs. by the Constitution (Thirtieth Amendment) Act, 1972, sec. 2, for clause (1) (w.e.f. 27-2-1973).

7 Subs. by the Constitution (Forty-fourth Amendment) Act, 1978, sec.18, for "if the High Court certifies" (w.e.f. 1-8-1979).

(2) Notwithstanding anything in article 132, any party appealing to the Supreme Court under clause (1) may urge as one of the grounds in such appeal that a substantial question of law as to the interpretation of this Constitution has been wrongly decided.

(3) Notwithstanding anything in this article, no appeal shall, unless Parliament by law otherwise provides, lie to the Supreme Court from the judgement, decree or final order of one Judge of a High Court.

Notes on Article 133

Ordinarily the Supreme Court would interfere with the exercise of discretion in the matter of grant of temporary injunction only when the discretion was exercised arbitrarily or perversely or capriciously or where the settled principles of law regulating grant or refusal of interlocutory injunction were ignored.

Application of Constitutional Right

The question in regard to application of constitutional right and in particular fundamental right cannot be thwarted only by reason of a concession made by a counsel; *Election Commission of India v. St. Mary's School*, AIR 2008 SC 655

Building Plan

The extension of constitution is a question of fact. Where the High Court after examining records concluded that there was no excess construction, the Supreme Court cannot re – examine the said question of fact; *(Indore Municipal Corporation v. Dr. Hemalata)* AIR 2010.

Interlocutory Appeal

Interlocutory application is maintainable only during pendency of case but not after case is finally disposed of, *except* for correcting clerical or accidental mistakes; *Narpat Singh v. Rajasthan Financial Corporation*, AIR 2008 SC 77.

134. Appellate jurisdiction of Supreme Court in regard to criminal matters.-

(1) An appeal shall lie to the Supreme Court from any judgement, final order or sentence in a criminal proceeding of a High Court in the territory of India if the High Court-

(a) has on appeal reversed an order of acquittal of an accused person and sentenced him to death; or

(b) has withdrawn for trial before itself any case from any court subordinate to its authority and has in such trial convicted the accused person and sentenced him to death; or

(c) [1][certifies under article 134A] that the case is a fit one for appeal to the Supreme Court:

Provided that an appeal under sub-clause (c) shall lie subject to such provisions as may be made in that behalf under clause (1) of article 145 and to such conditions as the High Court may establish or require.

(2) Parliament may by law confer on the Supreme Court any further powers to entertain and hear appeals from any judgement, final order or sentence in a criminal proceeding of a High Court in the territory of India subject to such conditions and limitations as may be specified in such law.

Appeal against conviction

Non filling of appeal by co – accused cannot be treated as a factor against accused. It would not be in any event take away right of accused to file appeal; Vadamalai v. Syed Thastha Keer, AIR 2009

1 Subs. by the Constitution (Forty-fourth Amendment) Act, 1978, sec. 19 for "certifies" (w.e.f. 1-8-1979).

Appellate Jurisdiction of Supreme Court: Quashing of F.I.R.

Where the accused is foster sister and is not relative of husband by blood, marriage or adoption, then she cannot be tried for offence under section 498A of Indian Penal Code. The FIR can be quashed; Vijeta Gajra v. State of NCT of Delhi AIR 2010.

[1][**134A. Certificate for appeal to the Supreme Court.**- Every High Court, passing or making a judgement, decree, final order, or sentence, referred to in clause (1) of article 132 or clause (1) of article 133, or clause (1) of article 134.-

(a) may, if it deems fit so to do, on its own motion; and

(b) shall, if an oral application is made, by or on behalf of the party aggrieved, immediately after the passing or making of such judgement, decree, final order or sentence,

determine, as soon as may be after such passing or making, the question whether a certificate of the nature referred to in clause (1) of article 132, or clause (1) of article 133 or, as the case may be, sub-clause (c) of clause (1) of article 134, may be given in respect of that case].

Maintenance Claim be Illegitimate Child

The illegitimate child has no other right the except right to claim maintenance section 125 of Cr. P.C.; *Dimple Gupta (Minor) v. Rajiv Gupta*, AIR 2008 SC 239

Where the High Court has examined all the evidence, the Supreme Court will not interfere on technical ground; *Ajit v. State of Punjab*, (1991) Cri. LJ 2008 (SC): AIR 1991 Sc 1738, paragraphs 3 and 4.

Re-appreciation of evidence

Re-appreciation of evidence is permissible only if an error of law or procedure and conclusions arrived at are perverse; *Radha Mohan Singh@ Lal Saheb v. State of Uttar Pradesh*, AIR 2006 SC 951.

135. Jurisdiction and powers of the Federal Court under existing law to be exercisable by the Supreme Court.- Until Parliament by law otherwise provides, the Supreme Court shall also have jurisdiction and powers with respect to any matter to which the provisions of article 133 or article 134 do not apply if jurisdiction and powers in relation to that matter were exercisable by the Federal Court immediately before the commencement of this Constitution under any existing law.

136. Special leave to appeal by the Supreme Court.-

(1) Notwithstanding anything in this chapter, the Supreme Court may, in its discretion, grant special leave to appeal from any judgement, decree, determination, sentence or order in any cause or matter passed or made by any court or tribunal in the territory of India.

(2) Nothing in clause (1) shall apply to any judgement, determination, sentence or order passed or made by any court or tribunal constituted by or under any law relating to the Armed Forces.

Notes on Article 136

This is an extraordinary power of the Supreme Court to be exercised in exceptional circumstances. While there are provisions for regular appeals to the Supreme court from the decisions of the High Court in Art. 32-34, there may still remain some cases where justice might require interference of the Supreme Court with decisions of the High Courts outside the purview of Art. 32-34 or any other court or tribunal within the territory of India. Thus, Article 136 vests in the Supreme Court a plenary jurisdiction in the matter of entertaining and hearing appeals, by

1 Ins. by the Constitution (Forty-fourty Amendment) Act, 1978, sec.20 (w.e.f. 1-8-1979).

granting special leave, against any kind of judgement, sentence or order made by any court or tribunal (except a military tribunal). The exercise of the power under this article is left entirely to the discretion of the Supreme Court not hedged around by restrictions. However, the Supreme Court has laid down the principles which must be the basis for the exercise of this power, e.g. where there has been a violation of the principles of natural justice. In civil cases the special leave to appeal would not be granted unless it involves a substantial question of law or general public interest. Likewise, in criminal cases the Supreme Court will interfere only when it is shown that exceptional and special circumstances exist, that substantial and grave injustice has been done. Further, the Supreme Court would interfere to quash the decision of a quasi-judicial tribunal when it has either exceeded its jurisdiction or has adopted a procedure which runs counter to the established rules of natural justice. The decisions below illustrate the propositions:

(*i*) *Pritam Singh v. State*, AIR 1950 SC 169.
(*ii*) *D.C. Mills v. Commissioner of I.T.*, AIR 1955 SC 65.

Fraud

Where the petitioner succeeds in obtaining a special leave by suppressing the fact that an earlier petition by him was dismissed, the Supreme Court can direct recall of the order releasing him on bail.

Suraj v. Bharat (1990) 1 UJSC, 135 para 3.

Likewise, bail was withdrawn on the basis of fraud practised upon the court;

Surinder v. Delhi Administration, (1990) Supp. SCC 610.

Interference of Supreme Court in service matter when High Court has properly understood purport, object and purpose of a government order and arrived at a correct conclusion, the Supreme Court's interference is not warranted;

L. Muhammed Aslam v. State of Kerala 2009.

Power of Supreme Court:- In respect of compounding of offence of dishonour of cheques of Supreme Court is empowered to pass appropriate order in line with section 328 of criminal procedure court in application under section 147 of Negotiable Instruments Act 1881;

(K.M Ibrahim v. K.P Mohammed), AIR 2010.

137. Review of judgements or orders by the Supreme Court.- Subject to the provisions of any law made by Parliament or any rules made under article 145, the Supreme Court shall have power to review any judgement pronounced or order made by it.

Remand of Matter

The Court would not pass any order which would make a statutory authority to comply with only useless formalities; *Chandrakant Hargovindas Shah v. Deputy Commissioner of police* (2009).

Special Leave Petition

The special leave petition against order admitting second appeal is not maintainable. *(S. B Minerals U.M/S MSPL Ltd.)* AIR 2010.

Review

Order passed by Chief Justice of India or his nominee under section 11(6) of Arbitration Act is an order within the meaning of Article 137 and is subject to review; *Jain Studios Ltd. v. Shin Satellite Public Co. Ltd.*, AIR 2006 SC 2686

138. Enlargement of the jurisdiction of the Supreme Court.-

(1) The Supreme Court shall have such further jurisdiction and powers with respect to any of the matters in the Union List as Parliament may by law confer.

(2) The Supreme Court shall have such further jurisdiction and powers with respect to any matter as the Government of India and the Government of any State may by special agreement confer, if Parliament by law provides for the exercise of such jurisdiction and powers by the Supreme Court.

139. Conferment on the Supreme Court of powers to issue certain writs.- Parliament may by law confer on the Supreme Court power to issue directions, orders, or writs, including writs in the nature of *habeas corpus, mandamus,* prohibition, *quo warranto and certiorari*, or any of them, for any purposes other than those mentioned in clause (2) of article 32.

[1][**139A. Transfer of certain Cases.-**

[2][(1) Where cases involving the same or substantially the same questions of law are pending before the Supreme Court and one or more High Courts or before two or more High Courts and the Supreme Court is satisfied on its own motion or an application made by the Attorney-General of India or by a party to any such case that such questions are substantial questions of general importance, the Supreme Court may withdraw the case or cases pending before the High Court or High Courts and dispose of all the cases itself;

Provided that the Supreme Court may after determining the said questions of law return any case so withdrawn together with a copy of its judgement on such questions to the High Court from which the case has been withdrawn, and the High Court shall on receipt thereof, proceed to dispose of the case in conformity with such judgement.]

(2) The Supreme Court may, if it deems it expedient so to do for the ends of justice, transfer any case, appeal or other proceedings pending before any High Court to any other High Court].

140. Ancillary powers of Supreme Court.- Parliament may by law make provisions for conferring upon the Supreme Court such supplemental powers not inconsistent with any of the provisions of this Constitution as may appear to be necessary or desirable for the purpose of enabling the court more effectively to exercise the jurisdiction conferred upon it by or under this Constitution.

141. Law declared by Supreme Court to be binding on all courts.- The law declared by the Supreme Court shall be binding on all courts within the territory of India.

Notes on Article 141

Binding Jurisdiction of the Supreme court:

It is almost unthinkable for the High Courts to overrule the decisions of the Supreme Court. Article 141 of the constitution states in no uncertain terms that the law declared by the Supreme Court shall be binding on all courts within the territory of India. In other words, this Article serves as an inviolable discipline to be observed by all the courts.

Suganthi Suresh Kumar v. Jagdeeshan, (2002) 2 SCC 420.

Central Board of Dawoodi Bohra Community v. State of Maharashtra AIR 2005

A ruling making specific reference to earlier binding precedent may or may not be correct; *Central Board of Dawoodi Bohra Committee v. State of Maharashtra,* AIR 2005 Sc 752.

1 Ins. by the Constitution (Forty – Second Amendment) Act, 1976, sec. 24 (w.e.f. 1-2-1977).

2 Subs. by the Constitution (Forty-fourth Amendment) Act, 1978, sec. 21, for clause (1) (w.e.f. 1-8-1979).

Law declared

It is of no consequence that the conclusion of the majority is arrived at by several judges on different grounds or different processes of reasoning. What is binding is the ratio of the decision and no other thing should be taken into consideration. *Ramesh v. Union of India*, AIR 1990 SC 560 paragraph 20.

Obiter dicta

The following categories of the decisions of the Supreme Court as laid down by it, have no binding force:

a. Obiter dicta i.e. statements which have nothing to do with *ratio decidendi.*

b. A decision per incurium i.e. a decision given without taking into account the terms of a statute.

c. A decision given sub-silento i.e. without any argument or debate on the relevant question.

   (*i*) *Municipal Corporation v. Gurnam* (1989) 1 SCR 101 (paragraphs 10-11).

   (*ii*) *State of Uttar Pradesh v. Synthetics* (1991) 4 SCC 139.

Stare decisis

Consistency is the cornerstone of the administration of justice. It is rather sine qua non for the administration of justice. Consistency gives legitimacy to the system and inspires confidence therein. But this consistency can never be attained without respect to the rule of finality. In order to achieve this ideal of 'consistency' in judicial pronouncements, the courts have evolved the rule of precedents, the doctrine of stare decisis etc. These rules and principles have their roots in public policy and if courts fail to observe (follow) these (rules and principles) there will be chaos in the administration of justice.

Government of Andhra Pradesh v. A.P. Jaiswal, AIR 2001, SC 499.

Chik Kusappa v. State of Karnataka, AIR 2006

Judicial Discipile

(*i*) The Judicial discipline to abide by Supreme Court decision cannot be forsaken under any pretext by any authority or court, be it even High Court; State of Himachal Pradesh v. ParasRam, AIR 2008

(*ii*) High Court distinguishing the judgement of Apex Court on ground that there was no elaborate discussion and therefore no reason is discernible, is clearly violative of judicial discipline; special Deputy Collector v. N. Vasudeva Rao AIR 2008

Precedent

Decision in election petition cannot be treated as Judicial precedent;

Satrucharla Vijaya Rama Raju v. Nimmaka Jaya Raju, AIR 2006

Oriental Insurance Company Ltd. v. Laxmi Rani Biswas AIR 2008.

President: Observation made in Judgement: The observation made in judgement is not to be applied mechanically; *Bihar School Examination Board v. Suresh Prasad Sinha* AIR 2010.

Decision cannot be considered as binding authority in view of statutory provisions having undergone legislative changes; *Chikkusappa v. State of Karnataka*, AIR 2006 (NOC) 472 (Kar).

Foreign case law-Precedent

When law in India is clear and settled no occasion arises to rely upon foreign case laws laying down a wider proposition; *BSES Ltd. (Now Reliance Energy Ltd.) v. Fenner India Ltd.*, AIR 2006 SC 1148

Judicial Discipline

(*i*) The judicial discipline to abide by Supreme Court decision cannot be forsaken under any pretext by any authority or court, be it even High Court; *State of Himachal Pradesh v. Paras Ram*, AIR 2006 SC 930

(*ii*) High Court distinguishing the judgment of Apex Court on ground that there was no elaborate discussion and therefore, no reason is discernible, is clearly violative of judicial discipline; *Special Deputy Collector (LA) v. N. Vasudeva Rao*, AIR 2008 SC 944.

Precedent

Decision in election petition cannot be treated to be a judicial precedent; *Satrucharla Vijaya Rama Raju v. Nimaka Jay Rajua*, AIR 2006, SC 543

Stare decisis is not a dogmatic rule allergic to logic and reason. It does not prohibit a fresh look in changed facts and circumstances; *State of Gujarat v. Mirzapur Moti Kureshi Kasab Jamat*, AIR 2006 SC 212.

Supreme Court decision is binding on lower courts. It cannot be distinguished merely because some facts allegedly escaped its attention, more so when Supreme Court had before it the factual aspects in toto; *Gladhurst Co-op. Housing Society Ltd. v. Dr. (Mrs.) V.B. Shah*, AIR 2006 (NOC) 1217 (Bom)

The principles on which a question before court is decided constitutes precedent but not every observation made in judgment; *Oriental Insurance Co. Ltd. v. Raj Kumari*, AIR 2008 SC 403.

The decision is precedent on its own facts. What is binding in a decision is the principle on which it is decided. The reliance on a decision without looking into factual background of case before it is clearly impermissible; *State of Rajasthan v. Ganeshi Lal*, AIR 2008 SC 690

The precedents are to be a binding authority or precedent on any specific issue, must be at least raised and answered directly or by implication; *Oriental Insurance Co. Ltd. v. Laxmi Rani Biswas*, AIR 2008 Gau 13.

142. Enforcement of decrees and orders of Supreme Court and orders as to discovery, etc.-

(1) The Supreme Court in the exercise of its jurisdiction may pass such decree or make such order as is necessary for doing complete justice in any cause or matter pending before it, and any decree so passed or order so made shall be enforceable throughout the territory of India in such manner as may be prescribed by or under any law made by Parliament and, until provision in that behalf is so made, in such manner as the President may by order[1] prescribe.

(2) Subject to the provisions of any law made in this behalf by Parliament, the Supreme Court shall, as respects the whole of the territory of India, have all and every power to make any order for the purpose of securing the attendance of any person, the discovery or production of any documents, or the investigation or punishment of any contempt of itself.

Complete Justice

The Court can grant equitable relief to eradicate injustice; *Manish Goel v. Rohini Goel*, AIR 2010

Power to docomplete justice

The Supreme Court cannot by pass the provisions of the Arbitration and Conciliation Act, 1996 while exercising power under Article 142; *Bharat Sewa Sansthan v. U.P. Electricity Corpn. Ltd.* (2007) 7 SCC 737

---

1 See the Supreme Court (Decrees and Orders) Enforcement Order, 1954 (C.O. 47).

143. Power of President to consult Supreme Court.-

(1) If at any time it appears to the President that a question of law or fact has arisen, or is likely to arise, which is of such a nature and of such public importance that it is expedient to obtain the opinion of the Supreme Court upon it, he may refer the question to that court for consideration and the court may, after such hearing as it thinks fit, report to the President its opinion thereon.

(2) The President may, notwithstanding anything in [1][***] the proviso to article 131, refer a dispute of the kind mentioned in the [2][said proviso] to the Supreme Court for opinion and the Supreme Court shall, after such hearing as it thinks fit, report to the President its opinion thereon.

144. Civil and judicial authorities to act in aid of the Supreme Court- All authorities, civil and judicial, in the territory of India shall act in aid of the Supreme Court.

[3]**[144A. Special provisions as to disposal of questions relating to constitutional validity of laws.**- *[Rep. by the Constitution (Forty-third Amendment) Act, 1977, sec. 5 (w.e.f. 13-4-1978)].*

145. Rules of Court, etc.

(1) Subject to the provisions of any law made by Parliament, the Supreme Court may from time to time, with the approval of the President, make rules for regulating generally the practice and procedure of the court including-

(a) rules as to the persons practising before the court;

(b) rules as to the procedure for hearing appeals and other matters pertaining to appeals including the time within which appeals to the Court are to be entered;

(c) rules as to the proceedings in the court for the enforcement of any of the rights conferred by Part III;

[4][(cc) rules as to the proceedings in the court under [5][article 139A];]

(d) rules as to the entertainment of appeals under sub-clause (c) of clause (1) of article 134;

(e) rules as to the conditions subject to which any judgement pronounced or order made by the court may be reviewed and the procedure for such review including the time within which applications to the court for such review are to be entered;

(f) rules as to the costs of and incidental to any proceedings in the court and as to the fees to be charged in respect of proceedings therein;

(g) rules as to the granting of bail;

(h) rules as to stay of proceedings;

(i) rules providing for the summary determination of any appeal which appears to the court to be frivolous or vexatious or brought for the purpose of delay;

(j) rules as to the procedure for inquiries referred to in clause (1) of article 317.

---

1 The words, brackets and figure "clause (I) of" omitted by the Constitution (Seventh Amendment) Act, 1956, sec. 29 and Sch (w.e.f. 1.11.1956).

2 Subs. by the Constitution (Seventh Amendment) Act, 1956, sec.29, and Sch., for "said clause" (w.e.f. 1.11.1956).

3 Ins. by the Constitution (Forty-second Amendment) Act, 1976, sec. 25 (w.e.f. 1-2-1977).

4 Ins. by the Constitution (Forty-second Amendment) Act, 1976, sec. 26 (w.e.f. 1-2-1977).

5 Subs. by the Constitution (Forty-third Amendment) Act, 1977, sec. 6, for "articles 131A and 139A" (w.e.f. 13-4-1978).

(2) Subject to the [1][provisions of [2][***] clause (3)], rules made under this article may fix the minimum number of Judges who are to sit for any purpose, and may provide for the powers of single Judges and Division Courts.

(3) [3][[4][***]The minimum number] of Judges who are to sit for the purpose of deciding any case involving a substantial question of law as to the interpretation of this Constitution or for the purpose of hearing any reference under article 143 shall be five;

Provided that, where the court, hearing an appeal under any of the provisions of this Chapter other than article 132 consists of less than five Judges and in the course of the hearing of the appeal the Court is satisfied that the appeal involves a substantial question of law as to the interpretation of this Constitution the determination of which is necessary for the disposal of the appeal, such court shall refer the question for opinion to a court constituted as required by this clause for the purpose of deciding any case involving such a question and shall on receipt of the opinion dispose of the appeal in conformity with such opinion.

(4) No judgement shall be delivered by the Supreme Court save in open Court, and no report shall be made under article 143 save in accordance with an opinion also delivered in open Court.

(5) No judgement and no such opinion shall be delivered by the Supreme Court save with the concurrence of a majority of the Judges present at the hearing of the case, but nothing in this clause shall be deemed to prevent a Judge who does not concur from delivering a dissenting judgement or opinion.

Notes on Article 145

The Supreme Court was given power to frame rules regarding the condition for practicing in the Supreme Court. But the disciplinary jurisdiction of Bar Councils have nothing to do with such a framed rule.

The single situation in which a two-judge bench may refer a matter directly to a Constitutional Bench is when the provisions of Clause (3) of Article 145 are attracted;

Pradip Chandra Parja v. Pramod Chandra Pattnaik, AIR 2002 SC 296.

146. Officers and servants and the expenses of the Supreme Court -

(1) Appointment of officers and servants of the Supreme Court shall be made by the Chief Justice of India or such other Judge or officer of the court as he may direct;

Provided that the President may by rule require that in such cases as may be specified in the rule, no person not already attached to the court shall be appointed to any office connected with the court, save after consultation with the Union Public Service Commission.

(2) Subject to the provisions of any law made by Parliament, the conditions of service of officers and servants of the Supreme Court shall be such as may be prescribed by rules made by the Chief Justice of India or by some other Judge or officer of the court authorised by the Chief Justice of India to make rules for the purpose:

Provided that the rules made under this clause shall, so far as they relate to salaries, allowances, leave or pensions, require the approval of the President.

---

1 Subs. by the Constitution (Forty-second Amendment) Act, 1976, sec.6, for "provisions of clause (3)" (w.e.f. 1-2-1977).

2 Certain words, figures and letters omitted by the Constitution (Forty-third Amendment) Act, 1977, sec.6. (w.e.f. 13-4-1978).

3 Subs. by the Constitution (Forty-second Amendment) Act, 1976, sec.26, for "The minimum number" (w.e.f. 1-2-1977).

4 Certain words, figures and letters omitted by the Constitution (Forty-third Amendment) Act, 1977, sec.6 (w.e.f. 13-4-1978).

(3) The administrative expenses of the Supreme Court, including all salaries, allowances and pensions payable to or in respect of the officers and servants of the court, shall be charged upon the Consolidated Fund of India, and any fees or other moneys taken by the Court shall form part of that Fund.

Notes on Article 146

This article gives power to the Supreme Court which is primarily of legislative nature; *Supreme Court Employees Welfare Association v. Union of India*; AIR 1990 SC 334, paragraph 46.

147. Interpretation. - In this chapter and in chapter V of Part VI, references to any substantial question of law as to the interpretation of this Constitution shall be construed as including references to any substantial question of law as to the interpretation of the Government of India Act, 1935 (including any enactment amending or supplementing that Act), or of any order in Council or order made thereunder, or of the Indian Independence Act, 1947 or of any order made thereunder.

CHAPTER V — COMPTROLLER AND AUDITOR-GENERAL OF INDIA

148. Comptroller and Auditor-General of India.-

(1) There shall be a Comptroller and Auditor - General of India who shall be appointed by the President by warrant under his hand and seal and shall only be removed from office in like manner and on the like grounds as a Judge of the Supreme Court.

(2) Every person appointed to be the Comptroller and Auditor-General of India shall, before he enters upon his office, make and subscribe before the President, or some person appointed in that behalf by him, an oath or affirmation according to the form set out for the purpose in the Third Schedule.

(3) The salary and other conditions of service of the Comptroller and Auditor General shall be such as may be determined by Parliament by law and, until they are so determined, shall be as specified in the Second Schedule;

Provided that neither the salary of the Comptroller and Auditor-General nor his rights in respect of leave of absence, pension or age of retirement shall be varied to his disadvantage after his appointment.

(4) The Comptroller and Auditor-General shall not be eligible for further office either under the Government of India or under the Government of any State after he has ceased to hold his office.

(5) Subject to the provisions of this Constitution and of any law made by Parliament, the conditions of service of persons serving in the Indian Audit and Accounts Department and the administrative powers of the Comptroller and Auditor-General shall be such as may be prescribed by rules made by the President after consultation with the Comptroller and Auditor-General.

(6) The administrative expenses of the office of the Comptroller and Auditor-General, including all salaries, allowances and pensions payable to or in respect of persons serving in that office, shall be charged upon the Consolidated Fund of India.

149. Duties and powers of the Comptroller and Auditor-General. - The Comptroller and Auditor-General shall perform such duties and exercise such powers in relation to the accounts of the Union and of the States and of any other authority or body as may be prescribed by or under any law made by Parliament and, until provision in that behalf is so made, shall perform such duties and exercise such powers in relation to the accounts of the Union and of the States as were conferred on or exercisable by the Auditor-General of India immediately before the commencement of this Constitution in relation to the accounts of the Dominion of India and of the Provinces respectively.

[1][**150. Form of accounts of the Union and of the States**- The accounts of the Union and of the States shall be kept in such form as the President may, [2][on the advice of the Comptroller and Auditor-General of India, prescribe.]

151. Audit reports. -

(1) The reports of the Comptroller and Auditor-General of India relating to the accounts of the Union shall be submitted to the President, who shall cause them to be laid before each House of Parliament.

(2) The reports of the Comptroller and Auditor-General of India relating to the accounts of a State shall be submitted to the Governor [3][***] of the State, who shall cause them to be laid before the Legislature of the State.

PART VI

THE STATES [4][***]

CHAPTER 1 - GENERAL

152. Definition- In this Part, unless the context otherwise requires, the expression "State" [5][does not include the State of Jammu and Kashmir].

CHAPTER II — THE EXECUTIVE

The Governor

153. Governors of States. - There shall be a Governor for each State:

[6][Provided that nothing in this article shall prevent the appointment of the same person as Governor for two or more States.]

154. Executive power of State. -

(1) The executive power of the State shall be vested in the Governor and shall be exercised by him either directly or through officers subordinate to him in accordance with this Constitution.

(2) Nothing in this article shall -

(a) be deemed to transfer to the Governor any functions conferred by any existing law on any other authority; or

(b) prevent Parliament or the Legislature of the State from conferring by law functions on any authority subordinate to the Governor.

Notes on Article 154

Central Govt's executive power

The Central Govt.'s executive power extends to the same subjects and to the same extent as that of the Parliament; *Satya Narain Shukla v. Union of India*, AIR 2006 SC 2511

1 Subs. by the Constitution (Forty-second Amendment) Act, 1976, sec. 27, for article 150 (w.e.f. 1-4-1977).

2 Subs. by the Constitution (Forty-fourth Amendment) Act, 1978, sec. 22, for "after consultation with" (w.e.f. 20-6-1979).

3 The word "or Rajpramukh" omitted by the Constitution (Seventh Amendment) Act, 1956, sec.29 and Sch (w.e.f. 1.11.1956).

4 The words 'IN PART A OF THE FIRST SCHEDULE' omitted by the Constitution (Seventh Amendment) Act, 1956, sec. 29 and Sch (w.e.f. 1.11.1956).

5 Subs. by the Constitution (Seventh Amendment) Act, 1956, sec.29 and Sch., for "means a State specified in Part A of the First Schedule. (w.e.f. 1.11.1956)"

6 Added by the Constitution (Seventh Amendment) Act, 1956, sec.6 (w.e.f. 1.11.1956).

155. Appointment of Governor. - The Governor of State shall be appointed by the President by warrant under his hand and seal.

156. Term of office of Governor.-

(1) The Governor shall hold office during the pleasure of the President.

(2) The Governor may, by writing under his hand addressed to the President, resign his office.

(3) Subject to the foregoing provisions of this article, a Governor shall hold office for a term of five years from the date on which he enters upon his office;

Provided that a Governor shall, notwithstanding the expiration of his term, continue to hold office until his successor enters upon his office.

157. Qualifications for appointment as Governor. - No person shall be eligible for appointment as Governor unless he is a citizen of India and has completed the age of thirty-five years.

158. Conditions of Governor's Office. -

(1) The Governor shall not be a member of either House of Parliament or of a House of the Legislature of any State specified in the First Schedule, and if a member of either House of Parliament or of a House of the Legislature of any such State be appointed Governor, he shall be deemed to have vacated his seat in that House on the date on which he enters upon his office as Governor.

(2) The Governor shall not hold any other office of profit.

(3) The Governor shall be entitled without payment of rent to the use of his official residences and shall be also entitled to such emoluments, allowances and privileges as may be determined by Parliament by law and, until provision in that behalf is so made, such emoluments, allowances and privileges as are specified in the Second Schedule.

[1][(3A) Where the same person is appointed as Governor of two or more States, the emoluments and allowances payable to the Governor shall be allocated among the States in such proportaion as the President may by order determine.]

(4) The emoluments and allowances of the Governor shall not be diminished during his term of office.

159. Oath or affirmation by the Governor.- Every Governor and every person discharging the function of the Governor shall, before entering upon his office, make and subscribe in the presence of the Chief Justice of the High Court exercising jurisdiction in relation to the State, or, in his absence, the seniormost Judge of that Court available, an oath or affirmation in the following form, that is to say —

"I, A.B., do <u>swear in the name of God</u> that I will faithfully execute the
solemnly affirm

office of Governor (or discharge the functions of the Governor) of....(name of the State) and will to the best of my ability preserve, protect and defend the Constitution and the law and that I will devote myself to the service and well-being of the people of..... (*name of the state*)".

160. Discharge of the functions of the Governor in certain contingencies. - The President may make such provision as he thinks fit for the discharge of the functions of the Governor of a State in any contingency not provided for in this Chapter.

161. Power of Governor to grant pardons etc. and to suspend, remit or commute sentences in certain cases. - The Governor of a State shall have the power to grant pardon, reprieves, respites or remissions of punishment or to suspend, remit or commute the sentence of any person convicted of any offence against any law relating to a matter to which the executive power of the State extends.

1 Ins. by the Constitution (Seventh Amendment) Act, 1956, sec.7 (w.e.f. 1.11.1956).

Notes on Article 161

The Governor's power under Article 161 is statutory which cannot be fettered by positions such as sections 432, 433, 433A of the Indian Penal Code, 1860; *State of Punjab v. Joginder*, AIR 1990, SC 1396.

The power of granting pardon in Governor's armoury is very wide and virtually not limited by time, occasion, and circumstances. However, this being a constitutional power, is subject to judicial review on certain limited grounds. The court, thus would be justified in interfering with an order passed by the Governor under this Article. The Court can look into whether :

(a) The Governor has exercised the power himself without being advised by the Government.

(b) Or the Governor has transgressed the jurisdiction in exercising this power

(c) Or the Governor has passed the order without application of mind

(d) Or the said order is a *mala fide* one;

Satpal v. State of Haryana, AIR 2000 SC 1702.

Sanaboina Saty anarayan v. Govt of Andhra Pradesh AIR 2003.

162. Extent of executive power of State. - Subject to the provisions of this Constitution, the executive power of a State shall extend to the matters with respect to which the Legislature of the State has power to make laws;

Provided that in any matter with respect to which the Legislature of a State and Parliament have power to make laws, the executive power of the State shall be subject to, and limited by, the executive power expressly conferred by this Constitution or by any law made by Parliament upon the Union or authorities thereof.

Notes on Article 162

Executive instructions

Where statutory rules govern the field, prior executive instructions cease to apply; *K.P. Sudhakaran v. State of Kerala*, AIR 2006 SC 2138.

Executive instructions can only fill in gaps not covered by rules and cannot be in derogation of statutory rules; *Union of India v. Central Electrical and Mechanical Engineering Service Group A (Direct Recruit) Association*, CPWD, AIR 2008 SC 3.

Council of Ministers

163. Council of Ministers to aid and advise Governor. -

(1) There shall be a Council of Ministers with the Chief Minister as the head to aid and advise the Governor in the exercise of his functions, except in so far as he is by or under this Constitution required to exercise his functions or any of them in his discretion.

(2) If any question arises whether any matter is or is not a matter as respects which the Governor is by or under this Constitution required to act in his discretion, the decision of the Governor in his discretion shall be final, and the validity of anything done by the Governor shall not be called in question on the ground that he ought or ought not to have acted in his discretion.

(3) The question whether any, and if so what, advice was tendered by ministers to the Governor shall not be inquired into in any court.

Notes on Article 163

As at the centre, Parliamentary system obtains in the states of the Indian Union. The position of the Governor is broadly akin to that of the President. However, discretionary powers of the Governor place him in a stronger position. He is empowered to act in his discretion in the following cases:

(a) The powers of the Governor of Assam under paragraph 9 of the 6th Schedule;

(b) The functions of a Governor appointed to be an administrator of a Union Territory under Article 239(2);

(c) The powers and functions under Articles 371(2), 371A (1)(b), 371 C (1), 371 F (g).

In other cases, Article 163 largely follows Article 74 (Council of Ministers in the Union) but unlike 74 as amended, Article 163 does not expressly require the Governor to accept Cabinet's advice. However, (except where the Governor is to exercise his powers in his discretion as noted above) the Governor is bound to act in accordance with the advice tendered by the State Council of Ministers as per the rulings in:

(i) *Kapoor v. State of Punjab* (1955) 1 SCR 577, 587.

(ii) *Sanjivee v. State of Madras*, AIR 1970 SC 1102.

(iii) *UP Public Service Commission v. Suresh*, AIR 1987 SC 1953.

However, the report of the Governor to the Centre under Article 356(1) which may precipitate the fall of the State government, cannot be given on the advice of the Cabinet.

164. Other provisions as to Ministers –

(1) The Chief Minister shall be appointed by the Governor and the other Ministers shall be appointed by the Governor on the advice of the Chief Minister and the Ministers shall hold office during the pleasure of the Governor.

Provided that in the states of [1][Chattisgarh, Jharkhand], Madhya Pradesh and [2][Odisha] there shall be a minister in charge of Tribal welfare who may in addition be in charge of the welfare of the scheduled castes and backward classes or any other work.

[3][1(A) The Total number of Minister including the chief Minister in the Council of Ministers in a state shall not exceed fifteen percent of the total number of members of the legislative Assembly of that state: Provided that the number of Ministers, including the Chief Minister, in a state shall not be less than twelve provided further that where the total number of Minister, including the Chief Minister, in the Council of Ministers in any state at the commencement of the Constitution (Ninety first Amendment) Act 2003 exceeds the said fifteen percent or the number specified in the first proviso, as the case may be, then the total number of Ministers in that state shall be brougnt in conformity with the provisions of this clause within six months from such date as the President may by public notification* appoint]

[3][(1B) A member of the Legislative Assembly of a State or either House of the Legislature of a State having Legislative Council belonging to any political party who is disqualified for being a member of that House under paragraph 2 of the Tenth Schedule shall also be disqualified to be appointed as a Minister under clause (1) for duration of the period commencing from the date of his disqualification till the date on which the term of his office as such member would expire or where he contests any election to the Legislative Assembly of a State or either House of the Legislature of a State having Legislative Council, as the case may be, before the expiry of such period, till the date on which he is declared elected, whichever is earlier.]

(2) The Council of Ministers shall be collectively responsible to the Legislative Assembly of the State.

---

1 Subs. by constitution (Ninety fourth amendment) Act, 2006, sec. 2, for "Bihar" (w.e.f. 12.6.2006).

2 Subs. by Orissa (Alteration of name) Act, 2011.

3 Ins. by the Constitution (Ninety-first Amendment) Act, 2003, sec. 3 (w.e.f. 1-1-2004).

* 7th January, 2004, *vide* S.O. 21(E), dated 7th Janaury, 2004.

(3) Before a Minister enters upon his office, the Governor shall administer to him the oaths of office and of secrecy according to the forms set out for the purpose in the Third Schedule.

(4) A Minister who for any period of six consecutive months is not a member of the Legislature of the State shall at the expiration of that period cease to be a Minister.

(5) The salaries and allowances of ministers shall be such as the Legislature of the State may from time to time by law determine and, until the Legislature of the State so determines, shall be as specified in the Second Schedule.

The Advocate-General for the State

165. Advocate-General for the State. -

(1) The Governor of each State shall appoint a person who is qualified to be appointed a Judge of a High Court to be Advocate-General for the State.

(2) It shall be the duty of the Advocate-General to give advice to the Government of the State upon such legal matters, and to perform such other duties of a legal character, as may from time to time be referred or assigned to him by the Governor, and to discharge the functions conferred on him by or under this Constitution or any other law for the time being in force.

(3) The Advocate-General shall hold office during the pleasure of the Governor, and shall receive such remuneration as the Governor may determine.

Appoinment of Advocate – General

The person beyond age of 62 years can be appointed as advocate – general; *State of Uttaranchal v. Balwant Singh Chauful* AIR 2010.

Conduct of Government Business

166. Conduct of business of the Government of a State.-

(1) All executive action of the Government of a State shall be expressed to be taken in the name of the Governor.

(2) Orders and other instruments made and executed in the name of the Governor shall be authenticated in such manner as may be specified in rules to be made by the Governor, and the validity of an order or instrument which is so authenticated shall not be called in question on the ground that it is not an order or instrument made or executed by the Governor.

(3) The Governor shall make rules for the more convenient transaction of the business of the Government of the State, and for the allocation among Ministers of the said business in so far as it is not business with respect to which the Governor is by or under this Constitution required to act in his discretion.[1][***]

167. Duties of Chief Minister as respects the furnishing of information to Governor, etc. - It shall be the duty of the Chief Minister of each State-

(a) to communicate to the Governor of the State all decisions of the Council of Ministers relating to the administration of the affairs of the State and proposals for legislation;

(b) to furnish such information relating to the administration of the affairs of the State and proposals for legislation as the Governor may call for; and

(c) if the Governor so requires, to submit for the consideration of the Council of Ministers any matter on which a decision has been taken by a Minister but which has not been considered by the Council.

---

1 Clause (4) was ins. by the Constitution (Forty-second Amendment) Act, 1976, sec.28 (w.e.f. 3-1-1977) and omitted by the constitution (Forty-fourth Amendment) Act, 1978, sec23 (w.e.f. 20-6-1979)

CHAPTER III—THE STATE LEGISLATURE

General

168. Constitution of Legislature in States:

(1) For every state there shall be a legislature which shall consist of the Governor and –

(a) in the states of [1][Andhra Pradesh], Bihar [2][***], [3][***], [4][***], [5][Maharashtra], [6][Karnataka], [7][Tamilnadu], [8] [***], [9][Uttar Pradesh], two houses

(b) in other States, one House

(2) Where there are two Houses of the Legislature of a State, one shall be known as the Legislative Council and the other as the Legislative Assembly, and where there is only one House, it shall be known as the Legislative Assembly.

169. Abolition or creation of Legislative Councils in States. -

(1) Notwithstanding anything in article 168, Parliament may by law provide for the abolition of the Legislative Council of a State having such a Council or for the creation of such a Council in a State having no such Council, if the Legislative Assembly of the State passes a resolution to that effect by a majority of the total membership of the Assembly and by a majority of not less than two-thirds of the members of the Assembly present and voting.

(2) Any law referred to in clause (1) shall contain such provisions for the amendment of this Constitution as may be necessary to give effect to the provisions of the law and may also contain such supplemental, incidental and consequential provisions as Parliament may deem necessary.

(3) No such law as aforesaid shall be deemed to be an amendment of this Constitution for the purposes of Article 368.

[9][170. Composition of the Legislative Assemblies. -

(1) Subject to the provisions of article 333, the Legislative Assembly of each State shall consist of not more than five hundred, and not less than sixty, members chosen by direct election from territorial constituencies in the State.

(2) For the purposes of clause (1), each State shall be divided into territorial constituencies in such manner that the ratio between the population of each constituency and the number of seats allotted to it shall, so far as practicable, be the same throughout the State.

---

1 Ins. by the Andhra Pradesh Legislative Council Act, 2005 (1 of 2006), sec. 3(1) (w.e.f. 30-3-2007). Earlier the words "Andhra Pradesh" were omitted by the Andhra Pradesh Legislative Council (Abolition) Act, 1985 (34 of 1985), sec. 4 (w.e.f. 1-6-1986).

2 The word "Bombay" omitted by the Bombay Reorganisation Act, 1960 (11 of 1960), sec.20 (w.e.f. 1-5-1960)

3 For the insertion of the words "Madhya Pradesh" in this sub-clause, no date has been appointed under sec. 8(2) of the Constitution (Seventh Amendment) Act, 1956.

5 Ins. by the Bombay Reorganisation Act, 1960 (11 of 1960), sec. 20 (w.e.f. 1-5-1960).

6 Subs. by the Mysore State (Alteration of Name) Act, 1973 (31 of 1973), sec. 4, for "Mysore " (w.e.f. 1-11-1973), which was inserted by the Constitution (Seventh Amendment) Act, 1956, sec. 8(1).

7 The words "Tamil Nadu", inserted by the Tamil Nadu Legislative Council Act, 2010 (16 of 2010), sec. 3(1).

8 Subs. by the West Bengal Legislative Council (Abolition) Act, 1969 (20 of 1969), sec. 4, for "Uttar Pradesh and West Bengal " (w.e.f. 1-8-1969).

9 Subs. by the Constitution (Seventh Amendment) Act, 1956, sec.9, for article 170 (w.e.f. 1-11-1956).

[1][Explanation—In this clause, the expression 'population' means the population as ascertained at the last preceding census of which the relevant figures have been published:

Provided that the reference in this *Explanation* to the last preceding census of which the relevant figures have been published shall, until the relevant figures for the first census taken after the year [2][2026] have been published, be construed as a reference to the [3][2001] census].

(3) Upon the completion of each census, the total number of seats in the Legislative Assembly of each State and the division of each State into territorial constituencies shall be readjusted by such authority and in such manner as Parliament may by law determine:

Provided that such readjustment shall not affect representation in the Legislative Assembly until the dissolution of the then existing Assembly:

[4][Provided further that such readjustment shall take effect from such date as the President may, by order, specify and until such readjustment takes effect, any election to the Legislative Assembly may be held on the basis of the territorial constituencies existing before such readjustment:

Provided also that until the relevant figures for the first census taken after the year [2][2026] have been published, it shall not be necessary to [5][readjust-

(i) the total number of seats in the Legislative Assembly of each State as readjusted on the basis of the [6][1971] census;

(ii) the division of such State into territorial constituencies as may be readjusted on the basis of the [7][2001] census, under this clause]].

171. Composition of the Legislative Councils. -

(1) The total number of members in the Legislative Council of a State having such a Council shall not exceed [8][one -third] of the total number of members in the Legislative Assembly of that State:

Provided that the total number of members in the Legislative Council of a State shall in no case be less than forty.

(2) Until Parliament by law otherwise provides, the composition of the Legislative Council of a State shall be as provided in clause (3).

(3) Of the total number of members of the Legislative Council of a State-

(a) as nearly as may be, one-third shall be elected by electorates, consisting of members of municipalities, district boards and such other local authorities in the State as Parliament may by law specify;

---

1 Subs. by the Constitution (Forty-second Amendment) Act, 1976, sec. 29(a), for the Explanation (w.e.f. 3-1-1977).

2 Subs. by the Constitution (Eighty Fourth Amendment) Act, 2001, sec.5(a), for "2000" (w.e.f. 21-2-2002).

3 Subs. by the Constitution (Eighty fourth Amendment) Act, 2003, sec.4(1) for "1991" (w.e.f. 22-6-2003) Earlier the figures "1991" were substituted by the Constitution (Eighty-fourth Amendment) Act, 2001, sec. 5(d) for '1971' (w.e.f. 21-2-2002).

4 Ins. by the Constitution (Forty-second Amendment) Act, 1976, sec. 29(b) (w.e.f. 3-1-1977).

5 Subs. by the Constitution (Eighty fourth Amendment) Act, 2001, sec. 5(a)(*i*), for certain words (w.e.f. 21.02.2002).

6 Subs. by the Constitution (Eighty Fourth Amendment) Act, 2001, sec.5 for "1971" (w.e.f. 21-2-2002) and again subs. by the Constitution (Eighty-seventh Amendment) Act, 2002, for '1991' (w.e.f. 22-6-2003).

7 Subs. by the Constitution (Eighty seventh Amendment) Act, 2003, for '1991' (w.e.f. 22.06.2003).

8 Subs. by the Constitution (Seventh Amendment) Act, 1956, sec.10, for "one-fourth"(w.e.f. 1-11-1956).

(b) as nearly as may be, one-twelfth shall be elected by electorates consisting of persons residing in the State who have been for at least three years graduates of any university in the territory of India or have been for at least three years in possession of qualifications prescribed by or under any law made by Parliament as equivalent to that of a graduate of any such university.

(c) as nearly as may be, one-twelfth shall be elected by electorates consisting of persons who have been for at least three years engaged in teaching in such educational institutions within the State, not lower in standard than that of a secondary school, as may be prescribed by or under any law made by Parliament;

(d) as nearly as may be, one-third shall be elected by the members of the Legislative Assembly of the State from amongst persons who are not members of the Assembly;

(e) the remainder shall be nominated by the Governor in accordance with the provisions of clause (5).

(4) The members to be elected under sub-clauses (a), (b) and (c) of clause (3) shall be chosen in such territorial constituencies as may be prescribed by or under any law made by Parliament, and the elections under the said sub-clauses and under sub-clause (d) of the said clause shall be held in accordance with the system of proportional representation by means of the single transferable vote.

(5) The members to be nominated by the Governor under sub-clause (e) of clause (3) shall consist of persons having special knowledge or practical experience in respect of such matters as the following, namely:–

Literature, science, art, co-operative movement and social service.

172. Duration of State Legislatures. -

(1) Every Legislative Assembly of every State, unless sooner dissolved, shall continue for [1][five years] from the date appointed for its first meeting and no longer and the expiration of the said period of [1][five years] shall operate as a dissolution of the Assembly;

Provided that the said period may, while a Proclamation of Emergency is in operation, be extended by Parliament by law for a period not exceeding one year at a time and not extending in any case beyond a period of six months after the Proclamation has ceased to operate.

(2) The Legislative Council of a State shall not be subject to dissolution, but as nearly as possible one-third of the members thereof shall retire as soon as may be on the expiration of every second year in accordance with the provisions made in that behalf by Parliament by law.

173. Qualifications for membership of the State Legislature. - A person shall not be qualified to be chosen to fill a seat in the Legislature of a State unless he-

[2][(a) is a citizen of India, and makes and subscribes before some person authorised in that behalf by the Election Commission an oath or affirmation according to the form set out for the purpose in the Third Schedule;].

(b) is, in the case of a seat in the Legislative Assembly, not less than twenty-five years of age and, in the case of a seat in the Legislative Council, not less than thirty years of age; and

(c) possesses such other qualifications as may be prescribed in that behalf by or under any law made by Parliament.

---

1 Subs. by the Constitution (Forty-fourth Amendment) Act, 1978, sec. 24, for "six years" (w.e.f. 6-9-1979). The words "six years" were subs. for the original words "five years" by the Constitution (Forty-second Amendment) Act, 1976, sec.30 (w.e.f. 3-1-1977).

2 Subs. by the Constitution (Sixteenth Amendment) Act, 1963, sec.4, for clause (a).(w.e.f. 5.10.1963).

Notes on Article 173

The crucial date for applying this article, read with Section 36(2). Representation of the People Act, 1951, is the date fixed for the scrutiny of nomination paper. We can see the following cases.

(i) *Pashupati v. Harihar,* AIR 1968 SC 1064.

(ii) *Hussain v. Janalingappa,* AIR 1969 SC 1034.

Nomination of a candidate may be rejected by the Returning Officer if he has failed to take the oath prescribed; *Laxmi Narain v. Ram Ratan,* (1990) 2 SCC 673.

A person cannot be permitted to occupy an office for which he is disqualified under the Constitution. The endeavour of the court shall therefore be to see that a disqualified person should not hold the office but should not at the same time, unseat a person qualified therefore; *Sushil Kumar v. Rakesh Kumar,* AIR 2004 SC 230: (2003) 8 SCC 673

[1][174. **Sessions of the State Legislature, prorogation and dissolution.-**

(1) The Governor shall from time to time summon the House or each House of the Legislature of the State to meet at such time and place as he thinks fit, but six months shall not intervene between its last sitting in one session and the date appointed for its first sitting in the next session.

(2) The Governor may from time to time-

(a) prorogue the House or either House;

(b) dissolve the Legislative Assembly.

Notes on Article 174

Dissolution of Assembly

Dissolution can not be resorted for good governance or cleansing of politics; *Rameshwar Prasad v. Union of India* AIR 2006. On 7th of December, 1988, the Division Bench of Chief Justice A. Raghubir and Mr. Justice B.L. Hansaria (High Court, Guahati) pronounced an important judgement in the case relating to dissolution of the Nagaland Assembly holding that the report of the Governor recommending dissolution of the said Assembly was not tenable. Mr. Vamuzo, leader of the Joint Regional Legislative Party, had filed a writ petition challenging the validity of the Presidential Proclamation of 17th August, 1988. The viable contention of the petitioner was that he was enjoying the support of the majority of 35 MLAs in the 60 member House and legally should have been invited to form the Government after the split in the Congress-I. The petitioner, further, said that in spite of the Speaker's ruling that it was a split, the Governor took into consideration extraneous and irrelevant aspects. The Attorney General submitted three points apposing the writ petition. First, the President acted as per the advice of the Council of Ministers and Court could not look into such advice. Secondly, the Governor gets protection under Article 361. Thirdly, as the proclamation had already been approved by Parliament, no relief could be given to the petitioner.

Despite the above arguments the court gave its ruling that the action of the Governor was justiciable thus diluting and qualifying Article 361. The court observed that political tricks cannot bar the court from looking into justiciability of any action;

Vamuzo v. Union of India, 1988. (2) GLJ 468. See also *S.R. Bommai v. Union of India,* 1994 (3) SCC 1 See also notes on Article 356.

Dissolution cannot be resorted to for good governance or cleansing of politics; *Rameshwar Prasad v. Union of India,* AIR 2006 SC 980.

---

1 Subs. by the Constitution (First Amendment) Act, 1951, sec. 8, for Article 174(w.e.f. 18.6.1951)

Ground for dissolution- Immorality

Immorality is not a ground recognized by Constitution for formation of satisfaction to dissolve assembly; *Rameshwar Prasad v. Union of India*, AIR 2006 SC 980

175. Right of Governor to address and send messages to the House or Houses. -

(1) The Governor may address the Legislative Assembly or, in the case of a State having a Legislative Council, either House of the Legislature of the State, or both Houses assembled together, and may for that purpose require the attendance of members.

(2) The Governor may send messages to the House or Houses of the Legislature of the State, whether with respect to a Bill then pending in the Legislature or otherwise, and a House to which any message is so sent shall with all convenient dispatch consider any matter required by the message to be taken into consideration.

176. Special address by the Governor. -

(1) At the commencement of [1][the first session after each general election to the Legislative Assembly and at the commencement of the first session of each year], the Governor shall address the Legislative Assembly or, in the case of a State having a Legislative Council, both Houses assembled together and inform the Legislature of the causes of its summons.

(2) Provision shall be made by the rules, regulating the procedure of the House or either House for the allotment of time for discussion of the matters referred to in such address. [2][***]

177. Rights of Ministers and Advocate-General as respects the Houses. - Every Minister and the Advocate -General for a State shall have the right to speak in, and otherwise to take part in the proceedings of, the Legislative Assembly of the State or, in the case of a State having a Legislative Council, both Houses, and to speak in, and otherwise to take part in the proceedings of any committee of the Legislature of which he may be named a member, but shall not by virtue of this article, be entitled to vote.

Officers of the State Legislature

178. The Speaker and Deputy Speaker of the Legislative Assembly. - Every Legislative Assembly of a State shall, as soon as may be, choose two members of the Assembly to be respectively Speaker and Deputy Speaker thereof and, so often as the office of Speaker or Deputy Speaker becomes vacant, the Assembly shall choose another member to be Speaker or Deputy Speaker, as the case may be.

179. Vacation and resignation of, and removal from, the offices of Speaker and Deputy Speaker.- A member holding office as Speaker or Deputy Speaker of an Assembly-

(a) shall vacate his office if he ceases to be a member of the Assembly;

(b) may at any time by writing under his hand addressed, if such member is the Speaker, to the Deputy Speaker, and if such member is the Deputy Speaker, to the Speaker, resign his office; and

(c) may be removed from his office by a resolution of the Assembly passed by a majority of all the then Members of the Assembly.

Provided that no resolution for the purpose of clause (c) shall be moved unless at least fourteen days notice has been given of the intention to move the resolution;

Provided further that, whenever the Assembly is dissolved, the Speaker shall not vacate his office until immediately before the first meeting of the Assembly after the dissolution.

1 Subs. by the Constitution (First Amendment) Act, 1951, sec.9(1), for "every session".(w.e.f. 18.6.1951)

2 The words "and for the precedence of such discussion over other business of the House" omitted by the Constitution (First Amendment) Act, 1951, sec.9(2).(w.e.f. 18.6.1951)

180. Power of the Deputy Speaker or other person to perform the duties of the office, or to act as, Speaker. -

(1) While the office of Speaker is vacant, the duties of the office shall be performed by the Deputy Speaker or, if the office of Deputy Speaker is also vacant, by such member of the Assembly as the Governor may appoint for the purpose.

(2) During the absence of the Speaker from any sitting of the Assembly the Deputy Speaker or, if he is also absent, such person as may be determined by the rules of procedures of the Assembly, or if no such person is present, such other person as may be determined by the Assembly, shall act as Speaker.

181. The Speaker or the Deputy Speaker not to preside while a resolution for his removal from office is under consideration.-

(1) At any sitting of the Legislative Assembly, while any resolution for the removal of the Speaker from his office is under consideration, the Speaker, or while any resolution for the removal of the Deputy Speaker from his office is under consideration, the Deputy Speaker, shall not, though he is present, preside, and the provisions of clause (2) of article 180 shall apply in relation to every such sitting as they apply in relation to a sitting from which the Speaker or, as the case may be, the Deputy Speaker, is absent.

(2) The Speaker shall have the right to speak in and otherwise to take part in the proceedings of, the Legislative Assembly while any resolution for his removal from office is under consideration in the Assembly and shall, notwithstanding anything in article 189, be entitled to vote only in the first instance on such resolution or on any other matter during such proceedings but not in the case of an equality of votes.

182. The Chairman and Deputy Chairman of the Legislative Council. The Legislative Council of every State having such Council shall, as soon as may be, choose two members of the Council to be respectively Chairman and Deputy Chairman thereof and, so often as the office of Chairman or Deputy Chairman becomes vacant, the Council shall choose another member to be Chairman or Deputy Chairman, as the case may be.

183. Vacation and resignation of, and removal from, the offices of Chairman and Deputy Chairman.- A member holding office as Chairman or Deputy Chairman of a Legislative Council -

(a) shall vacate his office if he ceases to be a member of the Council;

(b) may at any time by writing under his hand addressed, if such member is the Chairman, to the Deputy Chairman, and if such member is the Deputy Chairman, to the Chairman, resign his office; and

(c) may be removed from his office by a resolution of the Council passed by a majority of all the then members of the Council;

Provided that no resolution for the purpose of clause (c) shall be moved unless at least fourteen days notice has been given of the intention to move the resolution.

184. Power of the Deputy Chairman or other person to perform the duties of the office of, or to act as, Chairman. -

(1) While the office of Chairman is vacant, the duties of the office shall be performed by the Deputy Chairman or, if the office of Deputy Chairman is also vacant, by such member of the Council as the Governor may appoint for the purpose.

(2) During the absence of the Chairman from any sitting of the Council the Deputy Chairman or, if he is also absent, such person as may be determined by the rules of procedure of the Council, or, if no such person is present, such other person as may be determined by the Council, shall act as Chairman.

185. The Chairman or the Deputy Chairman not to preside while a resolution for his removal from office is under consideration.-

(1) At any sitting of the Legislative Council, while any resolution for the removal of the Chairman from his office is under consideration, the Chairman, or while any resolution for the removal of the Deputy Chairman from his office is under consideration, the Deputy Chairman, shall not, though he is present, preside, and the provisions of clause (2) of article 184 shall apply in relation to every such sitting as they apply in relation to a sitting from which the Chairman or, as the case may be, the Deputy Chairman is absent.

(2) The Chairman shall have the right to speak in, and otherwise to take part in the proceedings of the Legislative Council while any resolution for his removal from office is under consideration in the Council and shall, notwithstanding anything in article 189, be entitled to vote only in the first instance on such resolution or on any other matter during such proceedings but not in the case of an equality of votes.

186. Salaries and allowances of the Speaker and Deputy Speaker and the Chairman and Deputy Chairman.- There shall be paid to the Speaker and the Deputy Speaker of the Legislative Assembly, and to the Chairman and the Deputy Chairman of the Legislative Council, such salaries and allowances as may be respectively fixed by the Legislature of the State by law and, until provision in that behalf is so made, such salaries and allowances as are specified in the Second Schedule.

187. Secretariat of State Legislature.-

(1) The House or each House of the Legislature of a State shall have a separate secretarial staff:

Provided that nothing in this clause shall, in the case of the Legislature of a State having a Legislative Council, be construed as preventing the creation of posts common to both Houses of such Legislature.

(2) The Legislature of a State may by law regulate the recruitment, and the conditions of service of persons appointed, to the secretarial staff of the House or Houses of the Legislature of the State.

(3) Until provision is made by the Legislature of the State under clause (2), the Governor may, after consultation with the Speaker of the Legislative Assembly or the Chairman of the Legislative Council, as the case may be, make rules regulating the recruitment and the conditions of service of persons appointed, to the secretarial staff of the Assembly or the Council and any rules so made shall have effect subject to the provisions of any law made under the said clause.

Conduct of Business

188. Oath or affirmation by members.- Every member of the Legislative Assembly or the Legislative Council of a State shall, before taking his seat, make and subscribe before the Governor, or some person appointed in that behalf by him, an oath or affirmation according to the form set out for the purpose in the Third Schedule.

189. Voting in Houses, power of Houses to act notwithstanding vacancies and quorum. -

(1) Save as otherwise provided in this Constitution, all questions at any sitting of a House of the Legislature of State shall be determined by a majority of votes of the members present and voting, other than the Speaker or Chairman, or person acting as such.

The Speaker or Chairman, or person acting as such, shall not vote in the first instance, but shall have and exercise a casting vote in the case of an equality of votes.

(2) A House of the Legislature of a State shall have power to act notwithstanding any vacancy in the membership thereof, and any proceedings in the Legislature of a State shall be valid notwithstanding that it is discovered subsequently that some person who was not entitled so to do sat or voted or otherwise took part in the proceedings.

(3) Until the Legislature of the State by law otherwise provides, the quorum to constitute a meeting of a House of the Legislature of State shall be ten members or one-tenth of the total number of members of the House, whichever is greater.

(4) If at any time during a meeting of the Legislative Assembly or the Legislative Council of a State there is no quorum, it shall be the duty of the Speaker or Chairman, or person acting as such, either to adjourn the House or to suspend the meeting until there is a quorum.

Disqualifications of Members

190. Vacation of seats.-

(1) No person shall be a member of both Houses of the Legislature of State and provision shall be made by the Legislature of the State by law for the vacation by a person who is chosen a member of both Houses of his seat in one House or the other.

(2) No person shall be a member of the Legislatures of two or more States specified in the First Schedule and if a person is chosen member of the Legislatures of two or more such States, then at the expiration of such period as may be specified in rules[1] made by the President, the person's seat in the Legislatures of all such States shall become vacant, unless he has previously resigned his seat in the Legislatures of all but one of the States.

(3) If a member of a House of the Legislature of a State –

(a) becomes subject to any of the disqualifications mentioned in [2][clause (1) or clause (2) of article 191]; or

[3][(b) resigns his seat by writing under his hand addressed to the Speaker or the Chairman, as the case may be, and his resignation is accepted by the Speaker or the Chairman, as the case may be,]

his seat shall thereupon become vacant;

[4][Provided that in the case of any resignation referred to in sub-clause (b), if from information received or otherwise and after making such inquiry as he thinks fit, the Speaker or the Chairman, as the case may be, is satisfied that such resignation is not voluntary or genuine, he shall not accept such resignation.]

(4) If for a period of sixty days a member of a House of the Legislature of a State is without permission of the House absent from all meetings thereof, the House may declare his seat vacant;

Provided that in computing the said period of sixty days no account shall be taken of any period during which the House is prorogued or is adjourned for more that four consecutive days.

191. Disqualifications for membership.

(1) A person shall be disqualified for being chosen as, and for being, a member of the Legislative Assembly or Legislative Council of a State-

(a) if he holds any office of profit under the Government of India or the Government of any State specified in the First Schedule, other than an office declared by the Legislature of the State by law not to disqualify its holders;

---

1 See the Prohibitionof Simultaneous Membership Rules, 1950 published with the Ministry of Law, Notification No.F.46/50-C, dated the 26th January, 1950, Gazette of India, Extra., p. 678.

2 Subs. by the Constitution (Fifty-second Amendment) Act, 1985, sec. 4, for the words, brackets and figures "clause (1) of article 191" (w.e.f. 1-3-1985).

3 Subs. by the Constitution (Thirty-third Amendment) Act, 1974, sec. 3(1), for sub- clause (b) (w.e.f. 19.5.1974).

4 Ins. by the Constitution (Thirty-third Amendment) Act, 1974, sec.3(2) (w.e.f. 19.5.1974).

(b) if he is of unsound mind and stands so declared by a competent court;

(c) if he is an undischarged insolvent;

(d) if he is not a citizen of India, or has voluntarily acquired the citizenship of a foreign State, or is under any acknowledgment of allegiance or adherence to a foreign State;

(e) If he is so disqualified by or under any law made by Parliament.

[1][*Explanation.*— For the purposes of this clause], a person shall not be deemed to hold an office of profit under the Government of India or the government of any State specified in the First Schedule by reason only that he is a Minister either for the Union or for such State.

[2][(2). A person shall be disqualified for being a member of the Legislative Assembly or Legislative Council of a State if he is so disqualified under the Tenth Schedule.]

[3][192. Decision on questions as to disqualifications of members.-

(1) If any question arises as to whether a member of a House of the Legislature of a State has become subject to any of the disqualifications mentioned in clause (1) of article 191, the question shall be referred for the decision of the Governor and his decision shall be final.

(2) Before giving any decision on any such question, the Governor shall obtain the opinion of the Election Commission and shall act according to such opinion.

193. Penalty for sitting and voting before making oath or affirmation under article 188 or when not qualified or when disqualified.- If a person sits or votes as a member of the Legislative Assembly or the Legislative Council of State before he has complied with the requirements of article 188, or when he knows that he is not qualified or that he is disqualified for membership thereof, or that he is prohibited from so doing by the provisions of any law made by Parliament or the Legislature of the State, he shall be liable in respect of each day on which he so sits or votes to a penalty of five hundred rupees to be recovered as a debt due to the State.

Powers, Privileges and Immunities of State Legislatures and their Members

194. Powers, Privileges, etc., of the Houses of Legislatures and of the members and committees thereof.-

(1) Subject to the provisions of this Constitution and to the rules and standing orders regulating the procedure of the Legislature, there shall be freedom of speech in the Legislature of every State.

(2) No member of the Legislature of a State shall be liable to any proceedings in any court in respect of anything said or any vote given by him in the Legislature or any committee thereof, and no person shall be so liable in respect of the publication by or under the authority of a House of such a Legislature of any report, paper, votes or proceedings.

(3) In other respects, the powers, privileges and immunities of a House of the Legislature of a State, and of the members and the committees of a House of such Legislature, shall be such as may from time to time be defined by the Legislature by law, and until so defined; [4][shall be those of that House and of its members and committees immediately before the coming into force of section 26 of the Constitution (Forty-fourth Amendment) Act, 1978].

(4) The provisions of clauses (1), (2) and (3) shall apply in relation to persons who by

---

1 Subs. by the Constitution (Fifty-second Amendment) Act, 1985, sec.5(a), For the brackets, figures and words "(2) for the purpose of this article" (w.e.f. 1-3-1985).

2 Ins. by the Constitution (Fifty-second Amendment) Act, 1985, sec. 5(b) (w.e.f. 1-3-1985).

3 Subs. by the Constitution (Forty-fourth Amendment) Act, 1978, sec. 25, for article 192 (w.e.f. 20-6-1979). Earlier article 192 was substituted by the Constitution (Forty second Amendment) Act, 1976, sec. 33 (w.e.f. 3-1-1977)

4 Subs. by the Constitution (Forty-fourth Amendment) Act, 1978, sec. 26, for certain words (w.e.f. 20-6-1979).

virtue of this Constitution have the right to speak in, and otherwise to take part in the proceedings of a House of the Legislature of State or any Committee thereof as they apply in relation to members of that Legislature.

Notes on Article 194

The provisions of Tenth Schedule, paragraph 2, in no way violate Articles 105(1) or 194(1); *Kihota v. Zachillhu*, AIR 1993 SC 412 (CB).

Powers and Priviledges of Member of Legislature :- The members of legislature being protected by priviledges under article 194 are not answerable to court for voting in a particular manner in legislature. No person can claim any legal right to have a rule framed in a particular manner and rule making authority does not owe any corresponding duty to do same;

Advocate M.L. George v. High Court of Kerala AIR 2010.

195. Salaries and allowances of members.- Members of the Legislative Assembly and the Legislative Council of State shall be entitled to receive such salaries and allowances as may from time to time be determined, by the Legislature of the State by law and, until provision in that respect is so made, salaries and allowances at such rates and upon such conditions as were immediately before the commencement of the Constitution applicable in the case of members of the Legislative Assembly of the corresponding province.

Legislative Procedure

196. Provisions as to introduction and passing of Bills.-

(1) Subject to the provisions of articles 198 and 207 with respect to Money Bills and other Financial Bills, a Bill may originate in either House of the Legislature of a State which has a Legislative Council.

(2) Subject to the provisions of articles 197 and 198, a Bill shall not be deemed to have been passed by the Houses of the Legislature of a State having a Legislative Council unless it has been agreed to by both Houses, either without amendment or with such amendments only as are agreed to by both Houses.

(3) A Bill pending in the Legislature of a State shall not lapse by reason of the prorogation of the House or Houses thereof.

(4) A Bill pending in the Legislative Council of a State which has not been passed by the Legislative Assembly shall not lapse on a dissolution of the Assembly.

(5) A Bill which is pending in the Legislative Assembly of a State, or which having been passed by the Legislative Assembly is pending in the Legislative Council, shall lapse on a dissolution of the Assembly.

197. Restriction on powers of Legislative Council as to Bills other than Money Bills.-

(1) If after a Bill has been passed by the Legislative Assembly of a State having a Legislative Council and transmitted to the Legislative Council -

(a) The bill is rejected by the Council; or

(b) More than three months elapse from the date on which the Bill is laid before the Council without the Bill being passed by it; or

(c) The Bill is passed by the Council with amendments to which the Legislative Assembly does not agree;

the Legislative Assembly may, subject to the rules regulating its procedures, pass the Bill again in the same or in any subsequent session with or without such amendments, if any, as have been made, suggested or agreed to by the Legislative Council and then transmit the Bill as so passed to the Legislative Council.

(2) If after a Bill has been so passed for the second time by the Legislative Assembly and transmitted to the Legislative Council-

a. The Bill is rejected by the Council; or

b. More than one month elapses from the date on which the Bill is laid before the Council without the Bill being passed by it; or

c. The Bill is passed by the Council with amendments to which the Legislative Assembly does not agree;

the Bill shall be deemed to have been passed by the Houses of the Legislature of the State in the form in which it was passed by the Legislative Assembly for the second time with such amendments, if any, as have been made or suggested by the Legislative Council and agreed to by the Legislative Assembly.

(3) Nothing in this article shall apply to a Money Bill.

198. Special procedure in respect of Money Bills.-

(1) A Money Bill shall not be introduced in a Legislative Council.

(2) After a Money Bill has been passed by the Legislative Assembly of a State having a Legislative Council, it shall be transmitted to the Legislative Council for its recommendations, and the Legislative Council shall within a period of fourteen days from the date of its receipt of the Bill return the Bill to the Legislative Assembly with its recommendations, and the Legislative Assembly may thereupon either accept or reject all or any or the recommendations of the Legislative Council.

(3) If the Legislative Assembly accepts any of the recommendations of the Legislative Council, the Money Bill shall be deemed to have been passed by both Houses with the amendments recommended by the Legislative Council and accepted by the Legislative Assembly.

(4) If the Legislative Assembly does not accept any of the recommendations of the Legislative Council, the Money Bill shall be deemed to have been passed by both Houses in the form in which it was passed by the Legislative Assembly without any of the amendments recommended by the Legislative Council.

(5) If a Money Bill passed by the Legislative Assembly and transmitted to the Legislative Council for its recommendations is not returned to the Legislative Assembly within the said period of fourteen days, it shall be deemed to have been passed by both Houses at the expiration of the said period in the form in which it was passed by the Legislative Assembly.

199. Definition of "Money Bills".-

(1) For the purposes of this chapter, a Bill shall be deemed to be a Money Bill if it contains only provisions dealing with all or any of the following matters, namely:-

a. the imposition, abolition, remission, alteration or regulation of any tax;

b. the regulation of the borrowing of money or the giving of any guarantee by the State, or the amendment of the law with respect to any financial obligations undertaken or to be undertaken by the State;

c. the custody of the Consolidated Fund or the Contingency Fund of the State, the payment of moneys into or the withdrawal of moneys from any such Fund;

d. the appropriation of moneys out of the Consolidated Fund of the State.

e. the declaring of any expenditure to be expenditure charged on the Consolidated Fund of the State, or the increasing of the amount of any such expenditure.

f. the receipt of money on account of the Consolidated Fund of the State or the public account of the State or the custody or issue of such money; or

g. any matter incidental to any of the matters specified in sub-clauses (a) to (f).

(2) A Bill shall not be deemed to be a Money Bill by reason only that it provides for the imposition of fines or other pecuniary penalties, or for the demand or payment of fees for licences or fees for services rendered, or by reason that it provides for the imposition, abolition, remission, alteration or regulation of any tax by any local authority or body for local purposes.

(3) If any question arises whether a Bill introduced in the Legislature of a State which has a Legislative Council is a Money Bill or not, the decision of the Speaker of the Legislative Assembly of such State thereon shall be final.

(4) There shall be endorsed on every Money Bill when it is transmitted to the Legislative Council under article 198, and when it is presented to the Governor for assent under article 200, the certificate of the Speaker of the Legislative Assembly signed by him that it is a Money Bill.

200. Assent to Bills.- When a Bill has been passed by the Legislative Assembly of a State or, in the case of State having a Legislative Council, has been passed by both Houses of the Legislature of the State, it shall be presented to the Governor and the Governor shall declare either that he assents to the Bill or that he withholds assent therefrom or that he reserves the Bill for the consideration of the President:

Provided that the Governor may, as soon as possible after the presentation to him of the Bill for assent, return the bill if it is not a Money Bill together with a message requesting that the House or Houses will reconsider the Bill or any specified provisions thereof and, in particular, will consider the desirability of introducing any such amendments as he may recommend in his message and, when a Bill is so returned, the House or Houses shall reconsider the Bill accordingly, and if the Bill is passed again by the House or Houses with or without amendment and presented to the Governor for assent, the Governor shall not withhold assent therefrom:

Provided further that the Governor shall not assent to, but shall reserve for the consideration of the President, any Bill which in the opinion of the Governor would, if it became law, so derogate from the powers of the High Court as to endanger the position which that Court is by this Constitution designed to fill.

201. Bills reserved for consideration.- When a Bill is reserved by a Governor for the consideration of the President, the President shall declare either that he assents to the Bill or that he withholds assent therefrom:

Provided that where the Bill is not a Money Bill, the President may direct the Governor to return the Bill to the House or as the case may be, the Houses of the Legislature of the State together with such a message as is mentioned in the first proviso to article 200 and, when a Bill is so returned, the House or Houses shall reconsider it accordingly within a period of six months from the date of receipt of such message and, if it is again passed by the House or Houses with or without amendment, it shall be presented again to the President for his consideration.

Procedure in Financial Matters

202. Annual financial statement.-

(1) The Governor shall in respect of every financial year cause to be laid before the House or Houses of the Legislature of the State a statement of the estimated receipts and expenditure of the State for that year, in this Part referred to as the "annual financial statement".

(2) The estimates of expenditure embodied in the annual financial statement shall show separately-

(a) The sums required to meet expenditure described by this Constitution as expenditure charged upon the Consolidated Fund of the State; and

(b) The sums required to meet other expenditure proposed to be made from the Consolidated Fund of the State, and shall distinguish expenditure on revenue account from other expenditure.

(3) The following expenditure shall be expenditure charged on the Consolidated Fund of each State-

(a) the emoluments and allowances of the Governor and other expenditure relating to his office;

(b) the salaries and allowances of the Speaker and the Deputy Speaker of the Legislative Assembly and, in the case of State having a Legislative Council, also of the Chairman and the Deputy Chairman of the Legislative Council;

(c) debt charges for which the State is liable including interest, sinking fund charges and redemption charges, and other expenditure relating to the raising of loans and the service and redemption of debts;

(d) expenditure in respect of the salaries and allowances of Judges of any High Court:

(e) any sums required to satisfy any judgement, decree or award of any court or arbitral tribunal;

(f) any other expenditure declared by this Constitution, or by the Legislature of the State by law, to be so charged.

203. Procedure in Legislature with respect to estimates.-

(1) So much of the estimates as relates to expenditure charged upon the Consolidated Fund of a State shall not be submitted to the vote of the Legislative Assembly, but nothing in this clause shall be construed as preventing the discussion in the Legislature of any of those estimates.

(2) So much of the said estimates as relates to other expenditure shall be submitted in the form of demands for grants to the Legislative Assembly, and the Legislative Assembly shall have power to assent, or to refuse to assent, to any demand, or to assent to any demand subject to a reduction of the amount specified therein.

(3) No demand for a grant shall be made except on the recommendation of the Governor.

204. Appropriation Bills.-

(1) As soon as may be after the grants under article 203 have been made by the Assembly, there shall be introduced a bill to provide for the appropriation out of the Consolidated Fund of the State of all moneys required to meet-

(a) the grants so made by the Assembly; and

(b) the expenditure charged on the Consolidated Fund of the State but not exceeding in any case the amount shown in the statement previously laid before the House or Houses.

(2) No amendment shall be proposed to any such Bill in the House or either House of the Legislature of the State which will have the effect of varying the amount or altering the destination of any grant so made or of varying the amount of any expenditure charged on the Consolidated Fund of the State, and the decision of the person presiding as to whether an amendment is inadmissible under this clause shall be final.

(3) Subject to the provisions of Articles 205 and 206, no money shall be withdrawn from the Consolidated Fund of the State except under appropriation made by law passed in accordance with the provisions of this Article.

205. Supplementary, additional or excess grants.-

(1) The Governor shall -

(a) if the amount authorised by any law made in accordance with the provisions of article 204 to be expended for a particular service for the current financial year is found to be insufficient for the purposes of that year or when a need has arisen during the current financial year for supplementary or additional expenditure upon some new service not contemplated in the annual financial statement for that year, or

(b) if any money has been spent on any service during a financial year in excess of the amount granted for that service and for that year.

Cause to be laid before the House or the Houses of the Legislature of the State another statement showing the estimated amount of that expenditure or cause to be presented to the Legislative Assembly of the State a demand for such excess, as the case may be.

(2) The provisions of articles 202, 203 and 204 shall have effect in relation to any such statement and expenditure or demand and also to any law to be made authorizing the appropriation of moneys out of the Consolidated Fund of the State to meet such expenditure or the grant in respect of such demand as they have effect in relation to the annual financial statement and the expenditure mentioned therein or to a demand for a grant and the law to be made for the authorization of appropriation of moneys out of the Consolidated Fund of the State to meet such expenditure or grant.

206. Votes on account, votes of credit and exceptional grants.-

(1) Notwithstanding anything in the foregoing provisions of this Chapter, the Legislative Assembly of a State shall have power-

(a) to make any grant in advance in respect of the estimated expenditure for a part of any financial year pending the completion of the procedure prescribed in article 203 for the voting of such grant and the passing of the law in accordance with the provisions of article 204 in relation to that expenditure;

(b) to make a grant for meeting an unexpected demand upon the resources of the State when on account of the magnitude or the indefinite character of the service the demand cannot be stated with the details ordinarily given in an annual financial statement;

(c) to make an exceptional grant which forms no part of the current service of any financial year.

And the Legislature of the State shall have power to authorise by law the withdrawal of moneys from the Consolidated Fund of the State for the purposes for which the said grants are made.

(2) The provisions of articles 203 and 204 shall have effect in relation to the making of any grant under clause (1) and to any law to be made under that clause as they have effect in relation to the making of a grant with regard to any expenditure mentioned in the annual financial statement and the law to be made for the authorization of appropriation of moneys out of the Consolidated Fund of the State to meet such expenditure.

207. Special provisions as to financial Bills.-

(1) A Bill or amendment making provision for any of the matters specified in sub-clauses (a) to (f) of clause (1) or article 199 shall not be introduced of moved except on the recommendation of the Governor, and a Bill making such provision shall not be introduced in a Legislative Council;

Provided that no recommendation shall be required under this clause for the moving of an amendment making provision for the reduction or abolition of any tax.

(2) A Bill or amendment shall not be deemed to make provision for any of the matters aforesaid by reason only that it provides for the imposition of fines or other pecuniary penalties, or for the demand or payment, of fees for licences or fees for services rendered, or by reason that it provides for the imposition, abolition, remission, alteration or regulation of any tax by any local authority or body for local purposes.

(3) A Bill which, if enacted and brought into operation, would involve expenditure from the Consolidated Fund of a State shall not be passed by a House of the Legislature of the State unless the Governor has recommended to that House the consideration of the Bill.

Procedure Generally

208. Rules of procedure.

(1) A House of the Legislature of a State may make rules for regulating, subject to the provisions of this Constitution, its procedure and the conduct of its business.

(2) Until rules are made under clause (1), the rules of procedure and standing orders in force immediately before the commencement of this Constitution with respect to the Legislature for the corresponding province shall have effect in relation to the Legislature of the State subject to such modifications and adaptations as may be made therein by the Speaker of the Legislative Assembly, or the Chairman of the Legislative Council, as the case may be.

(3) In a State having a Legislative Council the Governor, after consultation with the Speaker of the Legislative Assembly and the Chairman of the Legislative Council, may make rules as to the procedure with respect to communications between the two Houses.

209. Regulation by law of procedure in the Legislature of the State in relation to financial business.- The Legislature of a State may, for the purpose of the timely completion of financial business, regulate by law the procedure of, and the conduct of business in, the House or Houses of the Legislature of the State in relation to any financial matter or to any Bill for the appropriation of moneys out of the Consolidated Fund of the State, and, if and so far as any provision of any law so made is inconsistent with any rule made by the House or either House of the Legislature of the State under clause (1) of article 208 or with any rule or standing order having effect in relation to the Legislature of the State under clause (2) of that article, such provision shall prevail.

210. Language to be used in the Legislature.-

(1) Notwithstanding anything in Part XVII, but subject to the provisions of article 348, business in the Legislature of a State shall be transacted in the official language or languages of the State or in Hindi or in English.

Provided that the Speaker of the Legislative Assembly or Chairman of the Legislative Council, or person acting as such, as the case may be, may permit any member who cannot adequately express himself in any of the languages aforesaid to address the House in his mother tongue.

(2) Unless the Legislature of the State by law otherwise provides, this article shall, after the expiration of a period of fifteen years from the commencement of this Constitution have effect as if the words 'or in English' were omitted therefrom;

[1][Provided that in relation to the [2][Legislatures of the States of Himachal Pradesh, Manipur, Meghalaya and Tripura] this clause shall have effect as if for the words 'fifteen years' occurring therein, the words "twenty-five years" were substituted:]

[3][Provided further that in relation to the [4][Legislatures of the States of [5][Arunachal Pradesh, Goa and Mizoram]] this clause shall have effect as if for the words "fifteen years" occurring therein, the words "forty years" were substituted.]

---

1 Ins. by the State of Himachal Pradesh Act, 1970 (53 of 1970), sec. 46 (w.e.f. 25-1-1971).

2 Subs. by the North-Eastern Areas (Reorganisation) Act, 1971 (81 of 1971), sec. 71, for "Legislature of the State of Himachal Pradesh " (w.e.f. 21-1-1972).

3 Ins. by the State of Mizoram Act, 1986 (34 of 1986), sec. 39 (w.e.f. 20-2-1987).

4 Subs. by the State of Arunachal Pradesh Act, 1986 (69 of 1986), sec. 42, for "Legislature of the State of Mizoram " (w.e.f. 20-2-1987).

5 Subs. by the Goa, Daman and Diu Reorganization Act, 1987 (18 of 1987), sec. 63 for "Arunachal Pradesh and Mizoram" (w.e.f. 30-5-1987).

211. Restriction on discussion in the Legislature.- No discussion shall take place in the Legislature of a State with respect to the conduct of any Judge of the Supreme Court or of a High Court in the discharge of his duties.

212. Courts not to inquire into proceedings of the Legislature.-

(1) The validity of any proceedings in the Legislature of a State shall not be called in question on the ground of any alleged irregularity of procedure.

(2) No officer or member of the Legislature of a State in whom powers are vested by or under this Constitution for regulating procedure or the conduct of business, or for maintaining order, in the Legislature shall be subject to the jurisdiction of any court in respect of the exercise by him of those powers.

CHAPTER IV—LEGISLATIVE POWER OF THE GOVERNOR

213. Power of Governor to promulgate Ordinances during recess of Legislature.-

(1) If at any time, except when the Legislative Assembly of a State is in session, or where there is Legislative Council in a State, except when both Houses of the Legislature are in session, the Governor, is satisfied that circumstances exist which render it necessary for him to take immediate action, he may promulgate such Ordinances as the circumstances appear to him to require:

Provided that the Governor shall not, without instructions from the President, promulgate any such Ordinance if-

(a) a Bill containing the same provisions would under this Constitution have required the previous sanction of the President for the introduction thereof into the Legislature; or

(b) he would have deemed it necessary to reserve a Bill containing the same provisions for the consideration of the President; or

(c) an Act of the Legislature of the State containing the same provisions would under this Constitution have been invalid unless, having been reserved for the consideration of the President, it had received the assent of the President.

(2) An Ordinance promulgated under this article shall have the same force and effect as an Act of Legislature of the State assented to by the Governor, but every such Ordinance-

(a) shall be laid before the Legislative Assembly of the State, or where there is a Legislative Council in the State, before both Houses, and shall cease to operate at the expiration of six weeks from the reassembly of the Legislature, or if before the expiration of that period a resolution disapproving it is passed by the Legislative Assembly and agreed to by the Legislative Council, if any, upon the passing of the resolution or, as the case may be, on the resolution being agreed to by the Council; and

(b) may be withdrawn at any time by the Governor.

Explanation: Where the Houses of the Legislature of a State having a Legislative Council are summoned to reassemble on different dates, the period of six weeks shall be reckoned from the later of those dates for the purposes of this clause.

(3) If and so far as an Ordinance under this article makes any provision which would not be valid if enacted in an act of the Legislature of the State assented to by the Governor, it shall be void:

Provided that, for the purposes of the provisions of this Constitution relating to the effect of an Act of the Legislature of a State which is repugnant to an Act of Parliament or an existing law with respect to a matter enumerated in the Concurrent List, an Ordinance promulgated under this article in pursuance of instructions from the President shall be deemed to be an Act of the Legislature of the State which has been reserved for the consideration of the President and assented to by him.[1][***]

Notes on Article 213

This Article should be read alongwith article 123 (power of the President to promulgate ordinances). The most important decision of the Supreme Court on this Article is *D.C. Wadhwa v. State of Bihar.* The Supreme Court observed that an ordinance can be put to judicial scrutiny if the Governor —

a. directly violates a constitutional provision; or

b. exceeds his authority to promulgate an Ordinance; or

c. has made a colourable use of such power e.g. (successive repromulgation of Ordinance without resort to formal legislation by the Legislature).

These grounds are sufficient for declaring an Ordinance null and void;

D.C. Wadhwa v. State of Bihar, AIR 1987 SC 579, paragraphs 6-8.

CHAPTER V — THE HIGH COURTS IN THE STATES

214. High Courts for States.- [2][***]There shall be a High Court for each State. [3][***]

Notes on Article 214

In federation of Bar Association in *Karnataka V. Union of India*, AIR 2000 SC 2544, it was held that no litigant can claim a fundamental right to have the high court located within proximal distance of his residence.

215. High Courts to be courts of record.- Every High Court shall be a court of record and shall have all the powers of such a court including the power to punish for contempt of itself.

Notes on Article 215

The Supreme Court and High courts are courts of record and the power to punish for contempt was given to them by the constitution. Any legislation which stultifies or abrogates that power cannot be regarded as validly enacted. (*Pallow sheth V. Custodian*) AIR 2001 SC 2763

216. Constitution of High Courts.- Every High Court shall consist of a Chief Justice and such other Judges as the President may from time to time deem it necessary to appoint.[4][***]

217. Appointment and Conditions of the office of a Judge of a High Court.- (1) Every Judge of a High Court shall be appointed by the President by warrant under his hand and seal after consultation with the Chief Justice of India, the Governer of the State, and, in case of appointment of a Judge other than the Chief Justice,the Chief Justice of the High Court and [5][shall hold office in the case of an additional or acting Judge, as provided in article 224, and in any other case, until he attains the age of [6][sixty-two years]].

---

1 Clause (4) omitted by the Constitution (Forty-fourth Amendment) Act, 1978,sec. 27 (w.e.f.20-6-1979). Earlier clause (4) was inserted by the Constitution (Thirty-eighth Amendment) Act, 1975, sec. 3 (retrospectively).

2 The brackets and figures "(1)" omitted by the Constitution (Seventh Amendment) Act, 1956, sec. 29 and Sch. (w.e.f. 1-11-1956)

3 Clauses (2) and (3) omitted by the Constitution (Seventh Amendment) Act, 1956, sec. 29and Sch. (w.e.f. 1-11-1956)

4 Proviso omitted by the Constitution (Seventh Amendment) Act, 1956, sec. 11 (w.e.f. 1-11-1956).

5 Subs. by the Constitution (Seventh Amendment) Act, 1956, sec. 12, for "shall hold office until he attains the age of sixty years" (w.e.f. 1-11-1956).

6 Subs. by the Constitution (Fifteenth Amendment) Act, 1963, sec.4(a), for "sixty years". (w.e.f. 5-10-1963).

Provided that-

(a) a Judge may, by writing under his hand addressed to the President, resign his office;

(b) a Judge may be removed from his office by the President in the manner provided in clause (4) of article 124 for the removal of a Judge of the Supreme Court;

(c) the office of a Judge shall be vacated by his being appointed by the President to be a Judge of the Supreme Court or by his being transferred by the President to any other High Court within the territory of India.

(2) A person shall not be qualified for appointment as a Judge of a High Court unless he is a citizen of India and—

(a) has for at least ten years held a judicial office in the territory of India; or

(b) has for at least ten years been an advocate of a High Court [1][***] or of two or more such courts in succession; [2][***]

Explanation — For the purposes of this clause—

[3][(a) in computing the period during which a person has held judicial office in the territory of India, there shall be included any period, after he has held any judicial office, during which the person has been an advocate of a High Court or has held the office of a member of a tribunal or any post, under the Union or a State, requiring special knowledge of law;]

[4][aa)] in computing the period during which a person has been an advocate of a High Court, there shall be included any period during which the person [5][has held judicial office or the office of a member of a tribunal or any post, under the Union or a State, requiring special knowledge of law] after he became an advocate;

(b) in computing the period during which a person has held judicial office in the territory of India or been an advocate of a High Court, there shall be included any period before the commencement of this Constitution during which he has held judicial office in any area which was comprised before the fifteenth day of August, 1947, within India as defined by the Government of India Act,1935, or has been an advocate of any High Court in any such area, as the case may be.

[6][(3) If any question arises as to the age of a Judge of a High Court, the question shall be decided by the President after consultation with the Chief Justice of India and the decision of the President shall be final.]

Notes on Article 217

The requirement of consultation with the chief justice of the High Court and his opinion as per the proviso in section 16(1)(a) of the consumer protection Act, 1986 must have the same status as in the matter of the appointment of High Court under Article 217 of the constitution.

N. Kannadasan V. Ajay Khose (2009)

---

1 The words "in any State specified in the First Schedule" omitted by the Constitution (Seventh Amendment) Act, 1956, sec. 29 and Sch (w.e.f. 1-11-1956).

2 The word "or" and sub-clause (c) were ins. by the Constitution (Forty-second Amendment) Act, 1976, sec. 36 (w.e.f. 3-1-1977) and omitted by the Constitution (Forty-fourth Amendment) Act, 1978, sec. 28(c), (w.e.f. 20-6-1979).

3 Ins. by the Constitution (Forty-fourth Amendment) Act, 1978, sec. 28 (w.e.f. 20-6-1979).

4 Clause (a) re-lettered as clause (aa) by the Constitution (Forty-fourth Amendment) Act, 1978, sec. 28(c) (w.e.f. 20-6-1979).

5 Subs. by the Constitution (Forty-second Amendment) Act, 1976, sec.36(c), for "has held judicial office" (w.e.f. 3-1-1977).

6 Ins. by the Constitution (Fifteenth Amendment) Act, 1963, sec.4(b) (with retrospective effect).

218. Application of certain provisions relating to Supreme Court to High Courts.- The provisions of clauses (4) and (5) of article 124 shall apply in relation to a High Court as they apply in relation to the Supreme Court with the substitution of references to the High Court for references to the Supreme Court.

219. Oath or affirmation by Judges of High Courts.- Every person appointed to be a Judge of a High Court [1][***] shall, before he enters upon his office, make and subscribe before the Governor of the State, or some person appointed in that behalf by him, an oath or affirmation according to the form set out for the purpose in the Third Schedule.

[2][**220. Restriction on practice after being a permanent Judge. -** No person who, after the commencement of this Constitution, has held office as a permanent Judge of a High Court shall plead or act in any court or before any authority in India except the Supreme Court and the other High Courts.

Explanation: In this article, the expression "High Court" does not include a High Court for a State specified in Part B of the First Schedule as it existed before the commencement[3] of the Constitution (Seventh Amendment) Act, 1956.]

221. Salaries, etc. of Judges.-

[4][(1) There shall be paid to the Judges of each High Court such salaries as may be determined by Parliament by law, and, until provision in that behalf is so made, such salaries as are specified in the Second Schedule.]

(2) Every Judge shall be entitled to such allowances and to such rights in respect of leave of absence and pension as may from time to time be determined by or under law made by Parliament and, until so determined, to such allowances and rights as are specified in the Second Schedule:

Provided that neither the allowances of a Judge nor his rights in respect of leave of absence or pension shall be varied to his disadvantage after his appointment.

222. Transfer of a Judge from one High Court to another.-

(1) The President may, after consultation with the Chief Justice of India, transfer a Judge from one High Court to any other High Court. [5][***]

[6][(2) When a Judge has been or is so transferred, he shall, during the period he serves, after the commencement of the Constitution (Fifteenth Amendment) Act, 1963, as a Judge of the other High Court, be entitled to receive in addition to his salary such compensatory allowance as may be determined by Parliament by law and, until so determined, such compensatory allowance as the President may by order fix.]

223. Appointment of acting Chief Justice.- When the office of Chief Justice of a High Court is vacant or when any such Chief Justice is by reason of absence or otherwise, unable to perform the duties of his office, the duties of the office shall be performed by such one of the other Judges of the Court as the President may appoint for the purpose.

[7][**224. Appointment of additional and acting Judges.-**

(1) If by reason of any temporary increase in the business of a High Court or by reason of arrears of work therein, it appears to the President that the number of the Judges of that

1 The words "in a State" omitted by the Constitution (Seventh Amendment) Act, 1956, sec. 29 and Sch (w.e.f. 1-11-1956).

2 Subs. by the Constitution (Seventh Amendment) Act, 1956, sec. 13, for article 220.

3 1st day of November, 1956.

4 Subs. by the Constitution (Fifty-fourth Amendment) Act, 1986, sec. 3, for clause (1) (w.e.f. 1-4-1986).

5 The words "within the territory of India "omitted by the Constitution (Seventh Amendment) Act, 1956, sec. 14 (w.e.f. 1-11-1956).

6 Ins. by the Constitution (Fifteenth Amendment) Act, 1963, sec.5 (w.e.f. 5-10-1963), original clause (2) was omitted by the Constitution (Seventh Amendment) Act, 1956, sec.14 (w.e.f. 1-11-1956).

7 Subs. by the Constitution (Seventh Amendment) Act, 1956, sec. 15 for article 224 (w.e.f. 1-11-1956).

Court should be for the time being increased, the President may appoint duly qualified persons to be additional Judges of the Court for such period not exceeding two years as he may specify.

(2) When any Judge of a High Court other than the Chief Justice is by reason of absence or for any other reason unable to perform the duties of his office or is appointed to act temporarily as Chief Justice, the President may appoint a duly qualified person to act as a Judge of that Court until the permanent Judge has resumed his duties.

(3) No person appointed as an additional or acting Judge of a High Court shall hold office after attaining the age of [1][sixty-two years].

[2][**224A. Appointment of retired Judges at sittings of High Courts.-** Notwithstanding anything in this Chapter, the Chief Justice of a High Court for any State may at any time, with the previous consent of the President, request any person who has held the office of a Judge of that Court or of any other High Court to sit and act as a Judge of the High Court for that state, and every such person so requested shall, while so sitting and acting, be entitled to such allowances as the President may by order determine and have all the jurisdiction, powers and privileges of, but shall not otherwise be deemed to be, a Judge of that High Court :

Provided that nothing in this article shall be deemed to require any such person as aforesaid to sit and act as a Judge of that High Court unless he consents so to do.]

225. Jurisdiction of existing High Courts- Subject to the provisions of this Constitution and to the provisions of any law of the appropriate Legislature made by virtue of powers conferred on that Legislature by this constitution, the jurisdiction of, and the law administered in, any existing High Court, and the respective powers of the judges thereof in relation to the administration of Justice in the court, including any power to make rules of Court and to regulate the sittings of the Court and of members thereof sitting alone or in Division Courts, shall be the same as immediately before the commencement of this Constitution:

[3][Provided that any restriction to which the exercise of original jurisdiction by any of the High Courts with respect to any matter concerning the revenue or concerning any act ordered or done in the collection thereof was subject immediately before the commencement of this Constitution shall no longer apply to the exercise of such jurisdiction.]

[4][**226. Power of High Courts to issue certain writs.-** Nothwithstanding anything in article 32 [5][***], every High Court shall have powers, throughout the territories in relation to which it exercises jurisdiction, to issue to any person or authority, including in appropriate cases, any Government, within those territories, directions, orders or writs, including [6][writs in the nature of *habeas corpus*, *mandamus*, prohibition, *quo warranto* and *certiorari*, or any of them, for the enforcement of any of the rights conferred by Part III and for any other purpose.]

---

1 Subs. by the Constitution (Fifteenth Amendment) Act, 1963, sec. 6, for "sixty years" (w.e.f. 5-10-1963).

2 Ins. by the Constitution (Fifteenth Amendment) Act, 1963, sec.7 (w.e.f. 5-10-1963).

3 Ins. by the Constitution (Forty-fourth Amendment) Act, 1978, sec. 29 (w.e.f. 20-6-1979). Original proviso was omitted by the Constitution (Forty-second Amendment) Act, 1976, sec. 37 (w.e.f. 1-2-1977).

4 Subs. by the Constitution (Forty-second Amendment) Act, 1976, sec. 38, for article 226 (w.e.f. 1-2-1977). Earlier article 226 amended by the Constitution (Fifteenth Amendment) Act, 1963, sec. 8 (w.e.f. 5-10-1963).

5 The words, figures and letters "but subject to the provisions of article 131A and article 226A" omitted by the Constitution (Forty-third Amendment) Act, 1977, sec. 7 (w.e.f.13-4-1978).

6 Subs. by the Constitution (Forty-fourth Amendment) Act, 1978, sec. 30, for the portion beginning with the words "writs in the nature of habeas corpus, mandamus, prohibition, quo warranto and certiorari, or any of them" and ending with the words "such illegalityhas resulted in substantial failure of justice". (w.e.f. 1-8-1979).

(2) The power conferred by clause (1) to issue directions, orders or writs to any Government, authority or person may also be exercised by any High Court exercising jurisdiction in relation to the territories within which the cause of action, wholly or in part, arises for the exercise of such power, notwithstanding that the seat of such Government or authority or the residence of such person is not within those territories.

[1][(3) Where any party against whom an interim order, whether by way of injunction or stay or in any other manner, is made on, or in any proceedings relating to, a petition under clause (1), without-

a. furnishing to such party copies of such petition and all documents in support of the plea of such interim order; and

b. giving such party an opportunity of being heard,

makes an application to the High Court for the vacation of such order and furnishes a copy of such application to the party in whose favour such order has been made or the counsel of such party, the High Court shall dispose of the application within a period of two weeks from the date on which it is received or from the date on which the copy of such application is so furnished, whichever is later, or where the High Court is closed on the last day of that period, before the expiry of the next day afterwards on which the High Court is open; and if the application is not so disposed of, the interim order shall, on the expiry of that period, or, as the case may be, the expiry of the said next day, stand vacated].

[2][(4) The power conferred on a High Court by this article shall not be in derogation of the power conferred on the Supreme Court by clause (2) of article 32]

[3][**226A. Constitutional validity of Central laws not to be considered in proceedings under article 226.**- *[Rep. by the Constitution (Forty-Third Amendment) Act, 1977, sec. 8 (w.e.f. 13-4-1978)]*.

Notes on Article 226

Scope

The power of the High Court to issue to any person or authority directions, order or writs is wider than that of the Supreme Court. While the Supreme Court's writ jurisdiction extends only to cases of violation of fundamental rights, the High Courts can issue writs not only for the enforcement of fundamental rights, but also for any ordinary legal right. The use of the term " for any other purpose" makes it amply clear that the High Courts can issue writs in all cases of breach of any right. Thus, the High Court is armed with the power of setting aside an illegal order, of declaring the law or the right and of ordering relief by way of, for example, refund of illegal tax etc. Just as the law declared by Supreme Court is binding on all Courts in India, that declared by the High Court is binding on all subordinate Courts within the state or within the territory covered by the jurisdiction of the High Court. We may cite relevant decisions on this point.

(i) *State of Orissa v. Madan Gopal Rungta (1952) SCR 28.*

(ii) *Rambhadraiah v. Secretary, AIR 1981 SC 1653*

(iii) *Desai v. Roshan, AIR 1976, SC 578*

(iv) *State of M.P. v. Bhailal, AIR 1964 SC 1006.*

---

1 Subs. by the Constitution (Forty-fourth Amendment) Act, 1978, sec. 30, for clauses (3), (4), (5) and (6) (w.e.f. 1-8-1979).

2 Clause (7) renumbered as clause (4) by the Constitution (Forty-fourth Amendment) Act, 1978, sec. 30 (w.e.f. 1.8.1979).

3 Ins. by the Constitution (Forty-second Amendment) Act, 1976, sec. 39 (w.e.f. 1-2-1977).

The important thing to be borne in mind is that the remedy through a writ in cases other than those of violation of fundamental rights is an extraordinary one and is not expected to be granted as a matter of routine This extraordinary writ should be resorted to in special circumstances and only under the discretion of the Court. The undermentioned decisions are reflective of the propositions stated above:

(i) *Himmat Lal Shah v. State of U.P. AIR 1954 SC 403.*

(ii) *Abraham v. IT, AIR 1961 SC 609.*

(iii) *Bhopal Sugar Industry v. ITO, AIR 1967 SC 549*

(iv) *State of Rajasthan v. Karam Chand, Thappar and Bros. AIR 1965 SC 913.*

The power to issue writs has been vested in the Supreme Court and the High Courts to ensure quicker justice and early relief to persons whose rights are violated with impunity. The concerned court ensures that a speedy remedy is made available to such harassed persons without going into avoidable technicalities. A brief account of writs, which are five in number, would be desirable.

Habeas corpus:

The words '*habeas corpus*' literally means 'to have a body'. It applies in a case where a person is alleged to have been detained unlawfully. It is in the nature of an order calling upon the detaining authority or person to physically present before the Court the detained person and show the ground of his detention so that the Court can determine its legality or otherwise. If there is no lawful justification for detention, the Court sets free the detained person. After the 44th Amendment Act, 1978, the right to personal liberty under Article 21 cannot be suspended even during the Proclamation of Emergency. Thus, the writ of *habeas corpus* is a powerful instrument to safeguard the personal liberty of the individual. The writ of '*habeas corpus*' is granted only if the detention is illegal. Principal grounds for questioning the legality of detention may be enumerated here as under:

(a) The law which forms the basis of detention is invalid.

(b) The executive order under which the detention has been ordered, is invalid.

(c) Detention is not in conformity with the law or order mentioned above. The defect may arise with application of law or order in its entirety i.e. where the law prescribes certain limits as regards period, procedure etc. which have not been observed or where the officer passing the order for detention is not competent under the law.

   (i) *Durgadas v. Empl., AIR 1979 All 148 (FB)*

   (ii) *Tilak Raj v. Reg. AIR 1979 All 28*

(d) The order of detention is malafide.

(e) The order of detention is based on irrelevant or extraneous considerations.

   Mahindra v. King, AIR 1950 FC 129.

(f) The order is passed without application of mind.

   Kishore Mohan v. State of Bengal, AIR 1972 SC 1749

Generally, the writ of '*habeas corpus*' applies only after a person has been arrested. However, in exceptional cases, it may be granted even when detention is threatened (not yet carried out). Those cases in which threatened detention may entail the issuance of the writ are where the Court is satisfied about one of the following circumstances:

(a) The order of detention is not passed under the relevant act,

(b) It is passed against a wrong person.

(c) for a wrong purpose.

(d) on extraneous and irrelevant grounds.

   Additional Secretary v. Alka Subhash Gadia, (1990) 2 SC ALE 1352.

Here, this is worth remembering that while the Supreme Court can issue writ of 'habeas corpus' only against the state (as defined in Article 12) in cases of violation of fundamental rights, the High Courts can issue it also against private individuals illegally or arbitrarily detaining any other person.

Preventive Detention

See notes under Article 32

Mandamus

Mandamus literally means a command to act lawfully and to desist from perpetrating an unlawful act. The writ demands some activity on the part of the body or person to whom it is addressed. We may illustrate it thus. Where 'A' has a legal right, which casts certain obligations on 'B', 'A' can seek issuance of a writ of 'mandamus' directing and compelling 'B' to perform its legal duty. In short, mandamus may lie against any authority, officers, government or even judicial bodies failing or refusing to perform a public duty. However, it is to be kept in mind that this is an extraordinary remedy and the High Court may refuse to grant it where there is an alternative remedy for the redressal of grievances. The Supreme Court and High Courts can issue the writ of mandamus to enforce a fundamental right in case an act or governmental order violates any of the rights under Part III.

But the power of the High Court under Article 226 goes a step further and it may issue this writ, as discussed above, to direct an officer to exercise his constitutional and legal powers and also to compel him to perform public duties cast on him. Appropriate proceedings against the government can be brought under Article 226 and 361. The writ can also be issued against inferior courts or other judicial bodies when they have refused to exercise their jurisdiction and thus to perform their duty.

Here again, the scope of the writ of mandamus to be issued by the High Court is wider than that of the Supreme Court which issues this writ only in cases of violation of a fundamental right. Apart from the enforcement of fundamental rights, the High Court issues the writ of mandamus for various other purposes as mentioned above. We may illustrate this by citing a few judicial cases:

Mandamus will issue against an inferior Court where it has refused to carry out the intra vires directions of its superior tribunal.

Union of India v. Kamalakshi (1991) 2 UJSC 617, paragraph 6.

Mandamus can be issued to cancel a seniority list or promotion and to make necessary adjustments where the list prepared is in conflict with the statutory rules.

Garg v. State of Uttar Pradesh, (1991) 2 UJSC 571, paragraphs 22 and 25

Mandamus would issue to command a statutory authority to perform its duty to exercise its discretion according to law but not to exercise its discretion in a particular manner unless that is expressly required by the law;

U.P S.R.T.C. v. Mohammad Ismail, (1991) 3 SCC 239, paragraph 12

Employer has the right to fill all posts or not to fill them. The writ of Mandamus cannot be issued unless discrimination is made in regard to filling up of vacancies S.S Balu V. State of Kerela AIR 2009.

Court Martial

Mandamus may be issued to prevent Court Martials from exceeding their jurisdiction but not to interfere with their proper functioning e.g. on issues of military discipline, except in case of error of law;

Commander Ranvir Kumar v. Union of India, (1991) Cri LJ 1729 (Bom) paragraph 9.

The Supreme Court and the High Courts under articles 32 and 226 can interfere with proceedings before a court martial and grant relief when the impugned order has infringed the fundamental rights of the party aggrieved;

S.N. Mukherjee v. Union of India, (1990) 3 SCJ 193, paragraph 4

The above courts can also interfere in a situation where the sentence awarded by a Court martial is disproportionate to the offence committed.

Ex-Naik Sardar Singh v. Union of India, (1991) 2 UJSC 466, paragraph 6

Natural justice

The doctrine of natural justice is the outcome of the several judicial interpretations of the fundamental rights of the individuals. Natural justice is the collective name for some precious basic rights. Naturally the principles or rules of natural justice have come to be recognized by each and all. Article 20 of the Constitution has given birth to a basic principle of natural justice that no one can be penalised on the ground of conduct which was not penal on the day it was committed. Thus, no law can be applied retrospectively. The applicability of the rules of natural justice depends on the statutory provisions serving as the basis of action to be taken and also on the perusal of the facts and circumstances of each case. Principles of natural justice have been extended to administrative orders when civil rights are infringed or civil consequences ensue;

Union of India v. Nambudri (1991) 3 SCC 38, paragraph 7.

The principles of natural justice are now increasingly being applied in administrative inquiries. The requirement of "reasonableness and fair play" is observed in such inquires; *Union of India v. Nambudri (1991) 3 SCC 38, paragraph 7.*

The rule of natural justice stipulates that an opportunity to be heard must be given to the accused for enhancing the sentence;

Govind v. State of Maharashtra (1990) 4 SCC 718, paragraph 15.

Nemo judex in causa sua

The maxim *"nemo judex in causa sua"* (no one should be a judge in his own case) is one of the cardinal principles of natural justice. Its genesis can be traced to Lord Coke's pronouncement in Dr. Bonham's case (1910) 8 Co. Rep. 1142. The inference accrued from this maxim is that a person must be prohibited from trying a matter if he has a bias.

Prohibition:

The writ of prohibition is a writ issued by the Supreme Court and a High Court to a lower Court or tribunal and is intended to prohibit the latter from exceeding its jurisdiction. This writ is not issued against administrative agencies. It is available only against judicial and quasi-judicial bodies. This writ differs from the writ of mandamus in that while mandamus commands activity, prohibition commands inactivity. In India, a writ of prohibition is issued not only in cases of absence or excess of jurisdiction but also in cases where the court or tribunal assumes jurisdiction under a law which itself infringes any of the fundamental rights enshrined in Part III.

Certiorari

Originally, the writ of certiorari also lies against judicial and quasi-judicial bodies— courts and tribunals. The difference is that certiorari is issued to quash the order or decision of the tribunal while prohibition is issued to prohibit the tribunal from making ultra vires order or decision. In short, it can be said that while prohibition is available at an earlier stage, certiorari is available at a later stage, on similar grounds.

But the writ of certiorari has undergone a fundamental change so far as its application is concerned. The decisions of the Court have obliterated the distinction between administrative and quasi-judicial bodies. The current view is that even if the statute does not so require opportunity must be given to an individual before making any order capable of affecting his civil rights. To deny this is to deny natural justice and in such cases, the High Court may quash the so called administrative decision by invoking the writ of certiorari under article 226.

In *Union of India v. Nambudri, (1991) 2 UJSC 303, paragraph 9*, the Court observed that the writ of '*certiorari*' would be available even against administrative bodies not having any quasi-judicial obligation, if they affect rights of individuals without conforming to the principles of 'fair play'.

Defect of jurisdiction

Defect of jurisdiction is the principal ground for the issuance of the writ of 'certiorari'. But this would not be issued merely because the decision of a tribunal on an item within its jurisdiction is considered to be wrong. We can see the following cases:-

(*i*) *Basappa v. Nagappa (1955) 1 SCR 250, 257, 258.*

(*ii*) *Syed Yaqoob v. Radhakrishnan, AIR 1964 SC 477*

Certiorari can be issued for rectifying errors of jurisdiction committed by lower courts or tribunals. In other words, this writ would issue if the Court or tribunal acts illegally or improperly in exercising its jurisdiction. Two important grounds for quashing an order are – (i) when a lower court decides a question without giving an opportunity to be heard to the party affected by the said order and (ii) where the procedure adopted in dealing with the dispute is contrary to the principles of natural justice;

Syed Yaqoob v. Radhakrishnan, AIR 1964 SC 477.

Consumer Disputes Redressal Commission

If the State Consumer Disputes Redressal Commission entertains some complaint in excess of the jurisdiction and gives some order, it may be quashed by the High Court;

Larson and Toubro Ltd. v. State Consumer Disputes Redressal Commission, AIR 1998 Cal 313.

Error of law

Where justice is meted out by the erroneous interpretation of law, the High Court is not expected to do away with such justice in the name of "correcting the error of law".

Roshan Deen v. Preeti Lal, AIR 2002 SC 33.

Fraud

Natural justice is not violated in a case where a person has obtained an order from the High Court by fraud and that order has subsequently been cancelled;

U.P. Junior Doctors v. Nandwani, AIR 1991 SC 909, Paragraph 5.

Quo – warranto

Quo – warranto is a proceeding whereby the Court inquires into the legality of a person's claim to hold a public office. An application seeking such a writ may be made by any person provided.

(*i*) the office in question is a substantive public office created by a statute or by the Constitution itself, and

(*ii*) there has been a contravention of any provision of the Constitution or a statute in appointing a person to that office.

The fundamental objective of the writ of *Quo-warranto* is to ensure that an unlawful claimant does not usurp a public office. It is however, a discretionary remedy, which the Court may grant or refuse according to the facts and circumstances of each case. Thus, the Court may refuse it where the application is found to be vexatious or is made with ulterior motive;

Mokhtiar v. State Punjab, AIR 1991 P & H 20, paragraph 6.

Public Interest Litigation

See notes under Article 32.

Numerous judicial decisions in the light of Article 226 have fortified the fundamental rights and other legal rights of the people. No right can be violated with impurity. The concept of natural justice has come to occupy the centerstage in every judicial decision. Several fundamental rights particularly rights under articles 20, 21 and 22 have been interpreted to contain elements of natural justice. The judicial decisions have given birth to several other basic rights, which find no mention in the Constitution. Likewise Article 32 has also ensured the enjoyment of various fundamental rights and the decisions of the Supreme Court have added several new rights to the list of fundamental rights. Naturally, therefore, there is bound to be some overlapping between articles 226 and Hence, article 226 should be read along with article 32 and the case laws on various fundamental rights particularly articles 20, 21, and 22.

Administrative action

While exercising power of judicial review of administrative action, the Court is not an appellate authority and the Court cannot direct or advise the executive in matter of policy; *Ekta Shakti Foundation v. Govt. of NCT of Delhi*, AIR 2006 SC 2609

Alternative remedy

Writ petition once allowed can be dismissed in appeal on facts of case, on ground of alternative remedy; *S.N. J. Abdul Hakeem v. Assirathul Musthakeem Etheemkhana Trust*, AIR 2006 Mad 67.

Cases of non-statutory matters

Writ petition lies only where State or its instrumentality acts in exercise of statutory power under certain Act or Rules made thereunder; *Uktazl Highways v. State of Chhattisgarh*, AIR 2006 Chhat 29

Exercise of writ jurisdiction

Whether to exercise discretion or not arises only in cases where a mandatory provision of law is said to be violated and not in case of directory provisions which is not enforceable; *Poorvanchal Caterers v. Indian Railway Catering and Tourism Corporation Ltd.*, AIR 2006 (NOC) 455 (Del).

Extraordinary Jurisdiction

The power to summon Chief Secretary, Secretary to Government and other Senior Government officials is to be exercised only in rare and exceptional cases. In case higher official has to be and is summoned he should be shown due respect and should not be made to stand all the time during hearing; *State of Gujarat v. Turabai Gulamhussain Hirani*, AIR 2008 SC 86.

Image of Judiciary

Petition by Association of lawyers that court scenes projected in some motion pictures lowers down the image of judiciary is maintainable as PIL; *Rajasthan Chapter of Indian Association of Lawyers v. Union of India*, AIR 2008 (NOC) 533 (Raj)

Judicial Activism

Judicial activism should be resorted to in exceptional circumstances when situation forcefully demands it in interest of nation; *All India Council For Technical Education v. Ombir Kaushik*, AIR 2006 (NOC) 496 (Del).

Judicial Review vis-à-vis Legislative Policy

A policy decision should not be lightly interfered with but it is difficult to accept that courts cannot exercise this power of judicial review at all; *Bombay Dyeing & Mfg. Co. Ltd. v. Bombay Environmental Action Group*, AIR 2006 SC 1489

Jurisdiction

Ouster clause in contract can oust jurisdiction only of civil court and not of High Court under Article 226; *P.R. Transport Agency v. Union of India*, AIR 2006 All 23.

Jurisdiction of High Court

High Court while deciding appeal is bound to act within four corners of statute. However, while exercising power of judicial review the High Court exercises a wider Jurisdiction; *Shiv Kumar Sharma v. Santosh Kumari*, AIR 2008 SC 171.

Mala fides

Mala fides should be established only by direct evidence; *Union of India v. Ashok Kumar*, AIR 2006, SC 124.

Action taken by State in undue haste may be held to be *mala fide*; *Inderpreet Singh Kahlon v. State of Punjab*, AIR 2006 SC 2571

Order of Arbitral Tribunal

Orders passed by Arbitral Tribunal are not open to challenge under Articles 226, 227; *S.B. P. & Co. v. Patel Engineering Ltd.*, AIR 2006 SC 450

Particular Writs

The matter involving the private law remedy cannot be entertained by High Court except for good reasons; *Moran M. Baselios Marthona Mathews v. State of Kerala*, (2007) 6 SCC 517.

Plea before Single Judge of High Court

The plea abandoned before the Single Judge in High Court could be raised before Division Bench. Such plea is not barred by estoppel because writ appeal is in continuation of the original order passed by the Single Judge in writ jurisdiction; *Bongaigaon Refinery & Petrochemicals Ltd. v. Girish Chandra Sharma*, (2007) 7 SCC 206.

PIL – delay in filing

Delay in filing PIL can be fatal when parties have altered their position and third party interests have been created. However, considering magnitude of public interest court may relax rigours; *Bombay Dyeing & Mfg. Co. Ltd. v. Bombay Environmental Action Group*, AIR 2006 SC 1489.

Restoration of writ petition

Writ petition dismissed for want of prosecution can be restored; *Ratan Singh v. State of Rajasthan*, AIR 2006 NOC 129 (Raj).

Writ Jurisdiction

The High Courts exercise original jurisdiction under Article 226 of the Constitution and supervisory jurisdiction and the power of superintendence under Article 227 of the Constitution; *Manoj Kumar v. Board of Revenue*, AIR 2008 MP 22.

227. Power of superintendence over all courts by the High Court.-

[1][(1) Every High Court shall have superintendence over all courts and tribunals throughout the territories in relation to which it exercises jurisdiction.]

(2) Without prejudice to the generality of the foregoing provisions, the High Court may-

(a) call for returns from such courts;

---

1 Clause (1) has been successively subs. by the Constitution (Forty-second Amendment) Act, 1976, sec. 40 (w.e.f. 21-2-1977) and the Constitution (Forty-fourty Amendment) Act, 1978, sec. 31 to read as above (w.e.f. 20-6-1979).

(b) make and issue general rules and prescribe forms for regulating the practice and proceedings of such courts; and

(c) prescribe forms in which books, entries and accounts shall be kept by the officers of any such courts.

(3) The High Court may also settle tables of fees to be allowed to the sheriff and all clerks and officers of such courts and to attorneys, advocates and pleaders practising therein: Provided that any rule made, forms prescribed or tables settled under clause (2) or clause (3) shall not be inconsistent with the provision of any law for the time being in force, and shall require the previous approval of the Governor.

(4) Nothing in this article shall be deemed to confer on a High Court powers of superintendence over any court or tribunal constituted by or under any law relating to the Armed Forces.[1][***]

ARTICLE 226

Administrative Action: While exercising power of Judicial review of

administrative action, the Court is not an appellate authority and the court cannot direct or advise the executive in matter of policy, Ekta Shakti Foundation V. Govt of NCT of Delhi AIR 2006.

Alternative Remedy: The Alternative remedy is not an absolute bar; Committee of Management V. Vice chancellor AIR 2009.

Delay and Laches: Three to four years is reasonable period for challenging seniority. The delay in approaching adjudicatory forum beyond same should be satisfactorily explained, Shiba Shankar Mohapatra V. State of Orissa AIR 2010.

Exercise of Power: The writ court is bound to consider all relevant parameters and authentic facts of the case; Sity Industrial Development Corporation V. Dosu Aardeshir Bhiwandiwala 2009.

Extraordinary Jurisdiction: The power to summon chief secretary, Secretary to Government and other Senior Government officials is to be exercised only in rare and exceptional cases. In case higher official has to be and is summoned, he should be shown due respect and should not be made to stand all the time during hearing; State of Gujarat V. Turabai Gulamhussain Hirani AIR 2008.

Image of Judiciary: Petition by Association of lawyers that court scenes projected in some motion pictures lowers down the image of Judiciary is maintainable as PIL; Rajasthan chapter of Indian Association of Lawyers V. Union of India AIR 2008.

Judicial Activism: Judicial activism should be resorted to in exceptional circumstances when situation forcefully demands it in interest of nation. All India Council for Technical Education V. Ombir Kaushik AIR 2006.

Jurisdiction of High Court: High Court while deciding appeal is bound to act within four corners of statue. However while exercising power of Judicial review the High Court exercises a wider jurisdiction, Shiv Kumar Sharma V. Santosh Kumar AIR 2008.

Public Interest Litigation: Public Interest Litigation during pendency of civil suit is not maintainable; Santosh sood V. Gajendra Singh AIR 2010.

Writ Petition – Maintainability: Writ petition to rectify grave procedural error is maintainable; Gujarat Electricity Board V. Thakar Hasmukhhai Khelshanker, AIR 2006.

Writ Jurisdiction: The High Courts exercise original jurisdiction under Article 226 of the constitution and supervisory jurisdiction and the power of superitendence under article 227 of the coustitution. Manoj Kumar V. Board of Revenue AIR 2008.

---

1 Clause (5) was ins. by Constitution (Forty-second Amendment) Act, 1976, sec. 40 (w.e.f. 1-2-1977) and omitted by the Constitution (Forty-Fourth Amendment) Act, 1978, sec. 31 (w.e.f. 20-6-1979).

Correction of Facts

Finding of fact reached in improper manner can be corrected under Article 227; *Kishore Kumar Khaitan v. Parveen Kumar Singh*, AIR 2006 SC 1474

Jurisdiction of Court

The higher courts should observe restraint in making disparaging remarks against member of lower judiciary; "K" A judicial officer V. Registrar General, High Court of Andhra Pradesh AIR 2010.

Supervisory Jurisdiction

Where there is no concurrent findings of fact in question, the High Court can set the writ petition; state of Haryana V. Manoj Kumar AIR 2010.

Writ Petition–Maintainability

Writ petition to rectify grave procedural error is maintainable; *Gujarat Electricity Board v. Thakar Hasmukhbhai Khelshanker*, AIR 2006 Guj 16.

228. Transfer of certain cases to High Court.- If the High Court is satisfied that a case pending in a court subordinate to it involves a substantial question of law as to the interpretation of this Constitution the determination of which is necessary for the disposal of the case, [1][it shall withdraw the case and [2][***] may —].

(a) either dispose off the case itself, or

(b) determine the said question of law and return the case to the court from which the case has been so withdrawn together with a copy of its judgement on such question, and the said court shall on receipt thereof proceed to dispose off the case in conformity with such judgement.

[3]**228A. Special provisions as to disposal of questions relating to constitutional validity of State Laws.-** *[Rep. by the Constitution (Forty-third Amendment) Act, 1977, sec. 10 (w.e.f. 13-4-1978)].*

229. Officers and servants and the expenses of High Courts.-

(1) Appointments of officers and servants of a High Court shall be made by the Chief Justice of the Court or such other Judge or officer of the court as he may direct:

Provided that the Governor of the State [4][***] may by rule require that in such cases as may be specified in the rule no person not already attached to the court shall be appointed to any office connected with the court save after consultation with the State Public Service Commission.

(2) Subject to the provisions of any law made by the Legislature of the State, the conditions of service of officers and servants of a High Court shall be such as may be prescribed by rules made by the Chief Justice of the Court or by some other Judge or officer of the court authorised by the Chief Justice to make rules for the purpose;

Provided that the rules made under this clause shall, so far as they relate to salaries, allowances, leave or pensions, require the approval of the Governor of the State. [5][***]

---

1 Subs. by the Constitution (Forty-second Amendment) Act, 1976, sec. 41, for "it shall withdraw the case and may—" (w.e.f. 1-2-1977).

2 The words, figure and letter, "subject to the Provisions of article 131A", omitted by the Constitution (Forty-third Amendment) Act, 1977, sec. 9 (w.e.f. 13-4-1978).

3 Ins. by the Constitution (Forty-second Amendment) Act, 1976, sec. 42 (w.e.f. 1-2-1977).

4 The words "in which the High court has its principal seat" omitted by the Constitution (Seventh Amendment) Act, 1956, sec. 29 and Sch (w.e.f. 1.11.1956).

5 Omitted by the Constitution (Seventh Amendment) Act, 1956, sec. 29 and Sch.

(3) The administrative expenses of a High Court, including all salaries, allowances and pensions payable to or in respect of the officers and servants of the court, shall be charged upon the Consolidated Fund of the State, and any fees or other money taken by the court shall form part of that Fund.

[1][230. Extension of jurisdiction of High Courts to Union territories.-

(1) Parliament may by law extend the jurisdiction of a High Court to, or exclude the jurisdiction of a High Court from, any Union territory.

(2) Where the High Court of a State exercises jurisdiction in relation to a Union territory-

(a) nothing in this Constitution shall be construed as empowering the Legislature of the State to increase, restrict or abolish that jurisdiction; and

(b) the reference in article 227 to the Governor shall, in relation to any rules, forms or tables for subordinate courts in that territory, be construed as a reference to the President.]

231. Establishment of a common High Court for two or more States.-

(1) Notwithstanding anything contained in the preceding provisions of this Chapter, Parliament may by law establish a common High Court for two or more States or for two or more States and a Union Territory.

(2) In relation to any such High Court,-

(a) the reference in article 217 to the Governor of the State shall be construed as a reference to the Governors of all the States in relation to which the High Court exercises jurisdiction.

(b) the reference in article 227 to the Governor shall, in relation to any rules, forms or tables for subordinate courts, be construed as a reference to the Governor of the State in which the Subordinate Courts are situated; and

(c) the references in articles 219 and 229 to the State shall be construed as a reference to the State in which the High Court has its principal seat:

Provided that if such principal seat is in a Union Territory, the references in articles 219 and 229 to the Governor, Public Service Commission, Legislature and Consolidated Fund of the State shall be construed respectively as references to the President, Union Public Service Commission, Parliament and Consolidated Fund of India.]

232. Interpretation—*[Rep. by Constitution (7th Amendment) Act, 1956.]*

CHAPTER VI — SUBORDINATE COURTS

233. Appointment of district Judges.-

(1) Appointments of persons to be, and the posting and promotion of, district judges in any State shall be made by the Governor of the State in cosultation with the High Court exercising jurisdiction in relation to such State.

(2) A person not already in the service of the Union or of the State shall only be eligible to be appointed a district judge if he has been, for not less than seven years an advocate or a pleader and is recommended by the High Court for appointment.

Appointment of District Judges

Anticipated vacancies cannot be considered when statutory rules do not provide so; *Rakhi Ray V. High Court of Delhi* AIR 2010.

1 Subs. by the Constitution (Seventh Amendment) Act, 1956, sec. 16, for articles 230 (w.e.f. 1.11.1956).

Control of High Court over subordinate Judiciary

The control of High Court over subordinate judiciary is comprehensive, exclusive and effective and it is to subserve a basic feature of the Constitution i.e. independence of judiciary; *Prakash Singh Badal v. State of Punjab*, (2007) 1 SCC 1.

[1][**233A. Validation of appointments of, and judgements, etc., delivered by, certain District Judges.**- Notwithstanding any judgement, decree or order of any court,-

(a) (*i*) no appointment of any person already in the judicial service of a State or of any person who has been for not less than seven years an advocate or a pleader, to be a district judge in that State, and

(*ii*) no posting, promotion or transfer of any such person as a District Judge,

made at any time before the commencement of the Constitution (Twentieth Amendment) Act, 1966, otherwise than in accordance with the provisions of article 233 or article 235 shall be deemed to be illegal or void or ever to have become illegal or void by reason only of the fact that such appointment, posting, promotion or transfer was not made in accordance with the said provisions;

(b) no jurisdiction exercised, no judgement, decree, sentence or order passed or made, and no other act or proceeding done or taken, before the commencement of the Constitution (Twentieth Amendment) Act, 1966 by, or before, any person appointed, posted, promoted or transferred as a District Judge in any State otherwise than in accordance with the provisions of article 233 or article 235 shall be deemed to be illegal or invalid or ever to have become illegal or invalid by reason only of the fact that such appointment, posting, promotion or transfer was not made in accordance with the said provisions.]

234. Recruitment of persons other than Districts Judges to the judicial service.- Appointments of persons other than District Judges to the judicial service of a State shall be made by the Governor of the State in accordance with rules made by him in that behalf after consultation with the State Public Service Commission and with the High Court exercising jurisdiction in relation to such State.

235. Control over subordinate courts.- The control over district courts and courts subordinate thereto including the posting and promotion of, and the grant of leave to, persons belonging to the judicial service of a State and holding any post inferior to the post of District Judge shall be vested in the High Court, but nothing in this article shall be construed as taking away from any such person any right of appeal which he may have under the law regulating the conditions of his service or as authorising the High Court to deal with him otherwise than in accordance with the conditions of his service prescribed under such law.

236. Intrepretation — In this chapter—

(a) the expression 'District Judge' includes judge of a city civil court, additional district judge, joint district judge, assistant district judge, chief judge of a small cause court, chief presidency magistrate, additional chief presidency magistrate, sessions judge, additional sessions judge and assistant sessions judge;

(b) the expression "judicial service" means a service consisting exclusively of persons intended to fill the post of district judge and other civil judicial posts inferior to the post of district judge.

237. Application of the provisions of this Chapter to certain class or classes of magistrates.— The Governor may by public notification direct that the foregoing provisions of this chapter and any rules made thereunder shall with effect from such date as may be fixed by him in that behalf apply in relation to any class or classes of magistrates in the State as they apply in relation to persons appointed to the judicial service of the State subject to such exceptions and modifications as may be specified in the notification.

1 Ins. by the Constitution (Twentieth Amendment) Act, 1966, sec.2 (w.e.f. 22.12.1966).

PART VII

The States in Part B of the First Schedule.— *[Rep. by the Constitution (Seventh Amendment) Act, 1956, sec. 29 and Sch.]* (w.e.f. 1.11.1956).

238. Application of provisions of Part VI to States in Part B of the First Schedule.—*[Rep. by the Constitution (Seventh Amendment) Act, 1956, sec. 29 and Sch. (w.e.f. 1-11-1956)]*

PART VIII

[1]THE UNION TERRITORIES

[2][**239. Administration of Union territories.-**

(1) Save as otherwise provided by Parliament by law, every Union Territory shall be administered by the President acting, to such extent as he thinks fit, through an administrator to be appointed by him with such designation as he may specify.

(2) Nothwithstanding anything contained in Part VI, the President may appoint the Governor of a State as the administrator of an adjoining Union Territory, and where a Governor is so appointed, he shall exercise his functions as such administrator independently of his Council of Ministers.]

[3][**239A. Creation of local Legislatures or Council of Ministers or both for certain Union territories.-**

(1) Parliament may by law create [4][for the Union territory of [5][Puducherry].

(a) a body, whether elected or partly nominated and partly elected, to function as a Legislature for the Union territory, or

(b) a Council of Ministers,

or both with such constitution, powers and functions, in each case as may be specified in the law.

(2) Any such law as is referred to in clause (1) shall not be deemed to be an amendment of this Constitution for the purposes of article 368 notwithstanding that it contains any provision which amends or has the effect of amending this Constitution.]

[6][**239AA.Special provisions with respect to Delhi.-**

(1) As from the date of commencement of the Constitution (sixty ninth Amendment), Act, 1991 the Union territory of Delhi shall be called the National Capital Territory of Delhi (hereafter in this Part referred to as the National Capital Territory) and the administrator thereof appointed under article 239 shall be designated as the Lieutenant Governor.

(2) (a) There shall be a Legislative Assembly for the National Capital Territory and the seats in such Assembly shall be filled by members chosen by direct election from territorial constituencies in the National Capital Territory.

(b) The total number of seats in the Legislative Assembly, the number of seats reserved for Scheduled Castes, the division of the National Capital Territory into territorial constituencies (including the basis for such division) and all other matters relating to the functioning of the Legislative Assembly shall be regulated by law made by Parliament.

---

1 Subs. by the Constitution (Seventh Amendment) Act, 1956, sec. 17, for the heading "THE STATES IN PART C OF THE FIRST SCHEDULE' (w.e.f. 1.11.1956).

2 Subs. by the Constitution (Seventh Amendment) Act, 1956, sec. 17, for articles 239 and 240 (w.e.f. 1.11.1956).

3 Ins. by the Constitution (Fourteenth Amendment) Act, 1962, sec. 4 (w.e.f. 28.12.1962).

4 Subs. by the Goa, Daman and Diu Reorganisation Act, 1987 (18 of 1987), sec. 63(c), for certain words (w.e.f. 30-5-1987). Earlier those words were amended by the State of Himachal Pradesh Act, 1970 (53 of 1970), sec. 46 (b) (w.e.f. 25-1-1971); by the North Eastern Areas (Reorganisation) Act, 1971 (81 of 1971), sec. 71(b) (w.e.f. 21-1-1972); by the Constitution (Twenty-seventh Amendment) Act 1971, sec. 2 (w.e.f. 30-12-1971) and by the Constitution (Thirty-seventh Amendment) Act, 1975, sec. 2 (w.e.f.5-5-1975).

5 Subs. by the Pondicherry (alteration of name) Act, 2006 (44 of 2006), sec. 4, for "Pondicherry" (w.e.f. **1-10-2006**).

6 Ins. by the Constitution (Sixty-ninth Amendment) Act, 1991, sec. 2. (w.e.f. 1-2-1972).

* 1st February, 1992.

(c) The provisions of articles 324 to 327 and 329 shall apply in relation to the National Capital Territory, the Legislative Assembly of the National Capital Territory and the members thereof as they apply, in relation to a State, the Legislative Assembly of a State and the members thereof respectively; and any reference in articles 326 and 329 to "appropriate Legislature" shall be deemed to be a reference to Parliament.

(3) (a) Subject to the provisions of this Constitution, the Legislative Assembly shall have power to make laws for the whole or any part of the National Capital Territory with respect to any of the matters enumerated in the State List or in the Concurrent List in so far as any such matter is applicable to Union territories except matters with respect to Entries, 1, 2 and 18 of the State List and Entries 64, 65 and 66 of that List in so far as they relate to the said Entries 1, 2 and 18.

(b) Nothing in sub-clause (a) shall derogate from the powers of Parliament under this Constitution to make laws with respect to any matter for a Union territory or any part thereof.

(c) If any provision of a law made by the Legislative Assembly with respect to any matter is repugnant to any provision of a law made by Parliament with respect to that matter, whether passed before or after the law made by the Legislative Assembly, or of an earlier law, other than a law made by the Legislative Assembly, then, in either case, the law made by Parliament, or, as the case may be, such earlier law, shall prevail and the law made by the Legislative Assembly shall, to the extent of the repugnancy, be void;

Provided that if any such law made by the Legislative Assembly has been reserved for the consideration of the President and has received his assent, such law shall prevail in the National Capital Territory:

Provided further that nothing in this sub-clause shall prevent Parliament from enacting at any time any law with respect to the same matter including a law adding to, amending, varying or repealing the law so made by the Legislative Assembly.

4. There shall be a Council of Ministers consisting of not more than ten per cent of the total number of members in the Legislative Assembly, with the Chief Minister at the head to aid and advise the Lieutenant Governor in the exercise of his functions in relation to matters with respect to which the Legislative Assembly has power to make laws, except in so far as he is, by or under any law, required to act in his discretion:

Provided that in the case of difference of opinion between the Lieutenant Governor and his Ministers on any matter, the Lieutenant Governor shall refer it to the President for decision and act according to the decision given thereon by the President and pending such decision it shall be competent for the Lieutenant Governor in any case where the matter, in his opinion is so urgent that it is necessary for him to take immediate action, to take such action or to give such direction in the matter as he deems necessary.

5. The Chief Minister shall be appointed by the President and the other Ministers shall be appointed by the President on the advice of the Chief Minister and the Ministers shall hold office during the pleasure of the President.

6. The Council of Ministers shall be collectively responsible to the Legislative Assembly.

[1][7a. Parliament may, by law, make provisions for giving effect to or supplementing the provisions contained in the foregoing clauses and for all matters incidental or consequential thereto.

1 Subs. by the Constitution (Seventieth Amendment) Act, 1992, sec. 3 (i), for the brackets and figures "(7)" (w.e.f. 21-12-1991).

[1][b. Any such law as is referred to in sub-clause (a) shall not be deemed to be an amendment of this constitution for the purposes of article 368 notwithstanding that it contains any provision which amends or has the effect of amending, this constitution.]

8. The provision of article 239B shall be, so far as may be, apply in relation to the National Capital Territory, the Lieutenant Governor and the Legislative Assembly, as they apply in relation to the Union territory of [2][Puducherry], the administer and its Legislature, respectively, and any reference in that article to "clause (1) of article 239A" shall be deemed to be reference to this article or article 239 AB, as the case may be.

[3]**239AB.Provision in case of failure of constitutional machinery.**- If the President, on receipt of a report from the Lieutenant Governor or otherwise, is satisfied-

(a) that a situation has arisen in which the administration of the National Capital Territory cannot be carried on in accordance with the provisions of article 239AA or of any law made in pursuance of that article; or

(b) that for the proper administration of the National Capital Territory it is necessary or expedient so to do,

the President may by order suspend the operation of any provision of article 239AA or of all or any of the provisions of any law made in pursuance of that article for such period and subject to such conditions as may be specified in such law and make such incidental and consequential provisions as may appear to him to be necessary or expedient for administering the National Capital Territory in accordance with the provisions of article 239 and article 239AA.]

[4]**[239B. Power of administrator to promulgate Ordinances during recess of Legislature.-**

(1) If at any time, except when the Legislature of [5][the Union territory of Puducherry] is in session, the administrator thereof is satisfied that circumstances exist which render it necessary for him to take immediate action, he may promulgate such Ordinances as the circumstances appear to him to require:

Provided that no such Ordinance shall be promulgated by the administrator except after obtaining instructions from the President in that behalf:

Provided further that whenever the said Legislature is dissolved, or its functioning remains suspended on account of any action taken under any such law as is referred to in clause (1) of article 239A, the administrator shall not promulgate any Ordinance during the period of such dissolution or suspension.

(2) An Ordinance promulgated under this article in pursuance of instructions from the President shall be deemed to be an Act of the Legislature of the Union territory which has been duly enacted after complying with the provisions in that behalf contained in any such law as is referred to in clause (1) of article 239A, but every such Ordinance-

(a) shall be laid before the Legislature of the Union territory and shall cease to operate at the expiration of six weeks from the reassembly of the Legislature or if, before the expiration of that period, a resolution disapproving it is passed by the Legislature, upon the passing of the resolution; and

(b) may be withdrawn at any time by the administrator after obtaining instructions from the President in that behalf.

---

1 Ins. by the Constitution (Seventieth Amendment) Act, 1992, sec. 3 (iii) (w.e.f. 21-12-1991).

2 Sub by the Pondichary (alteration of name) Act, 2006.

3 Ins. by the Constitution (Sixty - ninth Amendment) Act, 1991, sec. 2 (w.e.f. 1-2-1992).

4 Ins. by the Constitution (Twenty-seventh Amendment) Act, 1971, sec. 3 (w.e.f 30-12-1971).

5 Subs. by the Goa, Daman and Diu Reorganisation Act, 1987 (18 of 1987), sec. 63, for "a Union territory referred to in clause (1) of article 239A" (w.e.f. 30-5-1987).

(3) If and so far as an Ordinance under this article makes any provision which would not be valid if enacted in an Act of the Legislature of the Union territory made after complying with the provisions in that behalf contained in any such law as is referred to in clause (1) of article 239A, it shall be void.] [1][***]

[2][240. Power of President to make regulations for certain Union territories.-

(1) The President may make regulations for the peace, progress and good governance of the Union Territory of-

a. the Andaman and Nicobar Islands;

[3][b. Lakshadweep

[4][c. Dadra and Nagar Haveli

[5][[6]d. Daman & Diu;

[7][e. Puducherry.[8][***]

[9][Provided that when any body is created under article 239A to function as a Legislature for the [10][Union territory of [11][[12][[13]Puducherry]] [14][***] the President shall not make any regulation for the peace, progress and good governance of that Union territory with effect from the date appointed for the first meeting of the Legislature.]

[15][Provided further that whenever the body functioning as a Legislature for the Union Territory of [3][[4][[5]Puducherry] [6][***] is dissolved, or the functioning of that body as such Legislature remains suspended on account of any action taken under any such law as is referred to in clause (1) of article 239A, the President may, during the period of such dissolution or suspension, make regulations for the peace progress and good government of that Union territory.]

(2) Any regulation so made may repeal or amend any Act made by Parliament or [16][any other law], which is for the time being applicable to the Union territory and, when promulgated by the President, shall have the same force and effect as an Act of Parliament which applies to that territory.

---

1 Clause (4) was ins. by the Constitution (Thirty-eighth Amendment) Act, 1975, sec. 4 (retrospectively) and omitted by the Constitution (Forty-fourth Amendment) Act, 1978, sec. 32 (w.e.f. 20-6-1979).

2 Subs. by the Constitution (7th Amendment) Act, 1956, Sec. 17, for Article 240.

3 Subs. by the Laccadive, Minicoy and Amindivi Islands (Alteration of Name), Act, 1973 (34 of 1973), sec. 4, for entry (d) (w.e.f. 1-11-1973).

4 Ins. by the Constitution (Tenth Amendment) Act, 1961, sec. 3.

5 Subs. by Goa, Daman and Diu Reorganisation Act, 1987 (18 of 1987), sec. 63, for entry (d) (w.e.f. 30-5-1987).

6 Ins. by the Constitution (Twelfth Amendment) Act, 1962, sec. 3.

7 Sub by Pondicherry (Alteration of name) Act, 2006 (AA of 2006).

8 Entries (f) and (g) which were ins. by the Constitution (Twenty-seventh Amendment) Act, 1972, sec. 4 (w.e.f. 15-2-1972) omitted by the State of Mizoram Act, 1986 (34 ot 1986), sec. 39 (w.e.f. 20-2-1987) and the State of Arunachal Pradesh Act, 1986 (69 of 1986), sec. 42 (w.e.f. 20-2-1987) respectively.

9 Ins. by the Constitution (fourteenth Amendment) Act, 1962, sec. 5.

10 Ins. by Constitution (Twenty-seventh Amendment) Act, 1971, sec. 4. (w.e.f. 15-2-1972).

11 Subs. by theGoa, Daman and Diu Reorganisation Act, 1987 (18 of 1987), sec. 63, for "Goa, Daman and Diu or Pondicherry" (w.e.f. 30-5-1987).

12 Subs. by the Constitution (Thirty-seventh Amendment) Act, 1975, sec. 3, for "Pondicherry or Mizoram".

13 Subs. by the State of Arunachal Pradesh Act, 1986 (69 of 1986), sec. 42, for "Pondicherry or Arunachal Pradesh" (w.e.f. 20-2-1987).

14 The word, "Mizoram" omitted by the State of Mizoram Act, 1986 (34 of 1986), sec. 39 (w.e.f. 20-2-1987).

15 Ins. by the Constitution (Twenty-seventh Amendment) Act, 1971, sec. 4 (w.e.f. 15-2-1972).

16 Subs. by the Constitution (Twenty-seventh Amendment) Act, 1971, sec. 4, for "any existing law" (w.e.f. 15-2-1972).

241. High Courts for Union Territory. -

(1) Parliament may by law constitute a High Court for a [1][Union Territory] or declare any court in any [2][such territory] to be a High Court for all or any of the purposes of this Constitution.

(2) The provisions of Chapter V of Part VI shall apply in relation to every High Court referred to in clause(1) as they apply in relation to a High Court referred to in article 214 subject to such modifications or exceptions as Parliament may be law provide.

[3][(3) Subject to the provisions of this Constitution and to the provisions of any law of the appropriate Legislature made by virtue of powers conferred on that Legislature by or under this Constitution, every High Court exercising jurisdiction immediately before the commencement of the Constitution (Seventh Amendment) Act 1956, in relation to any Union territory shall continue to exercise such jurisdiction in relation to that territory after such commencement.

(4) Nothing in this article derogates from the power of Parliament to extend or exclude the jurisdiction of a High Court for a State to, or from, any Union territory or part thereof.]

242. Coorg. - *[Rep. by the Constitution (Seventh Amendment) Act, 1956, sec. 29 and Sch.].*

[4][PART IX*The Panchayats

243. Definitions.- In this Part, unless the context otherwise requires,-

(a) "district" means a district in a State:

(b) "Gram Sabha" means a body consisting of persons registered in the electoral rolls relating to a village comprised within the area of Panchayat at the village level;

(c) "intermediate level" means a level between the village and district levels specified by the Governor of a State by public notification to be the intermediate level for the purposes of this Part;

(d) "Panchayat" means an institution (by whatever name called) of self-government constituted under Article 243B, for the rural areas;

(e) "Panchayat area" means the territorial area of a Panchayat;

(f) "Population" means the population as ascertained at the last preceding census of which the relevant figures have been published.

(g) "village" means a village specified by the Governor by public notification to be a village for the purposes of this Part and includes a group of villages so specified.

243A. Gram Sabha. - A Gram Sabha may exercise such powers and perform such functions at the village level as the Legislature of a State may by law, provide.

---

1 Subs. by the Constitution (Seventh Amendment) Act, 1956, sec. 29 and Sch. for "State Specified in part C of the First Schedule" (w.e.f. 1.11.1956).

2 Subs. by the Constitution (Seventh Amendment) Act, 1956, sec. 29 and Sch., for "such State" (w.e.f. 1.11.1956).

3 Subs. by the Constitution (Seventh Amendment) Act, 1956, sec. 29 and Sch., for clause (3) and (4) (w.e.f. 1.11.1956).

4 Part IX (containing articles 243, 243A to 343-O) ins. by the Constitution (Seventy-third Amendment) Act, 1992, sec. 2 (w.e.f. 24-4-1993). Earlier Part IX dealing with territories in Part D of the First Sechedule was repealed by the Constitution (Seventh Amendment) Act, 1956, sec. 29 and Sch. (w.e.f. 1.11.1956).

243B. Constitution of Panchayats. -

(1) There shall be constituted in every State, Panchayats at the Village, intermediate and district levels in accordance with the provisions of this Part.

(2) Notwithstanding anything in Clause (1), Panchayats at the intermediate level may not be constituted in a State having a population not exceeding twenty lakhs.

243C. Composition of Panchayats. -

(1) Subject to the provisions of this Part, the Legislature of a state may, by law, make provisions with respect to the composition of Panchayats;
Provided that the ratio between the population of the territorial area of a Panchayat at any level and the number of seats in such Panchayat to be filled by election shall, so far as practicable, be the same throughout the State.

(2) All the seats in a Panchayat shall be filled by persons chosen by direct election from territorial constituencies in the Panchayat area and, for this purpose, each Panchayat area shall be divided into teritorial constituencies in such manner that the ratio between the population of each constituency and the number of seats allotted to it shall, so far as practicable, be the same throughout the Panchayat area.

(3) The Legislature of a State may, by law, provide for the representation-

(a) of the Chairpersons of the Panchayats at the village level, in the Panchayats at the intermediate level or in the case of a State not having Panchayats at the intermediate level, in the Panchayats at the district level;

(b) of the Chairpersons of the Panchayats at the intermediate level, in the Panchayats at the district level;

(c) of the members of the House of the People and the members of the Legislative Assembly of the State representing constituencies which comprise wholly or partly a Panchayat area at a level other than the village level, in such Panchayat;

(d) of the members of the Council of States and the members of the Legislative Council of the State, where they are registered as electors within-

(*i*) a Panchayat area at the intermediate level, in Panchayat at the intermediate level.

(*ii*) a Panchayat area at the district level, in Panchayat at the district level;

(4) The Chairperson of a Panchayat and other members of a Panchayat whether or not chosen by direct election from territorial constituencies in the Panchayat area shall have the right to vote in the meetings of the Panchayats.

(5) The Chairperson of-

(a) Panchayat at the village level shall be elected in such manner as the Legislature of a State may, by law, provide; and

(b) a Panchayat at the intermediate level or district level, shall be elected by, and from amongst, the elected members thereof,

243D. Reservation of seats. -

(1) Seats shall be reserved for-

(a) the Scheduled Castes and

(b) the Scheduled Tribes,

in every Panchayat and the number of seats so reserved shall bear, as nearly as may be, the same proportion to the total number of seats to be filled by direct election in that Panchayat as the population of the Scheduled Castes in that Panchayat area or of the Scheduled Tribes in that Panchayat area bears to the total population of that area and such seats may be allotted by rotation to different constituencies in a Panchayat.

(2) Not less than one-third of the total number of seats reserved under clause(1) shall be reserved for women belonging to the Scheduled Castes or, as the case may be, the Scheduled Tribes.

(3) Not less than one-third (including the number of seats reserved for women belonging to the Scheduled Castes and the Scheduled Tribes) of the total number of seats to be filled by direct election in every Panchayat shall be reserved for women and such seats may be allotted by rotation to different constituencies in a Panchayat.

(4) The offices of the Chairpersons in the Panchayats at the village or any other level shall be reserved for the Scheduled Castes, the Scheduled Tribes and women in such manner as the Legislature of a State may, by law, provide:

Provided that the number of offices of Chairpersons reserved for the Scheduled Castes and the Scheduled Tribes in the Panchayats at each level in any State shall bear, as nearly as may be, the same proportion to the total number of such offices in the Panchayats at each level as the population of the Scheduled Castes in the State or of the Scheduled Tribes in the State bears to the total population of the State;

Provided further that not less than one-third of the total number of offices of Chairpersons in the Panchayats at each level shall be reserved for women:

Provided also that the number of offices reserved under this clause shall be allotted by rotation to different Panchayats at each level.

(5) The reservation of seats under Clause(1) and (2) and the reservation of offices of Chairpersons (other than the reservation of women) under clause (4) shall cease to have effect on the expiration of the period specified in Article 334.

(6) Nothing in this part shall prevent the Legislature of a State from making any provision for reservation of seats in any Panchayat or offices of Chairpersons in the Panchayats at any level in favour of backward class of citizens.

243E. Duration of Panchayats, etc. -

(1) Every Panchayat, unless sooner dissolved under any law for the time being in force, shall continue for five years from the date appointed for its first meeting and no longer.

(2) No amendment of any law for the time being in force shall have the effect of causing dissolution of a Panchayat at any level, which is functioning immediately before such amendment, till the expiration of its duration specified in clause(1).

(3) An election to constitute a Panchayat shall be completed-

(a) before the expiry of its duration specified in clause(1);

(b) before the expiration of a period of six months from the date of its dissolution:

Provided that where the remainder of the period for which the dissolved Panchayat would have continued is less than six months, it shall not be necessary to hold any election under this clause for constituting the Panchayat for such period.

(4) A Panchayat constituted upon the dissolution of a Panchayat before the expiration of its duration shall continue only for the remainder of the period for which the dissolved Panchayat would have continued under Clause(1) had it not been so dissolved.

243F. Disqualifications for membership. -

(1) A person shall be disqualified for being chosen, as, and for being, a member of a Panchayat.-

(a) if he is so disqualified by or under any law for the time being in force for the purposes of elections to the Legislature of the State concerned;

Provided that no person shall be disqualified on the ground that he is less than twenty-five years of age, if he has attained the age of twenty-one years;

(b) if he is so disqualified by or under any law made by the Legislature of the State.

(2) if any question arises as to whether a member of Panchayat has become subject to any of the disqualifications mentioned in Clause(1), the question shall be referred for the decision of such authority and in such manner as the Legislature of a State may, by law, provide.

243G. Powers authority and responsibilities of Panchayat. - Subject to the provisions of this Constitution, the Legislature of a State may, by law, endow the Panchayats with such powers and authority as may be necessary to enable them to function as institutions of self-government and such law may contain provisions for the devolution of powers and responsibilities upon Panchayats at the appropriate level, subject to such conditions as may be specified therein, with respect to-

(a) the preparation of plans for economic development and social justice;

(b) the implementation of schemes for economic development and social justice as may be entrusted to them including those in relation to the matters listed in the Eleventh Schedule.

243H. Powers to impose taxes by, and Funds of, the Panchayats.- The Legislature of a State may, by law,-

(a) authorise a Panchayat to levy, collect and appropriate such taxes, duties, tolls and fees in accordance with such procedure and subject to such limits;

(b) assign to a Panchayat such taxes, duties, tolls and fees levied and collected by the State Government for such purposes and subject to such conditions and limits;

(c) provide for making such grants-in-aid to the Panchayats from the Consolidated Fund of the State; and

(d) provide for constitution of such Funds for crediting all moneys received, respectively by or on behalf of the Panchayats and also for the withdrawal of such moneys therefrom,

as may be specified in the law.

243-I. Constitution of Finance Commission to review financial position. -

(1) The Governor of a State shall, as soon as may be within one year from the commencement of the Constitution (Seventy-third Amendment) Act, 1992, and thereafter at the expiration of every fifth year, constitute a Finance Commission to review the financial position of the Panchayats and to make recommendations to the Governor as to-

(a) the principles which should govern-

(*i*) the distribution between the State and the Panchayats of the net proceeds of the taxes, duties, tolls and fees leviable by the State, which may be divided between them under this Part and the allocation between the Panchayats at all levels of their respective shares of such proceeds;

(*ii*) the determination of the taxes, duties, tolls and fees which may be assigned to, or appropriated by, the Panchayats.

(*iii*) the grants-in-aid to the Panchayats from the Consolidated Fund of the State;

(b) the measures needed to improve the financial position of the Panchayats;

(c) any other matter referred to the Finance Commission by the Governor in the interest of sound finance of the Panchayats.

(2) The Legislature of a State may, by law, provide for the composition of the Commission, the qualifications which shall be requisite for appointment as members thereof and the manner in which they shall be selected.

(3) The Commission shall determine their procedure and shall have such powers in the performance of their functions as the Legislature of the State may, by law, confer on them.

(4) The Governor shall cause every recommendation made by the Commission under this article together with an explanatory memorandum as to the action taken thereon to be laid before the Legislature of the State.

243J. Audit of accounts of Panchayats.- The Legislature of a State may, by law, make provisions with respect to the maintenance of accounts by the Panchayats and the auditing of such accounts.

243K. Elections to the Panchayats.-

(1) The superintendence, direction and control of the preparation of electoral rolls for, and the conduct of, all elections to the Panchayats shall be vested in a State Election Commission consisting of a State Election Commissioner to be appointed by the Governor.

(2) Subject to the provisions of any law made by the Legislature of a State, the conditions of service and tenure of office of the State Election Commissioner shall be such as the Governor may by rule determine;

Provided that the State Election Commissioner shall not be removed from his office except in like manner and on the like ground as a Judge of a High Court and the conditions of service of the State Election Commissioner shall not be varied to his disadvantage after his appointment.

(3) The Governor of a State shall, when so requested by the State Election Commission, make available to the State Election Commission such staff as may be necessary for the discharge of the functions conferred on the State Election Commission by Clause(1).

(4) Subject to the provisions of this Constitution, the Legislature of a State may, by law, make provision with respect to all matters relating to, or in connection with, elections to the Panchayats.

243L. Application to Union Territories.- The Provisions of this Part shall apply to the Union Territories and shall, in their application to a Union Territory, have effect as if the references to the Governor of a State were references to the Administrator of the Union territory appointed under Article 239 and references to the Legislature or the Legislative Assembly of a State were references, in relation to a Union territory having a Legislative Assembly, to that Legislative Assembly;

Provided that the President may, by public notification, direct that the provisions of this Part shall apply to any Union territory or part thereof subject to such exceptions and modifications as he may specify in the notification.

243M. Part not to apply to certain areas.-

(1) Nothing in this Part shall apply to the Scheduled Areas referred to in clause (1), and the tribal areas referred to in clause(2), of Article 244.

(2) Nothing in this Part shall apply to-

(a) the State of Nagaland, Meghalaya and Mizoram;

(b) the Hill Areas in the State of Manipur for which District Councils exist under any law for the time being in force.

(3) Nothing in this part-

(a) relating to Panchayats at the district level shall apply to the Hill areas of the District of Darjeeling in the State of West Bengal for which Darjeeling Gorkha Hill Council exists under any law for the time being in force;

(b) shall be construed to affect the functions and powers of the Darjeeling Gorkha Hill Council constituted under such law.

[1][(3A) Nothing in Article 243D, relating to reservation of seats for the Scheduled Castes, shall apply to the State of Arunachal Pradesh.]

---

1 Ins. by the Constitution (Eighty-third Amendment) Act, 2000, sec. 2 (w.e.f. 8.9.2000)

(4) Notwithstanding anything in this Constitution,-

(a) the Legislature of a State referred to in sub-clause(a) of Clause(2) may, by law, extend this Part to that State, except the areas, if any, referred to in Clause(1), if the Legislative Assembly of that State passes a resolution to that effect by a majority of the total membership of that House and by a majority of not less than 2/3rds of the members of that House present and voting;

(b) Parliament may, by law, extend the provisions of this Part to the Scheduled Areas and the tribal areas referred to in Clause(1) subject to such exceptions and modifications as may be specified in such law, and no such law shall be deemed to be an amendment of this Constitution for the purposes of Article 368.

243N. Continuance of existing laws and Panchayats.- Notwithstanding anything in this Part, any provision of any law relating to Panchayats in force in a State immediately before the commencement of the Constitution (Seventy-third Amendment) Act, 1992, which is inconsistent with the provisions of this Part, shall continue to be in force until amended or repealed by a competent Legislature or other competent authority or until the expiration of one year from such commencement, whichever is earlier:

Provided that all the Panchayats existing immediately before such commencement shall continue till the expiration of their duration, unless sooner dissolved by a resolution passed to that effect by the Legislative Assembly of that State or, in the case of a State having a Legislative Council, by each House of the Legislature of that State.

243-O. Bar to interference by courts in electoral matters.- Notwithstanding anything in this Constitution-

(a) the validity of any law relating to the delimitation of constituencies or the allotment of seats to such constituencies made or purporting to be made under Article 243K, shall not be called in question in any court;

(b) no election to any Panchayat shall be called in question except by an election petition presented to such authority and in such manner as is provided for by or under any law made by the Legislature of a State].

Notes on Article 243-O

Election process: Gram panchayats:

When the election process starts, the High court cannot.

(*i*) Direct the election officer to conduct the election process afresh or to stall the election proceedings or

(*ii*) Direct him to conduct a fresh poll for 20 persons, or

(*iii*) Direct him to declare the result of the gram panchayat election.

[1][PART IXA

THE MUNICIPALITIES

243P. Definitions.- In this part, unless the context otherwise requires,-

(a) "Committee" means a Committee constituted under Article 243S;

(b) "district" means a district in a State.

(c) "Metropolitan area" means an area having a population of ten lakhs or more, comprised in one or more districts and consisting of two or more Municipalities or Panchayats or other contiguous areas, specified by the Governor by public notification to be Metropolitan area for the purposes of this Part;

1 Ins. by the Constitution (Seventy-fourth Amendment) Act, 1992, sec. 2 (w.e.f. 1-6-1993).

(d) "Municipal area" means the territorial area of a Municipality as is notified by the Governor;

(e) "Municipality" means an institution of self-government constituted under Article 243Q;

(f) "Panchayat" means a Panchayat constituted under Article 243B;

(g) "population" means the population as ascertained at the last preceding census of which the relevant figures have been published.

243Q. Constitution of Municipalities.-

(1) There shall be constituted in every State-

(a) a Nagar Panchayat (by whatever name called) for a transitional area, that is to say, an area in transition from a rural area to an urban area;

(b) a Municipal Council for a smaller urban area; and

(c) a Municipal Corporation for a larger urban area,

in accordance with the provisions of this Part;

Provided that a Municipality under this clause may not be constituted in such urban area or part thereof as the Governor may, having regard to the size of the area and the Municipal services being provided or proposed to be provided by an industrial establishment in that area and such other factors as he may deem fit, by public notification, specify to be an industrial township.

(2) In this article, "a transitional area", "a smaller urban area" or " larger urban area" means such area as the Governor may, having regard to the population of the area, the density of the population therein, the revenue generated for local administration, the percentage of employment in non-agricultural activities, the economic importance or such other factors as he may deem fit, specify by public notification for the purposes of this part.

Notes on Article 243Q

For treating any area as "transitional area' governor has to issue public notification under clause (2) of article 243Q with respect to the population of the area, density of the population therein with other factors mentioned in the article 243Q(2).

243R. Composition of Municipalities.-

(1) Save as provided in Clause(2), all the seats in a Municipality shall be filled by persons chosen by direct election from the territorial constituencies in the Municipal area and for this purpose each Municipal area shall be divided into territorial constituencies to be known as wards.

(2) The Legislature of a State may, by law, provide-

(a) for the representation in a Municipality of-

(*i*) persons having special knowledge or experience in Municipal administration;

(*ii*) the members of the House of the People and the members of the Legislative Assembly of the State representing constituencies which comprise wholly or partly the Municipal area;

(*iii*) the members of the Council of States and the members of the Legislative Council of the state registered as electors within the Municipal area;

(*vi*) the Chairpersons of the Committees constituted under Clause(5) of Article 243S;

Provided that the persons referred to in paragraph (i) shall not have the right to vote in the meetings of the Municipality;

(b) the manner of election of the Chairperson of a Municipality.

243S. Constitution and composition of Wards Committees, etc.-

(1) There shall be constituted Wards Committees, consisting of one or more Wards, within the territorial area of a Municipality having a population of three lakhs or more.

(2) The Legislature of State may, by law, make provision with respect to-

(a) the composition and the territorial area of a Wards Committee;

(b) the manner in which the seats in a Wards Committee shall be filled.

(3) A member of a Municipality representing a ward within the territorial area of the Wards Committee shall be a member of that Committee.

(4) Where a Wards Committee consists of-

(a) one ward, the member representing that ward in the Municipality; or

(b) two or more wards, one of the members representing such wards in the Municipality elected by the members of the Wards Committee,

shall be the Chairperson of that Committee.

(5) Nothing in this article shall be deemed to prevent the Legislature of a State from making any provision for the constitution of Committees in addition to the Wards Committees.

243T. Reservation of seats.-

(1) Seats shall be reserved for the Scheduled Castes and the Scheduled Tribes in every Municipality and the number of seats so reserved shall bear, as nearly as may be, the same proportion of the total number of the seats to be filled by direct election in that Municipality as the population of the Schedule Castes in the Municipal area or of the Schedule Tribes in the Municipal area bears to the total population of that area and such seats may be allotted by rotation to different constituencies in a Municipality.

(2) Not less than one-third of the total number of seats reserved under clause (1) shall be reserved for women belonging to the Scheduled Castes or, as the case may be, the Scheduled Tribes.

(3) Not less than one-third (including the number of seats reserved for women belonging to the Scheduled Castes and the Scheduled Tribes) of the total number of seats to be filled by direct election in every Municipality shall be reserved for women and such seats may be allotted by rotation to different constituencies in a Municipality.

(4) The offices of Chairpersons in the Municipalities shall be reserved for the Scheduled Castes, the Scheduled Tribes and women in such manner as the Legislature of a State may, by law, provide.

(5) The reservation of seats under clauses (1) and (2) and the reservation of offices of Chairpersons (other than the reservation for women) under clause (4) shall cease to have effect on the expiration of the period specified in Article 334.

(6) Nothing in this part shall prevent the Legislature of a State from making any provision for reservation of seats in any Municipality or offices of Chairpersons in the Municipalities in favour of backward class of citizens.

243U. Duration of Municipalities.etc.-

(1) Every Municipality, unless sooner dissolved under any law for the time being in force, shall continue for five years from the date appointed for its first meeting and no longer:

Provided that a Municipality shall be given a reasonable opportunity of being heard before its dissolution.

(2) No amendment of any law for the time being in force shall have the effect of causing dissolution of a Municipality at any level, which is functioning immediately before such amendment, till the expiration of its duration specified in Clause (1).

(3) An election to constitute a Municipality shall be completed,-

(a) before the expiry of its duration specified in clause(1);

(b) before the expiration of a period of six months from the date of its dissolution;

Provided that where the remainder of the period for which the dissolved Municipality would have continued is less than six months, it shall not be necessary to hold any election under this clause for constituting the Municipality for such period.

(4) A Municipality constituted upon the dissolution of a Municipality before the expiration of its duration shall continue only for the remainder of the period for which the dissolved Municipality would have continued under clause(1) had it not been so dissolved.

243V. Disqualifications for membership.-

(1) A person shall be disqualified for being chosen as, and for being, a member of a Municipality-

(a) if he is so disqualified by or under any law for the time being in force for the purposes of elections to the Legislature of the State concerned;

Provided that no person shall be disqualified on the ground than he is less than twenty-five years of age; if he has attained the age of twenty-one years;

(b) if he is so disqualified by or under any law made by the Legislature of the State.

(2) If any question arises as to whether a member of a Municipality has become subject to any of the disqualifications mentioned in Clause(1), the question shall be referred for the decision of such authority and in such manner as the Legislature of a State may, by law, provide.

243W. Powers, authority and responsibilities of Municipalities, etc.- Subject to the provisions of this Constitution, the Legislature of a State may, by law, endow-

(a) the Municipalities with such powers and authority as may be necessary to enable them to function as institutions of self-government and such law may contain provisions for the devolution of powers and responsibilities upon Municipalities, subject to such conditions as may be specified therein, with respect to-

(*i*) the preparation of plans for economic development and social justice;

(*ii*) the performance of functions and the implementation of schemes as may be entrusted to them including those in relation to the matters listed in the Twelfth Schedule;

(b) the Committees with such powers and authority as may be necessary to enable them to carry out the responsibilities conferred upon them including those in relation to the matters listed in the Twelfth Schedule.

243X. Power to impose taxes by, and Funds of, the Municipalities.- The Legislature of a State may, by law,-

(a) authorise a Municipality to levy, collect and appropriate such taxes, duties, tolls and fees in accordance with such procedure and subject to such limits;

(b) assign to a Municipality such taxes, duties, tolls and fees levied and collected by the State Government for such purposes and subject to such conditions and limits;

(c) provide for making, such grants-in-aid to the Municipalities from the Consolidated Fund of the State; and

(d) provide for constitution of such Funds for crediting all moneys received, respectively, by or on behalf of the Municipalities and also for the withdrawal of such moneys therefrom, as may be specified in the law.

***243Y. Finance Commission.-**

(1) The Finance Commission constituted under article 243-I shall also review the financial position of the Municipalities and make recommendations to the Governor as to-

* In its application to the Union Territory of Dadra and Nagar Haveli, in clause (1) of Art. 243Y, for the word "Governor", at both the places, the word "President" shall be substituted. [vide S.O.615(E), dated 21st May 2004, Published in the Gazette of India, Extra, Pt. II, Sec 3(11), dated 21st May, 2004].

(a) the principles which should govern-

(*i*) the distribution between the State and the Municipalities of the net proceeds of the taxes, duties, tolls and fees leviable by the State, which may be divided between them under this Part and the allocation between the Municipalities at all levels of their respective shares of such proceeds;

(*ii*) the determination of the taxes, duties, tolls and fees which may be assigned to, or appropriated by, the Municipalities;

(*iii*) the grants-in-aid to the Municipalities from the Consolidated Fund of the State;

(b) the measures needed to improve the financial position of the Municipalities;

(c) any other matter referred to the Finance Commission by the Governor in the interests of sound finance of the Municipalities.

(2) The Governor shall cause every recommendation made by the Commission under this article together with an explanatory memorandum as to the action taken thereon to be laid before the Legislature of the State.

243Z. Audit of accounts of Municipalities.- The Legislature of a State may, by law, make provisions with respect to the maintenance of accounts by the Municipalities and the auditing of such accounts.

243ZA. Elections to the Municipalities.-

(1) The Superintendence, direction and control of the preparation of electoral rolls for, and the conduct of, all elections to the Municipalities shall be vested in the State Election Commission referred to in Article 243K.

(2) Subject to the provisions of this Constitution, the Legislature of a State may, by law, make provision with respect to all matters relating to, or in connection with, elections to the Municipalities.

243ZB. Application to Union territories.- The provisions of this Part shall apply to the Union territories and shall, in their application to a Union Territory have effect as if the references to the Governor of a State were references to the Administrator of the Union territory appointed under Article 239 and references to the Legislature or the Legislative Assembly of a State were references in relation to a Union territory having a Legislative Assembly, to that Legislative Assembly.

Provided that the President may, by public notification, direct that the provisions of this Part shall apply to any Union territory or part thereof subject to such exceptions and modifications as he may specify in the notification.

243ZC. Part not to apply to certain areas.-

(1) Nothing in this part shall apply to the Scheduled Areas referred to in Clause(1), and the tribal areas referred to in Clause (2), of Article 244.

(2) Nothing in this Part shall be construed to affect the functions and powers of the Darjeeling Gorkha Hill Council constituted under any law for the time being in force for the hill areas of the district of Darjeeling in the State of West Bengal.

(3) Notwithstanding anything in this Constitution, Parliament may, by law, extend the provisions of this part to the Scheduled Areas and the tribal areas referred to in clause (1) subject to such exceptions and modifications as may be specified in such law, and no such law shall be deemed to be an amendment of this Constitution for the purposes of Article 368.

[*]243ZD. Committee for district planning.-

(1) There shall be constituted in every State at the district level a District Planning Committee to consolidate the plans prepared by the Panchayats and the Municipalities in the district and to prepare a draft development plan for the district as a whole.

---

[*] The provisions of article 243ZD/243ZE shall not apply to the National Capital Territory of Delhi, vide S.O.1125(E) dated 12th November, 2001.

(2) The Legislature of a State may, by law, make provision with respect to-

(a) the composition of the District Planning Committees;

(b) the manner in which the seats in such Committees shall be filled;

Provided that not less than four-fifths of the total number of members of such Committees shall be elected by, and from amongst, the elected members of the Panchayat at the district level and of the Municipalities in the district in proportion to the ratio between the population of the rural and of the urban areas in the district;

(c) the functions relating to district planning which may be assigned to such Committees.

(d) the manner in which the Chairpersons of such Committees shall be chosen.

(3) Every District Planning Committee shall, in preparing the draft development plan,-

(a) have regard to-

(*i*) matters of common interest between the Panchayat and the Municipalities including spatial planning, sharing of water and other physical and natural resources; the integrated development of infrastructure and environmental conservation;

(*ii*) the extent and type of available resources whether financial or otherwise;

(b) consult such institutions and organizations as the Governor may, by order, specify.

(4) The Chairperson of every District Planning Committee shall forward the development plan, as recommended by such Committee, to the Government of the State.

***243ZE. Committee for Metropolitan planning.-**

(1) There shall be constituted in every metropolitan area a Metropolitan Planning Committee to prepare a draft development plan for the Metropolitan area as a whole.

(2) The Legislature of a State may, by law, make provisions with respect to-

(a) the composition of the Metropolitan Planning Committees,

(b) the manner in which the seats in such Committees shall be filled;

Provided that not less than two-thirds of the members of such Committee shall be elected, by, and from amongst, the elected members of the Municipalities and Chairpersons of the Panchayats in the Metropolitan area in proportion to the ratio between the population of the Municipalities and of the Panchayats in that area;

(c) the representation in such Committees of the Government of India and the Government of the State and of such organizations and institutions as may be deemed necessary for carrying out the functions assigned to such Committees;

(d) the functions relating to planning and coordination for the Metropolitan areas which may be assigned to such Committees;

(e) the manner in which the Chairpersons of such Committees shall be chosen.

(3) Every Metropolitan Planning Committee shall, in preparing the draft development plan,-

(a) have regard to-

(*i*) the plans prepared by the Municipalities and the Panchayats in the Metropolitan area;

---

* The provisions of article 243ZD/243ZE shall not apply to the National Capital Territory of Delhi, vide S.O.1125(E) **dated** 12th November, 2001.

(*ii*) matters of common interest between the Municipalities and the Panchayats, including co-ordinated spatial planning of the area, sharing of water and other physical and natural resources, the integrated development of infrastructure and environmental conservation;

(*iii*) the overall objectives and priorities set by the Government of India and the Government of the States;

(*iv*) the extent and nature of investments likely to be made in the Metropolitan area by agencies of the Government of India and of the Government of the State and other available resources whether financial or otherwise;

(b) consult such institutions and organizations as the Governor may, by order, specify.

(4) The Chairperson of every Metropolitan Planning Committee shall forward the development plan, as recommended by such Committee, to the Government of the State.

243ZF. Continuance of existing laws and Municipalities.- Notwithstanding anything in this Part, any provision of any law relating to Municipalities in force in a State immediately before the commencement of the Constitution (Seventy-fourth Amendment) Act, 1992, which is inconsistent with the provisions of this Part, shall continue to be in force until amended or repealed by a competent Legislature or other competent authority or until the expiration of one year from such commencement, whichever is earlier.

Provided that all the Municipalities existing immediately before such commencement shall continue till the expiration of their duration, unless sooner dissolved by a resolution passed to that effect by the Legislative Assembly of that State or in the case of a State having a Legislative Council, by each House of the Legislature of that State.

243ZG. Bar to interference by Courts in electoral matters.- Notwithstanding anything in this Constitution,-

(a) the validity of any law relating to the delimitation of constituencies or the allotment of seats to such constituencies, made or purporting to be made Article 243ZA shall not be called in question in any Court;

(b) no election to any Municipality shall be called in question except by an election petition presented to such authority and in such manner as is provided for by or under any law made by the Legislature of a State.]

[1][PART IXB

THE CO-OPERATIVE SECIETIES

243ZH Definitions– In this Part, unless the context otherwise requires,—

(a) "authorised person" means a person referred to as such in article 243ZQ;

(b) "board" means the board of directors or the governing body of a co-operative society, by whatever name called, to which the direction and control of the management of the affairs of a society is entrusted to;

(c) "co-operative society" means a society registered or deemed to be registered under any law relating to co-operative societies for the time being in force in any State;

1 Part IXB (containing Articles 243ZH to 243ZT) inserted by the Constitution (Ninety-seventh Amendment) Act, 2011, sec. 4 (w.e.f. 15.2.2012).

(d) "multi-State co-operative society" means a society with objects not confined to one State and registered or deemed to be registered under any law for the time being in force relating to such co-operatives;

(e) "office bearer" means a President, Vice-President, Chairperson, Vice-Chairperson, Secretary or Treasurer of a co-operative society and includes any other person to be Treasurer of a co-operative society;

(f) "Registrar" means the Central Registrar appointed by the Central Government in relation to the multi-State co-operative societies and the Registrar for co-operative societies appointed by the State Government under the law made by the Legislature of a State in relation to co-operative societies;

(g) "State Act" means any law made by the Legislature of a State;

(h) "State level co-operative society" means a co-operative society having its area of operation extending to the whole of a State and defined as such in any law made by the Legislature of a State.

243ZI Incorporation of co-operative societies– Subject to the provisions of this Part, the Legislature of a State may, by law, make provisions with respect to the incorporation, regulation and winding-up of co-operative societies based on the principles of voluntary formation, democratic member-control, member-economic participation and autonomous functioning.

243ZJ Number and term of members of board and its office bearers–

(1) The board shall cosist of such number of directors as may be provided by the Legislature of a State, by law:

Provided that the maximum number of directors of a co-operative society shall not exceed twenty-one;

Provided further that the Legislature of a State shall, by law, provide for the reservation of one seat for the Scheduled Castes or the Scheduled Tribes and two seats for women on board of every co–operative society consisting of individuals as members and having members from such class or category of persons.

(2) The terms of office of elected members of the board and its office bearers shall be five years from the date of election and the term of office bearers shall be [1][coterminous]with the term of the board:

Provided that the board may fill a casual vacancy on the board by nomination out of the same class of members in respect of which the casual vacancy has arisen, if the term of office of the board is less than half of its original term.

(3) The Legislature of a State shall, by law, make provisions for co–option of persons to be members of the board having experience in the field of banking, management, finance or specialisation in any other field relating to the objects and activities undertaken by the co–operative society, as members of the board of such society:

Provided that the number of such co–opted members shall not exceed two in addition to twenty–one directors specified in the first proviso to clause (1):

Provided further that number of such co–opted members shall not have the right to vote in any election of the co–operative society in their capacity as such member or to be eligible to be elected as office bearers of the board:

Provided also that the functional directors of a co–operative society shall also be the members of the board and such members shall be excluded for the purpose of counting the total number of directors specified in the first proviso to clause (1).

1 Corrected for "conterminous" vide corrigendum dated 129th March, 2012, ublished along with Act 19 of 2012 in the Gazette of India, Extra., Pt II, Sec. I, No. 21, dated 29th March, 2012.

243ZK. Election of members of board–

(1) Notwithstanding anything contained in any law made by the Legislature of a State, the election of a board shall be conduted before the expiry of the term of the board so as to ensure that the newly elected members of the board assume office immediately on the expiry of [1][the term of the office] of members of the outgoing board.

(2) The superintendence, direction and control of the preparation of eletoral rolls for, and the conduct of, all elections to a co–operative society shall vest in such an authority or body, as may be provided by the Legislature of a State, by law:

Provided that the Legislature of a State may, by law, provide for the procedure and guidelines for the conduct of such election.

243ZL.Supersession and suspension of board and interim management –

(1) Notwithstanding anything contained in any law for the time being in force, no board shall be superseded or kept under suspension for a period exceeding six months:

Provided that the board may be superseded or kept under suspension in case–

(*i*) of its persistent default; or

(*ii*) of negligence in the performance of its duties; or

(*iii*) the board has committed any act prejudicial to the interests of the co–operative society or its members; or

(*iv*) there [2][is a stalement] in the constitution or functions of the board; or

(*v*) the authority or body as provided by the Legislature of a State, by law, under clause (2) of article 243ZK, has failed to conduct elections in accordance with the provisions of the State Act:

Provided further that the board of any such co–operative society shall not be superseded or kept under suspension where there is no Government shareholding or loan or financial assistance or any guarantee by the Government:

Provided also that in case of a co–operative society carrying on the business of banking, the provisions of the Banking Regulation Act, 1949 (10 of 1949) shall also apply:

Provided also that in case of a co–operative society, other than a multi–State co–operative society, carrying on the business of banking, the provisions of this clause shall have the effect as if for the words "six months", the words "one year" had been substituted.

(2) In case of supersession of a board, the administrator appointed to manage the affairs of such co–operative society shall arrange for conduct of elections within the period specified in clause (1) and handover the management to the elected board.

(3) The Legislature of a State may, by law, make provisions for the conditions of service of the administrator.

243ZM. Audit of accounts of co–operative societies –

(1) The Legislature of a State may, by law, make provisions with respect to the maintenance of accounts by the co–operative societies and the auditing of such accounts at least once in each financial year.

(2) The Legislature of State shall, by law, lay down the minimum qualifications and experience of auditors and auditing firms that shall be eligible for auditing accounts of the co–operative societies.

---

1 Corrected for "the office" vide corrigendum dated 29th March 2012, published along with Act 19 of 2012 in the Gazette of India, Extra., Pt. II, Sec. 1, No. 21, dated 29th March, 2012.

2 Corrected for "is stalemate" vide corrigendum dated 29th March, 2012, published along with Act 19 of 2012 in the Gazette of India, Extra., Pt. II, Sec. 1, No. 21, dated 29th March, 2012.

(3) Every co–operative society shall cause to be audited by an auditor or auditing firms referred to in clause (2) appointed by the general body of the co–operative society:

Provided that such auditors or auditing firms shall be appointed from a panel approved by a State Government or authority authorised by the State Government in this behalf.

(4) The accounts of every co–operative society shall be audited within six months of the close of the financial year to which such accounts relate.

(5) The audit report of the accounts of an apex co–operative society, as may be defined by the State Act, shall be laid before the State Legislature in the manner, as may be provided by the State Legislature, by law.

243ZN. Convening of general body meetings– The Legislature of a State may, by law, make provisions that the annual general body meeting of every co–operative society shall be convened within a period of six months of close of the financial year to transact the business as may be provided in such law.

243ZO. Right of a member to get information –

(1) The Legislature of a State may, by law, provide for access to every member of a co–operative society to the books, information and accounts of the co–operative society kept in regular transaction of the business with such member.

(2) The Legislature of a State may, by law, make provisions to ensure the participation of members in the management of the co–operative society providing minimum requirement of attending meetings by the members and untilising the minimum level of services as may be provided in such law.

(3) The Legislature of a State may, by law, provide for co–operative education and training for its members.

243ZP. Returns– Every co–operative society shall file returns, within six months from the close of every finanical year, to the authority designated by the State Gaovernment including the following matters, namely:–

(a) annual report of its activities;

(b) its audited statement of accounts;

(c) plan for surplus disposal as approved by the general body of the co–operative society;

(d) list of amendments to the by–laws of the co–operative society, if any;

(e) declaration regading date of holding of its general body meeting and conduct of elections when due; and

(f) any other information required by the Registrar in pursuance of any of the provisions of the State Act.

243ZQ. Offences and penalties –

(1) The Legislature of a State may, by law, make provisions for the offences relating to the co–operative societies and penalties for such offences.

(2) A law made by the Legislature of a State under clause (1) shall include the commission of the following act or omission as offences, namely:–

(a) a co–operative society or an officer or member thereof wilfully makes a false return or furnishes false information, or any person willfully not furnishes any information required from him by a person authorised in this behalf under the provisions of the State Act;

(b) any person willfully or without any reasonable excuse disobeys any summons, requisition or lawful written order issued under the provisions of the State Act;

(c) any employer who, without sufficient cause, fails to pay to a co–operative society amount deducted by him from its employee within a period of fourteen days from the date on which such deduction is made;

(d) any officer or custodian who willfully fails to handover custody of books, accounts, documents, records, case, security and other property belonging to a co–operative society of which he is an officer or custodian, to an authorised person; and

(e) whoever, before, during or after the election of members of the board or office bearers, adopts any corrupt practice.

243ZR. Application to multi–State co–operative societies– The provisions of this Part shall apply to the multi–State co–operative societies subject to the modification that any reference to "Legislature of a State", "State Act" or "State Government" shall be construed as a reference to "Parliament", "Central Act" or "the Central Government" respectively.

243ZS. Application to Union territories– The provisions of this Part shall apply to the Union territories and shall, in their application to a Union territory, having no Legislative Assembly as if the referances to the Legislature of a State were a reference to the administrator thereof appointed under article 239 and, in relation to a Union territory having a Legislative Assembly, to that Legislative Assembly:

Provided that the President may, by notification in the Official Gazette, direct that the provisions of this Part shall not apply to any Union terriotry or part thereof as he may specify in the notification.

243ZT. Continuance of existing laws– Notwithstanding anything in this Part, any provision of any law relating to co–operative societies in force in a State immediately before the commencement of the Constitution (Ninety–seventh Amendment) Act, 2011, which is inconsistent with the provisions of this Part, shall continue to be in force until amended or repealed by a competent Legislature or other completent authority or until the expiration of one year from such commencement, whichever is less.

PART X

THE SCHEDULED AND TRIBAL AREAS

244. Administration of Scheduled Areas and Tribal Areas.-

(1) The provisions of the Fifth Schedule shall apply to the administration and control of the Scheduled Areas and Scheduled Tribes in any State [1][***] other than [2][the States of Assam, [3][Meghalaya, Tripura and Mizoram.]]]

(2) The provisions of the Sixth Schedule shall apply to the administration of the tribal areas in [2][the States of Assam, [4][[5][Meghalaya, Tripura and Mizoram]]].

[5][**244A. Formation of an autonomous State comprising certain tribal areas in Assam and creation of Local Legislature or Council of Ministers or both therefor.-** Notwithstanding anything in this Constitution, Parliament may, by law, form within the State of Assam an autonomous State comprising (whether wholly or in part) all or any of the tribal areas specified in [6][Part I] of the table appended to paragraph 20 of the Sixth Schedule and create therefor-

1 The words and letters "specified in Part A or Part B of the First Schedule" omitted by the Constitution (Seventh Amendment) Act, 1956, sec. 29 and Sch (w.e.f. 1.11.1956).

2 Sub. by the North-Eastern Areas (Reorganisation) Act, 1971 (81 of 1971), sec. 71, for "for State of Assam" (w.ef. 21-1-1972).

3 Subs. by the Constitution (Forty-ninth Amendment) Act 1984 sec.2 for "and Meghalaya"(w.e.f. 1-4-1985). (w.e.f. 20-2-1887).

4 Subs. by the State of Mizoram Act, 1986 (34 of 1986), sec. 39, for "Meghalaya and Tripura and the Union Territory of Mizoram" (w.e.f. 20-2-1987).

5 Ins. by the Constitution (Twenty-second Amendment) Act, 1969, sec. 2 (w.e.f. 25.9.1969).

6 Subs. by the North-Eastern Areas (Reorganisation) Act, 1971 (81 of 1971), sec. 71, for "part A" (w.e.f. 21-1-1972)

a. a body, whether elected or partly nominated and partly elected, to function as a Legislature for the autonomous State, or

b. a Council of Ministers,

or both with such constitution, powers and functions, in each case, as may be specified in the law.

2. Any such law as is referred to in clause (1) may, in particular,-

   a. specify the matters enumerated in the State List or the Concurrent List with respect to which the Legislature of the autonomous State shall have power to make laws for the whole or any part thereof, whether to the exclusion of the Legislature of the State of Assam or otherwise;

   b. define the matters with respect to which the executive power of the autonomous State shall extend;

   c. provide that any tax levied by the State of Assam shall be assigned to the autonomous State in so far as the proceeds thereof are attributable to the autonomous State;

   d. provide that any reference to a State in any article of this Constitution shall be construed as including a reference to the autonomous State; and

   e. make such supplemental, incidental and consequential provisions as may be deemed necessary.

(3) An amendment of any such law as aforesaid in so far as such amendment relates to any of the matters specified in sub-clause (a) or sub-clause(b) of clause (2) shall have no effect unless the amendment is passed in each House of Parliament by not less than two-thirds of the members present and voting.

(4) Any such law as is referred to in this article shall not be deemed to be an amendment of this Constitution for the purposes of article 368 notwithstanding that it contains any provision which amends or has the effect of amending this Constitution.]

PART XI

RELATIONS BETWEEN THE UNION AND THE STATES

CHAPTER I — LEGISLATIVE RELATIONS

Distribution of Legislative Powers

245. Extent of laws made by Parliament and by the Legislatures of States.-

(1) Subject to the provisions of this Constitution, Parliament may make laws for the whole or any part of the territory of India, and the Legislature of a State may make laws for the whole or any part of the State.

(2) No law made by Parliament shall be deemed to be invalid on the ground that it would have extra-territorial operation.

Notes on Article 245

Art. 245 deals with the essence of federalism i.e. division of powers between the centre and the units. This Article lays down the general scheme of division of legislative powers between the Parliament and the State Legislatures. This general provision is supposed to operate under certain limitations, which may be enumerated as follows:

a. the broad federal scheme of division of powers,

b. taking into consideration fundamental rights and other provisions of the Constitution while passing laws.

c. constitutional provisions as to prior sanction or subsequent approval of the President in respect of certain bills.

d. no extra-territorial legislation by State Legislatures

e. the doctrine that the Legislature cannot delegate matters of policy.

f. the guiding principle that legislation must not be a fraud on the Constitution.

g. the doctrine that the legislature must confine itself to the function of legislation only.

Limitation (a) above flows from Art. 246. Limitation (b) above can be located in articles 12 and 13 under fundamental rights Limitation (c) above has its manifestation in (i) the doctrine that all authority and power must be exercised in conformity with the Constitution, and (ii) in the words "subject to the provision of this Constitution" in Art. 245(I). Limitation (d) above springs from the words "for the whole or any part of the state", in article 245 (I) (as regards State Legislature) we can see the following decisions.

(*i*) *State of Bihar v. Charusila, AIR 1959 SC 1002*

(*ii*) *Tata Iron and Steel Co. v. State of Bihar, AIR 1958 SC 452.*

As regards Limitation (e), it flows from the general principle that power given to a body by the Constitution must in its essentials, be exercised by that body only. Limitation (f) is the outcome of another vital principle that constitutional and statutory powers must be exercised in pursuit of their intended purposes. *D.C. Wadhwa v. Union of India, AIR 1987 SC 579.*

Limitation (g) comes out of the interpretation of the word 'law' occuring in the text of article 245 (1), which confers the power to make 'laws' only. The decisions below illustrate this:

(*i*) *Indira v. Raj Narain, AIR 1975 SC 2299*

(*ii*) *Trinath v. State of Uttar Pradesh, AIR 1973 SC 405*

Legislation affecting judicial decisions

Legislations aimed at doing away with judgments, decrees and order of any court are impermissible and unconstitutional and thus void:

S.R. Bhagwat v. State of Mysore, AIR 1996 SC 188, paragraph 10, 18.

Legislation as will of the people

In an important case, the Supreme Court held that "an act of the Legislature represents the will of the people and cannot be lightly dismissed as void;

State of Bihar, v. Bihar Distillery Ltd., AIR 1997 SC 1811, paragraph 18.

Transgression of limits of power by legislature:

A legislature may transgress its limits of power under a federal Constitution. This transgression may be open, direct or overt which may be challenged judicially. But in some cases, it may be disguised, indirect and covert. This is called colourable legislation in a parliamentary usage. Recourse to Entries in the Seventh Schedule should be taken to avoid conflict.

Sub judice

There is nothing colourable if a Legislature wields its constituent power to amend a provision during the pendency of a writ petition questioning the validity of that provision in order to avoid possible adverse verdict in that writ petition;

Hotel Balaji v. State of Andhra Pradesh, AIR 1993 SC 1048

Constitutional Validity of Law

The Constitutional validity of law is to be decided as per societal conditions prevalent at relevant time. The changed social psyche and expectations are important factors to be considered in upkeep of law; *Anuj Garg v. Hotel Association of India*, AIR 2008 SC 663.

Conflict between Statues

One of the two Acts of Parliament enacted under List 1 Entry 66 and the other under List III Entry 25 cannot be repugnant to each other. *Annamalai University V. Secretary of Govt. Inf. and Tourism Department 2009.*

Lgislative Competence of State

It is within legislative competence of state of Maharashtra to enact provisions of "promoting insurgency" in section 2 (1) (e) of MCOCA under Entries 1 and 2 of List II read with Entries 1, 2 and 12 of List III of Seventh Schedule of Constitution; *Zameer Ahmed Latifur Rehman Sheikh V. State of Maharashtra AIR 2010.*

Rule Making Power

The states power to make rules wnder a central Act extends only to the extent provided for under the central Act; *V.V.S Rama Sharma V. State of Uttar Pradesh 2009.*

246. Subject-matter of laws made by Parliament and by the Legislatures of States.-

(1) Notwithstanding anything in clauses (2) and (3), Parliament has exclusive power to make laws with respect to any of the matters enumerated in List I in the Seventh Schedule (in this Constitution referred to as the 'Union List').

(2) Notwithstanding anything in clause (3), Parliament and, subject to clause (1), the Legislature of any State [1][***] also, have power to make laws with respect to any of the matters enumerated in List III in the Seventh Schedule (in this Constitution referred to as the Concurrent List').

(3) Subject to clauses (1) and (2), the Legislature of any State [1][***] has exclusive power to make laws for such State or any part thereof with respect to any of the matters enumerated in List II in the Seventh Schedule (in this Constitution referred to as the 'State List').

(4) Parliament has power to make laws with respect to any matter for any part of the territory of India not included [2][in a State] notwithstanding that such matter is a matter enumerated in the State List.

Notes on Article 246

Scope

Article 246 deals with the formal division of powers between the centre and the federated units (States). In a sense, this article establishes India as a federal State in the most comprehensive way. Generally two patterns of division of powers have been followed by various federal systems of the world:

a. American pattern and

b. Canadian Pattern

1 The words and letters "specified in Part A or Part B of the First Schedule" omitted by the Constitution (Seventh Amendment) Act, 1956, sec. 29 and Sch (w.e.f. 1.11.1956).

2 Subs. by the Constitution (Seventh Amendment) Act, 1956, sec. 29 and Sch., for "in Part A or Part B of the First Schedule" (w.e.f. 1.11.1956).

The Constitution of India has essentially followed the Canadian pattern of distribution of powers. Like Canada, in Indian constitution too, there are three Lists and the residuary powers have been vested in the Parliament. Matters of national importance have been incorporated into the Union List, on which the Parliament has exclusive power to make laws. Matters of local importance have been put under the State List, on which the State Legislature has been given exclusive powers to make laws. On matters mentioned in the Concurrent List, both Parliament and State Legislature have concurrent jurisdiction with a proviso that in case of a conflict between the law made by Parliament and the law made by the State Legislature, the law made by Parliament prevails. The constitution of Australia has also provided for concurrent jurisdiction. The Government of India Act, 1935 also embodied a similar provision. As noted at the very outset, matters not specifically mentioned in the Constitution constitute the residuum and these have been vested in the Parliament.

The doctrine of pith and substance

The doctrine of pith and substance is the most useful contrivance in settling crises in a federal setup. The significance of comparative approach can best be seen in the evolution of this doctrine. The doctrine has gained ground in India and it derives its genesis from the approach adopted by the Courts (including the Privy Council) in dealing with controversies arising in other federations. The celebrated commentator on Indian constitution, P.M. Bakshi, has defined the doctrine with illustrations like this:

"Briefly stated, what the doctrine means is this. Where the question arises of determining a particular law relates to a particular subject mentioned in one list or another, the Court looks to the substance of the matter. Thus, if the substance falls within Union List, then the incidental encroachment by the law on the State List does not make it invalid. This principle had come to be established by the Privy Council when it determined appeals from Canada or Australia involving the question of legislative competence of the federation or the States in those countries. In India, the doctrine came to be established in the pre-independence period under the Government of India Act 1935. The classical example is the Privy Council judgment in *Prafulla V. Bank of Commerce, AIR 1946 PC 60*, holding that a State law dealing with money lending (a State subject) is not invalid merely because it incidentally affects promissory notes (Union List, entry 46). The doctrine is sometimes expressed in terms of ascertaining the true character of legislation and it is also emphasised that the name given by the Legislature to the legislation in the short title is immaterial. Again, for applying the doctrine of pith and substance, regard is to be had (i) to the enactment as a whole, (ii) to its main objects, and (iii) to the scope and effect of its provisions"

The under mentioned decisions illustrate the above proposition:

(*i*) *Southern Pharmaceuticals v. State of Kerala, AIR 1981 SC 1865, paragraph 15 (incidental encroachment to be disregarded).*

(*ii*) *Prem v. Chhabra (1984) 2 SCC 302 paragraph 8.*

(*iii*) *State of Rajasthan v. Chawla, AIR 1959 SC 544, 547.*

(*iv*) *Amar Singh v. State of Rajasthan, (1955) 2 SCR 803 (extent of invasion immaterial).*

(*v*) *D.C.G.M. v. Union of India, AIR 1983 SC 937 paragraph 33 (Incidental encroachment immaterial).*

No question of conflict between the two lists will arise if the impugned legislation by the application of pith and substance seems to fall exclusively under one list, and the encroachment upon the other list is only incidental;

Viswanathiah v. State of Karnataka, (1991) 3 SCC 358, paragraph 9.

Effect of declaration: The ghost of public interest

Even if the Parliament makes a declaration vide Entry 52 of List I that the control of particular industry by the Union is expedient in the public interest, the State Legislature will not lose its power to legislation in regard to raw materials used in that industry;

Vishwanathia v. State of Karnataka, (1991) 3 SCC 358, paragraph 6. (Three Judge Bench).

Legislation by the Parliament under Entry 7 or 52 of List I does not mean absolute exclusion of the State Legislature. This would be confined only to those aspects of the industry, which are brought under the control of the Union;

Orissa Cement Co.v. State of Orissa (1991) Supp. SCC 430, paragraphs 42 and 43

Entry of goods

The State Legislature cannot make undue use of the phrase "within the competence of the State Legislature", and consequently cannot levy taxes on the entry of goods into local areas, which are not meant for consumption, use or sale therein.

Indian Oil Corporation v. Municipal Corporation, Jullunder AIR 1990 P & H 99.

Mines

Entry 54 under Union List and Entry 23 under State List deal with regulations of mines and mineral development but Entry 23 is subject to the provisions of the List I. If the Parliament declares that such regulation and development under the control of the Union is expedient in the public interest, any legislation by the State Legislature after such declaration is liable to be declared unconstitutional. We can see the following decisions:

(i) Nanganayaka v. State of Karnataka, AIR 1990 Kant. 97, 103, 104, paragraphs 10-13.

(ii) Baijnath v. State of Bihar, AIR 1970 SC 1436, 1443, 1444, 1445.

(iii) State of Tamil Nadu v. Hind Stones, AIR 1981, SC 711.

247. Power of Parliament to provide for the establishment of certain additional Courts.- Notwithstanding anything in this Chapter, Parliament may by law provide for the establishment of any additional courts for the better administration of laws made by Parliament or of any existing laws with respect to a matter enumerated in the Union List.

248. Residuary powers of legislation.-

(1) Parliament has exclusive power to make any law with respect to any matter not enumerated in the Concurrent List or State List.

(2) Such power shall include the power of making any law imposing a tax not mentioned in either of those Lists.

249. Power of Parliament to legislate with respect to a matter in the State list in the national interest.-

(1) Notwithstanding anything in the foregoing provisions of this Chapter, if the Council of States has declared by a resolution supported by not less than two-thirds of the members present and voting that it is necessary or expedient in national interest that Parliament should make laws with respect to any matter enumerated in the State List specified in the resolution, it shall be lawful for Parliament to make laws for the whole or any part of the territory of India with respect to that matter while the resolution remains in force.

(2) A resolution passed under clause (1) shall remain in force for such period not exceeding one year as may be specified therein:

Provided that, if and so often as a resolution approving the continuance in force of any such resolution is passed in the manner provided in clause (1), such resolution shall continue in force for a further period of one year from the date on which under this clause it would otherwise have ceased to be in force.

(3) A law made by Parliament which Parliament would not but for the passing of a resolution under clause (1) have been competent to make shall, to the extent of the incompetency, cease to have effect on the expiration of a period of six months after the resolution has ceased to be in force, except as respects things done or omitted to be done before the expiration of the said period.

250. Power of Parliament to legislate with respect to any matter in the State List if a Proclamation of Emergency is in operation .-

(1) Notwithstanding anything in this Chapter, Parliament shall, while a Proclamation of Emergency is in operation, have power to make laws for the whole or any part of the territory of India with respect to any of the matters enumerated in the State List.

(2) A law made by Parliament which Parliament would not but for the issue of a Proclamation of Emergency have been competent to make shall, to the extent of the incompetency, cease to have effect on the expiration of a period of six months after the Proclamation has ceased to operate, except as respects things done or omitted to be done before the expiration of the said period.

251. Inconsistency between laws made by Parliament under articles 249 and 250, and laws made by the Legislatures of States.-Nothing in articles 249 and 250 shall restrict the power of the Legislature of a State to make any law which under this Constitution it has power to make, but if any provision of a law made by the Legislature of a State is repugnant to any provision of a law made by Parliament which Parliament has under either of the said articles power to make, the law made by Parliament, whether passed before or after the law made by the Legislature of the State, shall prevail, and the law made by the Legislature of the State shall to the extent of the repugnancy, but so long only as the law made by Parliament continues to have effect, be inoperative.

252. Power of Parliament to legislate for two or more states by consent and adoption of such legislation by any other State.-

(1) If it appears to the Legislatures of two or more States to be desirable that any of the matters with respect to which Parliament has no power to make laws for the States except as provided in articles 249 and 250 should be regulated in such States by Parliament by law, and if resolutions to that effect are passed by all the Houses of the Legislatures of those States, it shall be lawful for Parliament to pass an Act for regulating that matter accordingly, and any Act so passed shall apply to such States and to any other State by which it is adopted afterwards by resolution passed in that behalf by the House or, where there are two Houses, by each of the Houses of the Legislature of that State.

(2) Any Act so passed by Parliament may be amended or repealed by an Act of Parliament passed or adopted in like manner but shall not, as respects any State to which it applies, be amended or repealed by an Act of the Legislature of that State.

Notes on Article 252

If a state legislature passes a resolution to empower the parliament to make laws relating to state subjects, the parliament can make such laws. But for this purpose, resolution must be passed.

253. Legislation for giving effect to international agreements.-Notwithstanding anything in the foregoing provisions of this Chapter, Parliament has power to make any law for the whole or any part of the territory of India for implementing any treaty, agreement or convention with any other country or countries or any decision made at any international conference, association or other body.

254. Inconsistency between laws made by Parliament and laws made by the Legislatures of States.-

(1) If any provision of a law made by the Legislature of a State is repugnant to any provision of a law made by Parliament which Parliament is competent to enact, or to any

provision of an existing law with respect to one of the matters enumerated in the Concurrent List, then, subject to the provisions of clause (2), the law made by Parliament, whether passed before or after the law made by the Legislature of such State, or, as the case may be, the existing law, shall prevail and the law made by the Legislature of the State shall, to the extent of the repugnancy, be void.

(2) Where a law made by the Legislature of a State [1][***] with respect to one of the matters enumerated in the Concurrent List contains any provision repugnant to the provisions of an earlier law made by Parliament or an existing law with respect to that matter, then, the law so made by the Legislature of such State shall, if it has been reserved for the consideration of the President and has received his assent, prevail in that State:

Provided that nothing in this clause shall prevent Parliament from enacting at any time any law with respect to the same matter including a law adding to, amending, varying or repealing the law so made by the Legislature of the State.

Notes on Article 254

Article 254 contains for resolution of conflict between central and state legislations enacted with respect to any matter enumerated in List III of 7th schedule of constitution; *Central Bank of India V. State of Kerala* 2009.

255. Requirements as to recommendations and previous sanction to be regarded as matters of procedure only.- No Act of Parliament or of the Legislature of a State [1][***] and no provision in any such Act, shall be invalid by reason only that some recommendation or previous sanction required by this Constitution was not given, if assent to that Act was given-

a. where the recommendation required was that of the Governor, either by the Governor or by the President;

b. where the recommendation required was that of the Rajpramukh, either by the Rajpramukh or by the President;

c. where the recommendation or previous sanction required was that of the President, by the President.

CHAPTER II — ADMINISTRATIVE RELATIONS

General

256. Obligation of States and the Union.-The executive power of every State shall be so exercised as to ensure compliance with the laws made by Parliament and any existing laws which apply in that State, and the executive power of the Union shall extend to the giving of such directions to a State as may, appear to the Government of India to be necessary for that purpose.

257. Control of the Union over States in certain cases.-

(1) The executive power of every State shall be so exercised as not to impede or prejudice the exercise of the executive power of the Union, and the executive power of the Union shall extend to the giving of such directions to a State as may appear to the Government of India to be necessary for that purpose.

(2) The executive power of the Union shall also extend to the giving of directions to a State as to the construction and maintenance of means of communication declared in the direction to be of national or military importance:

Provided that nothing in this clause shall be taken as restricting the power of Parliament

---

1 The words and letters "specified in Part A or Part B of the First Schedule" omitted by the Constitution (Seventh Amendment) Act, 1956 sec. 29 and Sch (w.e.f. 1.11.1956).

to declare highways or waterways to be national highways or national waterways or power of the Union with respect to highways or waterways so declared or the power of the Union to construct and maintain means of communication as part of its functions with respect to naval, military and air force works.

(3) The executive power of the Union shall also extend to the giving of directions to a State as to the measures to be taken for the protection of the railways within the State.

(4) Where in carrying out any direction given to a State under clause (2) as to the construction or maintenance of any means of communication or under clause (3) as to the measures to be taken for the protection of any railway, costs have been incurred in excess of those which would have been incurred in the discharge of the normal duties of the State if such direction had not been given, there shall be paid by the Government of India to the State such sum as may be agreed, or, in default of agreement, as may be determined by an arbitrator appointed by the Chief Justice of India, in respect of the extra costs so incurred by the State.

[1]**257A. Assistance to States by deployment of armed forces or other forces of the Union.-** *[Rep.by the Constitution (Forty-fouth Amendment) Act, 1978, sec.33 (w.e.f. 20-6-1979).]*

258. Power of the Union to confer powers, etc., on States in certain cases.-

1. Notwithstanding anything in this Constitution, the President may, with the consent of the Governor of a State, entrust either conditionally or unconditionally to that Government or to its officers functions in relation to any matter to which the executive power of the Union extends.
2. A law made by Parliament which applies in any State may, notwithstanding that it relates to a matter with respect to which the Legislature of the State has no power to make laws, confer powers and impose duties, or authorise the conferring of powers and the imposition of duties, upon the State or officers and authorities thereof.
3. Where by virtue of this article powers and duties have been conferred or imposed upon a State or officers or authorities thereof, there shall be paid by the Government of India to the State such sum as may be agreed, or, in default of agreement, as may be determined by an arbitrator appointed by the Chief Justice of India, in respect of any extra costs of administration incurred by the State in connection with the exercise of those powers and duties.

[2]**258A. Power of the States to entrust functions to the Union.-** Notwithstanding anything in this Constitution, the Governor of a State may, with the consent of the Government of India, entrust either conditionally or unconditionally to that Government or to its officers functions in relation to any matter to which the executive power of the State extends.

259. Armed Forces in States in Part B of the First Schedule.- *[Rep.by the Constitution (Seventh Amendment) Act, 1956, sec. 29 and Sch.]*

260. Jurisdiction of the Union in relation to territories outside India.-The Government of India may by agreement with the Government of any territory not being part of the territory of India undertake any executive, legislative or judicial functions vested in the Government of such territory, but every such agreement shall be subject to, and governed by, any law relating to the exercise of foreign jurisdiction for the time being in force.

261. Public acts, records and judicial proceedings.-

1. Full faith and credit shall be given throughout the territory of India to public acts, records and judicial proceedings of the Union and of every State.
2. The manner in which and the conditions under which the acts, records and proceedings

---

1 Ins. by the Constitution(Forty-second Amendment) Act, 1976, sec. 43 (w.e.f. 3-1-1977).

2 Ins. by the Constitution (Seventh Amendment) Act, 1956, sec. 18 (w.e.f. 1.11.1956).

referred to in clause (1) shall be proved and the effect thereof determined shall be as provided by law made by Parliament.

3. Final judgments or orders delivered or passed by civil courts in any part of the territory of India shall be capable of execution anywhere within that territory according to law.

Disputes relating to Waters

262. Adjudication of disputes relating to waters of inter-State rivers or river valleys.-

(1) Parliament may by law provide for the adjudication of any dispute or complaint with respect to the use, distribution or control of the waters of, or in, any inter-State river or river valley.

(2) Notwithstanding anything in this Constitution, Parliament may by law provide that neither the Supreme Court nor any other court shall exercise jurisdiction in respect of any such dispute or complaint as is referred to in clause (1).

Notes on Article 262

Section 11 of the inter state water disputes Act, 1956, which is passed under Article 262, excludes the jurisdiction of the Supreme Court in matter of water dispute referred to the Tribunal. But the Central government can be directed by the Supreme Court to fulfill the statutory obligation under section 4 of the Act. Fulfilling the statutory obligation is mandatory.

Co-ordination between States

263. Provisions with respect to an inter-State Council.-If at any time it appears to the President that the public interests would be served by the establishment of a Council charged with the duty of-

(a) inquiring into and advising upon disputes which may have arisen between States;

(b) investigating and discussing subjects in which some or all of the States, or the Union and one or more of the States, have a common interest; or

(c) making recommendations upon any such subject and, in particular, recommendations for the better co-ordination of policy and action with respect to that subject,

it shall be lawful for the President by order to establish such a Council, and to define the nature of the duties to be performed by it and its organization and procedure.

Notes on Article 263

Once it is found by the Central government that the dispute referred to in the request by the state government cannot be settled by negotiations, the constitution of a tribunal becomes mandatory. The dispute will be adjudicated by the tribunal. If such reference is not made by the central government, mandamus can be issued by the court under Article 32 to the Central Government.

PART XII

FINANCE, PROPERTY, CONTRACTS AND SUITS

Chapter 1

Finance

General

[1][264. **Interpretation.-** In this Part, "Finance Commission" means a Finance Commission constituted under article 280.

1 Subs. by the Constitution (Seventh Amentment) Act, 1956, sec. 29 and Sch., for article 264.

265. Taxes not to be imposed save by authority of law.-No tax shall be levied or collected except by authority of law.

266. Consolidated Funds and Public Accounts of India and of the States.-

(1) Subject to the provisions of article 267 and to the provisions of this Chapter with respect to the assignment of the whole or part of the net proceeds of certain taxes and duties to States, all revenues received by the Government of India, all loans raised by that Government by the issue of treasury bills, loans or ways and means advances and all moneys received by that Government in repayment of loans shall form one consolidated fund to be entitled "the Consolidated Fund of India", and all revenues received by the Government of a State, all loans raised by that Government by the issue of treasury bills, loans or ways and means advances and all moneys received by that Government in repayment of loans shall form one consolidated fund to be entitled "the Consolidated Fund of the State".

(2) All other public moneys received by or on behalf of the Government of India or the Government of a State shall be credited to the public account of India or the public account ot the State, as the case may be.

(3) No moneys out of the Consolidated Fund of India or the Consolidated Fund of State shall be appropriated except in accordance with law and for the purposes and in the manner provided in this Constitution.

267. Contingency Fund.-

(1) Parliament may by law establish a Contingency Fund in the nature of an imprest to be entitled "the Contingency Fund of India" into which shall be paid from time to time such sums as may be determined by such law, and the said Fund shall be placed at the disposal of the President to enable advances to be made by him out of such Fund for the purposes of meeting unforeseen expenditure pending authorisation of such expenditure by Parliament by law under article 115 or article 116.

(2) The Legislature of a State may by law establish a Contingency Fund in the nature of an imprest to be entitled "the Contingency Fund of the State" into which shall be paid from time to time such sums as may be determined by such law, and the said Fund shall be placed at the disposal of the Governor [1][***] of the State to enable advances to be made by him out of such Fund for the purposes of meeting unforeseen expenditure pending authorisation of such expenditure by the Legislature of the State by law under article 205 or article 206.

Distribution of Revenues between the Union and the States

268. Duties levied by the Union but collected and appropriated by the States.-

(1) Such stamp duties and such duties of excise on medicinal and toilet preparations as are mentioned in the Union List shall be levied by the Government of India but shall be collected-

   (a) in the case where such duties are leviable within any [2][Union territory], by the Government of India, and

   (b) in other cases, by the States within which such duties are respectively leviable.

(2) The proceeds in any financial year of any such duty leviable within any State shall not form part of the Consolidated Fund of India, but shall be assigned to that State.

[3]**[268A. Service tax levied by Union and collected and appropriated by the Union and the States.–**

(1) Taxes on services shall be levied by the Government of India and such tax shall be collected and appropriated by the Government of India and the States in the manner provided in clause (2),

---

1 The words "or Rajpramukh" omitted by the Constitution (Seventh Amendment) Act, 1956, sec. 29 and Sch (w.e.f. 1.11.1956).

2 Subs. by the Constitution (Seventh Amendment) Act, 1956, sec. 29 and Sch., for "State specified in Part C of the First Schedule" (w.e.f. 1.11.1956).

3 Ins by constitution (Eighty Eight Amendment) Act 2003 (w.e.f. 19.2.2004).

(2) The proceeds in any financial year of any such tax levied in accordance with the provisions of clause (1) shall be–

(a) Collected by the Government of India and the States.

(b) Appropriated by the Government of India and the States.

in accordance with such principles of collection and appropriation as may be formulated by Parliament by law.

269. Taxes levied and collected by the Union but assigned to the States.-

[1][(1) Taxes on the sales or purchase of goods and taxes on the consignment of goods shall be levied and collected by the Government of India but shall be assigned and shall be deemed to have been assigned to the States on or after the 1st day of April, 1996 in the matter provided in clause (2).

Explanation,- For the purposes of this clause,-

(a) the expression "taxes on the sale or purchase of goods" shall mean taxes on sale or purchase of goods other than newspapers, where such sale or purchase takes place in the course of inter-State trade or commerce;

(b) the expression "taxes on the consignment of goods" shall mean taxes on the consignment of goods (whether the consignment is to the person making it or to any other person), where such consignment takes place in the course of inter-State trade or commerce.

(2) The net proceeds in any financial year of any such duty or tax, except in so far as those proceeds represent proceeds attributable to Union territories, shall not form part of the Consolidated Fund of India, but shall be assigned to the States within which that duty or tax is leviable in that year, and shall be distributed among those States in accordance with such principles of distribution as may be formulated by Parliament by law.]

[2][(3) Parliament may by law formulate principles for determining when a [3][sale or purchase of, or consignment of, goods] takes place in the course of inter-State trade or commerce.

[4][270. Taxes levied and collected by the Union and distributed between the Union and the States.-

(1) All taxes and duties referred to in the Union List, except the duties and taxes referred to in [5][articles 268, 268A and 269], respectively, surcharge on taxes and duties referred to in article 271 and any cess levied for specific purposes under any law made by Parliament shall be levied and collected by the Government of India and shall be distributed between the Union and the States in the manner provided in clause (2).

(2) Such percentage, as may be prescribed, of the net proceeds of any such tax or duty in any financial year shall not form part of the Consolidated Fund of India, but shall be assigned to the States within which that tax or duty is leviable in that year, and shall be distributed among those States in such manner and from such time as may be prescribed in the manner provided in Clause (3).

(3) In this article, "prescribed" means-

a. until a Finance Commission has been constituted, prescribed by the President by order, and

---

1 Subs. by the Constitution (Eightieth Amendment) Act, 2000, sec. 2, for clauses (1) & (2) (w.e.f. 9.6.2000).

2 Ins. by the Constitution (Sixth Amendment) Act, 1956, sec. 3 (w.e.f. 11.9.1956).

3 Subs. by the Constitution (Forty-sixth Amendment) Act, 1982, sec. 2, for "sale or purchase of goods" (w.e.f. 2.2.1983).

4 Sub. by the Constitution (Eightieth Amendment) Act, 2000, sec. 3, for article 270. (w.e.f. 1-4-1996).

5 Subs. by the Constitution (Eighty-eighth Amendment) Act, 2003, Sec.3 (w.e.f. 19.2.2004).

b. after a Finance Commission has been constituted, prescribed by the President by order after considering the recommendations of the Finance Commission.]

271. Surcharge on certain duties and taxes for purposes of the Union.-Notwithstanding anything in articles 269 and 270, Parliament may at any time increase any of the duties or taxes referred to in those articles by a surcharge for purposes of the Union and the whole proceeds of any such surcharge shall form part of the Consolidated Fund of India.

***272. Taxes which are levied and collected by the Union and may be distributed between the Union and the States.-** *[Rep. by the Constitution (Eightieth Amendment) Act, 2000, sec. (4) (w.e.f. 9.6.2000).]*

Notes on Article 272

The union duties of excise including additional duties and any other tax or duty collected and distributed by Central Government as grants-in-aid to States after 1.4.1996 and before 9.6.2000 shall be deemed to be distributed as if before 1.4.1996.

273. Grants in lieu of export duty on jute and jute products.-

(1) There shall be charged on the Consolidated Fund of India in each year as grants-in aid of the revenues of the States of Assam, Bihar, [1][Odisha] and West Bengal, in lieu of assignment of any share of the net proceeds in each year of export duty on jute and jute products to those States, such sums as may be prescribed.

(2) The sums so prescribed shall continue to be charged on the Consolidated Fund of India so long as any export duty on jute or jute products continues to be levied by the Government of India or until the expiration of ten years from the commencement of this Constitution, whichever is earlier.

(3) In this article, the expression "prescribed" has the same meaning as in article 270.

274. Prior recommendation of President required to Bills affecting taxation in which States are interested.-

(1) No Bill or amendment which imposes or varies any tax or duty in which States are interested, or which varies the meaning of the expression "agricultural income" as defined for the purposes of the enactments relating to Indian Income-tax, or which affects the principles on which under any of the foregoing provisions of this Chapter moneys are or may be distributable to State, or which imposes any surcharge for the purposes of the Union as is mentioned in the foregoing provisions of this Chapter, shall be introduced or moved in either House of Parliament except on the recommendation of the President.

(2) In this article, the expression "tax or duty in which States are interested" means-

(a) a tax or duty the whole or part of the net proceeds whereof are assigned to any State; or

(b) a tax or duty by reference to the net proceeds whereof sums are for the time being payable out of the Consolidated Fund of India to any State.

275. Grants from the Union to certain States.-

(1) Such sums as Parliament may by law provide shall be charged on the Consolidated Fund of India in each year as grants-in-aid of the revenues of such States as Parliament may determine to be in need of assistance, and different sums may be fixed for different States:

Provided that there shall be paid out of the Consolidated Fund of India as grants-in-aid of the revenues of a State such capital and recurring sums as may be necessary to

---

* The union duties of excise including additional duties and any other tax or duty collected and distributed by Central Government as grants-in-aid to States after 1-4-1996 and before 9-6-2000 shall be deemed to be distributed as if before 1-4-1996.

1 Subs. by the Orissa (Alteration of Name) Act, 2011 (15 of 2011), sec. 5, for "Orissa" (w.e.f. 1-11-2011), *vide* G.S.R. 791(E), dated 1st November, 2011).

enable that State to meet the costs of such schemes of development as may be undertaken by the State with the approval of the Government of India for the purpose of promoting the welfare of the Scheduled Tribes in that State or raising the level of administration of the Scheduled Areas therein to that of the administration of the rest of the areas of that State:

Provided further that there shall be paid out of the Consolidated Fund of India as grants-in-aid of the revenues of the State of Assam sums, capital and recurring, equivalent to-

(a) the average excess of expenditure over the revenues during the two years immediately preceding the commencement of this Constitution in respect of the administration of the tribal areas specified in [1][Part I] of the table appended to paragraph 20 of the Sixth Schedule; and

(b) the costs of such schemes of development as may be undertaken by that State with the approval of the Government of India for the purpose of raising the level of administration of the said areas to that of the administration of the rest of the areas of that State.

[2][(1A) On and from the formation of the autonomous State under article 244A,-

(i) any sums payable under clause (a) of the second proviso to clause (1) shall, if the autonomous State comprises of all the tribal areas referred to therein, be paid to the autonomous State, and, if the autonomous State comprises only some of those tribal areas, be apportioned between the State of Assam and the autonomous State as the President may, by order, specify;

(ii) there shall be paid out of the Consolidated Fund of India as grants -in aid of the revenues of the autonomous State sums, capital and recurring, equivalent to the costs of such schemes of development as may be undertaken by the autonomous State with the approval of the Government of India for the purpose of raising the level of administration of that State to that of the administration of the rest of the State of Assam.]

(2) Until provision is made by Parliament under clause (1), the powers conferred on Parliament under that clause shall be exercisable by the President by order and any order made by the President under this clause shall have effect subject to any provision so made by Parliament:

Provided that after a Finance Commission has been constituted no order shall be made under this clause by the President except after considering the recommendations of the Finance Commission.

276. Taxes on professions, trades, callings and employments.-

(1) Notwithstanding anything in article 246, no law of the Legislature of a State relating to taxes for the benefit of the State or of a municipality, district board, local board or other local authority therein in respect of professions, trades, callings or employments shall be invalid on the ground that it relates to a tax on income.

(2) The total amount payable in respect of any one person to the State or to any one municipality, district board, local board or other local authority in the State by way of taxes on professions, trades, callings and employments shall not exceed [3][two thousand and five hundred rupees] per annum.[4][***]

1 Subs. by the North-Eastern Areas (Reorganisation) Act, 1971 (81 of 1971), sec. 71, for "Part A" (w.e.f. 21-1-1972).

2 Ins. by the Constitution (Twenty-second Amendment) Act, 1969, sec. 3 (w.e.f. 25.9.1969).

3 Subs. by the Constitution (Sixtieth Amendment) Act, 1988, sec. 2, for "two hundred and fifty rupees" (w.e.f. 20.12.1988).

4 Proviso omitted by the Constitution (Sixtieth Amendment) Act, 1988, sec. 2 (w.e.f. 20-12-1988).

(3) The power of the Legislature of a State to make laws as aforesaid with respect to taxes on professions, trades, callings and employments shall not be construed as limiting in any way the power of Parliament to make laws with respect to taxes on income accruing from or arising out of professions, trades, callings and employments.

277. Savings.- Any taxes, duties, cesses or fees which, immediately before the commencement of this Constitution, were being lawfully levied by the Government of any State or by any municipality or other local authority or body for the purposes of the State, municipality, district or other local area may, notwithstanding that those taxes, duties, cesses or fees are mentioned in the Union List, continue to be levied and to be applied to the same purposes until provision to the contrary is made by Parliament by law.

278. Agreement with States in Part B of the First Schedule with regard to certain financial matters.- [*Rep., by the Constitution (Seventh Amendment) Act, 1956, sec. 29 and Sch.]* (w.e.f. 1.11.1956)

279. Calculation of "net proceeds", etc.-

(1) In the foregoing provisions of this Chapter, "net proceeds" means in relation to any tax or duty the proceeds thereof reduced by the cost of collection, and for the purposes of those provisions the net proceeds of any tax or duty or of any part of any tax or duty, in or attributable to any area shall be ascertained and certified by the Comptroller and Auditor- General of India, whose certificate shall be final.

(2) Subject as aforesaid, and to any other express provision of this Chapter, a law made by Parliament or an order of the President may, in any case where under this Part the proceeds of any duty or tax are, or may be, assigned to any State, provide for the manner in which the proceeds are to be calculated, for the time from or at which and the manner in which any payments are to be made, for the making of adjustment between one financial year and another, and for any other incidental or ancillary matters.

280. Finance Commission.-

(1) The President shall, within two years from the commencement of this Constitution and thereafter at the expiration of every fifth year or at such earlier time as the President considers necessary, by order constitute a Finance Commission which shall consist of a Chairman and four other members to be appointed by the President.

(2) Parliament may by law determine the qualifications which shall be requisite for appointment as members of the Commission and the manner in which they shall be selected.

(3) It shall be the duty of the Commission to make recommendations to the President as to-

(a) the distribution between the Union and the States of the net proceeds of taxes which are to be, or may be, divided between them under this Chapter and the allocation between the States of the respective shares of such proceeds;

(b) the principles which should govern the grants-in aid of the revenues of the States out of the Consolidated Fund of India;

[1][(bb) the measures needed to augment the Consolidated Fund of a State to supplement the resources of the Panchayats in the State on the basis of the recommendations made by the Finance Commission of the State;]

[2][(c) the measures needed to augment the Consolidated Fund of a State to supplement the resources of the Municipalities in the State on the basis of the recommendations made by the Finance Commission of the State;]

---

1 Sub-clause (bb) ins. by the Constitution (Seventy-third Amendment) Act, 1992, sec. 3 (w.e.f. 24-4-1993).

2 Sub-clause (c) ins. by the Constitution (Seventy-fourth Amendment) Act, 1992, sec.3 (w.e.f. 1-6-1993); previously sub-clause (c) was omitted by the Constitution (Seventh Amendment) Act, 1956, sec. 29 and Sch.

[1][(d)] any other matter referred to the Commission by the President in the interests of sound finance.

(4) The Commission shall determine their procedure and shall have such powers in the performance of their functions as Parliament may by law confer on them.

281. Recommendations of the Finance Commission.- The President shall cause every recommendation made by the Finance Commission under the provisions of this Constitution together with an explanatory memorandum as to the action taken thereon to be laid before each House of Parliament.

Miscellaneous Financial Provisions

282. Expenditure defrayable by the Union or a State out of its revenues.- The Union or a State may make any grants for any public purpose, notwithstanding that the purpose is not one with respect to which Parliament or the Legislature of the State, as the case may be, may make laws.

283. Custody, etc., of Consolidated Funds, Contingency Funds and moneys credited to the public accounts.-

(1) The custody of the Consolidated Fund of India and the Contingency Fund of India, the payment of moneys into such Funds, the withdrawal of moneys therefrom, the custody of public moneys other than those credited to such funds received by or on behalf of the Government of India, their payment into the public account of India and the withdrawal of moneys from such account and all other matters connected with or ancillary to matters aforesaid shall be regulated by law made by Parliament, and, until provision in that behalf is so made, shall be regulated by rules made by the President.

(2) The custody of the Consolidated Fund of a State and the Contingency Fund of a State, the payment of moneys into such Funds, the withdrawal of moneys therefrom, the custody of public moneys other than those credited to such Funds received by or on behalf of the Government of the State, their payment into the public account of the State and the withdrawal of moneys from such account and all other matters connected with or ancillary to matters aforesaid shall be regulated by law made by the Legislature of the State, and, until provision in that behalf is so made, shall be regulated by rules made by the Governor [2][***] of the State.

284. Custody of suitors' deposits and other moneys received by public servants and Courts.- All moneys received by or deposited with-

(a) any officer employed in connection with the affairs of the Union or of a State in his capacity as such, other than revenues or public moneys raised or received by the Government of India or the Government of the State, as the case may be; or

(b) any court within the territory of India to the credit of any cause, matter, account or persons,

shall be paid into the public account of India or the public account of the State, as the case may be.

285. Exemption of property of the Union from State taxation.-

(1) The property of the Union shall, save in so far as Parliament may by law otherwise provides, be exempt from all taxes imposed by a State or by any authority within a State.

1 Sub-clause (c) re-lettered as sub-clause (d) by the Constitution (Seventy-fourth Amendment) Act, 1992, sec. 3 (w.e.f. 1-6-1993); previously sub-clause (d) was re-lettered as sub-clause (c) by the Constitution (Seventh Amendment) Act, sec. 29 and Sch (w.e.f. 1.11.1956).

2 The words "or Rajpramukh" omitted by the Constitution (Seventh Amendment) Act, 1956, sec. 29 and Sch (w.e.f. 1.11.1956).

(2) Nothing in clause (1) shall, until Parliament by law otherwise provides, prevent any authority within a State from levying any tax on any property of the Union to which such property was immediately before the commencement of this Constitution liable or treated as liable, so long as that tax continues to be levied in that State.

286. Restrictions as to imposition of tax on the sale or purchase of goods.-

(1) No law of a State shall impose, or authorise the imposition of, a tax on the sale or purchase of goods where such sale or purchase takes place-

(a) outside the State; or

(b) in the course of the import of the goods into, or export of the goods out of, the territory of India. [1][***]

[2](2) Parliament may by law formulate principles for determining when a sale or purchase of goods takes place in any of the ways mentioned in clause (1).

[3](3) Any law of a State shall, in so far as it imposes, or authorises the imposition of,-

(a) a tax on the sale or purchase of goods declared by Parliament by law to be of special importance in inter-State trade or commerce; or

(b) a tax on the sale or purchase of goods, being a tax of the nature referred to in sub-clause (b), sub-clause(c), or sub-clause(d) of clause (29A) of article 366,

be subject to such restrictions and conditions in regard to the system of levy, rates and other incidents of the tax as Parliament may by law specify.]]

287. Exemption from taxes on electricity :- Save in so far as Parliament may by law otherwise provide, no law of a state shall impose, or authorise the imposition of, a tax on the consumption or sale of electricity (whether produced by a Government or other persons) which is-

(a) consumed by the government of India, or sold to the government of India for consumption by that government; or

(b) consumed in the construction, maintenance or operation of any railway by the Government of India or a railway company operating that railway, or sold to that Government or any such railway company for consumption in the construction, maintenance or operation of any railway,

and any such law imposing, or authorising the imposition of, a tax on the sale of electricity shall secure that the price of electricity sold to the Government of India for consumption by that Government, or to any such railway company as aforesaid for consumption in the costruction, maintenance or operation of any railway, shall be less by the amount of the tax than the price charged to other consumers of a substantial quantity of electricity.

288. Exemption from taxation by States in respect of water or electricity in certain cases.-

(1) Save in so far as the President may by order otherwise provide, no law of a State in force immediately before the commencement of this Constitution shall impose, or authorise the imposition of, a tax in respect of any water or electricity stored, generated, consumed, distributed or sold by any authority established by any existing law or any law made by Parliament for regulating or developing any inter-State river or river-valley.

Explanation — The expression "law of a State in force" in this clause shall include a law of a State passed or made before the commencement of this Constitution and not previously repealed, notwithstanding that it or parts of it may not be then in operation either at all or in particular areas.

1 Explanation to clause (1) omitted by the Constitution (Sixth Amendment) Act, 1956, sec. 4 (w.e.f. 11.9.1956).

2 Subs. by the Constitution (Sixth Amendment) Act, 1956, for clauses (2) and (3) (w.e.f. 11.9.1956).

3 Subs. by the Constitution (Forty-sixth Amendment) Act, 1982, sec. 3, for clause (3) (w.e.f. 12-2-1983).

(2) The Legislature of a State may by law impose, or authorise the imposition of, any such tax as is mentioned in clause(1), but no such law shall have any effect unless it has, after having been reserved for the consideration of the President, received his assent; and if any such law provides for the fixation of the rates and other incidents of such tax by means of rules or orders to be made under the law by any authority, the law shall provide for the previous consent of the President being obtained to the making of any such rule or order.

289. Exemption of property and income of a State from Union taxation.-

(1) The property and income of a State shall be exempt from Union taxation.

(2) Nothing in clause (1) shall prevent the Union from imposing, or authorising the imposition of, any tax to such extent, if any, as Parliament may by law provide in respect of a trade or business of any kind carried on by, or on behalf of, the Government of a State, or any operations connected therewith, or any property used or occupied for the purposes of such trade or business, or any income accruing or arising in connection therewith.

(3) Nothing in clause (2) shall apply to any trade or business, or to any class of trade or business, which Parliament may by law declare to be incidental to the ordinary functions of Government.

290. Adjustment in respect of certain expenses and pensions.- Where under the provisions of this Constitution the expenses of any court or Commission, or the pension payable to or in respect of a person who has served before the commencement of this Constitution under the Crown in India or after such commencement in connection with the affairs of the Union or of a State, are charged on the Consolidated. Fund of India or the Consolidated Fund of a State, then, if-

(a) in the case of a charge on the Consolidated Fund of India, the court or Commission serves any of the separate needs of a State, or the person has served wholly or in part in connection with the affairs of a State; or

(b) in the case of a charge on the Consolidated Fund of a State, the court or Commission serves any of the separate needs of the Union or another State, or the person has served wholly or in part in connection with the affairs of the Union or another State,

there shall be charged on and paid out of the Consolidated Fund of the State or, as the case may be, the Consolidated Fund of India or the Consolidated Fund of the other State, such contribution in respect of the expenses or pension as may be agreed, or as may in default of agreement be determined by an arbitrator to be appointed by the Chief Justice of India.

[1][**290A. Annual payment to certain Devaswom Funds.-** A sum of forty-six lakhs and fifty thousand rupees shall be charged on, and paid out of, the Consolidated Fund of the State of Kerala every year to the Travancore Devaswom Fund; and a sum of thirteen lakhs and fifty thousand rupees shall be charged on, and paid out of the Consolidated Fund of the State of [2][Tamil Nadu] every year to the Devaswom Fund established in that State for the maintenance of Hindu temples and shrines in the territories transferred to that State on the Ist day of November, 1956, from the State of Travancore-Cochin.]

[3]**291. Privy purse sums of Rulers.-** *[Rep. by the Constitution (Twenty-sixth Amendment) Act, 1971,sec. 2.]*

---

1 Ins. by the Constitution (Seventh Amendment) Act, 1956, sec. 19 (w.e.f. 1.11.1956).

2 Subs. by the Madras State (Alteration of Name) Act, 1968, (53 of 1968), sec. 4 for "Madras" (w.e.f. 14-1-1969).

3 Article 291 was earlier amended by the Constitution (Seventh Amendment) Act, 1956, sec. 29 and sch. (w.e.f. 1-11-1956).

CHAPTER II — BORROWING

292. Borrowing by the Government of India.-The executive power of the Union extends to borrowing upon the security of the Consolidated Fund of India within such limits, if any, as may from time to time be fixed by Parliament by law and to the giving of guarantees within such limits, if any, as may be so fixed.

293. Borrowing by States.-

(1) Subject to the provisions of this article, the executive power of a State extends to borrowing within the territory of India upon the security of the Consolidated Fund of the State within such limits, if any, as may from time to time be fixed by the Legislature of such State by law and to the giving of guarantees within such limits, if any, as may be so fixed.

(2) The Government of India may, subject to such conditions as may be laid down by or under any law made by Parliament, make loans to any State or, so long as any limits fixed under article 292 are not exceeded, give guarantees in respect of loans raised by any State, and any sums required for the purpose of making such loans shall be charged on the Consolidated Fund of India.

(3) A State may not without the consent of the Government of India raise any loan if there is still outstanding any part of a loan which has been made to the State by the Government of India or by its predecessor Government, or in respect of which a guarantee has been given by the Government of India or by its predecessor Government

(4) A consent under clause (3) may be granted subject to such conditions, if any, as the Government of India may think fit to impose.

CHAPTER III — PROPERTY, CONTRACTS, RIGHTS, LIABILITIES, OBLIGATIONS AND SUITS

294. Succession to property, assets, rights, liabilities and obligations in certain cases.- As from the commencement of this Constitution-

(a) all property and assets which immediately before such commencement were vested in His Majesty for the purposes of the Government of the Dominion of India and all property and assets which immediately before such commencement were vested in His Majesty for the purposes of the Government of each Governor's Province shall vest respectively in the Union and the corresponding State, and

(b) all rights, liabilities and obligations of the Government of the Dominion of India and of the Government of each Governor's Province, whether arising out of any contract or otherwise, shall be the rights, liabilities and obligations respectively of the Government of India and the Government of each corresponding State,

subject to any adjustment made or to be made by reason of the creation before the commencement of this Constitution of the Dominion of Pakistan or of the Provinces of West Bengal, East Bengal, West Punjab and East Punjab.

295. Succession to property, assets, rights, liabilities and obligations in other cases.-

(1) As from the commencement of this Constitution-

  (a) all property and assets which immediately before such commencement were vested in any Indian State corresponding to a State specified in Part B of the First Schedule shall vest in the Union, if the purposes for which such property and assests were held immediately before such commencement will thereafter be purposes of the Union relating to any of the matters enumerated in the Union List, and

  (b) all rights, liabilities and obligations of the Government of any Indian State corresponding to a State specified in Part B of the First Schedule, whether arising out of any contract or otherwise, shall be the rights, liabilities and obligations of the Government of India, if the purposes for which such rights were acquired or liabilities or obligations were incurred before such commencement will thereafter be purposes of the Government of India relating to any of the matters enumerated in the Union List,

subject to any agreement entered into in that behalf by the Government of India with the Government of that State.

(2) Subject as aforesaid, the Government of each State specified in Part B of the First Schedule shall, as from the commencement of this Constitution, be the successor of the Government of the corresponding Indian State as regards all property and assets and all rights, liabilities and obligations, whether arising out of any contract or otherwise, other than those referred to in clause (1).

296. Property accruing by escheat or lapse or as *bona vacantia*.- Subject as hereinafter provided any property in the territory of India which, if this Constitution had not come into operation, would have accrued to His Majesty or, as the case may be, to the Ruler of an Indian State by escheat or lapse, or as *bona vacantia* for want of a rightful owner, shall, if it is property situated in a State, vest in such State, and shall, in any other case, vest in the Union;

Provided that any property which at the date when it would have so accrued to His Majesty or to the Ruler of an Indian State was in the possession or under the control of the Government of India or the Government of a State shall, according as the purposes for which it was then used or held were purposes of the Union or a State, vest in the Union or in that state.

Explanation: In this article, the expressions "Ruler" and "Indian State" have the same meanings as in article 363.

[1][**297. Things of value within territorial waters or continental shelf and resources of the exclusive economic zone to vest in the Union.-**

(1) All lands, minerals and other things of value underlying the ocean within the territorial waters, or the continental shelf, or the exclusive economic zone, of India shall vest in the Union and be held for the purposes of the Union.

(2) All other resources of the exclusive economic zone of India shall also vest in the Union and be held for the purposes of the Union.

(3) The limits of the territorial waters, the continental shelf, the exclusive economic zone, and other maritime zones, of India shall be such as may be specified from time to time, by or under any law made by Parliament.]

[2][**298. Power to carry on trade, etc.-**The executive power of the Union and of each State shall extend to the carrying on of any trade or business and to the acquisition, holding and disposal of property and the making of contracts for any purpose:

Provided that-

(a) the said executive power of the Union shall, in so far as such trade or business or such purpose is not one with respect to which Parliament may make laws, be subject in each State to legislation by the State; and

(b) the said executive power of each State shall, in so far as such trade or business or such purpose is not one with respect to which the State Legislature may make laws, be subject to legislation by Parliament.]

1 Subs. by the Constitution (Fortieth Amendment) Act, 1976, sec. 2, for article 297 (w.e.f. 27-5-1976).

2 Subs. by the Constitution (Seventh Amendment) Act, 1956, sec. 20, for article 298 (w.e.f. 1.11.1956).

299. Contracts.-

(1) All contracts made in the exercise of the executive power of the Union or of a State shall be expressed to be made by the President, or by the Governor [1][***] of the State, as the case may, and all such contracts and all assurances of property made in the exercise of that power shall be executed on behalf of the President or the Governor [1][***] by such persons and in such manner as he may direct or authorise.

(2) Neither the President nor the Governor[2][***] shall be personally liable in respect of any contract or assurance made or executed for the purposes of this Constitution, or for the purposes of any enactment relating to the Government of India heretofore in force, nor shall any person making or executing any such contract or assurance on behalf of any of them be personally liable in respect thereof.

300. Suits and proceedings.-

(1) The Government of India may sue or be sued by the name of the Union of India and the Government of a State may sue or be sued by the name of the State and may, subject to any provisions which may be made by Act of Parliament or of the Legislature of such State enacted by virtue of powers conferred by this Constitution, sue or be sued in relation to their respective affairs in the like cases as the Dominion of India and the corresponding Provinces or the corresponding Indian States might have sued or been sued if this Constitution had not been enacted.

(2) If at the commencement of this Constitution-

(a) any legal proceedings are pending to which the Dominion of India is a party, the Union of India shall be deemed to be substituted for the Dominion in those proceedings; and

(c) any legal proceedings are pending to which a Province or an Indian State is a party, the corresponding State shall be deemed to be substituted for the Province or the Indian State in those proceedings.

Notes on Article 300

Government liability in tort

The guiding principle in this regard is that Government is not liable for torts of its employees committed in the course of performance of sovereign functions. This theoretical doctrine has gained ground and it is widely resorted to. However, it is applied in a very liberal manner under the cloak of the word 'sovereign'. The Courts interpret 'sovereign' in its proper perspective. The cases below can be seen:

(i) State of Rajasthan v. Vidhyawati, AIR 1962, SC 933

(ii) Shyam Sunder v. State of Rajasthan, AIR 1974 SC 980, paragraph 21.

(iii) Kasturi Lal v. State of UP, AIR 1965 SC 1039.

(iv) Virendra v. State of UP, (1955) 1 SCR 415, 436 (Act of State).

The Government may be sued for wrongs committed by public servants in the course of business, such as death or injury caused to a person by Police atrocities;

Saheli v. Commissioner of Police, AIR 1990 SC 513.

---

1 The words "or the Rajpramukh" omitted by the Constitution (Seventh Amendment) Act, 1956, sec. 29 and Sch (w.e.f. 1.11.1956).

2 The words "nor the Rajpramukh" omitted by the Constitution (Seventh Amendment) Act, 1956, sec. 29 and Sch. (w.e.f. 1.11.1956).

[1][CHAPTER IV—RIGHT TO PROPERTY

300A. Persons not to be deprived of property save by authority of law.- No person shall be deprived of his property save by authority of law.]

Notes on Article 300A

Nature of right

The right to property under article 300A, once a fundamental Right, has been relegated to the status of a constitutional right;

Bishamber v. State of UP, AIR 1982 SC 33.

Right to Property

The right to property includes within it the right to use the property in accordance with the law as it stands at that particular time; *Chairman, Indore Vikas Pradhikaran v. Pure Industrial Coke & Chemicals Ltd.*, (2007) 8 SCC 705

Deprivation of property

But under Section 69 (2A) (Maharashtra Amendment) of partnership Act instituting suit for dissolution of unregistered firm or recovery of property as well are arbitrary and unreasonable, *V. Subramaniam V. Rajesh Raghuvandra Rao* AIR 2009.

An order of the Government refusing sanction to construct a building does not deprive a person of his right to property within the meaning of Article 300A. A legal restriction on the enjoyment of right to property cannot be equated with the deprivation of property. However, prevention of user of a land without any legal sanction is a deprivation within the ambit of Art. 300A.

Girdhari Lal Soni v. Municipal Corporation, Calcutta Municipal Corporation, AIR 2001 Cal. 12.

State Finance Corporation Act, 1951

Section 29 of the State Finance Corporation Act, 1951 empowers the Corporation to take possession of the property of an individual concerned if he is a defaulter in payment of any loan. The said Act does not infringe articles 14, 19, 21 or 300A of the Constitution. The real test lies in the principles of natural justice, which have to be read into the section. The Board of the Corporation consists of high-ranking officials. An individual concerned is fully aware of the provision before entering into an agreement with the Corporation. If the Corporation acts in an unjust and unfair manner, its action can be challenged, but that does not vitiate the provision;

Alka Ceramics v. Gujarat State Finance Corporation, AIR 1990 Guj. 105 (DB)

Forty Fourth Amendment Act, 1978

The Constitution (Forty fourth Amendment) Act; 1978 dealt a severe blow to the right of property under Part III and made it merely a constitutional right. Unlike the fundamental rights under Part III, this right no longer forms part of the basic structure of the Constitution.

---

1 Ins. by the Constitution (Forty-fourth Amendment) Act, 1978, sec. 34 (w.e.f. 20-6-1979).

PART XIII

TRADE, COMMERCE AND INTERCOURSE WITHIN THE TERRITORY OF INDIA

301. Freedom of trade, commerce and intercourse.- Subject to the other provisions of this Part, trade, commerce and intercourse throughout the territory of India shall be free.

Notes on Article 301

Freedom of inter-state & intra-state trade & commerce

(a) Article 301 provides freedom not from all laws but freedom from such laws which restrict or affect activities of trade and commerce among the States; *Jindal Stainless Steel Ltd. v. State of Haryana*, AIR 2006 SC 2550

(b) Article 302 refers to freedom from laws which go beyond regulations which burdens, restricts or prevents the trade movements between states and within state; *Jindal Stainless Steel Ltd., v. State of Haryana*, AIR 2006 SC 2550

302. Power of Parliament to impose restrictions on trade, commerce and intercourse.- Parliament may by law impose such restrictions on the freedom of trade, commerce or intercourse between one State and another or within any part of the territory of India as may be required in the public interest.

303. Restrictions on the legislative powers of the Union and of the States with regard to trade and commerce.-

(1) Notwithstanding anything in article 302, neither Parliament nor the Legislature of a State shall have power to make any law giving, or authorising the giving of, any preference to one State over another, or making, or authorising the making of, any discrimination between one State and another, by virtue of any entry relating to trade and commerce in any of the Lists in the Seventh Schedule.

(2) Nothing in clause(1) shall prevent Parliament from making any law giving, or authorising the giving of, any preference or making, or authorising the making of, any discrimination if it is declared by such law that it is necessary to do so for the purpose of dealing with a situation arising from scarcity of goods in any part of the territory of India.

304. Restrictions on trade, commerce and intercourse among States.- Notwithstanding anything in article 301 or article 303, the Legislature of a State may by law-

(a) impose on goods imported from other States [1][or the Union Territories] any tax to which similar goods manufactured or produced in that State are subject, so, however, as not to discriminate between goods so imported and goods so manufactured or produced; and

(b) impose such reasonable restrictions on the freedom of trade, commerce or intercourse with or within that State as may be required in the public interest:

Provided that no Bill or amendment for the purposes of clause (b) shall be introduced or moved in the Legislature of a State without the previous sanction of the President.

[2][**305. Saving of existing laws and laws providing for State monopolies.-** Nothing in articles 301 and 303 shall affect the provisions of any existing law except in so far as the President may by order otherwise direct; and nothing in article 301 shall affect the operation of any law made before the commencement of the Constitution (Fourth Amendment) Act, 1955, in so far as it relates to, or prevent Parliament or the Legislature of a State from making any law relating to, any such matter as is referred to in sub-clause (ii) of clause(6) of article 19.]

---

1 Ins. by the Constitution (Seventh Amendment) Act, 1956, sec. 29 and Sch (w.e.f. 1.11.1956).

2 Subs. by the Constitution (Fourth Amendment) Act, 1955, sec. 4 (w.e.f. 27.4.1955).

306. Power of certain States in Part B of the First Schedule to impose restrictions on trade and commerce.- *[Rep. by the Constitution (Seventh Amendment) Act, 1956, sec. 29 and Sch.(w.e.f. 1.11.1956).]*

307. Appointment of authority for carrying out the purposes of articles 301 to 304. Parliament may by law appoint such authority as it considers appropriate for carrying out the purposes of articles 301,302, 303 and 304, and confer on the authority so appointed such powers and such duties as it thinks necessary.

PART XIV

SERVICES UNDER THE UNION AND THE STATES

CHAPTER I — SERVICES

308. Interpretation.- In this Part, unless the context otherwise requires, the expression "State" [1][does not include the State of Jammu and Kashmir].

309. Recruitment and conditions of service of persons serving the Union or a State.- Subject to the provisions of this Constitution, Acts of the appropriate Legislature may regulate the recruitment, and conditions of service of persons appointed to public services and posts in connection with the affairs of the Union or of any State:

Provided that it shall be competent for the President or such person as he may direct in the case of services and posts in connection with the affairs of the Union, and for the Governor [2][***] of a State or such person as he may direct in the case of services and posts in connection with the affairs of the State, to make rules regulating the recruitment and the conditions of service of persons appointed, to such services and posts until provision in that behalf is made by or under an Act of the appropriate Legislature under this article, and any rules so made shall have effect subject to the provisions of any such Act.

310. Tenure of office of persons serving the Union or a State.-

(1) Except as expressly provided by this Constitution, every person who is a member of a defence service or of a civil service of the Union or of an all-India service or holds any post connected with defence or any civil post under the Union holds office during the pleasure of the President, and every person who is a member of a civil service of a State or holds any civil post under a State holds office during the pleasure of the Governor [3][***] of the State.

(2) Notwithstanding that a person holding a civil post under the Union or a State holds office during the pleasure of the President or, as the case may be, of the Governor [4][***] of the State, any contract under which a person, not being a member of a defence service or of an all-India service or of a civil service of the Union or a State, is appointed under this Constitution to hold such a post may, if the President or the Governor [5][***] as the case may be, deems it necessary in order to secure the services of a person having special qualifications, provide for the payment to him of compensation, if before the expiration of an agreed period that post is abolished or he is, for reasons not connected with any misconduct on his part, required to vacate that post.

1 Subs. by the Constitution (Seventh Amendment) Act, 1956, sec. 29 and Sch., for "means a State specified in Part A or Part B of the First Schedule" (w.e.f. 1.11.1956).

2 The words "or Rajpramukh" omitted by the Constitution (Seventh Amendment) Act, 1956, sec. 29 and Sch (w.e.f. 1.11.1956).

3 The words "or the Rajpramukh as the case may be, "omitted by the Constitution (Seventh Amendment) Act, 1956, sec. 29 and Sch (w.e.f. 1.11.1956).

4 The words "or Rajpramukh" omitted by the Constitution (Seventh Amendment) Act, 1956, sec. 29and Sch (w.e.f. 1.11.1956).

5 The words "or, the Rajpramukh" omitted by the Constitution (Seventh Amendment) Act, 1956, sec. 29 and Sch (w.e.f. 1.11.1956).

311. Dismissal, removal or reduction in rank of persons employed in civil capacities under the Union or a State.-

(1) No person who is a member of a civil service of the Union or an all-India service or a civil service of a State or holds a civil post under the Union or a State shall be dismissed or removed by an authority subordinate to that by which he was appointed.

[1][(2) No such person as aforesaid shall be dismissed or removed or reduced in rank except after an inquiry in which he has been informed of the charges against him and given a reasonable opportunity of being heard in respect of those charges[2][***]:

[3][Provided that where it is proposed after such inquiry, to impose upon him any such penalty, such penalty may be imposed on the basis of the evidence adduced during such inquiry and it shall not be necessary to give such person any opportunity of making representation on the penalty proposed:

Provided further that this clause shall not apply-]

(a) where a person is dismissed or removed or reduced in rank on the ground of conduct which has led to his conviction on a criminal charge; or

(b) where the authority empowered to dismiss or remove a person or to reduce him in rank is satisfied that for some reason, to be recorded by that authority in writing, it is not reasonably practicable to hold such inquiry; or

(c) where the President or the Governor, as the case may be, is satisfied that in the interest of the security of the State it is not expedient to hold such inquiry.

[4](3) If, in respect of any such person as aforesaid, a question arises whether it is reasonably practicable to hold such inquiry as is referred to in clause(2), the decision thereon of the authority empowered to dismiss or remove such person or to reduce him in rank shall be final.]

Notes on Article 311

Disciplinary Enquiry

The uncommunicated past adverse entries om service record cannot be considered for imposition of punishment is respect of disciplinary enquiry; *Indu Bhushan Dwivedi V. State of Jharkhand* AIR 2010.

The 'authority' is a genericterm term and is used in different places with different meaning and purposes; *Union of India V. Alok Kumar* AIR 2010.

Disciplinary Proceedings

Power of Judicial review in respect of disciplinary proceedings by inquiry officer is confined to decision making process; *State of Uttar Pradesh V. Man Mohan Nath Sinha* AIR 2010.

312. All India Services.-

(1) Notwithstanding anything in [4][Chapter VI of Part VI or Part XI], if the Council of States has declared by resolution supported by not less than two-thirds of the members present and voting that it is necessary or expedient in the national interest so to do, Parliament may by law provide for the creation of one or more all-India services including an all-India judicial service common to the Union and the States; and, subject to the other provisions of this Chapter, regulate the recruitment, and the conditions of service of persons appointed, to any such service.

---

1 Subs. by the Constitution (Fifteenth Amendment) Act, 1963, sec. 10, for clauses(2) and (3) (w.e.f. 5.10.1963).

2 Certain words omitted by the Constitution (Forty-second Amendment) Act, 1976, sec. 44 (w.e.f. 3.1.1977).

3 Subs. by the Constitution (Forty Second Amendment) Act, 1976, sec. 44 for certain words (w.e.f. 3.1.1977).

4 Subs. by the Constitution (Forty-second Amendment) Act, 1963, sec. 10, for clause (3) (w.e.f. 5-10-1963).

(2) The services known at the commencement of this Constitution as the Indian Administrative Service and the Indian Police Service shall be deemed to be services created by Parliament under this article.

[1](3) The All-India judicial service referred to in clause(1) shall not include any post inferior to that of a district judge as defined in article 236.

(4) The law providing for the creation of the all-India judicial service aforesaid may contain such provisions for the amendment of Chapter VI of Part VI as may be necessary for giving effect to the provisions of that law and no such law shall be deemed to be an amendment of this Constitution for the purposes of article 368.]

Notes on Article 312

Central Staffing Scheme

The central staffing scheme as amended in 1996 is not ultravires section of the All India Services Act 1951 on ground of lack of consultation with state governments. Section 3 is an enabling power of the central government to make rules for the regulation of recruitment and conditions of service for persons appointed to the All India Services; *Satya Narain Shukla V. Union of India, AIR 2006.*

[2][312A. Power of Parliament to vary or revoke conditions of service of officers of certain services.-

(1) Parliament may by law-

(a) vary or revoke, whether prospectively or retrospectively, the conditions of service as respects remuneration, leave and pension and the rights as respects disciplinary matters of persons who, having been appointed by the Secretary of State or Secretary of State in Council to a civil service of the Crown in India before the commencement of this Constitution, continue on and after the commencement of the Constitution (Twenty-eighth Amendment) Act, 1972, to serve under the Government of India or of a State in any service or post;

(b) vary or revoke, whether prospectively or retrospectively, the conditions of service as respects pension of persons who, having been appointed by the Secretary of State or Secretary of State in Council to a civil service of the Crown in India before the commencement of this Constitution, retired or otherwise ceased to be in service at any time before the Commencement of the Constitution (Twenty-eight Amendment) Act, 1972:

Provided that in the case of any such person who is holding or has held the office of the Chief Justice or other judge of the Supreme Court or a High Court, the Comptroller and Auditor-General of India, the Chairman or other members of the Union or a State Public Service Commission or the Chief Election Commissioner, nothing in sub-clause (a) or sub-clause (b) shall be construed as empowering Parliament to vary or revoke, after his appointment to such post, the conditions of his service to his disadvantage except in so far as such conditions of service are applicable to him by reason of his being a person appointed by the Secretary of State or Secretary of State in Council to a civil service of the Crown in India.

(2) Except to the extent provided for by Parliament by law under this article, nothing in this article shall affect the power of any Legislature or other authority under any other provision of this Constitution to regulate the conditions of service of persons referred to in clause(1).

1 Ins. by the Constitution (Forty-second Amendment) Act, 1976, sec. 45. (w.e.f. 3-1-1977).

2 Ins. by the Constitution (Twenty-eighth Amendment) Act, 1972, sec. 2 (w.e.f. 29-8-1972).

(3) Neither the Supreme Court nor any other court shall have jurisdiction in-

(a) any dispute arising out of any provision of, or any endorsement on, any covenant, agreement or other similar instrument which was entered into or executed by any person referred to in clause(1), or arising out of any letter issued to such person, in relation to his appointment to any civil service of the Crown in India or his continuance in service under the Government of the Dominion of India or a Province thereof;

(b) any dispute in respect of any right, liability or obligation under article 314 as originally enacted.

(4) The provisions of the article shall have effect notwithstanding anything in article 314 as originally enacted or in any other provision of this Constitution.]

313. Transitional provisions.- Until other provision is made in this behalf under this Constitution, all the laws in force immediately before the commencement of this Constitution and applicable to any public service or any post which continues to exist after the commencement of this Constitution, as an all-India service or as service or post under the Union or a State shall continue in force so far as consistent with the provisions of this Constitution.

314. Provision for protection of existing officers of certain services.-*[Rep. by the Constitution (Twenty-eighth Amendment) Act, 1972, sec. 3, (w.e.f. 29-8-1972).]*

CHAPTER II PUBLIC SERVICE COMMISSIONS

315. Public Service Commissions for the Union and for the States.-

(1) Subject to the provisions of this article, there shall be a Public Service Commission for the Union and a Public Service Commission for each State.

(2) Two or more States may agree that there shall be one Public Service Commission for that group of States, and if a resolution to that effect is passed by the House or, where there are two Houses, by each House of Legislature of each of those States, Parliament may by law provide for the appointment of a joint State Public Service Commission (referred to in this Chapter as Joint Commission) to serve the needs of those States.

(3) Any such law as aforesaid may contain such incidental and consequential provisions as may be necessary or desirable for giving effect to the purposes of the law.

(4) The Public Service Commission for the Union, if requested so to do by the Governor [1][***] of a State, may, with the approval of the President, agree to serve all or any of the needs of the State.

(5) References in this Constitution to the Union Public Service Commission or a State Public Service Commission shall, unless the context otherwise requires, be construed as references to the Commission serving the needs of the Union or, as the case may be, the State as respects the particular matter in question.

Notes on Article 315

Essential Qualification for Appointment

The public service commission can relax essential qualification only if it is expressly given power of relaxation; *Sanjay Kumar Manjul V. Chairman V. UPSC AIR 2007.*

316. Appointment and term of office of members.-

(1) The Chairman and other members of a Public Service Commission shall be appointed, in the case of the Union Commission or a Joint Commission, by the President, and in the case of State Commission, by the Governor [1][***] of the State:

1 The words "or Rajpramukh" omitted by the Constitution (Seventh Amendment) Act, 1956, sec. 29 and Sch (w.e.f. 1.11.1956).

Provided that as nearly as may be one-half of the members of every Public Service Commission shall be persons who at the dates of their respective appointments have held office for at least ten years either under the Government of India or under the Government of a State, and in computing the said period of ten years any period before the commencement of this Constitution during which a person has held office under the Crown in India or under the Government of an Indian State shall be included.

[1][(1A) If the office of the Chairman of the Commission becomes vacant or if any such Chairman is by reason of absence or for any other reason unable to perform the duties of his office, those duties shall, until some person appointed under clause (1) to the vacant office has entered on the duties thereof or, as the case may be, until the Chairman has resumed his duties, be performed by such one of the other members of the Commission as the President in the case of the Union Commission or a Joint Commission, and the Governor of the State in the case of a State, may appoint for the purpose.]

(2) A member of Public Service Commission shall hold office for a term of six years from the date on which he enters upon his office or until he attains, in the case of the Union Commission, the age of sixty five years, and in the case of a State Commission or a Joint Commission, the age of [2][sixty-two years], whichever is earlier:

Provided that-

(a) a member of a Public Service Commission may, by writing under his hand addressed, in the case of the Union Commission or a Joint Commission, to the President, and in the case of a State Commission, to the Governor of the State, resign his office;

(b) a member of a Public Service Commission may be removed from his office in the manner provided in clause(1) or clause(3) of article 317.

(3) A person who holds office as a member of a Public Service Commission shall, on the expiration of his term of office, be ineligible for re-appointment to that office.

317. Removal and suspension of a member of a Public Service Commission.-

(1) Subject to the provisions of clause (3), the Chairman or any other member of a Public Service Commission shall only be removed from his office by order of the President on the ground of misbehaviour after the Supreme Court, on reference being made to it by the President, has, on inquiry held in accordance with the procedure prescribed in that behalf under article 145, reported that the Chairman or such other member, as the case may be, ought on any such ground to be removed.

(2) The President, in the case of the Union Commission or a Joint Commission, and the Governor [3][***] in the case of a State Commission, may suspend from office the Chairman or any other member of the Commission in respect of whom a reference has been made to the Supreme Court under clause(1) until the President has passed orders on receipt of the report of the Supreme Court on such reference.

(3) Notwithstanding anything in clause(1), the president may by order remove from office the Chairman or any other member of a Public Service Commission if the Chairman or such other member, as the case may be,-

(a) is adjudged an insolvent; or

(b) engages during his term of office in any paid employment outside the duties of his office; or

1 Ins. by the Constitution (Fifteenth Amendment) Act, 1963, sec. 11 (w.e.f. 5.10.1963).

2 Subs. by the Constitution (Forty-first Amendment) Act, 1976, sec. 2, for "sixty years".

3 Subs. by the Constitution (Forty-first Amendment) Act, 1976, sec. 2, for "sixty years" (w.e.f. 7.9.1976)

(c) is, in the opinion of the President, unfit to continue in office by reason of infirmity of mind or body.

(4) If the Chairman or any other member of a Public Service Commission is or becomes in any way concerned or interested in any contract or agreement made by or on behalf of the Government of India or the Government of a State or participates in any way in the profit thereof or in any benefit or emolument arising therefrom otherwise than as a member and in common with the other members of an incorporated company, he shall, for the purposes of clause (1), be deemed to be guilty of misbehaviour.

318. Power to make regulations as to conditions of service of members and staff of the commission.- In the case of the Union Commission or a Joint Commission, the President and, in the case of a State Commission, the Governor [1][***] of the state may by regulations-

(a) determine the number of members of the Commission and their conditions of service; and

(b) make provision with respect to the number of members of the staff of the Commission and their conditions of service:

Provided that the conditions of service of a member of a Public Service Commission shall not be varied to his disadvantage after his appointment.

319. Prohibition as to the holding of offices by members of Commission on ceasing to be such members.- On ceasing to hold office-

(a) the Chairman of the Union Public Service Commission shall be ineligible for further employment either under the Government of India or under the Government of a State;

(b) the Chairman of a State Public Service Commission shall be eligible for appointment as the Chairman or any other member of Union Public Service Commission, or as the Chairman of any other State Public Service Commission, but not for any other employment either under the Government of India or under the Government of a State;

(c) a member other than the Chairman of the Union Public Service Commission shall be eligible for appointment as the Chairman of the Union Public Service Commission or as the Chairman of a State Public Service Commission, but not for any other employment either under the Government of India or under the Government of a State;

(d) a member other than the Chairman of a State Public Service Commission shall be eligible for appointment as the Chairman or any other member of Union Public Service Commisson or as the Chairman of that or any other State Public Service Commission, but not for any other employment either under the Government of India or under the Government of a State.

320. Functions of Public Service Commissions.-

(1) It shall be the duty of the Union and the State Public Service Commissions to conduct examinations for appointments to the services of the Union and the services of the State respectively.

(2) It shall also be the duty of the Union Public Service Commission, if requested by any two or more States so to do, to assist those States in framing and operating schemes of joint recruitment for any services for which candidates possessing special qualifications are required.

(3) The Union Public Service Commission or the State Service Commission, as the case may be, shall be consulted-

(a) on all matters relating to methods of recruitment to civil services and for civil posts;

---

1 The words "or Rajprakumh" omitted by the Constitution (Seventh Amendment) Act, 1956, sec. 29 and Sch (w.e.f. 1.11.1956).

(b) on the principles to be followed in making appointments to civil services and posts and in making promotions and transfers from one service to another and on the suitability of candidates for such appointments , promotions or transfers;

(c) on all disciplinary matters affecting a person serving under the Government of India or the Government of a State in a civil capacity, including memorials or petitions relating to such matters;

(d) on any claim by or in respect of a person who is serving or has served under the Government of India or the Government of a State or under the Crown in India or under the Government of an Indian State, in a civil capacity, that any costs incurred by him in defending legal proceedings instituted against him in respect of acts done or purporting to be done in the execution of his duty should be paid out of the Consolidated Fund India, or, as the case may be, out of the Consolidated Fund of the State;

(e) on any claim for the award of a pension in respect of injuries sustained by a person while serving under the Government of India or the Government of a State or under the Crown in India or under the Government of an Indian State, in a civil capacity, and any question as to the amount of any such award, and it shall be the duty of Public Service Commissions to advise on any matter so referred to them and on any other matter which the President , or , as the case may be, the Governor [1][***] of the State, may refer to them:

Provided that the President as respects the all-India services and also as respects other services and posts in connection with the affairs of the Union and the Governor [2][***] as respects other services and posts in connection with the affairs of a State, may make regulations specifying the matters in which either generally, or in any particular class of case or in any particular circumstances, it shall not be necessary for a Public Service Commission to be consulted.

(4) Nothing in clause (3) shall require a Public Service Commission to be consulted as respects the manner in which any provision referred to in clause(4) of article 16 may be made or as respects the manner in which effect may be given to the provisions of article 335.

(5) All regulations made under the proviso to clause (3) by the President or the Governor [3][***] of a State shall be laid for not less than fourteen days before each House of Parliament or the House or each House of the Legislature of the State, as the case may be, as soon as possible after they are made, and shall be subject to such modifications, whether by way of repeal or amendment, as both Houses of Parliament or the House or both Houses of the Legislature of the State may make during the session in which they are so laid.

321. Power to extend functions of Public Service Commissions.- An Act made by Parliament or, as the case may be, the Legislature of a State may provide for the exercise of additional functions by the Union Public Service Commission or the State Public Service Commission as respects the services of the Union or the State and also as respects the services of any local authority or other body corporate constituted by law or of any public institution.

322. Expenses of Public Service Commissions.- The expenses of the Union or a State Public Service Commission, including any salaries, allowances and pensions payable to or in respect of the members or staff of the Commission, shall be charged on the Consolidated Fund of India or, as the case may be, the Consolidated Fund of the State.

---

1 The word "or Rajpramukh" omitted by the Constitution (Seventh Amendment) Act, 1956, sec. 29 and Sch (w.e.f. 1.11.1956).

2 The words "or Rajpramukh as the case may be" omitted by the Constitution (Seventh Amendment) Act, 1956, sec. 29 and Sch (w.e.f. 1.11.1956).

3 The word "or Rajpramukh" omitted by the Constitution (Seventh Amendment) Act, 1956, sec. 29 and Sch.

323. Reports of Public Service Commissions.-

(1) It shall be the duty of the Union Commission to present annually to the President a report as to the work done by the Commission and on receipt of such report the President shall cause a copy thereof together with a memorandum explaining, as respects the cases, if any, where the advice of the Commission was not accepted, the reasons for such non-acceptance to be laid before each House of Parliament.

(2) It shall be the duty of a State Commission to present annually to the Governor [1][***] of the State a report as to the work done by the Commission, and it shall be the duty of a Joint Commission to present annually to the Governor [1][***] of each of the States the needs of which are served by the Joint Commission a report as to the work done by the Commission in relation to that State, and in either case the Governor [2][***], shall, on receipt of such report, cause a copy thereof together with a memorandum explaining, as respects the cases, if any, where the advice of the Commission was not accepted, the reasons for such non-acceptance to be laid before the Legislature of the State.

[3][PART XIV - A

TRIBUNALS

323A. Administrative tribunals.-

(1) Parliament may, by law, provide for the adjudication or trial by administrative tribunals of disputes and complaints with respect to recruitment and conditions of service of persons appointed to public services and posts in connection with the affairs of the Union or of any State or of any local or other authority within the territory of India or under the control of the Government of India or of any corporation owned or controlled by the Government.

(2) A law made under clause (1) may-

  (a) provide for the establishment of an administrative tribunal for the Union and a separate administrative tribunal for each State or for two or more States;

  (b) specify the jurisdiction, powers (including the power to punish for contempt) and authority which may be exercised by each of the said tribunals;

  (c) provide for the procedure (including provisions as to limitation and rules of evidence) to be followed by the said tribunals;

  (d) exclude the jurisdiction of all courts, except the jurisdiction of the Supreme Court under article 136, with respect to the disputes or complaints referred to in clause (1);

  (e) provide for the transfer to each such administrative tribunal of any cases pending before any court or other authority immediately before the establishment of such tribunal as would have been within the jurisdiction of such tribunal if the cause of action on which such suits or proceedings are based had arisen after such establishment;

  (f) repeal or amend any order made by the President under clause (3) of article 371D;

  (g) contain such supplemental, incidental and consequential provisions (including provisions as to fees) as Parliament may deem necessary for the effective functioning of, and for the speedy disposal of cases by, and the enforcement of the orders of, such tribunals.

---

1 The words "or Rajpramukh" omitted by the Constitution (Seventh Amendment) Act, 1956, sec. 29 and Sch (w.e.f. 1.11.1956).

2 The words "or Rajpramukh as the case may be" omitted by the Constitution (Seventh Amendment) Act, 1956, sec. 29 and Sch (w.e.f. 1.11.1956).

3 Part XIV A (containing article 232A and 232B) ins. by the Constitution (Forty-second Amendment) Act, 1976, sec. 46 (w.e.f. 3.1.1977),

(3) The provisions of this article shall have effect notwithstanding anything in any other provision of this Constitution or in any other law for the time being in force.

323B. Tribunals for other matters.-

(1) The appropriate Legislature may, by law, provide for the adjudication or trial by tribunals of any disputes, complaints, or offences with respect to all or any of the matters specified in clause (2) with respect to which such Legislature has power to make laws.

(2) The matters referred to in clause (1) are the following, namely:-

(a) levy, assessment, collection and enforcement of any tax;

(b) foreign exchange, import and export across customs frontiers;

(c) industrial and labour disputes;

(d) land reforms by way of acquisition by the State of any estate as defined in article 31A or of any rights therein or the extinguishment or modification of any such rights or by way of ceiling on agricultural land or in any other way;

(e) ceiling on urban property;

(f) elections to either House of Parliament or the House or either House of the Legislature of a State, but excluding the matters referred to in article 329 and article 329A;

(g) production, procurement, supply and distribution of food-stuffs (including edible oilseeds and oils) and such other goods as the President may, by public notification, declare to be essential goods for the purpose of this article and control of prices of such goods.

[1][(h) rent, its regulation and control and tenancy issues including the rights, title and interest of landlords and tenants,]

[2][(i)] offences against laws with respect to any of the matters specified in sub-clauses (a) to [3][(h)] and fees in respect of any of those matters;

[1][(j)] any matter incidental to any of the matters specified in sub-clauses (a) to [2][(i)].

(3) A law made under clause (1) may-

(a) provide for the establishment of a hierarchy of tribunals;

(b) specify the jurisdiction, powers (including the power to punish for contempt) and authority which may be exercised by each of the said tribunals;

(c) provide for the procedure (including provisions as to limitation and rules of evidence) to be followed by the said tribunals;

(d) exclude the jurisdiction of all courts except the jurisdiction of the Supreme Court under 136, with respect to all or any of the matters falling within the jurisdiction of the said tribunals;

(e) provide for the transfer to each such tribunal of any cases pending before any court or any other authority immediately before the establishment of such tribunal as would have been within the jurisdiction of such tribunal if the causes of action on which such suits or proceedings are based had arisen after such establishment;

(f) contain such supplemental, incidental and consequential provisions (including provisions as to fees) as the appropriate Legislature may deem necessary for the effective functioning of, and for the speedy disposal of cases by, and the enforcement of the orders of, such tribunals.

---

1 Ins. by the Constitution (Seventy-fifth Amendment) Act, 1993 sec.2 (w.e.f. 15-5-1994).

2 Sub-clauses (h) and (i) relettered as sub-clause (i) and (j) by the Constitution (Seventy-fifth Amendment) Act, 1993 sec. 2 (w.e.f. 15-5-1994).

3 Subs. by ibid, for (g).

(4) The provisions of this article shall have effect notwithstanding anything in any other provision of this Constitution or in any other law for the time being in force.

Explanation: In this article, "appropriate Legislature", in relation to any matter, means Parliament or, as the case may be, a State Legislature competent to make laws with respect to such matter in accordance with the provisions of Part XI.]

PART XV

ELECTIONS

324. Superintendence, direction and control of elections to be vested in an Election Commission.-

(1) The superintendence, direction and control of the preparation of the electoral rolls for, and the conduct of, all elections to Parliament and to the Legislature of every State and of elections to the offices of President and Vice-President held under this Constitution [1][***] shall be vested in a Commission (referred to in this Constitution as the Election Commission).

(2) The Election Commission shall consist of the Chief Election Commissioner and such number of other Election Commissioners, if any, as the President may from time to time fix and the appointment of the Chief Election Commissioner and other Election Commissioners shall, subject to the provisions of any law made in that behalf by Parliament, be made by the President.

(3) When any other Election Commissioner is so appointed the Chief Election Commissioner shall act as the Chairman of the Election Commission.

(4) Before each general election to the House of the People and to the Legislative Assembly of each State, and before the first general election and thereafter before each biennial election to the Legislative Council of each State having such Council, the President may also appoint after consultation with the Election Commission such Regional Commissioners as he may consider necessary to assist the Election Commission in the performance of the functions conferred on the Commission by clause (1).

(5) Subject to the provisions of any law made by Parliament, the conditions of service and tenure of office of the Election Commissioners and the Regional Commissioners shall be such as the President may by rule determine:

Provided that the Chief Election Commissioner shall not be removed from his office except in like manner and on the like grounds as a Judge of the Supreme Court and the conditions of service of the Chief Election Commissioner shall not be varied to his disadvantage after his appointment:

Provided further that any other Election Commissioner or a Regional Commissioner shall not be removed from office except on the recommendation of the Chief Election Commissioner.

(6) The President, or the Governor [2][***] of a State, shall, when so requested by the Election Commission, make available to the Election Commission or to a Regional Commissioner such staff as may be necessary for the discharge of the functions conferred on the Election Commission by clause (1).

---

1 The words "including the appointment of election tribunals for the decision of doubts and disputes arising out of or in connection with elections to Parliament and to the Legislatures of States" omitted by the Constitution (Nineteenth Amendment) Act, 1966, sec.2 (w.e.f. 11-12-1966).

2 The words "or Rajpramukh" omitted by the Constitution (Seventh Amendment) Act, 1956, sec. 29 and Sch. (w.e.f. 1-11-1956)

Notes on Article 324

Abolition of post of election commissioners and consequential termination of the service of that post by the president is not illegal and it is not a ground of action. Though the election commission has got very wide power with respect to direction and control, the election commission cannot violate any law. However precautionary measures would not be illegal if it does not violate any statutory provision.

Article 175 viz a viz Article 324: Scope

Both these articles operate in different fields. As far as the time period between the live assemblies is concerned the provisions of Article 174 is mandatory. Article 174 does not deal with elections which is a primary function of the commission under Article 324.

325. No person to be ineligible for inclusion in, or to claim to be included in a special, electoral roll on grounds of religion, race, caste or sex.- There shall be one general electoral roll for every territorial constituency for election to either House of Parliament or to the House or either House of the Legislature of a State and no person shall be ineligible for inclusion in any such roll or claim to be included in any special electoral roll for any such constituency on grounds only of religion, race, caste, sex or any of them.

326. Elections to the House of the People and to the Legislative Assemblies of States to be on the basis of adult suffrage.- The elections to the House of the People and to the Legislative Assembly of every State shall be on the basis of adult suffrage; that is to say, every person who is a citizen of India and who is not less than [1][eighteen years] of age on such date as may be fixed in that behalf by or under any law made by the appropriate Legislature and is not otherwise disqualified under this Constitution or any law made by the appropriate Legislature on the ground of non-residence, unsoundness of mind, crime or corrupt or illegal practice, shall be entitled to be registered as a voter at any such election.

327. Power of Parliament to make provision with respect to elections to Legislatures.- Subject to the provisions of this Constitution, Parliament may from time to time by law make provision with respect to all matters relating to, or in connection with, elections to either House of Parliament or to the House or either House of the Legislature of a State including the preparation of electoral rolls, the delimitation of constituencies and all other matters necessary for securing the due constitution of such House or Houses.

328. Power of Legislature of a state to make provision with respect to elections to such Legislature.- Subject to the provisions of this Constitution and in so far as provision in that behalf is not made by Parliament, the Legislature of a State may from time to time by law make provision with respect to all matters relating to, or in connection with, the elections to the House or either House of the Legislature of the State including the preparation of electoral rolls and all other matters necessary for securing the due constitution of such House or Houses.

329. Bar to interference by courts in electoral matters.- [2][Notwithstanding anything in this Constitution [3][***]

(a) the validity of any law relating to the delimitation of constituencies or the allotment of seats to such constituencies, made or purporting to be made under article 327 or article 328 shall not be called in question in any court;

---

1 Subs. by the Constitution (Sixty-first Amendment) Act, 1988, sec. 2 for "for twenty- one years" (w.e.f. 28-3-1989).

2 Subs. by the Constitution (Thirty-ninth Amendment) Act, 1975, sec. 3, for certain words (w.e.f. 10.8.1975).

3 The words, figures and letter "but subject to the provisions of article 329A" omitted by the Constitution (Forty-fourth Amendment) Act, 1978, sec. 35 (w.e.f. 20-6-1979).

(b) no election to either House of Parliament or to the House or either House of the Legislature of a State shall be called in question except by an election petition presented to such authority and in such manner as may be provided for by or under any law made by the appropriate Legislature.

Notes on Article 329

When case falls under article 191 and 193 and the election process has been completed, bar of article 329(b) will not come into play.

[1][**329A. Special provision as to elections to Parliament in the case of Prime Minister and Speaker.-** [*Rep. by the Constitution (Forty-fourth Amendment) Act, 1978 sec. 36(w.e.f.20-6-1979).]]*

PART XVI

SPECIAL PROVISIONS RELATING TO CERTAIN CLASSES

330. Reservation of seats for Scheduled Castes and Scheduled Tribes in the House of the people.-

(1) Seats shall be reserved in the House of the People for-

(a) the Scheduled Castes;

[2][(b) the Scheduled Tribes except the Scheduled Tribes in the autonomous districts of Assam; and]

(c) the Scheduled Tribes in the autonomous districts of Assam.

(2) The number of seats reserved in any State [3][or Union territory] for the Scheduled Castes or the Scheduled Tribes under clause (1) shall bear, as nearly as may be, the same proportion to the total number of seats allotted to that State [3][or Union territory] in the House of the People as the population of the Scheduled Castes in the State [3][or Union territory) or of the Scheduled Tribes in the State [3][or Union territory] or part of the State [3][or Union territory], as the case may be, in respect of which seats are so reserved, bears to the total population of the State [3][or Union territory].

[4][(3) Notwithstanding anything contained in clause (2), the number of seats reserved in the House of the People for the Scheduled Tribes in the autonomous districts of Assam shall bear to the total number of seats allotted to that State a proportion not less than the population of the Scheduled Tribes in the said autonomous districts bears to the total population of the State.]

[5][*Explanation.* — In this article and in article 332, the expression "population" means the population as ascertained at the last preceding census of which the relevant figures have been published:

Provided that the reference in this *Explanation* to the last preceding census of which the relevant figures have been published shall, until the relevant figures for the first census taken after the year [6][2026] have been published, be construed as a reference to the [7][2001] census.]

---

1 Ins. by the Constitution (Thirty-ninth Amendment) Act, 1975, sec. 4 (w.e.f. 10.8.1975).

2 Subs. by the Constitution (Fifty-first Amendment) Act, 1984, sec. 2, for sub-clause (b) (w.e.f. 16-6-1986).

3 Ins. by the Constitution (Seventh Amendment) Act, 1956, sec. 29 and Sch (w.e.f. 1.11.1956).

4 Ins. by the Constitution (Thirty-first Amendment) Act, 1973, sec. 3 (w.e.f. 17-10-1973).

5 Ins. by the Constitution (Forty-second Amendment) Act, 1973, sec. 47 (w.e.f. 3-1-1977).

6 Subs. by the Constitution (Eighty Fourth Amendment) Act, 2001, sec.2, for "2000" (w.e.f. 21-2-2002).

7 Subs. by the Constitution (Eighty Fourth Amendment) Act, 2001, sec.5 for "1971" (w.e.f. 21-2-2002) and again subs. by the Constitution (Eighty-seventh Amendment) Act, 2002, for '1991' (w.e.f. 22-6-2003).

331. Representation of the Anglo-Indian community in the House of the People.- Notwithstanding anything in article 81, the President may, if he is of opinion that the Anglo-Indian community is not adequately represented in the House of the People, nominate not more than two members of that community to the House of the People.

332. Reservation of seats for Scheduled Castes and Scheduled Tribes in the Legislative Assemblies of the States.-

(1) Seats shall be reserved for the Scheduled castes and the Scheduled Tribes, [1][[2][except the scheduled Tribes in the autonomous districts of Assam, in the Legislative Assembly of every State [3][***].

(2) Seats shall be reserved also for the autonomous districts in the Legislative Assembly of the State of Assam.

(3) The number of seats reserved for the Scheduled Castes or the Scheduled Tribes in the Legislative Assembly of any State under clause (1) shall bear, as nearly as may be, the same proportion to the total number of seats in the Assembly as the population of the Scheduled Castes in the State or of the Scheduled Tribes in the State or part of the State, as the case may be, in respect of which seats are so reserved, bears to the total population of the State.

[4][(3A) Notwithstanding anything contained in clause (3), until the taking effect, under article 170, of the re-adjustment, on the basis of the first census after the year [5][2026], of the number of seats in the Legislative Assemblies of the States of Arunachal Pradesh, Meghalaya, Mizoram and Nagaland, the seats which shall be reserved for the Scheduled Tribes in the Legislative Assembly of any such State shall be —

(a) if all the seats in the Legislative Assembly of such State in existence on the date of coming into force of the Constitution (Fifty-Seventh Amendment) Act, 1987 hereafter in this clause referred to as the existing Assembly) are held by members of the Scheduled Tribes, all the seats except one;

(b) in any other case, such number of seats as bears to the total number of seats, a proportion not less than the number (as on the said date) of members belonging to the Scheduled Tribes in the existing Assembly bears to the total number of seats in existing Assembly.]

[6][(3B) Notwithstanding anything contained in clause (3), until the re-adjustment, under article 170, takes effect on the basis of the first census after the year 2026, of the number of seats in the Legislative Assembly of the State of Tripura, the seats which shall be, such number of seats as bears to the total number of seats, a proportion not less than the number, as on the date of coming into force of the Constitution (Seventy-Second Amendment) Act,1992, of members belonging to the Scheduled Tribes in the Legislative Assembly in existence on the said date bears to the total number of seats in that Assembly.]

(4) The number of seats reserved for an autonomous district in the Legislative Assembly of the State of Assam shall bear to the total number of seats in that Assembly a proportion not less than the population of the district bears to the total population of the State.

---

1 Subs. by the Constitution (Fifty-first Amendment) Act, 1984, sec. 3 for certain words (w.e.f. 16-6-1986).

2 Subs. by the Constitution (Thirty First Amendment) Act, 1973, sec. 4, for certain words.

3 The words and letters "specified in Part A or Part B of the First Schedule" omitted by the Constitution (Seventh Amendment) Act, 1956, sec. 29 and Sch (w.e.f. 1.11.1956).

4 Ins. by the Constitution (Fifty-seventh Amendment) Act, 1987, sec. 2 (w.e.f. 21-9-1987).

5 Subs. by the Constitution (Eighty fourth Amendment)Act, 2001, sec. 7 for "2000" (w.e.f. 21-2-2002).

6 Ins. by the Constitution (Seventy-second Amendment) Act, 1992, sec. 2.

(5) The constituencies for the seats reserved for any autonomous district of Assam shall not comprise any area outside that district. [1][***]

(6) No person who is not a member of a Scheduled Tribe of any autonomous district of the State of Assam shall be eligible for election to the Legislative Assembly of the State from any constituency of that district [1][***];

[2][Provided that for elections to the Legislative Assembly of the State of Assam, the representation of the Scheduled Tribes and non-scheduled Tribes in the constituencies included in the Bodoland Territorial Areas District, so notified, and existing prior to the constitution of the Bodoland Territorial Areas District, shall be maintained.]

333. Representation of the Anglo-Indian community in the Legislative Assemblies of the States.- Notwithstanding anything in article 170, the Governor [3][***] of a State may, if he is of opinion that the Anglo-Indian community needs representation in the Legislative Assembly of the State and is not adequately represented therein [4][nominate one member of that community to the Assembly.]

334. Reservation of seats and special representation to cease after [5][seventy years].- Notwithstanding anything in the foregoing provisions of this Part, the provisions of this Constitution relating to-

(a) the reservation of seats for the Scheduled Castes and the Scheduled Tribes in the House of the people and in the Legislative Assemblies of the States; and

(b) the representation of the Anglo-Indian community in the House of the People and in the Legislative Assemblies of the States by nomination,

shall cease to have effect on the expiration of a period of [5][Seventy years] from the commencement of the Constitution:

Provided that nothing in this article shall affect any representation in the House of the People or in the Legislative Assembly of a State until the dissolution of the then existing House or Assembly, as the case may be.

335. Claims of Scheduled Castes and Scheduled Tribes to services and posts.- The claims of the members of the Scheduled Castes and the Scheduled Tribes shall be taken into consideration, consistently with the maintenance of efficiency of administration, in the making of appointments to services and posts in connection with the affairs of the Union or of a State:

[6][Provided that nothing in this article shall prevent in making of any provision in favour of the members of the Scheduled Castes and the Scheduled Tribes for relaxation in qualifying marks in any examination or lowering the standards of evaluation, for reservation in matters of promotion to any class or classes of services or posts in connection with the affairs of the Union or of a State.]

Notes on Article 335

Article 335 is to be read with article 46. The majority judgment in a leading case on Mandal commission, it was held that a balance between reservation and efficiency with reference to

1 Certain words omitted by the North-Eastern Areas (Reorganisation) Act, 1971 (81 of 1971) sec. 71 (w.e.f. 21-1-1972).

2 Ins. by the Constitution (Ninetieth Amendment) Act, 2003, sec. 2 (w.e.f. 28.9.2003).

3 The words "or Rajpramukh" omitted by the Constitution (Seventh Amendment) Act, 1956 sec. 29 and sch (w.e.f. 1.11.1956).

4 Subs. by the Constitution (Twenty-third Amendment) Act, 1969, sec. 4 for "nominate such number of members of the community to the Assembly as he considers appropriate" (w.e.f. 23.1.1970).

5 Subs. by the Constitution (Ninety fifth Amendment) Act, 2009, sec. 2 for sixty year (w.e.f. 25.1.2010).

6 Ins. by the Constitution (Eighty-second Amendment) Act, 2000, sec. 2 (w.e.f. 8.9.2000).

Schedule Caste, Schedule Tribe and other backward classes should be maintained. Sacrifice of merit may be made for social justice. Whether a particular class has got adequate representation in the state service is a matter of subjective satisfaction of the state government.

336. Special provision for Anglo-Indian community in certain services.-

(1) During the first two years after the commencement of this Constitution, appointments of members of the Anglo-Indian community to posts in the railway, customs, postal and telegraph services of the Union shall be made on the same basis as immediately before the fifteenth day of August, 1947.

During every succeeding period of two years, the number of posts reserved for the members of the said community in the said services shall, as nearly as possible, be less by ten percent, than the numbers so reserved during the immediately preceding period of two years:

Provided that at the end of ten years from the commencement of this Constitution all such reservations shall cease.

(2) Nothing in clause (1) shall bar the appointment of members of the Anglo-Indian community to posts other than, or in addition to, those reserved for the community under that clause if such members are found qualified for appointment on merit as compared with the members of other communities.

337. Special provision with respect to educational grants for the benefit of Anglo-Indian community. During the first three financial years after the commencement of this Constitution, the same grants, if any, shall be made by the Union and by each State [1][***] for the benefit of the Anglo-Indian community in respect of education as were made in the financial year ending on the thirty-first day of March, 1948.

During every succeeding period of three years the grants may be less by ten percent than those for the immediately preceding period of three years:

Provided that at the end of ten years from the commencement of this Constitution such grants, to the extent to which they are a special concession to the Anglo-Indian community, shall cease:

Provided further that no educational institution shall be entitled to receive any grant under this article unless at least forty percent of the annual admissions therein are made available to members of communities other than the Anglo-Indian community.

[2][338. National Commission for Scheduled Castes.-

[3][[4][(1) There shall be a Commission for the Scheduled Castes to be known as the National Commission for the Scheduled Castes.

(2) Subject to the provisions of any law made in this behalf by Parliament, the Commission shall consist of a Chairperson, Vice-Chairperson and three other Members and the conditions of service and tenure of office of the Chairperson, Vice-Chairperson and other Members so appointed shall be such as the President may by rule determine.]

(3) The Chairperson, Vice-Chairperson and other members of the Commission shall be appointed by the President by warrant under his hand and seal.

1 The words and letters "specified in Part A or Part B of the First Schedule" omitted by the Constitution (Seventh Amendment) Act, 1956, sec. 29 and Sch (w.e.f. 1.11.1956).

2 Subs. by the Constitution (Sixty-fifth Amendment) Act, 1990 sec. 2 (w.e.f. 12-3-1992) and subs. by the Constitution (Eighty ninth Amendment) Act, 2003, sec. 2, for the marginal heading "National Commission for Scheduled Castes and Scheduled Tribes" (w.e.f. 12.3.1992).

3 Subs. by the Constitution (Sixty fifth Amendment) Act, 1990, sec. 2, for clauses (1) & (2) (w.e.f. 12.3.1992).

4 Subs. by the Constitution (Eighty ninth Amendment) Act, 2003, sec. 2 for clauses (1) & (2).

[1][(4) The Commission shall have the power to regulate its own procedure.]

[1][(5) It shall be the duty of the Commission-

(a) to investigate and monitor all matters relating to the safeguards provided for the Scheduled Castes [2][***] under this Constitution or under any other law for the time being in force or under any order of the Government and to evaluate the working of such safeguards;

(b) to inquire into specific complaints with respect to the deprivation of rights and safeguards of the Scheduled Castes [2][***];

(c) to participate and advise on the planning process of socio-economic development of the Scheduled Castes [2][***] and to evaluate the progress of their development under the Union and any State;

(d) to present to the President, annually and at such other times as the Commission may deem fit, reports upon the working of those safeguards;

(e) to make in such reports recommendations as to the measures that should be taken by the Union or any State for the effective implementation of those safeguards and other measures for the protection, welfare and socio-economic development of the Scheduled Castes [2][***]; and

(f) to discharge such other functions in relation to the protection, welfare and development and advancement of the Scheduled Castes [2][***] as the President may, subject to the provisions of any law made by Parliament, by the rule specify.]

[1][(6) The President shall cause all such reports to be laid before each House of Parliament along with a memorandum explaining the action taken or proposed to be taken on the recommendations relating to the Union and the reasons for the non-acceptance, if any, of any of such recommendations.]

[1][(7) Where any such report, or any part thereof, relates to any matter with which any State Government is concerned, a copy of such report shall be forwarded to the Governor of the State who shall cause it to be laid before the Legislature of the State along with a memorandum explaining the action taken or proposed to be taken on the recommendations relating to the State and the reasons for the non-acceptance, if any, of any of such recommendations.]

[1][(8) The Commission shall, while investigating any matter referred to in sub-clause (a) or inquiring into any complaint referred to in sub-clause (b) of clause (5), have all the powers of a civil court trying a suit and in particular in respect of the following matters, namely:-

(a) summoning and enforcing the attendance of any person from any part of India and examining him on oath;

(b) requiring the discovery and production of any documents;

(c) receiving evidence on affidavits;

(d) requisitioning any public record or copy thereof from any court or office;

(e) issuing commissions for the examination of witnesses and documents;

(f) any other matter which the President may. by rule, determine.]

[1][(9) The Union and every State Government shall consult the Commission on all major policy matters affecting Scheduled Castes[2][***].]

---

1 Subs. by the Constitution (Sixty-fifth Amendment) Ac, 1990, sec. 2(b), for clauses (1) and (2) (w.e.f. 12.3.1992)

2 The words "and Scheduled Tribes" omitted by the Constitution (Eighty-ninth-Amendment) Act, 2003 sec. 2(c) (w.e.f. 19.2.2004).

[1][(10) In this article, references to the Scheduled Castes shall be construed as including references to such other backward classes as the President may, on receipt of the report of a Commission appointed under clause(1) of article 340 by order specify and also to the Anglo-Indian community.

[2][338A. **National Commission for Scheduled Tribes.-**

(1) There shall be a Commission for the Scheduled Tribes to be known as the National Commission for the Scheduled Tribes.

(2) Subject to the provisions of any law made in this behalf by Parliament, the Commission shall consist of a Chairperson, Vice-Chairperson and three other Members and the conditions of service and tenure of office of the Chairperson, Vice-Chairperson and other members so appointed shall be such as the President may by rule determine.

(3) The Chairperson, Vice-Chairperson and other members of the Commission shall be appointed by the President by warrant under his hand and seal.

(4) The Commission shall have the power to regulate its own procedure.

(5) It shall be the duty of the Commission-

(a) to investigate and monitor all matters relating to the safeguards provided for the Scheduled Tribes [3][***] under this Constitution or under any other law for the time being in force or under any order of the Government and to evaluate the working of such safeguards;

(b) to inquire into specific complaints with respect to the deprivation of rights and safeguards of the Scheduled Tribes;

(c) to participate and advise on the planning process of socio-economic development of the Scheduled Tribes and to evaluate the progress of their development under the Union and any State;

(d) to present to the President, annually and at such other times as the Commission may deem fit, reports upon the working of those safeguards;

(e) to make in such reports recommendations as to the measures that should be taken by the Union or any State for the effective implementation of those safeguards and other measures for the protection, welfare and socio-economic development of the Scheduled Tribes; and

(f) to discharge such other functions in relation to the protection, welfare and development and advancement of the Scheduled Tribes as the President may, subject to the provisions of any law made by Parliament, by the rule specify.

(6) The President shall cause all such reports to be laid before each House of Parliament along with a memorandum explaining the action taken or proposed to be taken on the recommendations relating to the Union and the reasons for the non-acceptance, if any, of any of such recommendations.

(7) Where any such report, or any part thereof, relates to any matter with which any State Government is concerned, a copy of such report shall be forwarded to the Governor of the State who shall cause it to be laid before the Legislature of the State along with a memorandum explaining the action taken or proposed to be taken on the recommendations relating to the State and the reasons for the non-acceptance, if any, of any of such recommendations.

---

1 Clause (3) renumbered as clause (10) by the Constitution (Sixty-fifth Amendment) Act, 1990, sec. 2, (w.e.f. 12-3-1992).

2 Ins. by the Constitution (Eighty ninth Amendment) Act, 2003, sec. 3 (w.e.f. 19.2.2004).

3 The words "and Scheduled Tribes" omitted by the Constutution "Eighty ninth Amendment) Act, 2003, sec. 2. (w.e.f. 19.2.2004)

(8) The Commission shall, while investigating any matter referred to in sub-clause (a) or inquiring into any complaint referred to in sub-clause (b) of clause (5), have all the powers of a civil court trying a suit and in particular in respect of the following matters, namely:-

(a) summoning and enforcing the attendance of any person from any part of India and examining him on oath;

(b) requiring the discovery and production of any documents;

(c) receiving evidence on affidavits;

(d) requisitioning any public record or copy thereof from any court or office;

(e) issuing commissions for the examination of witnesses and documents;

(f) any other matter which the President may by rule, determine.

(9) The Union and every State Government shall consult the Commission on all major policy matters affecting Scheduled Tribes.]

339. Control of the Union over the administration of Scheduled Areas and the welfare of Scheduled Tribes.-

(1) The President may at any time and shall, at the expiration of ten years from the commencement of this Constitution by order appoint a Commission to report on the administration of the Scheduled Areas and the welfare of the Scheduled Tribes in the States [1][***].

The order may define the composition, powers and procedure of the Commission and may contain such incidental or ancillary provisions as the President may consider necessary or desirable.

(2) The executive power of the Union shall extend to the giving of directions to [2][a State] as to the drawing up and execution of schemes specified in the direction to be essential for the welfare of the Scheduled Tribes in the state.

340. Appointment of a Commission to investigate the conditions of backward classes.-

(1) The President may by order appoint a Commission consisting of such persons as he thinks fit to investigate the conditions of socially and educationally backward classes within the territory of India and the difficulties under which they labour and to make recommendations as to the steps that should be taken by the Union or any State to remove such difficulties and to improve their condition and as to the grants that should be made for the purpose by the Union or any state and the conditions subject to which such grants should be made, and the order appointing such Commission shall define the procedure to be followed by the Commission.

(2) A Commission so appointed shall investigate the matters referred to them and present to the President a report setting out the facts as found by them and making such recommendations as they think proper.

(3) The President shall cause a copy of the report so presented together with a memorandum explaining the action taken thereon to be laid before each House of Parliament.

---

1 The words and letters "specified in Part A and Part B of the First Schedule" omitted by the Constitution (Seventh Amendment) Act, 1956, sec. 29 and Sch (w.e.f. 1.11.1956).

2 Subs. by the Constitution (Seventh Amendment) Act, 1956, sec. 29 and Sch., for "any such State" (w.e.f. 1.11.1956).

341. Scheduled Castes.-

(1) The President [1][may with respect to any State [2][or Union territory], and where it is a State [3][***] after consultation with the Governor [4][***] thereof], by public notification[5], specify the castes, races or tribes or parts of or groups within castes, races or tribes which shall for the purposes of this Constitution be deemed to be Scheduled Castes in relation to that State [6][or Union territory, as the case may be.]

(2) Parliament may by law include in or exclude from the list of Scheduled Castes specified in a notification issued under clause (1) any caste, race or tribe or part of or group within any caste, race or tribe, but save as aforesaid a notification issued under the said clause shall not be varied by any subsequent notification.

342. Scheduled Tribes.-

(1) The President [7][may with respect to any State [8][or Union territory], and where it is a State [9][***] after consultation with the Governor [10][***] thereof], by public notification[11], specify the tribes or tribal communities or parts of or groups within tribes or tribal communities which shall for the purposes of this Constitution be deemed to be Scheduled Tribes in relation to that State [12][or Union territory, as the case may be].

(2) Parliament may by law include in or exclude from the list of Scheduled Tribes specified in a notification issued under clause (1) any tribe or tribal community or part of or group within any tribe or tribal community, but save as aforesaid a notification issued under the said clause shall not be varied by any subsequent notification.

Notes on Article 342

Conversion: Schedule Caste status cannot be claimed by a person who is converted to another religion.

Under article 342, the order of the President is final regarding schedule tribes. Court cannot add to, modify or subtract from the Presidential Order. Enquiry can be made before the presidential order. Amendment to the president order can be made only through legislation.

The President can declare that a caste shall be Schedule Caste in particular part of the State and not in other part.

---

1 Subs. by the Constitution (First Amendment) Act, 1951, sec.10 for "may, after consultation with the Governor or Rajpramukh of a State".

2 Ins. by the Constitution (Seventh Amendment) Act, 1956, sec. 29 and Sch.

3 The words and letters "specified in Part A or Part B of the First Schedule" omitted by the Constitution (Seventh Amendment) Act, 1956, sec. 29 and Sch.

4 The words "or Rajpramukh" omitted by the Constitution (Seventh Amendment) Act, 1956, sec. 29 and Sch.

5 See the Constitution (Scheduled Castes) order, 1950 (C.O. 19), the Constitution (Scheduled Castes) (Union Territories) Order, 1951 (C.O. 32), the Constitution (Jammu and Kashmir) Scheduled Castes Order, 1956 (C.O. 52), the Constitution (Dadra and Nagar Haveli) Scheduled Castes Order, 1962 (C.O. 64), the Constitution (Pondicherry) Scheduled Castes Order, 1964 (C.O. 68), the Constitution (Goa, Daman and Diu) Scheduled Castes Order, 1968 (C.O. 81) and the Constitution (Sikkim) Scheduled Castes Order, 1978 (C.O. 110).

6 Ins. by the Constitution (Seventh Amendment) Act, 1956, sec. 29 and Sch. (w.e.f. 1.11.1956).

7 Subs. by the Constitution (First Amendment) Act, 1951, sec. 11, for "may, after consultation with the Governor or Rajpramukh of a State".

8 Ins. by the Constitution (Seventh Amendment) Act, 1956, sec. 29 and Sch.

9 The words and letters "specified in Part A or Part B of the First Schedule" omitted by the Constitution (Seventh Amendment) Act, 1956, sec. 29 and Sch. (w.e.f. 1.11.1956).

10 The words "or Rajpramukh" omitted by the Constitution (Seventh Amendment) Act, 1956, sec. 29 and Sch (w.e.f. 1.11.1956).

11 See the Constitution (Scheduled Tribes) Order, 1950 (C.O. 22), the Constitution (Scheduled Tribes) (Union Territories) Order, 1951 (C.O. 33), the Constitution (Andaman and Nicobar Islands) Scheduled Tribes Order, 1959 (C.O. 58), the Constitution (Dadra and Nagar Haveli) Scheduled Tribes Order, 1962 (C.O. 65), the Constitution (Scheduled Tribes) (Uttar Pradesh) Order, 1967, (C.O. 78), the Constitution (Goa, Daman and Diu) Scheduled Tribes Order, 1968 (C.O. 82), the Constitution (Nagaland) Scheduled Tribes Order, 1970 (C.O. 88) and the Constitution (Sikkim) Scheduled Tribes Order, 1978 (C.O. 111).

12 Ins. by the Constitution (Seventh Amemdment) Act, 1956, sec.29 and Sch.

Scheduled Tribe – Acquisition of Status

The offshoots of the wedlock of tribal woman married to a non tribal husband cannot claim Scheduled Tribe status; *Anjan Kumar V. Union of India AIR 2006.*

PART XVII

OFFICIAL LANGUAGE

CHAPTER 1 — LANGUAGE OF THE UNION

343. Official language of the Union.-

(1) The official language of the Union shall be Hindi in Devanagri script.

The form of numerals to be used for the official purposes of the Union shall be the international form of Indian numerals.

(2) Notwithstanding anything in clause (1), for a period of fifteen years from the commencement of this Constitution, the English language shall continue to be used for all the official purposes of the Union for which it was being used immediately before such commencement:

Provided that the President may, during the said period, by order[1] authorise the use of the Hindi language in addition to the English language and of the Devanagri form of numerals in addition to the international form of Indian numerals for any of the official purposes of the Union.

(3) Notwithstanding anything in this article, Parliament may by law provide for the use, after the said period of fifteen years, of-

(a) the English language, or

(b) the Devanagri form of numerals,

for such purposes as may be specified in the law.

344. Commission and Committee of Parliament on official language.-

(1) The President shall, at the expiration of five years from the commencement of this Constitution and thereafter at the expiration of ten years from such commencement, by order constitute a Commission which shall consist of a Chairman and such other members representing the different languages specified in the Eighth Schedule as the President may appoint, and the order shall define the procedure to be followed by the Commission.

(2) It shall be the duty of the Commission to make recommendations to the President as to-

(a) the progressive use of the Hindi language for the official purposes of the Union;

(b) restrictions on the use of the English language for all or any of the official purposes of the Union;

(c) the language to be used for all or any of the purposes mentioned in article 348;

(d) the form of numerals to be used for any one or more specified purposes of the Union;

(e) any other matter referred to the Commission by the President as regards the official language of the Union and the language for communication between the Union and a State or between one State and another and their use.

1 See C.O. 41.

(3) In making their recommendations under clause (2), the Commission shall have due regard to the industrial, cultural and scientific advancement of India, and the just claims and the interests of persons belonging to the non-Hindi speaking areas in regard to the public services.

(4) There shall be constituted a Committee consisting of thirty members, of whom twenty shall be members of the House of the People and ten shall be members of the Council of States to be elected respectively by the members of the House of the People and the members of the Council of States in accordance with the system of proportional representation by means of the single transferable vote.

(5) It shall be the duty of the Committee to examine the recommendations of the Commission constituted under clause (1) and to report to the President their opinion thereon.

(6) Notwithstanding anything in article 343, the President may, after consideration of the report referred to in clause (5), issue directions in accordance with the whole or any part of that report.

CHAPTER II — REGIONAL LANGUAGES

345. Official language or languages of a State.- Subject to the provisions of articles 346 and 347, the Legislature of a State may by law adopt any one or more of the languages in use in the State or Hindi as the language or languages to be used for all or any of the official purposes of that State:

Provided that, until the Legislature of the State otherwise provides by law, the English language shall continue to be used for those official purposes within the State for which it was being used immediately before the commencement ot this Constitution.

Notes on Article 345

Language for Right to information

In case of supply of information, the public authority is under obligation to give information to citizen in language which he understands; State consumer Dispute Redressal Commission, Uttarakhand State information commission AIR 2010.

346. Official language for communication between one State and another or between a State and the Union.- The language for the time being authorised for use in the Union for official purposes shall be the official language for communication between one State and another State and between a State and the Union:

Provided that if two or more States agree that the Hindi language should be the official language for communication between such States, that language may be used for such communication.

347. Special provision relating to language spoken by a section of the population of a State.- On a demand being made in that behalf the president may, if he is satisfied that a substantial proportion of the population of a State desires the use of any language spoken by them to be recognized by that State, direct that such language shall also be officially recognized throughout that State or any part thereof for such purpose as he may specify.

CHAPTER III — LANGUAGE OF THE SUPREME COURT, HIGH COURTS, ETC.

348. Language to be used in the Supreme Court and in the High Courts and for Acts, Bills, etc.-

(1) Notwithstanding anything in the foregoing provisions of this Part, until Parliament by law otherwise provides-

(a) all proceedings in the Supreme Court and in every High Court,

(b) the authoritative texts-

(i) of all Bills to be introduced or amendments thereto to be moved in either House of Parliament or in the House or either House of the Legislature of a State,

(ii) of all Acts passed by Parliament or the Legislature of a State and of all Ordinances promulgated by the President or the Governor [1][***] of a State, and

(iii) of all orders, rules, regulations and bye-laws issued under this Constitution or under any law made by Parliament or the Legislature of a State,

shall be in the English language.

(2) Notwithstanding anything in sub-clause (a) of clause (1), the Governor of a State may, with the previous consent of the President, authorise the use of the Hindi language, or any other language used for any official purposes of the State, in proceedings in the High Court having its principal seat in that State:

Provided that nothing in this clause shall apply to any judgement, decree or order passed or made by such High Court.

(3) Notwithstanding anything in sub-clause (b) of clause (1), where the Legislature of a State has prescribed any language other than the English language for use in Bills introduced in, or Acts passed by, the Legislature of the State or in Ordinances promulgated by the Governor [1][***] of the State or in any order, rule, regulation or bye-law referred to paragraph (iii) of that sub-clause, a translation of the same in the English language published under the authority of the Governor [1][***] of the State in the Official Gazette of that State shall be deemed to be the authoritative text thereof in the English language under this article.

349. Special procedure for enactment of certain laws relating to language.- During the period of fifteen years from the commencement of this Constitution, no Bill or amendment making provision for the language to be used for any of the purposes mentioned in clause (1) of article 348 shall be introduced or moved in either House of Parliament without the previous sanction of the President, and the President shall not give his sanction to the introduction of any such Bill or the moving of any such amendment except after he has taken into consideration the recommendations of the Commission constituted under clause (1) of article 344, and the report of the Committee constituted under clause (4) of that article.

CHAPTER IV — SPECIAL DIRECTIVES

350. Language to be used in representations for redress of grievances.- Every person shall be entitled to submit a representation for the redress of any grievance to any officer or authority of the Union or a State in any of the languages used in the Union or in the State, as the case may be.

[2][**350A. Facilities for instruction in mother-tongue at primary stage.-** It shall be the endeavour of every State and of every local authority within the State to provide adequate facilities for instruction in the mother-tongue at the primary stage of education to children belonging to linguistic minority groups; and the President may issue such directions to any State as he considers necessary or proper for securing the provision of such facilities.]

[2][**350B. Special Officer for linguistic minorities.-**

(1) There shall be a Special Officer for liguistic minorities to be appointed by the President.

---

1 The words "or Rajpramukh" omitted by the Constitution (Seventh Amendment) Act, 1956, sec. 29 and Sch.(w.e.f. 1.11.1956)

2 Ins. by the Constitution (Seventh Amendment) Act, 1956, sec. 21 (w.e.f. 1.11.1956).

(2) It shall be the duty of the Special Officer to investigate all matters relating to the safeguards provided for linguistic minorities under this Constitution and report to the President upon those matters at such intervals as the President may direct, and the President shall cause all such reports to be laid before each House of Parliament, and send to the Governments of the States concerned.]

351. Directive for development of the Hindi language.- It shall be the duty of the Union to promote the spread of the Hindi language, to develop it so that it may serve as a medium of expression for all the elements of the composite culture of India and to secure its enrichment by assimilating without interfering with its genius, the forms, style and expressions used in Hindustani and in the other languages of India specified in the Eighth Schedule, and by drawing, wherever necessary or desirable, for its vocabulary, primarily on Sanskrit and secondarily on other languages.

PART XVIII

EMERGENCY PROVISIONS

352. Proclamation of Emergency.-

(1) If the President is satisfied that a grave emergency exists whereby the security of India or of any part of the territory thereof is threatened, whether by war or external aggression or [1][armed rebellion], he may, by proclamation, make a declaration to that effect [2][in respect of the whole of India or of such part of the territory as may be specified in the Proclamation.]

[3][*Explanation* — A Proclamation of Emergency delcaring that the security of India or any part of the territory thereof is threatened by war or by external aggression or by armed rebellion may be made before the actual occurrence of war or of any such aggression or rebellion, if the President is satisfied that there is imminent danger thereof.]

[4][(2) A Proclamation issued under clause (1) may be varied or revoked by a subsequent Proclamation.

(3) The President shall not issue a Proclamation under clause (1) or a Proclamation varying such Proclamation unless the decision of the Union Cabinet (that is to say, the Council consisting of the Prime Minister and other Ministers of Cabinet rank appointed under article 75) that such a Proclamation may be issued has been communicated to him in writing.

(4) Every Proclamation issued under this article shall be laid before each House of Parliament and shall, except where it is a Proclamation revoking a previous proclamation, cease to operate at the expiration of one month unless before the expiration of that period it has been approved by resolutions of both Houses of Parliament:

Provided that if any such Proclamation (not being a Proclamation revoking a previous Proclamation) is issued at a time when the House of the People has been dissolved, or the dissolution of the House of the People takes place during the period of one month referred to in this clause, and if a resolution approving the Proclamation has been

---

1 Subs. by the Constitution (Forty-fourth Amendment) Act, 1978, sec. 37, for "internal disturbance" (w.e.f. 20-6-1979).

2 Ins. by the Constitution (Forty-second Amendment) Act, 1976, sec. 48 (w.e.f. 3-1-1977).

3 Ins. by the Constitution (Forty-fourth Amendment) Act, 1978, sec. 37 (w.e.f. 20-6-1979).

4 Subs. by the Constitution (Forty-fourth Amendment) Act, 1978, sec. 37, for clauses (2), (2A) and (3), (w.e.f. 20-6-1979).

passed by the Council of States, but no resolution with respect to such Proclamation has been passed by the House of the People before the expiration of that period, the Proclamation shall cease to operate at the expiration of thirty days from the date on which the House of the People first sits after its reconstitution, unless before the expiration of the said period of thirty days a resolution approving the Proclamation has been also passed by the House of the People.

(5) A Proclamation so approved shall, unless revoked, cease to operate on the expiration of a period of six months from the date of the passing of the second of the resolutions approving the Proclamation under clause (4):

Provided that if and so often as a resolution approving the continuance in force of such a Proclamation is passed by both Houses of Parliament the Proclamation shall, unless revoked, continue in force for a further period of six months from the date on which it would otherwise have ceased to operate under this clause:

Provided further that if the dissolution of the House of the People takes place during any such period of six months and a resolution approving the continuance in force of such Proclamation has been passed by the Council of States but no resolution with respect to the continuance in force of such Proclamation has been passed by the House of the People during the said period, the Proclamation shall cease to operate at the expiration of thirty days from the date on which the House of the People first sits after its reconstitution unless before the expiration of the said period of thirty days, a resolution approving the continuance in force of the Proclamation has been also passed by the House of the People.

(6) For the purposes of clauses (4) and (5), a resolution may be passed by either House of Parliament only by a majority of the total membership of that House and by a majority of not less than two-thirds of the members of that House present and voting.

(7) Notwithstanding anything contained in the foregoing clauses, the President shall revoke a Proclamation issued under clause (1) or a Proclamation varying such Proclamation if the House of the People passes a resolution disapproving, or, as the case may be, disapproving the continuance in force of, such Proclamation.

(8) Where a notice in writing signed by not less than one-tenth of the total number of members of the House of the People has been given, of their intention to move a resolution for disapproving, or, as the case may be, for disapproving the continuance in force of, a Proclamation issued under clause (1) or a Proclamation varying such Proclamation,-

(a) to the Speaker, if the House is in session; or

(b) to the President, if the House is not in session,

a special sitting of the House shall be held within fourteen days from the date on which such notice is received by the Speaker, or, as the case may be, by the President, for the purpose of considering such resolution.]

[1][[2][(9) The Power conferred on the President by this article shall include the power to issue different Proclamations on different grounds, being war or external aggression or [3][armed rebellion] or imminent danger of war or external aggression or [armed rebellion], whether or not there is a Proclamation already issued by the President under clause (1) and such Proclamation is in operation.][4][***]

1 Ins. by the Constitution (Thirty-eighth Amendment) Act, 1975, sec. 5 (retrospectively.).

2 Clause (4) re-numbered as clause (9) by the Constitution (Forty-fourth Amendment) Act, 1978, sec. 37 (w.e.f. 20-6-1979).

3 Subs. by the Constitution (Forty-fourth Amendment) Act, 1978, sec. 37, for internal disturbance" (w.e.f 20-6-1979).

4 Clause (5) omitted by the Constitution (Forty-fourth Amendment) Act, 1978, sec. 37 (w.e.f. 20-6-1979)

353. Effect of Proclamation of Emergency.- While a Proclamation of Emergency is in operation, then-

(a) notwithstanding anything in this Constitution, the executive power of the Union shall extend to the giving of directions to any State as to the manner in which the executive power thereof is to be exercised;

(b) the power of Parliament to make laws with respect to any matter shall include power to make laws conferring powers and imposing duties, or authorising the conferring of powers and the imposition of duties, upon the Union or officers and authorities of the Union as respects that matter, notwithstanding that it is one which is not enumerated in the Union List:

[1][Provided that where a Proclamation of Emergency is in operation only in any part of the territory of India,-

(i) the executive power of the Union to give directions under clause (a), and

(ii) the power of Parliament to make laws under clause (b),

shall also extend to any State other than a State in which or in any part of which the Proclamation of Emergency is in operation if and in so far as the security of India or any part of the territory thereof is threatened by activities in or in relation to the part of the territory of India in which the Proclamation of Emergency is in operation.]

354. Application of provisions relating to distribution of revenues while a Proclamation of Emergency is in operation.-

(1) The President may, while a Proclamation of Emergency is in operation, by order direct that all or any of the provisions of articles 268 to 279 shall for such period, not extending in any case beyond the expiration of the financial year in which such Proclamation ceases to operate, as may be specified in the order, have effect subject to such exceptions or modifications as he thinks fit.

(2) Every order made under clause (1) shall, as soon as may be after it is made, be laid before each House of Parliament.

355. Duty of the Union to protect States against external aggression and internal disturbance.- It shall be the duty of the Union to protect every State against external aggression and internal disturbance and to ensure that the government of every State is carried on in accordance with the provisions of this Constitution.

356. Provisions in case of failure of constitutional machinery in States.-

(1) If the President, on receipt of a report from the Governor [2][***] of a State or otherwise, is satisfied that a situation has arisen in which the Government of the State cannot be carried on in accordance with the provisions of this Constitution, the President may by Proclamation-

(a) assume to himself all or any of the functions of the Government of the State and all or any of the powers vested in or exercisable by the Governor [3][***] or any body or authority in the State other than the Legislature of the State;

(b) declare that the powers of the Legislature of the State shall be exercisable by or under the authority of Parliament;

(c) make such incidental and consequential provisions as appear to the President to be necessary or desirable for giving effect to the objects of the Proclamation, including provisions for suspending in whole or in part the operation of any provisions of this Constitution relating to any body or authority in the State:

---

1 Ins. by the Constitution (Forty-second Amendment) Act, 1976, sec. 49 (w.e.f. 3-1-1977).

2 The words "or Rajpramukh" omitted by the Constitution (Seventh Amendment) Act, 1956, sec. 29 and Sch. (w.e.f. 1.11.1956)

3 The words "or Rajpramukh, as the case may be" omitted by the Constitution (Seventh Amendment) Act, 1956, sec. 29 and Sch.

Provided that nothing in this clause shall authorise the President to assume to himself any of the powers vested in or exercisable by a High Court, or to suspend in whole or in part the operation of any provision of this Constitution relating to High Courts.

(2) Any such Proclamation may be revoked or varied by a subsequent Proclamation.

(3) Every Proclamation under this article shall be laid before each House of Parliament and shall, except where it is a Proclamation revoking a previous Proclamation, cease to operate at the expiration of two months unless before the expiration of that period it has been approved by resolutions of both Houses of Parliament:

Provided that if any such Proclamation (not being a Proclamation revoking a previous Proclamation) is issued at a time when the House of the People is dissolved or the dissolution of the House of the People takes place during the period of two months referred to in this clause, and if a resolution approving the Proclamation has been passed by the Council of States, but no resolution with respect to such proclamation has been passed by the House of the People before the expiration of that period, the Proclamation shall cease to operate at the expiration of thirty days from the date on which the House of the People first sits after its reconstitution unless before the expiration of the said period of thirty days a resolution approving the Proclamation has been also passed by the House of the People.

(4) A Proclamation so approved shall, unless revoked, cease to operate on the expiration of a period of [2][six months from the date of issue of the Proclamation]:

Provided that if and so often as a resolution approving the continuance in force of such a Proclamation is passed by both Houses of Parliament, the Proclamation shall, unless revoked, continue in force for a further period of [1][six months] from the date on which under this clause it would otherwise have ceased to operate, but no such Proclamation shall in any case remain in force for more than three years:

Provided further that if the dissolution of the House of the People takes place during any such period of [2][six months] and a resolution approving the continuance in force of such Proclamation has been passed by the Council of States, but no resolution with respect to the continuance in force of such Proclamation has been passed by the House of the People during the said period, the Proclamation shall cease to operate at the expiration of thirty days, from the date on which the House of the People first sits after its reconstitution unless before the expiration of the said period of thirty days a resolution approving the continuance in force of the Proclamation has been also passed by the House of the People:

[3][Provided also that in the case of the Proclamation issued under clause (1) on the 11th day of May, 1987 with respect to the State of Punjab the reference in the first proviso to this clause to "three years" shall be construed as reference to [4][Five years].]

---

1 Subs. by the Constitution (Forty-fourth Amendment) Act, 1978, sec. 38, for "one year" from the date of the passing of the second of the resolutions approving the Proclamation under clause (3)" (w.e.f. 20-6-1979). The words, "one year" were subs. for the original words "six months" by the Constitution (Forty-second Amendment) Act, 1976, sec. 50 (w.e.f. 3-1-1977).

2 Subs. by the Constitution (Forty-fourth Amendment) Act, 1978, sec. 38, for "one year" (w.e.f. 20-6-1979). The words "one year" were subs. for the original words "six months" by the Constitution (Forty-second Amendment) Act, 1976, sec. 50 (w.e.f. 3-1-1977).

3 Ins. by the Constitution (Sixty-fourth Amendment) Act, 1990, sec. 2(a) (w.e.f. 16-4-1992).

4 Successively subs. by the Constitution (Sixty-seventh Amendment) Act 1990 sec.2 and the Constitution (sixty-eighth Amendment) Act,1991, sec.2 to read as above.

[5][(5) Notwithstanding anything contained in clause (4), a resolution with respect to the continuance in force of a Proclamation approved under clause (3) for any period beyond the expiration of one year from the date of issue of such Proclamation shall not be passed by either House of Parliament unless-

(a) a Proclamation of Emergency is in operation, in the whole of India or, as the case may be, in the whole or any part of the State, at the time of the passing of such resolution, and

(b) the Election Commission certifies that the continuance in force of the Proclamation approved under clause (3) during the period specified in such resolution is necessary on account of difficulties in holding general elections to the Legislative Assembly of the State concerned:][2]

[6][Provided that nothing in this clause shall apply to the Proclamation issued under clause (1) on the 11th day of May, 1987 with respect to the State of Punjab.

357. Exercise of legislative powers under Proclamation issued under article 356.-

(1) Where by a Proclamation issued under clause (1) of article 356, it has been declared that the powers of the Legislature of the State shall be exercisable by or under the authority of Parliament, it shall be competent-

(a) for Parliament to confer on the President the power of the Legislature of the State to make laws, and to authorise the President to delegate, subject to such conditions as he may think fit to impose, the power so conferred to any other authority to be specified by him in that behalf;

(b) for Parliament, or for the President or other authority in whom such power to make laws is vested under sub-clause (a), to make laws conferring powers and imposing duties, or authorising the conferring of powers and the imposition of duties, upon the Union or officers and authorities thereof;

(c) for the President to authorise when the House of the People is not in session expenditure from the Consolidated Fund of the State pending the sanction of such expenditure by Parliament.

[1][(2) Any law made in exercise of the power of the Legislature of the State by Parliament or the President or other authority referred to in sub-clause (a) of clause (1) which Parliament or the President or such other authority would not, but for the issue of a Proclamation under article 356, have been competent to make shall, after the Proclamation has ceased to operate, continue in force until altered or repealed or amended by a competent Legislature or other authority.]

Notes on Article 356 and 357

Judicial Review

The Constitution Forty Second Amendment Act, 1976 had made the President's satisfaction for the making of a Proclamation under article 356 immune from judicial review. But the Forty fourth Amendment Act, 1978 removed this fetter paving the way for the courts to enjoy the

1 Subs. by the Constitution (Forty-fourth Amendment) Act, 1978, sec. 38, for clause (5) w.e.f. 20-6-1979). Clause (5) was ins. by the Constitution (Thirty-eighth Amendment) Act, 1975, sec. 6 (retrospectively).

2 Omitted by the Constitution (Sixty Third Amendment) Act, 1989, sec. 2 (w.e.f. 6-1-1990) which was earlier subs. by the Constitution (Fifty-ninth Amendment) Act, 1988, sec. 2.

3 Proviso subs. by the Constitution (Fifty-ninth Amendment) Act, 1988, sec. 2 and omitted by the Constitution (Sixty-third Amendment) Act, 1989, sec. 2 (w.e.f. 6-1-1990) and similar proviso ins. by the Constitution (Sixty fourth Amendment) Act, 1990, sec. 2 (w.e.f. 16-4-1990).

4 Subs. by the Constitution (Forty-second Amendment) Act, 1976, sec. 51, for clause (2) (w.e.f. 3-1-1977).

power of judicial review. *Dr. Basu, in "The Constitutional Law of India (1988)" pages, 403,* 404 has pointed out that judicial review of a Proclamation under article 356 would lie on any of the grounds upon which any executive determination founded on subjective satisfaction can be questionable. By way of example, he has cited the following grounds:-

(a) That the Proclamation has been made upon a consideration which is wholly extraneous or irrelevant to the purpose for which the power under article 356 had been conferred by the Constitution, namely, a breakdown of the constitutional machinery in a State, or, in other words, where there is no 'reasonable nexus' between the reasons disclosed and the satisfaction of the President, because in such a case, it can be said that there has been no 'satisfaction' of the President which is a condition for exercise of the power under article 356.

(b) That the exercise of the power under article 356 has been *mala fide*, because a statutory order which lacks *bona fides* has no existence in law.

State of Rajasthan v. Union of India, AIR 1977 SC 1361, paragraph 124 (Chandrachud, J., paragraph 144 Bhagwati and Gupta, JJ.) (allowed in Roy v. Union of India, AIR 1982 SC 710, paragraph 27: *State of Rajasthan v. Union of India, AIR 1977 SC 1361, paragraph 123* (Chandrachud, J), 170 (Goswami, J.) 178-179 (Untwalia, J). 203, 206, 208 (Fazal Ali, J.).

Mere dissolution of the Assembly on the advice of the Chief Minister does not bring the case within article 356 of the Constitution; *Arun v. Union of India, AIR 1992 All 1, paragraph 7.*

In *S.R. Bommai v. Union of India, JT (1994) 2 SC 215* the following propositions have been laid down by the Supreme Court dealing with article 356:-

(i) Presidential Proclamation dissolving a State Legislative Assembly is subject to judicial review,

(ii) Burden lies on the Government of India to prove that relevant material existed (to justify the issue of Proclamation).

(iii) Courts would not go into the correctness of the material.

(iv) If the court strikes down the Proclamation it has power to restore the dismissed State Government to office.

(v) A State Government pursuing anti-secular politics is liable to action under article 356.

358. Suspension of provisions of article 19 during emergencies.-

[1][(1)] [2][While a Proclamation of Emergency declaring that the security of India or any part of the territory thereof is threatened by war or by external aggression is in operation], nothing in article 19 shall restrict the power of the State as defined in Part III to make any law or to take any executive action which the State would but for the provisions contained in that Part be competent to make or to take, but any law so made shall, to the extent of the incompetency, cease to have effect as soon as the Proclamation ceases to operate, except as respects things done or omitted to be done before the law so ceases to have effect:

[3][Provided that [4][where such Proclamation of Emergency] is in operation only in any part of the territory of India, any such law may be made, or any such executive action may be taken, under this article in relation to or in any State or Union territory in which

1 Art. 358 re-numbered as clause. (1) thereof by the Constitution (Forty-fourth Amendment) Act, 1978, sec. 39 (w.e.f. 20-6-1979).

2 Subs. by the sec. 39, ibid, for "While a Proclamation of Emergency is in operation" (w.e.f. 20-6-1979).

3 Ins. by the Constitution (Forty-second Amendment) Act, 1976, sec. 52 (w.e.f 3-1-1977).

4 Subs. by the Constitution (Forty-fourth Amendment) Act, 1978, sec. 39, for "where a Proclamation of Emergency" (w.e.f. 20-6-1979).

or in any part of which the Proclamation of Emergency is not in operation, if and in so far as the security of India or any part of the territory thereof is threatened by activities in or in relation to the part of the territory of India in which the Proclamation of Emergency is in operation.]

[5][(2) Nothing in clause (1) shall apply-

(a) to any law which does not contain a recital to the effect that such law is in relation to the Proclamation of Emergency in operation when it is made; or

(b) to any executive action taken otherwise than under a law containing such a recital.]

359. Suspension of the enforcement of the rights conferred by Part III during emergencies.-

(1) Where a Proclamation of emergency is in operation, the President may by order declare that the right to move any court for the enforcement of such of [2][the rights conferred by Part III (except articles 20 and 21)] as may be mentioned in the order and all proceedings pending in any court for the enforcement of the rights so mentioned shall remain suspended for the period during which the Proclamation is in force or for such shorter period as may be specified in the order.

[3][(1A) While an order made under clause (1) mentioning any of [4][the rights conferred by Part III (except articles 20 and 21)] is in operation, nothing in that Part conferring those rights shall restrict the power of the State as defined in the said Part to make any law or to take any executive action which the State would but for the provisions containig in that Part be competent to make or to take, but any law so made shall, to the extent of the incompetency, cease to have effect as soon as the order aforesaid ceases to operate, except as respects things done or omitted to be done before the law so ceases to operate, except as respects things done or omitted to be done before the law so ceases to have effect:]

[5][Provided that where a Proclamation of Emergency is in operation only in any part of the territory of India, any such law may be made, or any such executive action may be taken, under this article in relation to or in any State or Union territory in which or in any part of which the Proclamation of Emergency is not in operation, if and is so far as the security of India or any part of the territory thereof is threatened by activities in or in relation to the part of the territory of India in which the Proclamation of Emergency is in operation.]

[6][(1B) Nothing in clause (1A) shall apply-

(a) to any law which does not contain a recital to the effect that such law is in relation to the Proclamation of Emergency in operation when it is made; or

(b) to any executive action taken otherwise than under a law containing such a recital.]

(2) An order made as aforesaid may extend to the whole or any part of the territory of India:

[7]Provided that where a Proclamation of Emergency is in operation only in a part of the territory of India, any such order shall not extend to any other part of the territory of

1 Ins. by the Constitution (Forty-fourth Amendment) Act, 1978, sec. 39 (w.e.f. 20-6-1979).

2 Subs. by the Constitution (Forty-fourth Amendment) Act, 1978, sec. 40, for "the rights conferred by Part III" (w.e.f. 20-6-1979).

3 Ins. by the Constitution (Thirty-eighth Amendment) Act, 1975, sec. 7 (retrospectively).

4 Subs. by the Constitution (Forty-fourth Amendment) Act, 1978, sec. 40, for "the rights conferred by Part III" (w.e.f. 20-6-1979).

5 Ins. by the Constitution (Forty-second Amendment) Act, 1976, sec. 53 (w.e.f. 3-1-1977).

6 Ins. by the Constitution (Forty-fourth Amendment) Act, 1978, sec. 40 (w.e.f. 20-6-1979).

7 Ins by the Constitution (Forty-second Amendment) Act,1976, sec.53 (w.e.f. 3-1-1977).

India unless the President, being satisfied that the security of India or any part of the territory thereof is threatened by activities in or in relation to the part to the territory of India in which the Proclamation of Emergency is in operation, considers such extension to be necessary.]

(3) Every order made under clause (1) shall, as soon as may be after it is made, be laid before each House of Parliament.

[1]**359A. Application of this Part to the State of Punjab.**-[*Rep. by the Constitution (Sixty Third Amendment) Act, 1989, sec. 3 (w.e.f. 6.1.1990).*]]

360. Provisions as to financial emergency.-

(1) If the President is satisfied that a situation has arisen whereby the financial stability or credit of India or of any part of the territory thereof is threatened, he may by a Proclamation make a declaration to that effect.

[2][(2) A Proclamation issued under clause (1)-

(a) may be revoked or varied by a subsequent Proclamation;

(b) shall be laid before each House of Parliament;

(c) shall cease to operate at the expiration of two months, unless before the expiration of that period it has been approved by resolutions of both Houses of the Parliament:

Provided that if any such Proclamation is issued at the time when the House of the People has been dissolved or the dissolution of the House of the People takes place during the period of two months referred to in sub-clause (c), and if a resolution approving the Proclamation has been passed by the Council of States, but no resolution with respect to such Proclamation has been passed by the House of the People before the expiration of that period, the Proclamation shall cease to operate at the expiration of thirty days from the date on which the House of the People first sits after its reconstitution, unless before the expiration of the said period of thirty days a resolution approving the Proclamation has been also passed by the House of the People.]

(3) During the period any such Proclamation as is mentioned in clause (1) is in operation, the executive authority of the Union shall extend to the giving of directions to any State to observe such canons of financial propriety as may be specified in the directions, and to the giving of such other directions as the President may deem necessary and adequate for the purpose.

(4) Notwithstanding anything in this Constitution-

(a) any such direction may include -

(i) a provision requiring the reduction of salaries and allowances of all or any class of persons serving in connection with the affairs of a State;

(ii) a provision requiring all Money Bills or other Bills to which the provisions of article 207 apply to be reserved for the consideration of the President after they are passed by the Legislature of the State;

(b) it shall be competent for the President during the period any Proclamation issued under this article is in operation to issue directions for the reduction of salaries and allowances of all or any class of persons serving in connection with the affairs of the Union including the Judges of the Supreme Court and the High Courts.

[3][***]

1 Ins by the Constitution (Fifty-ninth Amendment) Act,1988, sec. 3 (w.e.f. 30-3-1988).

2 Subs. by the Constitution (Forty-fourth Amendment) Act, 1978, sec. 41, for clause (2) (w.e.f. 20-6-1979).

3 Clause (5) was ins. by the Constitution (Thirty-eighth Amendment) Act, 1975, sec. 8 (retrospectively) and omitted by the Constitution (Forty-fourth Amendment) Act, 1978, sec. 41 (w.e.f. 20-6-1979).

PART XIX

MISCELLANEOUS

361. Protection of President and Governors and Rajpramukhs.-

(1) The President, or the Governor or Rajpramukh of a State, shall not be answerable to any court for the exercise and performance of the powers and duties of his office or for any act done or purporting to be done by him in the exercise and performance of those powers and duties:

Provided that the conduct of the President may be brought under review by any court, tribunal or body appointed or designated by either House of Parliament for the investigation of a charge under article 61:

Provided further that nothing in this clause shall be construed as restricting the right of any person to bring appropriate proceedings against the Government of India or the Government of a State.

(2) No criminal proceedings whatsoever shall be instituted or continued against the President, or the Governor [1][***] of a State, in any court during his term of office.

(3) No process for the arrest or imprisonment of the President, or the Governor [1][***] of a State, shall issue from any court during his term of office.

(4) No civil proceedings in which relief is claimed against the President, or the Governor [1][***] of a State, shall be instituted during his term of office in any court in respect of any act done or purporting to be done by him in his personal capacity, whether before or after he entered upon his office as President, or as Governor [1][***] of such State, until the expiration of two months next after notice in writing has been delivered to the President or the Governor [1][***] as the case may be, or left at his office stating the nature of the proceedings, the cause of action therefor, the name, description and place of residence of the party by whom such proceedings are to be instituted and the relief which he claims.

[2][**361A. Protection of publication of proceedings of Parliament and State Legislatures.-**

(1) No person shall be liable to any proceedings, civil or criminal, in any court in respect of the publication in a newspaper of a substantially true report of any proceedings of either House of Parliament or the Legislative Assembly, or, as the case may be, either House of the Legislature, of a State, unless the publication is proved to have been made with malice:

Provided that nothing in this clause shall apply to the publication of any report of the proceedings of a secret sitting of either House of Parliament or the Legislative Assembly, or, as the case may be, either House of the Legislature, of a State.

(2) Clause (1) shall apply in relation to reports or matters broadcast by means of wireless telegraphy as part of any programme or service provided by means of a broadcasting station as it applies in relation to reports or matters published in a newspaper.

Explanation— In this article, 'newspaper' includes a news agency report containing material for publication in a newspaper.]

[3][**361B Disqualification for appointment on remunerative political post** – A member of a House belonging to any political party 0who is disqualified for being a member of the House under paragraph 2 of the Tenth Schedule shall also be disqualified to hold any remu-

---

1 The words "or Rajpramukh" omitted by the Constitution (Seventh Amendment) Act, 1956, sec. 29 and Sch (w.e.f. 1.11.1956).

2 Ins. by the Constitution (Forty-fourth Amendment) Act, 1978, sec. 42 (w.e.f. 20-6-1979).

3 Ins by the constitution (Ninety first Amendment Act 2003) (w.e.f. 1.1.2004)

nerative political post for duration of the period commencing from the date of his disqualification till the date on which the term of his office as such member would expire or till the date on which he contests an election to a house and is declared elected, whichever is earlier.

Explanation – For the purpose of this article –

(a) the expressio "House" has the meaning assigned to it in clause (a) of paragraph 1 of the Tenth schedule.

(b) the expression "remunerative political post" mean any office –

  (i) under the Government of India or the Government of a state where the salary or remunration for such office is paid out the public revenue of the Government of India or the Government of the state, as the case may be, or

  (ii) under a body, whether incorporated or not, which is wholly or partially owned by the Government of India or the Government of a state and the salary or remuneration for such office is paid by such body.

362. Rights and privileges of Rulers of Indian States.- *[Rep.by the Constitution (Twenty-sixth Amendment) Act, 1971,sec.2.(w.e.f. 28.12.1971).]*

363. Bar to interference by courts in disputes arising out of certain treaties, agreements, etc.-

(1) Notwithstanding anything in this Constitution but subject to the provisions of article 143, neither the Supreme Court nor any other court shall have jurisdiction in any dispute arising out of any provision of a treaty, agreement, convenant, engagement, *sanad* or other similar instrument which was entered into or executed before the commencement of this Constitution by any Ruler of an Indian State and to which the Government of the Dominion of India or any of its predecessor Governments was a party and which has or has been continued in operation after such commencement, or in any dispute in respect of any right accruing under or any liability or obligation arising out of any of the provisions of this Constitution relating to any such treaty, agreement, covenant, engagement, *sanad* or other similar instrument.

(2) In this article-

  (a) 'Indian State' means any territory recognized before the commencement of this Constitution by His Majesty or the Government of the Dominion of India as being such a State; and

  (b) 'Ruler' includes the Prince, Chief or other person recognized before such commencement by His Majesty or the Government of the Dominion of India as the Ruler of any Indian State.

Notes on Article 363

Dispute Arising out of Treaties

The Treaty of Mandaur entered into in 1818 by Maharaja Holkar is not shown to have continued in operation after commencement of constitution. Hence the source of right claimed does not relate specifically to treaty of Mandsaur. Article 353 does not create bar for court to interfere. *Association of the residents of Mhow V. Union of India AIR 2010.*

[1][**363A. Recognition granted to Rulers of Indian States to cease and privy purses to be abolished.-** Notwithstanding anything in this Constitution or in any law for the time being in force-

(a) the Prince, Chief or other person who, at any time before the commencement of the Constitution (Twenty-sixth Amendment) Act, 1971, was recognized by the President

1 Ins. by the Constitution (Twenty-sixth Amendment) Act, 1971, sec. 3 (w.e.f. 28-12-1971).

as the Ruler of an Indian State or any person who, at any time before such commencement, was recognized by the President as the successor of such Ruler shall, on and from such commencement, cease to be recognized as such Ruler or the successor of such Ruler;

(b) on and from the commencement of the Constitution (Twenty-sixth Amendment) Act, 1971, privy purse is abolished and all rights, liabilities and obligations in respect of privy purse are extinguished and accordingly the Ruler or, as the case may by, the successor of such Ruler, referred to in clause (a) or any other person shall not be paid any sum as privy purse.]

364. Special provisions as to major ports and aerodromes.-

(1) Notwithstanding anything in this Constitution, the President may by public notification direct that as from such date as may be specified in the notification-

(a) any law made by Parliament or by the Legislature of a State shall not apply to any major port or aerodrome or shall apply thereto subject to such exceptions or modifications as may be specified in the notification, or

(b) any existing law shall cease to have effect in any major port or aerodrome except as respects things done or omitted to be done before the said date, or shall in its application to such port or aerodrome have effect subject to such exceptions or modifications as may be specified in the notification.

(2) In this article-

(a) 'major port' means a port declared to be a major port by or under any law made by Parliament or any existing law and includes all areas for the time being included within the limits of such port;

(b) 'aerodrome' means aerodrome as defined for the purposes of the enactments relating to airways, aircraft and air navigation.

365. Effect of failure to comply with, or to give effect to, directions given by the Union.- Where any State has failed to comply with, or to give effect to, any directions given in the exercise of the executive power of the Union under any of the provisions of this Constitution, it shall be lawful for the President to hold that a situation has arisen in which the government of the State cannot be carried on in accordance with the provisions of this Constitution.

366. Definitions.- In this Constitution, unless the context otherwise requires, the following expressions have the meanings hereby respectively assigned to them, that is to say-

(1) 'agricultural income' means agricultural income as defined for the purposes of the enactments relating to Indian income-tax;

(2) 'an Anglo-Indian' means a person whose father or any of whose other male progenitors in the male line is or was of European descent but who is domiciled within the territory of India and is or was born within such territory of parents habitually resident therein and not established there for temporary purposes only;

(3) 'article' means an article of this Constitution;

(4) 'borrow' includes the raising of money by the grant of annuities, and 'loan' shall be construed accordingly; [1][***]

(5) 'clause'means a clause of the article in which the expression occurs;

(6) 'corporation tax' means any tax on income, so far as that tax is payable by the companies and is a tax in the case of which the following conditions are fulfilled:-

---

1 Clause (4A) was ins. by the Constitution (Forty-second Amendment) Act, 1976, sec. 54 (w.e.f. 3-1-1977) and omitted by the Constitution (Forty-third Amendment) Act, 1977, sec.11 (w.e.f. 13-4-1978).

(a) that it is not chargeable in respect of agricultural income;

(b) that no deduction in respect of the tax paid by companies is, by any enactments which may apply to the tax, authorised to be made from dividends payable by the companies to individuals;

(c) that no provision exists for taking the tax so paid into account in computing for the purposes of Indian income-tax the total income of individuals receiving such dividends, or in computing the Indian income-tax payable by, or refundable to, such individuals;

(7) 'corresponding Province', 'corresponding Indian State' or 'corresponding State' means in cases of doubt such Province, Indian State or State as may be determined by the President to be the corresponding Province, the corresponding Indian state or the corresponding State, as the case may be, for the particular purpose in question;

(8) 'debt' includes any liability in respect of any obligation to repay capital sums by way of annuity and any liability under any guarantee, and 'debt charges' shall be construed accordingly;

(9) 'estate duty' means a duty to be assessed on or by reference to the principal value, ascertained in accordance with such rules as may be prescribed by or under laws made by Parliament or the Legislature of a State relating to the duty, of all property passing upon death or deemed, under the provisions of the said laws, so to pass;

(10) 'existing law' means any law, Ordinance, order, bye-law, rule or regulation passed or made before the commencement of this Constitution by any Lgislature, authority or person having power to make such a law, Ordinance, order, bye-law, rule or regulation;

(11) 'Federal Court' means the Federal Court constituted under the Government of India Act, 1935;

(12) 'goods' includes all materials, commodities, and articles;

(13) 'guarantee' includes any obligation undertaken before the commencement of this Constitution to make payments in the event of the profits of an undertaking falling short of a specified amount;

(14) 'High Court' means any court which is deemed for the purposes of this Constitution to be a High Court for any State and includes-

(a) any court in the territory of India constituted or reconstituted under this Constitution as a High Court, and

(b) any other court in the territory of India which may be declared by Parliament by law to be a High Court for all or any of the purposes of this Constitution;

(15) 'Indian State' means any territory which the Government of the Dominion of India recognized as such a State;

(16) 'Part' means a part of this Constitution;

(17) 'pension' means a pension, whether contributory or not, of any kind whatsoever payable to or in respect of any person, and includes retired pay so payable, a gratuity so payable and any sum or sums so payable by way of the return, with or without interest thereon or any other addition thereto, of subscriptions to a provident fund;

(18) 'Proclamation of Emergency' means a Proclamation issued under clause (1) of article 352;

(19) 'public notification' means a notification in the Gazette of India, or, as the case may be, the Official Gazette of a State;

(20) 'railway' does not include-

(a) a tramway wholly within a municipal area, or

(b) any other line of communication wholly situated in one State and declared by Parliament by law not to be railway;[1][***]

[2][(22) 'Ruler' means the Prince, Chief or other person who, at any time before the commencement of the Constitution (Twenty-sixth Amendment) Act, 1971, was recognized by the President as the Ruler of an Indian State or any person who at any time before such commencement, was recognized by the President as the successor of such Ruler;]

(23) 'Schedule' means a Schedule to this Constitution;

(24) 'Scheduled Castes' means such castes, races or tribes or parts of or groups within such castes, races or tribes as are deemed under article 341 to be Scheduled Castes for the purposes of this Constitution;

(25) 'Scheduled Tribes' means such tribes or tribal communities or parts of or groups within such tribes or tribal communities as are deemed under article 342 to be Scheduled Tribes for the purposes of this Constitution;

(26) 'securities' includes stock;[3][***]

(27) 'sub-clause' means a sub-clause of the clause in which the expression occurs;

(28) 'taxation' includes the imposition of any tax or impost, whether general or local or special, and "tax" shall be construed accordingly;

(29) ' tax on income' includes a tax in the nature of an excess profits tax;

[4][(29A) 'tax on the sale or purchase of goods' includes-

(a) a tax on the transfer, otherwise than in pursuance of a contract, of property in any goods for cash, deferred payment or other valuable consideration;

(b) a tax on the transfer of property in goods (whether as goods or in some other form) involved in the execution of a works contract;

(c) a tax on the delivery of goods on hire-purchase or any system of payment by instalments;

(d) a tax on the transfer of the right to use any goods for any purpose (whether or not for a specified period) for cash, deferred payment or other valuable consideration;

(e) a tax on the supply of goods by any unincorporated association or body of persons to a member thereof for cash, deferred payment or other valuable consideration;

(f) a tax on the supply, by way of or as part of any service or in any other manner whatsoever, of goods, being food or any other article for human consumption or any drink (whether or not intoxicating), where such supply or service is for cash, deferred payment or other valuable consideration,

and such transfer, delivery or supply of any goods shall be deemed to be a sale of those goods by the person making the transfer, delivery or supply and a purchase of those goods by the person to whom such transfer, delivery or supply is made;]

[5][(30) 'Union territory' means any Union territory specified in the First Schedule and includes any other territory comprised within the territory of India but not specified in that Schedule.]

---

1 Clause (21) omitted by the Constitution (Seventh Amendment) Act, 1956, sec. 29 and Sch (w.e.f. 1.11.1956).

2 Subs. by the Constitution (Twenty-sixth Amendment) Act, 1971, sec. 4, for clause (22) (w.e.f. 28.12.1971).

3 Clause (26A) was ins. by the Constitution (Forty-second Amendment) Act, 1976, sec. 54 (w.e.f. 1-2-1977) and omitted by the Constitution (Forty-third Amendment) Act, 1977, sec. 11 (w.e.f. 13-4-1978).

4 Ins. by the Constitution (Forty-sixth Amendment) Act, 1982, sec. 4 (w.e.f. 2.2.1983).

5 Subs. by the Constitution (Seventh Amendment) Act, 1956, sec. 29 and Sch, for clause (30) (w.e.f. 1.11.1956).

367. Interpretation.-

(1) Unless the context otherwise requires, the General Clauses Act, 1897, shall, subject to any adaptations and modifications that may be made therein under article 372, apply for the interpretation of this Constitution as it applies for the interpretation of an Act of the Legislature of the Dominion of India.

(2) Any reference in this Constitution to Acts or laws of, or made by, Parliament, or to Acts or laws of, or made by, the Legislature of a State [1][***], shall be construed as including a reference to an Ordinance made by the President or, to an Ordinance made by a Governor [2][***] as the case may be.

(3) For the purposes of this Constitution 'foreign State' means any State other than India: Provided that, subject to the provisions of any law made by Parliament, the President may by order[3] declare any State not to be a foreign State for such purposes as may be specified in the order.

PART XX

AMENDMENT OF THE CONSTITUTION

368. [4][Power of Parliament to amend the Constitution and procedure therefor].-

[5][(1) Notwithstanding anything in this Constitution, Parliament may in exercise of its constituent power amend by way of addition, variation or repeal any provision of this Constitution in accordance with the procedure laid down in this article.]

[6][(2)] An amendment of this Constitution may be initiated only by the introduction of a Bill for the purpose in either House of Parliament, and when the Bill is passed in each House by a majority of the total membership of that House and by a majority of not less than two-thirds of the members of that House present and voting, [7][it shall be presented to the President who shall give his assent to the Bill and thereupon] the Constitution shall stand amended in accordance with the terms of the Bill:

Provided that if such amendment seeks to make any change in-

(a) article 54, article 55, article 73, article 162, or article 241, or

(b) Chapter IV of Part V, Chapter V of Part VI, or Chapter I of Part XI, or

(c) any of the Lists in the Seventh Schedule, or

(d) the representation of States in Parliament, or

(e) the provisions of this article,

1 The words and letters "specified in Part A or Part B of the first Schedule" omitted by the Constitution (Seventh Amendment) Act, 1956, sec. 29 and Sch.(w.e.f. 1-11-1956)

2 The words "or Rajpramukh" omitted by the Constitution (Seventh Amendment) Act, 1956, sec. 29 and and Sch.(w.e.f. 1-11-1956)

3 See the Constitution (Declaration as to Foreign States) Order, 1950 (C.O.2.).

4 Subs. by the Constitution (Twenty-fourth Amendment) Act, 1971, sec. 3, for "Procedure for amendment of the Constitution".(w.e.f. 5-11-1971)

5 Ins. by the Constitution (Twenty-fourth Amendment) Act, 1971, sec. 3.(w.e.f. 5-11-1971)

6 Article 368 renumbered as clause (2) by the Constitution (Twenty-fourth Amendment) Act, 1971, sec. 3.(w.e.f. 5-11-1971). Earlier article 368 was amended by the constitution (Seventh Amendment) Act, 1956, sec 29 and sch. (w.e.f. 1-11-1956)

7 Subs. by the Constitution (Twenty-fourth Amendment) Act, 1971, sec. 3(c), for to the certain words. (w.e.f. 5-11-1971)

the amendment shall also require to be ratified by the Legislatures of not less than one-half of the States [1][***] by resolutions to that effect passed by those Legislatures before the Bill making provision for such amendment is presented to the President for assent.

[2][(3) Nothing in article 13 shall apply to any amendment made under this article.]

[3][(4) No amendment of this Constitution (including the provisions of Part III) made or purporting to have been made under this article [whether before or after the commencement of section 55 of the Constitution (Forty-second Amendment) Act, 1976] shall be called in question in any court on any ground.]

[3][5. For the removal of doubts, it is hereby declared that there shall be no limitation whatever on the constituent power of Parliament to amend by way of addition, variation or repeal the provisions of this Constitution under this article.]

Notes on Article 368

Article 368 dealing with the amendent of the Constitution makes the Indian Parliament the sole repository of the constituent power. As outlined in the provisions, a 'facile procedure' for amendment has been adopted in India. Hence, the elements of flexibility were imported into a federal Constitution which is inherently rigid in nature. Until the case of Golaknath Vs. State of Punjab, Constitution Amendment Acts were not ordinary laws and were passed by Parliament in exercise of its constituent powers as distinct from ordinary legislative powers. There was no limitation on the constituent power of the Parliament. Under Article 368, the Parliament could amend any provision of the Constitution including the fundamental rights and Article 368 itself.

In *Shankari Prasad v.Union of India, AIR 1951 SC 458*, the Supreme Court held that the 'law' in Article 13 meant ordinary legislation made by Parliament and hence would not include an amendment of the Constitution. This was also upheld in the case of *Sajjan Singh Vs. State of Rajasthan (AIR 1965 SC 845).*

But in the *Golakh Nath v. State of Punjab (AIR 1967 SC 1643)* case, the Supreme Court by a special majority reversed its earlier decisions and held that the fundamental rights contained in Part III of the Constitution were unamendable and transcendental. The Court further ruled that article 368 just dealt with procedure of amendment and did not give Parliament any susbtantive power to amend the Constitution. The power to amend the Constitution was also a legislative power conferred by article 245, hence a Constitution Amendment Act was a "law" within the purview of Article 13(2).

The Golakhnath case created some sort of a furore in the Indian political system. The Parliament sought to supersede it by amending Article 368 itself vide the Constitution Twenty fourth Amendment Act, 1971. The said Amendment Act provided that an amendment of the Constitution passed in accordance with Article 368, will not be 'law' within the meaning of Article 13 and that its validity cannot be questioned on the ground that it contravenes any of the fundamental rights. In 1973, the validity of the 24th Amendment was challenged in *Keshavanand Bharati v. State of Kerala, AIR (1973 SC 1461)*. The Supreme Court reviewed the decision in the Golak Nath case and ten of 13 Thirteen judges upheld the validity of the 24th Amendment Act and overruled the law declared in case of Golak Nath. Thus, it was established again that a Constitution Amendment Act, passed by Parliament, is not a 'law' within the meaning of Article 13. The case upheld the validity of clause (4) of Article 13 which reads "Nothing in this Article (i.e. Article 13) shall apply to any amendment made under article 368".

---

1 The words and letters "specified in Parts A and B of the First Schedule" omitted by Constitution (Seventh Amendment) Act, 1956, sec. 29 and Sch. (w.e.f. 1-11-1956)

2 Ins. by the Constitution (Twenty-fourth-Amendment) Act, 1971, sec. 3(d). (w.e.f. 5-11-1971)

3 Clauses 4 & 5 inserted by the Constitution (Forty-second-Amendment) Act, 1976, sec. 55. (w.e.f. 3-1-1977)

But on the question whether the amending power under article 368 is absolute and unlimited, by a majority of 7:6 the Supreme Court ruled that Article 368 does not enable Parliament to alter the 'basic structure' of the Constitution. What comes within the ambit of 'basic structure' was not defined.

Emboldened by the favourable decision in the *Keshavanand* case, the Parliament vide Forty second Amendment Act, 1976 added clauses 4 & 5 to article 368 to dilute the limitation of 'basic features' to the amending powers of Parliament. These clauses established the unlimited constituent power of the Parliament and made the Constitution Amendments immune from judicial review.

Decisive shift

The whole scenario was turned turtle in the *Minerva Mills v. Union of India, AIR 1980 SC (1789)*. The Supreme Court invoked the "doctrine of basic structure" by holding clauses 4 and 5 as void on the ground that the amendment sought to obliterate the judical review which is a basic feature of the Constitution.

The present position of the doctrine of 'basic features' is that so long as the decision of the Keshavanand Bharti case is not overturned by another full bench of the Supreme Court, any amendment to the Constitution can be questioned on the ground of infringement of one or the other basic features of the Constitution.

Basic Features

No list of basic features has been prepared by the Courts. Judicial decisions have pointed out several basic features. A few judgments dealing with basic featrues are as under:

(i) Election free and fair *Kihota Hollahon v. Zachilhu, AIR 1993 SC 412 paragraphs 18, 46 and 104.*

(ii) Principal of equality not every feature of equality, but (the quintessence of equal justice); *Raghunath Rao v. Union of India, AIR 1993 SC 1267 paragraphs 96, 176,185*

(iii) Judicial Review;*Subhash v. Union of India, AIR 1990 SC 631 paragraph 44.*

(iv) Rule of law; *Shri Kumar v. Union of India, (1992) AIR 2 SCC 428, paragraph 37.*

From the various decisions of the Supreme Court the following list of basic features may be drawn up:

(i) Supremacy of the Constitution

(ii) Rule of law

(iii) Preamble

(iv) Judicial review, Arts. 32 and 226

(v) The essence of Fundamental rights under Part III

(vi) Federation

(vii) Secularism

(viii) The Parliamentary system of Government

(ix) Independence of the judiciary

(x) Powers of the Supreme Court under Articles 32, 136, 141 and 142

The present scenario is that the Supreme Court and the High Courts can look into any amendment of the Constitution and can declare it *ultravires* if it is inconsistent with any of the provisions of the Constitution. Article13 determines the constitutionality of any Constitution Amendment. Similarly, the Supreme Court under Article 32 and the High Courts under article 226 enjoy the power of judicial review which acts as a limitation on the constituent power of the Parliament. Hence, amending procedure under article 368 should be read alongwith articles 13, 32 and 226 and also with various judicial decisions.

PART XXI

[1][TEMPORARY, TRANSITIONAL AND SPECIAL PROVISIONS]

369. Temporary power to Parliament to make laws with respect to certain matters in the State List as if they were matters in the Concurrent List.-Notwithstanding anything in this Constitution, Parliament shall, during a period of five years from the commencement of this Constitution, have power to make laws with respect to the following matters as if they were enumerated in the Concurrent List, namely:

(a) trade and commerce within a State in, and the production, supply and distribution of, cotton and woollen textiles, raw cotton (including ginned cotton and unginned cotton or kapas), cotton seed, paper (including newsprint), food stuffs (including edible oil-seeds and oil), cattle fodder (including oil-cakes and other concentrates), coal (including coke and derivatives of coal), iron, steel and mica;

(b) offences against laws with respect to any of the matters mentioned in clause (a), jurisdiction and powers of all courts except the Supreme Court with respect to any of those matters, and fees in respect of any of those matters but not including fees taken in any court,

but any law made by Parliament, which Parliament would not but for the provisions of this article have been competent to make, shall, to the extent of the incompetency, cease to have effect on the expiration of the said period, except as respects things done or omitted to be done before the expiration thereof.

[2][**370. Temporary provisions with respect to the State of Jammu and Kashmir.-**

(1) Notwithstanding anything in this Constitution,-

(a) the provisions of article 238 shall not apply in relation to the State of Jammu and Kashmir;*

(b) the power of Parliament to make laws for the said State shall be limited to-

(i) those matters in the Union List and the Concurrent List which, in consultation with the Government of the State, are declared by the President to correspond to matters specified in the Instrument of Accession governing the accession of the State to the Dominion of India as the matters with respect to which the Dominion Legislature may make laws for that State; and

(ii) such other matters in the said Lists, as, with the concurrence of the Government of the State, the President may by order specify.

Explanation: For the purposes of this article, the Government of the State means the person for the time being recognised by the President as the Maharaja of Jammu and Kashmir acting on the advice of the Council of Ministers for the time being in office under the Maharaja's Proclamation dated the fifth day of March, 1948;

---

1 Sub. by the Constitution (Thirteenth Amendment) Act, 1962, sec. 2(a), for "TEMPORARY AND TRANSITIONAL PROVISIONS" (w.e.f. 1-12-1963).

2 In exercise of the powers conferred by this article the President, on the recommendation of the Constituent Assembly of the State of Jammu and Kashmir, declared that, as from the 17th day of November, 1952, the said article 370 shall be operative with the modification that for the Explanation in clause (1) thereof the folloiwng Explanation is substituted, namely:—Explanation: For the purposes of this article, the Government of the State means the person for the time being recognized by the President on the recommendation of the Legislative Assembly of the State as the "Sadar-i-Riyasat" of Jammu & Kashmir, acting on the advice of Council of Ministers of the State for the time being in office.

**Now "Governor" (Ministry of Law Order No. C.O. 44, dated the 15th November, 1952.)

* Article 238 which was included in Part vii has been repealed by the constitution (Seventh Amendment) Act 1956, Sec 29 and Sch. (w.e.f. 1.11.1956)

(c) the provisions of article 1 and of this article shall apply in relation to that State;

(d) such of the other provisions of this Constitution shall apply in relation to that State subject to such exceptions and modifications as the President may by order[1] specify:

Provided that no such order which relates to the matters specified in the Instrument of Accession of the State referred to in paragraph (i) of sub-clause (b) shall be issued except in consultation with the Government of the State:

Provided further that no such order which relates to matters other than those referred in the last preceding proviso shall be issued except with the concurrence of that Government.

(2) If the concurrence of the Government of the State referred to in paragraph (ii) of sub-clause (b) of clause (1) or in second proviso to sub-clause (d) of that clause be given before the Constituent Assembly for the purpose of framing the Constitution of the State is convened, it shall be placed before such Assembly for such decision as it may take thereon.

(3) Notwithstanding anything in the foregoing provisions of this article, the President may, by pubic notification, declare that this article shall cease to be operative or shall be operative only with such exceptions and modifications and from such date as he may specify:

Provided that the recommendation of the Constituent Assembly of the State referred to in clause (2) shall be necessary before the President issues such a notification.

[2]371. Special provisions with respect to the State of [3][***] Maharashtra and Gujarat.— [4][***]

(2) Notwithstanding anything in this Constitution, the President may by order made with respect to [5][the State of Maharashtra or Gujarat], provide for any special responsibility of the Governor for-

(a) the establishment of separate development boards for Vidarbha, Marathwada, [6][and the rest of Maharashtra or, as the case may be,] Saurashtra, Kutch and the rest of Gujarat with the provision that a report on the working of each of these boards will be placed each year before the State Legislative Assembly:

(b) the equitable allocation of funds for developmental expenditure over the said areas, subject to the requirements of the State as a whole; and

(c) an equitable arrangement providing adequate facilities for technical education and vocational training, and adequate opportunities for employment in service under the control of the State Government, in respect of all the said areas, subject to the requirements of the State as a whole.]

[7][371A. Special provision with respect to the State of Nagaland.-

(1) Notwithstanding anything in this Constitution,-

---

1 See the Constitution (Application to Jammu and Kashmir) Order, 1954, (C.O. 48), as amended from time to time.

2 Subs. by the Constitution (Seventh Amendment) Act, 1956, sec. 22, for article 371. (w.e.f. 1-11-1956)

3 The words "Andhra Pradesh", omitted by the Constitution (Thirty-second Amendment) Act, 1973, sec. 2 (w.e.f. 1-7-1974).

4 Clause (1) omitted by the Constitution (Thirty-second Amendment) Act, 1973, sec. 2 (w.e.f. 1-7-1974).

5 Subs. by the Bombay Reorganisation Act, 1960 (11 of 1960), sec. 85(a) for "the State of Bombay" (w.e.f. 1-5-1960).

6 Subs. by the Bombay Reorganization Act, 1960 (11 of 1960), sec. 85(b), for "the rest of Maharashtra". (w.e.f. 1-5-1960).

7 Ins. by the Constitution (Thirteenth Amendment) Act, 1962, sec. 2(b) (w.e.f. 1-12-1963).

(a) no Act of Parliament in respect of-
  (i) religious or social practices of the Nagas,
  (ii) Naga customary law and procedure,
  (iii) administration of civil and criminal justice involving decisions according to Naga customary law,
  (iv) Ownership and transfer of land and its resources,

  shall apply to the State of Nagaland unless the Legislative Assembly of Nagaland by a resolution so decides;

(b) the Governor of Nagaland shall have special responsibility with respect to law and order in the State of Nagaland for so long as in his opinion internal disturbances occurring in the Naga Hills- Tuensang Area immediately before the formation of that State continue therein or in any part thereof and in the discharge of his functions in relation thereto the Governor shall, after consulting the Council of Ministers, exercise his individual judgment as to the action to be taken:

  Provided that if any question arises whether any matter is or is not a matter as respects which the Governor is under this sub-clause required to act in the exercise of his individual judgment, the decision of the Governor in his discretion shall be final, and the validity of anything done by the Governor shall not be called in question on the ground that he ought or ought not to have acted in the exercise of his individual judgment:

  Provided further that if the President on receipt of a report from the Governor or otherwise is satisfied that it is no longer necessary for the Governor to have special responsibility with respect to law and order in the State of Nagaland he may by order direct that the Governor shall cease to have such responsibility with effect from such date as may be specified in the order;

(c) in making his recommendation with respect to any demand for a grant, the Governor of Nagaland shall ensure that any money provided by the Government of India out of the Consolidated Fund of India for any specific service or purpose is included in the demand for a grant relating to that service or purpose and not in any other demand;

(d) as from such date as the Governor of Nagaland may by public notification in this behalf specify, there shall be established a regional council for Tuensang district consisting of thirty-five members and the Governor shall in his discretion make rules providing for-
  (i) the composition of the regional council and the manner in which the members of the regional council shall be chosen:

    Provided that the Deputy Commissioner of the Tuensang district shall be Chairman *ex-officio* of the regional council and the Vice-Chairman of the regional council shall be elected by the members thereof from amongst themselves;
  (ii) the qualifications for being chosen as, and for being, members of the regional council;
  (iii) the term of office of, and the salaries and allowances, if any, to be paid to members of, the regional council;
  (iv) the procedure and conduct of business of the regional council;
  (v) the appointment of officers and staff of the regional council and their conditions of services; and
  (vi) any other matter in respect of which it is necessary to make rules for the constitution and proper functioning of the regional council.

(2) Notwithstanding anything in this Constitution, for a period of ten years from the date of the formation of the State of Nagaland or for such further period as the Governor may, on the recommendation of the regional council, by public notification specify in this behalf,-

(a) the administration of the Tuensang district shall be carried on by the Governor;

(b) where any money is provided by the Government of India to the Government of Nagaland to meet the requirements of the State of Nagaland as a whole, the Governor shall in his discretion arrange for an equitable allocation of that money between the Tuensang district and the rest of the State;

(c) no Act of the Legislature of Nagaland shall apply to Tuensang district unless the Governor, on the recommendation of the regional council, by public notification so directs, and the Governor in giving such direction with respect to any such Act may direct that the Act shall in its application to the Tuensang district or any part thereof have effect subject to such exceptions or modifications as the Governor may specify on the recommendation of the regional council:

Provided that any direction given under this sub-clause may be given so as to have retrospective effect;

(d) the Governor may make regulations for the peace, progress and good government of the Tuensang district and any regulations so made may repeal or amend with retrospective effect, if necessary, any Act of Parliament or any other law which is for the time being applicable to that district;

(e) (i) one of the members representing the Tuensang district in the Legislative Assembly of Nagaland shall be appointed Minister for Tuensang affairs by the Governor on the advice of the Chief Minister and the Chief Minister in tendering his advice shall act on the recommendation of the majority of the members as aforesaid;[1]

(ii) the Minister for Tuensang affairs shall deal with, and have direct access to the Governor on, all matters relating to the Tuensang district but he shall keep the Chief Minister informed about the same;

(f) notwithstanding anything in the foregoing provisions of this clause, the final decision on all matters relating to the Tuensang district shall be made by the Governor in his discretion;

(g) in articles 54 and 55 and clause (4) of article 80, references to the elected members of the Legislative Assembly of a State or to each such member shall include references to the members or member of the Legislative Assembly of Nagaland elected by the regional council established under this article;

(h) in article 170-

(i) clause(1) shall, in relation to the Legislative Assembly of Nagaland, have effect as if for the word 'sixty', the words 'forty-six' had been substituted;

(ii) in the said clause, the reference to direct election from territorial constituencies in the State shall include election by the members of the regional council established under this article;

(iii) in clauses (2) and (3), references to territorial constituencies shall mean references to territorial constituencies in the Kohima and Mokokchung districts.

---

1 Paragraph 2 of the Constitution (Removal of Difficulties) Order No.X provides (w.e.f. 1-12-1963) that article 371A of the Constitution of India shall have effect as if the following proviso were added to paragraph (i) of sub-clause (e) of clause (2) thereof, namely:

—"Provided that the Governor may, on the advice of the Chief Minister, appoint any person as Minister for Tuensang affairs to act as such until such time as persons are chosen in accordance with law to fill the seats allocated to the Tuensang district in the Legislative Assembly of Nagaland."

(3) If any difficulty arises in giving effect to any of the foregoing provisions of this article, the President may by order do anything (including any adaptation or modification of any other article) which appears to him to be necessary for the purpose of removing that difficulty:

Provided that no such order shall be made after the expiration of three years from the date of the formation of the State of Nagaland.

Explanation — In this article, the Kohima, Mokokchung and Tuensang districts shall have the same meanings as in the State of Nagaland Act, 1962.]

[1][**371B. Special provision with respect to the State of Assam.-** Notwithstanding anything in this Constitution, the President may, by order made with respect to the State of Assam, provide for the constitution and functions of a Committee of the Legislative Assembly of the State consisting of members of that Assembly elected from the tribal areas specified in [2][Part 1] of the table appended to paragraph 20 of the Sixth Schedule and such number of other members of that Assembly as may be specified in the order and for the modifications to be made in the rules of procedure of that Assembly for the constitution and proper functioning of such Committee.]

[3][**371C. Special provision with respect to the State of Manipur.-**

(1) Notwithstanding anything in this Constitution, the President may, by order made with respect to the State of Manipur, provide for the constitution and functions of a committee of the Legislative Assembly of the State consisting of members of that Assembly elected from the Hill Areas of that State, for the modifications to be made in the rules of business of the Government and in the rules of procedure of the Legislative Assembly of the State and for any special responsibility of the Governor in order to secure the proper functioning of such Committee.

(2) The Governor shall annually, or whenever so required by the President, make a report to the President regarding the administration of the Hill Areas in the State of Manipur and the executive power of the Union shall extend to the giving of directions to the State as to the administration of the said areas.

Explanation— In this article, the expression 'Hill Areas' means such areas as the President may, by order, declare to be Hill Areas.]

[4][**371D. Special provisions with respect to the State of Andhra Pradesh.-**

(1) The President may by order made with respect to the State of Andhra Pradesh provide, having regard to the requirements of the State as a whole, for equitable opportunities and facilities for the people belonging to different parts of State, in the matter of public employment and in the matter of education, and different provisions may be made for various parts of the State.

(2) An order made under clause (1) may, in particular,-

(a) require the State Government to organise any class or classes of posts in a civil service of, or any class or classes of civil posts under, the State into different local cadres for different parts of the State and allot in accordance with such principles and procedure as may be specified in the order the persons holding such posts to the local cadres so organised;

---

1 Ins. by the Constitution (Twenty-second Amendment) Act, 1969, sec. 4 (w.e.f. 25.9.1969).

2 Subs. by the North-Eastern Areas (Reorganisation) Act, 1971 (81 of 1971), sec. 71, for "Part A" (w.e.f. 21-1-1972).

3 Ins. by the Constitution (Twenty-seventh Amendment) Act, 1971, sec.5 (w.e.f. 15-2-1972).

4 Ins. by the Constitution (Thirty-second Amendment) Act, 1973, sec. 3 (w.e.f. 1-7-1974).

(b) specify any part or parts of the State which shall be regarded as the local area-

(i) for direct recruitment to posts in any local cadre (whether organised in pursuance of an order under this article or constituted otherwise) under the State Government;

(ii) for direct recruitment to posts in any cadre under any local authority within the State ;and

(iii) for the purposes of admission to any University within the State or to any other educational institution which is subject to the control of the State Government;

(c) specify the extent to which, the manner in which and the conditions subject to which, preference or reservation shall be given or made-

(i) in the matter of direct recruitment to posts in any such cadre referred to in sub-clause (b) as may be specified in this behalf in the order;

(ii) in the matter of admission to any such University or other educational institution referred to in sub-clause (b) as may be specified in this behalf in the order,

to or in favour of candidates who have resided or studied for any period specified in the order in the local area in respect of such cadre, University or other educational institution, as the case may be.

(3) The President may, by order, provide for the constitution of an Administrative Tribunal for the State of Andhra Pradesh to exercise such jurisdiction, powers and authority including any jurisdiction, power and authority which immediately before the commencement of the Constitution (Thirty-second Amendment) Act, 1973, was exercisable by any court (other than the Supreme Court) or by any tribunal or other authority as may be specified in the order with respect to the following matters, namely:

(a) appointment, allotment or promotion to such class or classes of posts in any civil service of the State, or to such class or classes of civil posts under the State, or to such class or classes of posts under the control of any local authority within the State, as may be specified in the order;

(b) seniority of persons appointed, allotted or promoted to such class or classes of posts in any civil service of the State, or to such class or classes of civil posts under the State, or to such class or classes of posts under the control of any local authority within the State, as may be specified in the order;

(c) such other conditions of service of persons appointed, allotted or promoted to such class or classes of civil posts in any civil service of the State or such class or classes of civil posts under the State or to such class or classes of posts under the control of any local authority within the State, as may be specified in the order;

(4) An order made under clause (3) may-

(a) authorise the Administrative Tribunal to receive representations for the redress of grievances relating to any matter within its jurisdiction as the President may specify in the order and to make such orders thereon as the Administrative Tribunal deems fit;

(b) contain such provisions with respect to the powers and authorities and procedure of the Administrative Tribunal (including provisions with respect to the powers of the Administrative Tribunal to punish for contempt of itself) as the President may deem necessary;

(c) provide for the transfer to the Administrative Tribunal of such classes of proceedings, being proceedings relating to matters within its jurisdiction and pending before any court (other than the Supreme Court) or tribunal or other authority immediately before the commencement of such order, as may be specified in the order;

(d) contain such supplemental, incidental and consequential provisions (including provisions as to fees and as to limitation, evidence or for the application of any law for the time being in force subject to any exceptions or modifications) as the President may deem necessary.

[1](5) The order of the Administrative Tribunal finally disposing off any case shall become effective upon its confirmation by the State Government or on the expiry of three months from the date on which the order is made, whichever is earlier:

Provided that the State Government may, by special order made in writing and for reasons to be specified therein, modify or annul any order of the Administrative Tribunal before it becomes effective and in such a case, the order of the Administrative Tribunal shall have effect only in such modified form or be of no effect, as the case may be.

(6) Every special order made by the State Government under the proviso to clause (5) shall be laid, as soon as may be after it is made, before both Houses of the State Legislature.

(7) The High Court for the State shall not have any powers of superintendence over the Administrative Tribunal and no court (other than the supreme Court) or tribunal shall exercise any jurisdiction, power or authority in respect of any matter subject to the jurisdiction, power or authority of, or in relation to, the Administrative Tribunal.

(8) If the President is satisfied that the continued existence of the Administrative Tribunal is not necessary, the President may by order abolish the Administrative Tribunal and make such provisions in such order as he may deem fit for the transfer and disposal of cases pending before the Tribunal immediately before such abolition.

(9) Notwithstanding any judgment, decree or order of any court, tribunal or other authority,-

(a) no appointment, posting, promotion or transfer of any person-

(i) made before the 1st day of November, 1956, to any post under the Government of, or any local authority within, the State of Hyderabad as it existed before the date; or

(ii) made before the commencement of the Constitution (Thirty-second Amendment) Act, 1973 to any post under the Government of, or any local or other authority within, the State of Andhra Pradesh; and

(b) no action taken or thing done by or before any person referred to in sub-clause (a),

shall be deemed to be illegal or void or ever to have become illegal or void merely on the ground that the appointment, posting, promotion or transfer of such person was not made in accordance with any law, then in force, providing for any requirement as to residence within the State of Hyderbad or, as the case may be, within any part of the State of Andhra Pradesh, in respect of such appointment, posting, promotion or transfer.

(10) The provisions of this article and of any order made by the President thereunder shall have effect notwithstanding anything in any other provision of this Constitution or in any other law for the time being in force.]

Notes on Article 371D

Any order made by the President and Article 371 D(1) shall have effect in spite of anything in any provision of the Constitution or any other law for the time being in force.

1 In P. Sambamurthy v. State of A.P., AIR 1987 SC 663: (1987) 1 SCC 362, the Supreme Court declared clause (5) of Article 371D alongwith the proviso to be unconstitutional and void.

The expression "public employment" in article 371 D(1) includes direct recruitment as well as promotion. Article 371 D(1) is complementary to article 371 D(2).

If the President makes an order under articles 371 D(1) and (2), the inherent powers of the State Government is lost in matters relating to services.

[1]**371E. Establishment of Central University in Andhra Pradesh.-** Parliament may by law provide for the establishment of a University in the State of Andhra Pradesh.

[2][**371F. Special provisions with respect to the State of Sikkim.-** Notwithstanding anything in this Constitution,-

(a) the Legislative Assembly of the State of Sikkim shall consist of not less than thirty members;

(b) as from the date of commencement of the Constitution (Thirty-sixth Amendment) Act, 1975 (hereafter in this article referred to as the appointed day)-

(i) the Assembly for Sikkim formed as a result of the elections held in Sikkim in April, 1974 with thirty-two members elected in the said elections (hereinafter referred to as the sitting members) shall be deemed to be the Legislative Assembly of the State of Sikkim duly constituted under this Constitution;

(ii) the sitting members shall be deemed to be the members of the Legislative Assembly of the State of Sikkim duly elected under this Constitution; and

(iii) the said Legislative Assembly of the State of Sikkim shall exercise the powers and perform the functions of the Legislative Assembly of a State under this Constitution;

(c) in the case of the Assembly deemed to be the Legislative Assembly of the State of Sikkim under clause (b), the references to the period of [3][five years] in clause (1) of article 172 shall be construed as references to a period of [4][four years] and the said period of [2][four years] shall be deemed to commence from the appointed day;

(d) until other provisions are made by Parliament by law, there shall be allotted to the State of Sikkim one seat in the House of People and the State of Sikkim shall form one Parliamentary constituency to be called the Parliamentary constituency for Sikkim;

(e) the representative of the State of Sikkim in the House of the People in existence on the appointed day shall be elected by the members of the Legislative Assembly of the State of Sikkim;

(f) Parliament may, for the purpose of protecting the rights and interests of the different sections of the population of Sikkim make provision for the number of seats in the Legislative Assembly of the State of Sikkim which may be filled by candidates belonging to such sections and for the delimitation of the Assembly constituencies from which candidates belonging to such sections alone may stand for election to the Legislative Assembly of the State of Sikkim;

(g) the Governor of Sikkim shall have special responsibility for peace and for an equitable arrangement for ensuring the social and economic advancement of different sections of the population of Sikkim and in the discharge of his special responsibility under this clause, the Governor of Sikkim shall, subject to such directions as the President may, from time to time, deem fit to issue, act in his discretion;

---

1 Ins. by the constitution (thirty-second amendment) act: 1973, sec 3 (w.e.f. 1-7-1974)

2 Ins. by the Constitution (Thirty-sixth Amendment) Act, 1975, sec. 3 (w.e.f. 26-4-1975).

3 Subs. by the Constitution (Forty-fourth Amendment) Act, 1978, sec. 43, for "six years" (w.e.f. 6-9-1979). The words "six years" were substituted for the original words "five years" by the Constitution (Forty-second Amendment) Act, 1976, sec. 56 (w.e.f. 3-1-1977).

4 Subs. by the Constitution (Forty-fourth Amendment) Act, 1978, sec. 43, for "five years" (w.e.f. 6-9-1979). The words "five years" were substituted for the original words "four years" by the Constitution (Forty-second Amendment) Act, 1976, sec. 56 (w.e.f. 3-1-1977).

(h) all property and assets (whether within or outside the territories comprised in the State of Sikkim) which immediately before the appointed day were vested in the Government of Sikkim or in any other authority or in any person for the purposes of the Government of Sikkim shall, as from the appointed day, vest in the Government of the State of Sikkim;

(i) the High Court functioning as such immediately before the appointed day in the territories comprised in the State of Sikkim shall, on and from the appointed day, be deemed to be the High Court for the State of Sikkim;

(j) all courts of civil, criminal and revenue jurisdiction, all authorities and all officers, judicial, executive and ministerial, throughout the territory of the State of Sikkim shall continue on and from the appointed day to exercise their respective functions subject to the provisions of this Constitution;

(k) all laws in force immediately before the appointed day in the territories comprised in the State of Sikkim or any part thereof shall continue to be in force therein until amended or repealed by a competent Legislature or other competent authority;

(l) for the purpose of facilitating the application of any such law as is referred to in clause (k) in relation to the administration of the State of Sikkim and for the purpose of bringing the provisions of any such law into accord with the provisions of this Constitution, the President may, within two years from the appointed day, by order, make such adaptations and modifications of the law, whether by way of repeal or amendment, as may be necessary or expedient, and thereupon, every such law shall have effect subject to the adaptations and modifications so made, and any such adaptation or modification shall not be questioned in any court of law;

(m) neither the Supreme Court nor any other court shall have jurisdiction in respect of any dispute or other matter arising out of any treaty, agreement, engagement or other similar instrument relating to Sikkim which was entered into or executed before the appointed day and to which the Government of India or any of its predecessor Governments was a party, but nothing in this clause shall be construed to derogate from the provisions of article 143;

(n) the President may, by public notification, extend with such restrictions or modifications as he thinks fit to the State of Sikkim any enactment which is in force in a State in India at the date of the notification;

(o) if any difficulty arises in giving effect to any of the foregoing provisions of this article, the President may, by order[1], do anything (including any adaptation or modification of any other article) which appears to him to be necessary for the purpose of removing the difficulty:

Provided that no such order shall be made after the expiry of two years from the appointed day;

(p) all things done and all actions taken in or in relation to the State of Sikkim or the territories comprised therein during the period commencing on the appointed day and ending immediately before the date on which the Constitution (Thirty-sixth Amendment) Act, 1975, receives the assent of the President shall, in so far as they are in conformity with the provisions of this Constitution as amended by the Constitution (Thirty-sixth Amendment) Act, 1975, be deemed for all purposes to have been validly done or taken under this Constitution as so amended.]

1 See the Constitution (Removal of Difficulties) Order XI (C.O. 99).

[1][**371G. Special provision with respect to the State of Mizoram.-** Notwithstanding anything in this Constitution,-

(a) no Act of Parliament in respect of-

(i) religious or social practices of the Mizos,

(ii) Mizo customary law and procedure,

(iii) administration of civil and criminal justice involving decisions according to Mizo customary law,

(iv) ownership and transfer of land,

shall apply to the State of Mizoram unless the Legislative Assembly of the State of Mizoram by a resolution so decides:

Provided that nothing in this clause shall apply to any Central Act in force in the Union Territory of Mizoram immediately before the commencement of the Constitution (Fifty-third Amendment) Act, 1986;

(b) the Legislative Assembly of the State of Mizoram shall consist of not less than forty members.]

[2]**371H. Special provision with respect to the State of Arunachal Pradesh.-** Notwithstanding anything in this Constitution-

(a) the Governor of Arunachal Pradesh shall have special responsibility with respect to law and order in the State of Arunachal Pradesh and in the discharge of his functions in relation thereto, the Governor shall, after consulting the Council of Ministers, exercise his individual judgment as to the action to be taken:

Provided that if any question arises whether any matter is or is not a matter as respects which the Governor is under this clause required to act in the exercise of his individual judgment, the decision of the Governor in his discretion shall be final, and the validity of anything done by the Governor shall not be called in question on the ground that he ought or ought not to have acted in the exercise of his individual judgment:

Provided further that if the President on receipt of a report from the Governor or otherwise is satisfied that it is no longer necessary for the Governor to have special responsibility with respect to law and order in the State of Arunanchal Pradesh, he may by order direct that the Governor shall cease to have such responsibility with effect from such date as may be specified in the order;

(b) the Legislative Assembly of the State of Arunachal Pradesh shall consist of not less than thirty members.]

[3][**371-I. Special provision with respect to the State of Goa.-** Notwithstanding anything in this Constitution, the Legislative Assembly of the State of Goa shall consist of not less than thirty members.]

372. Continuance in force of existing laws and their adaptation.-

(1) Notwithstanding the repeal by this Constitution of the enactments referred to in article 395 but subject to the other provisions of this Constitution, all the law in force in the territory of India immediately before the commencement of this Constitution shall continue in force therein until altered or repealed or amended by a competent Legislature or other competent authority.

---

1 Ins. by the Constitution (Fifty-third Amendment) Act, 1986, sec. 2 (w.e.f. 20-2-1987).

2 Ins. by the Constitution (Fifty-fifth Amendment) Act, 1986, sec. 2 (w.e.f. 20-2-1987).

3 Ins. by the Constitution (Fifty-sixth Amendment) Act, 1987, sec. 2 (w.e.f. 30-5-1987).

(2) For the purpose of bringing the provisions of any law in force in the territory of India into accord with the provisions of this Constitution, the President may by order[1] make such adaptations and modifications of such law, whether by way of repeal or amendment, as may be necessary or expendient and provide that the law shall, as from such date as may be specified in the order, have effect subject to the adaptations and modifications so made, and any such adaptation or modification shall not be questioned in any court of law.

(3) Nothing in clause (2) shall be deemed-

(a) to empower the President to make any adaptation or modification of any law after the expiration of[2] [three years] from the commencement of this Constitution; or

(b) to prevent any competent Legislature or other competent authority from repealing or amending any law adapted or modified by the President under the said clause.

Explanation I— The expression 'law in force' in this article shall include a law passed or made by a Legislature or other competent authority in the territory of India before the commencement of this Constitution and not previously repealed, notwithstanding that it or parts of it may not be then in operation either at all or in particular areas.

Explanation II— Any law passed or made by a Legislature or other competent authority in the territory of India which immediately before the commencement of this Constitution had extra-territorial effect as well as effect in the territory of India shall, subject to any such adaptations and modifications as aforesaid, continue to have such extra-territorial effect.

Explanation III— Nothing in this article shall be construed as continuing any temporary law in force beyond the date fixed for its expiration or the date on which it would have expired if this Constitution had not come into force.

Explanation IV— An Ordinance promulgated by the Governor of a Province under section 88 of the Government of India Act, 1935, and in force immediately before the commencement of this Constitution shall, unless withdrawn by the Governor of the corresponding State earlier, cease to operate at the expiration of six weeks from the first meeting after such commencement of the Legislative Assembly of that State functioning under clause (1) of article 382, and nothing in this article shall be construed as continuing any such Ordinance in force beyond the said period.

Notes on Article 372

Expression "all the law in force" includes the enactments of the Indian legislative as well as the common law of land. This includes the personal law as well as common law.

[3][372A. Power of the President to adapt laws.-

(1) For the purposes of bringing the provisions of any law in force in India or in any part thereof, immediately before the commencement of the Constitution (Seventh Amendment) Act, 1956, into accord with the provisions of this Constitution as amended by that Act, the President may by order[4] made before the first day of November, 1957, make such adaptations and modifications of the law, whether by way of repeal or amend-

1 See the Adaptation of Laws Order, 1950 dated 26th January, 1950, Gazette of India, Extraordinary, p. 449 as amended by Notification S.R.O. 115, dated the 5th June, 1950, Gazette of India, Extraordinary, Part II, sec.3 p. 51, Notification S.R.O. 870, dated the 4th November, 1950, Gazette of India, Extraordinary, Part II, sec.3, p. 903, Notification S.R.O. 508, dated the 4th April, 1951, Gazette of India, Extraordinary, Part Ii sec. 3, p. 287, Notification S.R.O. 1140 B, dated 2nd July, 1952, Gazette of India, Extraordinary, Part II, sec. 3, p. 661/I; and the Adaptation of the Travancore-Cochin Land Acquisition Laws Order, 1952, dated the 20th November, 1952, Gazette of India, Extraordinary, Part II, sec. 3, p. 923.

2 Subs. by the Constitution (First Amendment) Act, 1951, sec. 12, for "two years" (w.e.f. 18.6.1951).

3 Ins. by the Constitution (Seventh Amendment) Act, 1956, sec. 23 (w.e.f. 1.11.1956).

4 See the Adaptation of Laws Orders of 1956 and 1957.

ment, as may be necessary or expedient, and provide that the law shall, as from such date as may be specified in the order, have effect subject to the adaptations and modifications so made, and any such adaptation or modification shall not be questioned in any court of law.

(2) Nothing in clause (1) shall be deemed to prevent a competent Legislature or other competent authority from repealing or amending any law adapted or modified by the President under the said clause.]

373. Power of President to make order in respect of persons under preventive detention in certain cases.- Until provision is made by Parliament under clause (7) of article 22, or until the expiration of one year from the commencement of this Constitution, whichever is earlier, the said article shall have effect as if for any reference to Parliament in clauses (4) and (7) thereof there were substituted a reference to the President and for any reference to any law made by Parliament in those clauses there were substituted a reference to an order made by the President.

374. Provisions as to Judges of the Federal Court and Proceedings pending in the Federal Court or before His Majesty in Council.-

(1) The Judges of the Federal Court holding office immediately before the commencement of this Constitution shall, unless they have elected otherwise, become on such commencement the Judges of the Supreme Court and shall thereupon be entitled to such salaries and allowances and to such rights in respect of leave of absence and pension as are provided for under article 125 in respect of the Judges of the Supreme Court.

(2) All suits, appeals and proceedings, civil or criminal, pending in the Federal Court at the commencement of this Constitution shall stand removed to the Supreme Court, and the Supreme Court shall have jurisdiction to hear and determine the same, and the judgements and orders of the Federal Court delivered or made before the commencement of this Constitution shall have the same force and effect as if they had been delivered or made by the Supreme Court.

(3) Nothing in this Constitution shall operate to invalidate the exercise of jurisdiction by His Majesty in Council to dispose of appeals and petitions from, or in respect of, any judgement, decree or order of any court within the territory of India in so far as the exercise of such jurisdiction is authorised by law, and any order of His Majesty in Council made on any such appeal or petition after the commencement of this Constitution shall for all purposes have effect as if it were an order or decree made by the Supreme Court in the exercise of the jurisdiction conferred on such Court by this Constitution.

(4) On and from the commencement of this Constitution the jurisdiction of the authority functioning as the Privy Council in a State specified in Part B of the First Schedule to entertain and dispose of appeals and petitions from or in respect of any judgement, decree or order of any court within that State shall cease, and all appeals and other proceedings pending before the said authority at such commencement shall be transferred to, and disposed of by, the Supreme Court.

(5) Further provision may be made by Parliament by law to give effect to the provisions of this article.

375. Courts, authorities and officers to continue to function subject to the provisions of the Constitution.-All courts of civil, criminal and revenue jurisdiction, all authorities and all officers, judicial, executive and ministerial, throughout the territory of India, shall continue to exercise their respective functions subject to the provisions of this Constitution.

376. Provisions as to Judges of High Courts.-

(1) Notwithstanding anything in clause (2) of article 217, the Judges of High Court in any Province holding office immediately before the commencement of this Constitution

shall, unless they have elected otherwise, become on such commencement the Judges of the High Court in the corresponding State, and shall thereupon be entitled to such salaries and allowances and to such rights in respect of leave of absence and pension as are provided for under article 221 in respect of the Judges of such High Court. [1][Any such Judge shall, notwithstanding that he is not a citizen of India, be eligible for appointment as Chief Justice of such High Court, or as Chief Justice or other Judge of any other High Court.]

(2) The Judges of a High Court in any Indian State corresponding to any State specified in Part B of the First Schedule holding office immediately before the commencement of this Constitution shall, unless they have elected otherwise, become on such commencement the Judges of the High Court in the State so specified and shall, notwithstanding anything in clauses (1) and (2) of article 217 but subject to the proviso to clause (1) of that article, continue to hold office until the expiration of such period as the President may by order determine.

(3) In this article, the expression 'Judge' does not include an acting Judge or an additional Judge.

377. Provisions as to Comptroller and Auditor-General of India.-The Auditor-General of India holding office immediately before the commencement of this Constitution shall, unless he has elected otherwise, become on such commencement the Comptroller and Auditor-General of India and shall thereupon be entitled to such salaries and to such rights in respect of leave of absence and pension as are provided for under clause (3) of article 148 in respect of the Comptroller and Auditor-General of India and be entitled to continue to hold office until the expiration of his term of office as determined under the provisions which were applicable to him immediately before such commencement.

378. Provisions as to Public Service Commissions.-

(1) The members of the Public Service Commission for the Dominion of India holding office immediately before the commencement of this Constitution shall, unless they have elected otherwise, become on such commencement the members of the Public Service Commission for the Union and shall, notwithstanding anything in clauses (1) and (2) of article 316 but subject to the proviso to clause (2) of that article, continue to hold office until the expiration of their term of office as determined under the rules which were applicable immediately before such commencement to such members.

(2) The members of a Public Service Commission of a Province or of a Public Service Commission serving the needs of a group of Provinces holding office immediately before the commencement of this Constitution shall, unless they have elected otherwise, become on such commencement the members of the Public Service Commission for the corresponding State or the members of Joint State Public Service Commission serving the needs of the corresponding States, as the case may be, and shall, notwithstanding anything in clauses (1) and (2) of article 316 but subject to the proviso to clause (2) of that article, continue to hold office until the expiration of their term of office as determined under the rules which were applicable immediately before such commencement to such members.

[2][**378A. Special provisions as to duration of Andhra Pradesh Legislative Assembly.-** Notwithstanding anything contained in article 172, the Legislative Assembly of the State of Andhra Pradesh as constituted under the provisions of sections 28 and 29 of the States Reorganisation Act, 1956, shall, unless sooner dissolved, continue for a period of five years from the date referred to in the said section 29 and no longer and the expiration of the said period shall operate as a dissolution of that Legislative Assembly.]

---

1 Added by the Constitution (First Amendment) Act, 1951, sec. 13 (w.e.f. 18.6.1951).

2 Ins. by the Constitution (Seventh Amendment) Act, 1956, sec. 24 (w.e.f. 1.11.1956).

379-391. *[Rep.by the Constitution (Seventh Amendment) Act, 1956, sec.29 and Sch. (w.e.f. 1.11.1956).]*

392. Power of the President to remove difficulties.-

(1) The President may, for the purpose of removing any difficulties, particularly in relation to the transition from the provisions of the Government of India Act, 1935, to the provisions of this Constitution, by order direct that this Constitution shall, during such period as may be specified in the order, have effect subject to such adaptations, whether by way of modification, addition or omission, as he may deem to be necessary or expedient: Provided that no such order shall be made after the first meeting of Parliament duly constituted under Chapter II of Part V.

(2) Every order made under clause (1) shall be laid before Parliament.

(3) The powers conferred on the President by this article, by article 324, by clause (3) of article 367 and by article 391 shall, before the commencement of this Constitution, be exercisable by the Governor-General of the Dominion of India.

PART XXII

SHORT TITLE, COMMENCEMENT, [1][AUTHORITATIVE TEXT IN HINDI] AND APPEALS

393. Short title.-This Constitution may be called the Constitution of India.

394. Commencement.-This article and articles 5, 6, 7, 8, 9, 60, 324, 366, 367, 379, 380, 388, 391, 392 and 393 shall come into force at once, and the remaining provisions of this Constitution shall come into force on the twenty-sixth day of January, 1950, which day is referred to in this Constitution as the commencement of this Constitution.

[2][**394A. Authoritative text in the Hindi language.-**

(1) The President shall cause to be published under his authority:—

(a) the translation of this Constitution in the Hindi language signed by members of the Constituent Assembly, with such modifications as may be necessary to bring it in conformity with the language, style and terminology adopted in the authoritative texts of Central Acts in the Hindi language, and incorporating therein all the amendments of this Constitution made before such publication; and

(b) the translation in the Hindi language of every amendment of this Constitution made in the English language.

(2) The translation of this Constitution and of every amendment thereof published under clause (1) shall be construed to have the same meaning as the original thereof and if any difficulty arises in so construing any part of such translation, the President shall cause the same to be revised suitably.

(3) The translation of this Constitution and of every amendment thereof published under this Article shall be deemed to be, for all purposes, the authoritative text thereof in the Hindi language.]

395. Repeals.- The Indian Independence Act, 1947 and the Government of India Act, 1935, together with all enactments amending or supplementing the latter Act, but not including the Abolition of Privy Council Jurisdiction Act, 1949 are hereby repealed.

---

1 Ins. by the Constitution (Fifty-eighth Amendment) Act, 1987, sec. 2 (w.e.f. 9-12-1987).

2 Ins. by the Constitution (Fifty-eighth Amendment) Act, 1987, sec. 3 (w.e.f. 9-12-1987).

[1][FIRST SCHEDULE]

[ARTICLES 1 AND 4]

I. THE STATES

	Name	Territories
1.	Andhra Pradesh	[2][The territories specified in sub-section (1) of section 3 of the Andhra State Act, 1953, sub-section (1) of section 3 of the States Reorganisation Act, 1956, the First Schedule to the Andhra Pradesh and Madras (Alteration of Boundaries) Act, 1959, and the Schedule to the Andhra Pradesh and Mysore (Transfer of Territory) Act, 1968, but excluding the territories specified in the Second Schedule to the Andhra Pradesh and Madras (Alteration of Boundaries) Act, 1959.]
2.	Assam	The territories which immediately before the commencement of this Constitution were comprised in the Province of Assam, the Khasi States and the Assam Tribal Areas, but excluding the territories specified in the Schedule to the Assam (Alteration of Boundaries) Act, 1951, [3][and the territories specified in sub-section (1) of section 3 of the State of Nagaland Act, 1962] [4][and the territories specified in sections 5, 6 and 7 of the North-Eastern Areas (Reorganisation) . Act, 1971.]
3.	Bihar	[5][The territories which immediately before the commencement of this Constitution were either comprised in the Province of Bihar or were being administered as if they formed part of that Province and the territories specified in clause (i) of sub-section (1) of section 3 of the Bihar and Uttar Pradesh (Alteration .of Boundaries) Act, 1968, but excluding the territories specified in sub-section (1) of section 3 of the Bihar and West Bengal (Transfer of Territories) Act, 1956, and the territories specified in clause (b) of sub-section (1) of section 3 of the first mentioned Act] [6][and the territories specified in section 3 of the Bihar Reorganisation Act, 2000].
[7][4.	Gujarat	The territories referred to in sub-section (1) of section 3 of the Bombay Reorganisation Act, 1960.]
5.	Kerala	The territories specified in sub-section (1) of section 5 of the States Reorganisation Act, 1956.
6.	Madhya Pradesh	The territories specified in sub-section (1) of section 9 of the States Reorganisation Act, 1956 [8][and the First Schedule to the Rajasthan and Madhya Pradesh (Transfer of Territories) Act, 1959] [9][but excluding the territories specified in section 3 of the Madhya Pradesh Reorganisation Act, 2000].

1 Subs. by the Constitution (Seventh Amendment) Act, 1956, sec. 2, for the First Schedule (w.e.f. 1.11.1956).
2 Subs. by the Andhra Pradesh and Mysore (Transfer of Territory) Act, 1968 (36 of 1968), sec. 4, for the former entry (w.e.f. 1-10-1968).
3 Added by the State of Nagaland Act, 1962 (27 of 1962), sec. 4 (w.e.f. 1-12-1963).
4 Added by the North-Eastern Areas (Reorganisation) Act, 1971 (81 of 1971), sec. 9 (w.e.f. 21-1-1972).
5 Subs. by the Bihar and Uttar Pradesh (Alteration of Boundaries) Act, 1968 (24 of 1968), sec. 4, for the former entry (w.e.f. 10-6-1970).
6 Added by the Bihar Reorganisation Act, 2000 (30 of 2000), sec. 5 (w.e.f. 15-11-2000).
7 Subs. by the Bombay Reorganisation Act, 1960 (11 of 1960), sec. 4, for entry 4 (w.e.f. 1-5-1960).
8 Ins. by the Rajasthan and Madhya Pradesh (Transfer of Territories) Act, 1959 (47 of 1959), sec. 4 (w.e.f. 1-10-1959).
9 Added by the Madhya Pradesh Reorganisation Act, 2000 (28 of 2000), sec. 5 (w.e.f. 1-11-2000).

Name	Territories
[1][7. Tamil Nadu]	The territories which immediately before the commencement of this Constitution were either comprised in the Province of Madras or were being administered as if they formed part of that Province and the territories specified in section 4 of the States Reorganisation Act, 1956, [2][and the Second Schedule to the Andhra Pradesh and Madras (Alteration of Boundaries) Act, 1959] but excluding the territories specified in sub-section (1) of section 3 and sub- section (1) of section 4 of the Andhra State Act, 1953 and [3][the territories specified in clause (b) of sub- section (1) of section 5, section 6 and clause (d) of sub- section (1) of section 7 of the States Reorganisation Act, 1956 and the territories specified in the First Schedule to the Andhra Pradesh and Madras (Alteration of Boundaries) Act, 1959]
[4][8. Maharashtra	The territories specified in sub-section (1) of section 8 of the States Reorganisation Act, 1956, but excluding the territories referred to in sub-section (1) of section 3 of the Bombay Reorganisation Act, 1960.]
[5][[6]9. Karnataka	The territories specified in sub-section (1) of section 7 of the States Reorganisation Act, 1956 [7][but excluding the territory specified in the Schedule to the Andhra Pradesh and Mysore (Transfer of Territory) Act, 1968].
[11][10. Odisha	The territories which immediately before the commencement of this Constitution were either comprised in the Province of Orissa or were being administered as if they formed part of that Province
[1][11. Punjab	The territories specified in section 11 of the States Reorganisation Act, 1956 [8][and the territories referred to in Part II of the First Schedule to the Acquired Territories (Merger) Act, 1960] [9][but excluding the territories referred to in Part II of the First Schedule to the Constitution (Ninth Amendment) Act, 1960] [10][and the territories specified in sub-section (1) of section 3, section 4 and sub-section (1) of section 5 of the Punjab Reorganisation Act, 1966].

1 Subs. by the Madras State (Alteration of Name) Act, 1968 (53 of 1968), sec.5, for "7. Madras" (w.e.f. 14-1-1969).

2 Ins. by the Andhra Pradesh and Madras (Alteration of Boundaries) Act, 1959 (56 of 1959), sec. 6 (w.e.f. 14-1-1960).

3 Subs. by the Andhra Pradesh and Madras (Alteration of Boundaries) Act, 1959 (56 of 1959), sec. 6, for certain words (w.e.f. 1-4-1960).

4 Ins. by the Bombay Reorganisation Act, 1960 (11 of 1960), sec. 4 (w.e.f: 1-5-1960).

5 Entries 8 to 14 renumbered as entries 9 to 15 by the Bombay Reorganisation Act, 1960. (11 of 1960), sec. 4 (w.e.f. 1-5-1960).

6 Subs. by the Mysore State (Alteration of Name) Act, 1973 (31 of 1973), sec. 5, for "9. Mysore" (w.e.f.1-10-1973).

7 Ins. by the Andhra Pradesh and Mysore (Transfer of Territory) Act, 1968 (36 of 1968), sec. 4 (w.e.f. 1-10-1968)

8 Ins. by the Acquired Territories (Merger) Act, 1960 (64 of 1960), sec. 4 (w.e.f. 17-1-1961).

9 Added *by* the Constitution (Ninth Amendment) Act, 1960, sec. 3 (w.e.f. 17-1-1961).

10 Ins. by the Punjab Reorganisation Act, 1966 (31 of 1966), sec. 7 (w.e.f. 1-11-1966).

11 Subs. by the Orissa (alteration of Name) Act 2011. (w.e.f. 1-11-2011).

Name	Territories
[1][12. Rajasthan	The territories specified in section 10 of the States Reorganisation Act, 1956 [1][but excluding the territories specified in the First Schedule to the Rajasthan and Madhya Pradesh (Transfer of Territories) Act, 1959].
[3][13. Uttar Pradesh	[2][The territories which immediately before the commencement of this Constitution were either comprised in the Province known as the United Provinces or were being administered as if they formed part of that Province, the territories specified " in clause (b) of sub-section (1) of section 3 of the Bihar and Uttar Pradesh (Alteration of Boundaries) Act, - 1968 , and the territories specified in clause (b) *of* sub-section (1) of section 4 of the Haryana and Uttar Pradesh (Alteration of Boundaries) Act, 1979, but excluding the territories specified in clause (a) of sub-section (1) of section 3 of the Bihar and Uttar Pradesh (Alteration of Boundaries) Act, 1968, [3][and the territories specified in section 3 of the Uttar Pradesh Reorganisation Act, 2000] and the territories specified in clause (a) of sub-section (1) of section 4 of the Haryana and Uttar Pradesh (Alteration of Boundaries) Act, 1979.]
[4][14. West Bengal	The territories which immediately before the commencement of this Constitution were either comprised in the Province of West Bengal or were being administered as if they formed part of that Province in the territory of Chandernagore as defined in clause (c) of section 2 of the Chandernagore (Merger) Act, 1954, and also the territories specified in sub-section (1) of section 3 of the Bihar and West Bengal (Transfer of Territories) Act, 1956.
[4][15. Jammu and Kashmir	The territory which immediately before the commencement of this Constitution are comprised in the Indian State of Jammu and Kashmir
[5][16. Nagaland	The territories specified in sub-section (1) of section 3 of the State of Nagaland Act, 1962.]
[6][17. Haryana	[7][The territories specified in sub-section (1) of section 3 of the Punjab Reorganisation Act, 1966 and the territories specified in clause (a) of sub-section (1) of section 4 of the Haryana and Uttar Pradesh (Alteration of Boundaries) Act, 1979, but excluding the territories specified in clause (b) of sub-section (1) of section 4 of that Act.)]
[8][18. Himachal Pradesh	The territories which immediately before the commencement of this Constitution were being administered as if they were Chief Commissioners' Provinces under the names of Himachal Pradesh and Bilaspur and the Territories specified in sub-section (1) of section 5 of the Punjab Reorganisation Act, 1966.]

1 Ins. by the Rajasthan and Madhya Pradesh (Transfer of Territories) Act, 1959 (47 of 1959), sec. 4 (w.e.f. 1-10-1959).

2 Subs. by the Haryana and Uttar Pradesh (Alteration of Boundaries) Act, 1979 (31 of 1979), sec. 5, for the former entry (w.e.f. 15-9-1983).

3 Ins. by the Uttar Pradesh Reorganisation Act, 2000 (29 of 2000), sec. 5 (w.e.f. 9-11-2000).

4 Entries 8 to 14 renumbered as entries 9 to 15 by the Bombay Reorganisation Act, 1960 (11 of 1960), sec. 4 (w.e.f. 1-5-1960).

5 Ins. by the State of Nagaland Act, 1962 (27 of 1962), sec. 4 (w.e.f. 1-12-1963).

6 Ins. by the Punjab Reorganisation Act, 1966 (31 of 1966), sec. 7 (w.e.f. 1-11-1966).

7 Subs. by the Haryana and Uttar Pradesh (Alteration of Boundaries) Act, 1979 (31 of 1979), sec. 5, for the former entry (w.e.f. 15-9-1983).

8 Ins. by the State of Himachal Pradesh Act; 1970 (53 of 1970), sec. 4 (w.e.f. 25-1-1971).

Name	Territories
[1][19. Manipur	The territory which immediately before the commencement of this Constitution was being administered as if it were a Chief Commissioner's Province under the name of Manipur.
20. Tripura	The territory which immediately before the commencement of this Constitution was being administered as if it were a Chief Commissioner's Province under the name of Tripura
21. Meghalaya	The territories specified in section 5 of the North- Eastern Areas (Reorganisation) Act, 1971.]
[2][22. Sikkim	The territories which immediately before the commencement of the Constitution (Thirty-sixth Amendment) Act, 1975, were comprised in Sikkim.]
[3][23. Mizoram	The territories specified in section 6 of the North Eastern Areas (Reorganisation) Act, 1971.]
[4][24. Arunachal Pradesh	The territories specified in section 7 of the North Eastern Areas (Reorganisation) Act, .1971.]
[5][25. Goa	The territories specified in section 3 of the Goa, Daman and Diu Reorganisation Act, 1987.]
[6][26. Chhattisgarh	The territories specified in section 3 of the Madhya Pradesh Reorganisation Act, 2000.]
[7][27. Uttarakhand	The territories specified in section 3 of the Uttar Pradesh Reorganisation Act, 2000.]
[8][28. Jharkhand	The territories specified in section 3 of the Bihar Reorganisation Act, 2000.]

II. THE UNION TERRITORIES

1. Delhi[9][***] [10][***]	The territory which immediately before the commencement of this Constitution was comprised in the Chief Commissioner's Province of Delhi.
[11][2.] The Andaman and Nicobar Islands	The territory which immediately before the commencement of this Constitution was comprised in the Chief Commissioner's Province of the Andaman and Nicobar Islands.

1 Ins. by the North-Eastern Areas (Reorganisation) Act, 1971 (81 of 1971), sec. 9 (w.e.f. 21-1-1972).

2 Ins. by the Constitution (Thirty-sixth Amendment) Act, 1975, sec. 2 (w.e.f. 26-4-1975).

3 Ins. by the State of Mizoram Act, 1986 (34 of 1986), sec. 4 (w.e.f. 20-2-1987).

4 Ins. by the State of Arunachal Pradesh Act, 1986 (69 of 1986), sec. 4 (w.e.f. 20-2-1987).

5 Ins. by the Goa, Daman and Diu Reorganisation Act, 1987 (18 of 1987), sec. 5 (w.e.f. 30-5-1987).

6 Ins. by the Madhya Pradesh Reorganisation Act, 2000 (28 of 2000), sec. 5.

7 Subs. by Uttaranchal (Alteration of Name) Act. 2006.

8 Ins. by the Bihar Reorganisation Act, 2000 (30 of 2000), sec. 5 (w.e.f. 15-11-2000).

9 Entry 2 relating to "Himachal Pradesh" omitted by the State of Himachal Pradesh Act, 1970 (53 of 1970), sec. 4 (w.e.f. 25-1-1971).

10 Entries relating to Manipur and Tripura omitted by the North-Eastern Areas (Reorganisation) Act, 1971 (81 of 1971), sec. 9 (w.e.f. 21-1-1972).

11 Entries 4 to 9 renumbered as entries 2 to 7 by the North-Eastern Areas (Reorganisation) Act, 1971 (81 of 1971), sec. 9 (w.e.f. 21-1-1972).

Name	Territories
[1][3.] [1][Lakshadweep]	The territory specified in section 6 of the States Reorganisation Act, 1956.
[2][[1][4.] Dadra and Nagar Haveli	The territory which immediately before the eleventh day of August, 1961 was comprised in Free Dadra and Nagar Haveli.]
[3][[4][[1][5.] Daman and Diu	The territories specified in section 4 of the Goa, Daman and Diu Reorganisation Act, 1987.]]
[5][[1][6.] Puducherry	The territories which immediately before the sixteenth day of August, 1962, were comprised in the French Establishments in India known as Pondicherry, Karikal, Mahe and Yanam.]
[6][[7][7.] Chandigarh	The territories specified in section 4 of the Punjab Reorganisation Act, 1966.]
[8][***][9][***]	

1 Subs. by the Laccadive, Minicoy and Amindivi Islands (Alteration of Name) Act, 1973 (34 of 1973), sec. 5, for "The Laccadive, Minicoy Amindivi and Amindivi Islands" (w.e.f. 1-11-1973).

2 Ins. by the Constitution (Tenth Amendment) Act, 1961, sec. 2.

3 Ins. by the Constitution (Twelfth Amendment) Act, 1962, sec. 2.

4 Subs. by the Goa, Daman and Diu Reorgnisation Act, 1987 (18 of 1987), sec. 5, for entry 5 (w.e.f. 30-5-1987).

5 Subs. by the pondicherry (Alteration of Name) Act 2006.

6 Ins. by the Punjab Reorganisation Act, 1966 (31 of 1966), sec. 7 (w.e.f. 1-11-1966).

7 Entries 4 to 9 renumbered as entries 2 to 7 by the North-Eastern Areas (Reorganisation) Act, 1971 (81 of 1971), sec. 9 (w.e.f. 21-1-1972).

8 Entry 8 'relating to Mizoram omitted "and entry 9 relating to Arunachal Pradesh renumbered as entry 8 by the State of Mizoram Act, 1986 (34 of 1986), sec. 4 (w.e.f. 20-2-1987).

9 Entry 8 relating to Arunachal Pradesh as renumbered by Act 34 of 1986, sec. 4 omitted by the State of Arunachal Pradesh Act, 1986 (69 of 1986), sec. 4 (w.e.f. 20-2-1987).

SECOND SCHEDULE

[ARTICLES 59(3), 65(3), 75(6), 97, 125, 148(3), 158(3), 164(5), 186 *and* 221]

PART A

PROVISIONS AS TO THE PRESIDENT AND THE GOVERNORS OF STATES [1][***]

1. There shall be paid to the President and to the Governors of the States [1][***] the following emoluments per mensem, that is to say:-

The President	[2][10,000 rupees]
The Governor of a State	[3][5,500 rupees]

2. There shall also be paid to the President and to the Governors of the States [4][***] such allowances as were payable respectively to the Governor-General of the Dominion of India and to the Governors of the corresponding Provinces immediately before the commencement of this Constitution.
3. The President and the Governors of [5][the States] throughout their respective terms of office shall be entitled to the same privileges to which the Governor-General and the Governors of the corresponding Provinces were respectively entitled immediately before the commencement of this Constitution.
4. While the Vice-President or any other person is discharging the functions of, or is acting as, President, or any person is discharging the functions of the Governor, he shall be entitled to the same emoluments, allowances and privileges as the President or the Governor whose functions he discharges or for whom he acts, as the case may be.

[6][PART B*]**

PART C

PROVISIONS AS TO THE SPEAKER AND THE DEPUTY SPEAKER OF THE HOUSE OF THE PEOPLE AND THE CHAIRMAN AND THE DEPUTY CHAIRMAN OF THE COUNCIL OF STATES AND THE SPEAKER AND THE DEPUTY SPEAKER OF THE LEGISLATIVE ASSEMBLY [7][***] AND THE CHAIRMAN AND THE DEPUTY CHAIRMAN OF THE LEGISLATIVE COUNCIL OF [8][A STATE].

7. There shall be paid to the Speaker of the House of the People and the Chairman of the Council of States such salaries and allowances as were payable to the Speaker of the Constituent Assembly of the Dominion of India immediately before the commencement of this Constitution, and there shall be paid to the Deputy Speaker of the House of the People and to the Deputy Chairman of the Council of States such salaries and allowances as were payable to the Deputy Speaker of the Constituent Assembly of the Dominion of India immediately before such commencement.

---

1 The words and letters "specified in Part A of the First Schedule" omitted by the Constitution (Seventh Amendment) Act, 1956, sec. 29 and Sch.

2 Raised to 1,50,000 rupees per mensem by the presidents emoluments and pension Act. 2008.

3 Raised to 1,10,000 repees per mensem by the Governor's (Emoluments allowances and privileges) amendment Act. 2008.

4 The. words "so specified" omitted by the Constitution (Seventh Amendment) Act, 1956, sec. 29 and Sch.

5 Subs. by the Constitution (Seventh Amendment) Act, 1956, sec. 29 and Sch., for "such States".

6 Part B omitted by the Constitution (Seventh Amendment) Act, 1956, sec. 29 and Sch.

7 The words and letters "or a State in Part A of the First Schedule" omitted by the Constitution (Seventh Amendment) Act, 1956, sec. 29 and Sch.

8 Subs. by the Constitution (Seventh Amendment) Act, 1956, sec. 29 and Sch., for "any such state.

8. There shall be paid to the Speaker and the Deputy Speaker of the Legislative Assembly [1][***] and to the Chairman and the Deputy Chairman of the Legislative Council of [2][a State] such salaries and allowances as were payable respectively to the Speaker and the Deputy Speaker of the Legislative Assembly and the President and the Deputy President of the Legislative Council of the corresponding Province immediately before the commencement of this Constitution and, where the corresponding Province had no Legislative Council immediately before such commencement, there shall be paid to the Chairman and the Deputy Chairman of the Legislative Council of the State such salaries and allowances as the Governor of the State may determine.

PART D

PROVISIONS AS TO THE JUDGES OF THE SUPREME COURT AND OF THE HIGH COURTS [3][***]

9. (1) There shall be paid to the Judges of the Supreme Court, in respect of time spent on actual service,. salary at the following rates per mensem, that is to say:-

The Chief Justice	[4][10,000 rupees]
Any other Judge	[5][9,000 rupees]:

Provided that if a Judge of the Supreme Court at the time of his appointment is in receipt of a pension (other than a disability or wound pension) in respect of any previous service under the Government of India or any of its predecessor Governments or under the Government of a State or any of its predecessor Governments, his salary in respect of service in the Supreme Court [6][shall be reduced-

(a) by the amount of that pension, and

(b) if he has, before such appointment, received in lieu of a portion of the pension due to him in respect of such previous service the commuted value thereof, by the amount of that portion of the pension, and

(c) if he has, before such appointment, received a retirement gratuity in respect of such previous service, by the pension equivalent of that gratuity].

(2) Every Judge of the Supreme Court shall be entitled without payment of rent to the use of an official residence.

(3) Nothing in sub-paragraph (2) of this paragraph shall apply to a Judge who, immediately before the commencement of this Constitution,-

(a) was holding office as the Chief Justice of the Federal Court and has become on such commencement the Chief Justice of the Supreme Court under clause (1) of article 374, or

---

1 The words and letters "of a State specified in Part A of the First Schedule" omitted by the Constitution (Seventh Amendment) Act, 1956, sec. 29 and Sch.

2 Subs. by the Constitution (Seventh Amendment) Act, 1956, sec. 29 and Sch., for "such State".

3 The words and letters "in States in Part A of the First Schedule" omitted by the Constitution (Seventh Amendment) Act, 1956, sec. 25.

4 Subs. by the Constitution (Fifty-fourth Amendment) Act, 1986, sec. 4, for "5,000 rupees" (w.e.f. 1-4-1986). Now Rs. 33,000 per mensem vide the High Court and Supreme Court Judges (Conditions of Service) Amendment Act, 1998 (18 of 1998), sec. 7 (w.r.e.f; 1-1-1996). Raised to Rs. 1,00,000 per mensem vide high court and supreme court judges (sa;aroes amd cpmdotopms pf servies) Amendement Act 2009.

5 Subs. by the Constitution (Fifty-fourth Amendment) Act, 1986, sec. 4, for "4,000 rupees" (w.e.f. 1-4-1986). Now Rs. 30,000 per mensem vide the High Court and Supreme Court Judges (Conditions of Service) Amendment Act, 1998 (18 of 1998), sec. 7 (w.r.e.f. 1-1-1996). Raised to Rs. 90,000 per mensem vide the High Court and Supreme Court Judges (Salries and Conditions of Service) Amendment Act. 2009.

6 Subs. by the Constitution (Seventh Amendment) Act, 1956, sec. 25, for "shall be reduced by the amount of that pension".

(b) was holding office as any other Judge of the Federal Court and has on such commencement become a Judge (other than the Chief Justice) of the Supreme Court under the said clause,

during the period he holds office as such Chief Justice or other Judge, and every Judge who so becomes the Chief Justice or other Judge of the Supreme Court shall, in respect of time spent on actual service as such Chief Justice or other Judge, as the case may be, be entitled to receive in addition to the salary specified in sub-paragraph (1) of this paragraph as special pay an amount equivalent to the difference between the salary so specified and the salary which he was drawing immediately before such commencement.

(4) Every Judge of the Supreme Court shall receive such reasonable allowances to reimburse him for expenses incurred in travelling on duty within the territory of India and shall be afforded such reasonable facilities in connection with travelling as the President may from time to time prescribe.

(5) The rights in respect of leave of absence (including leave allowances) and pension of the Judges of the Supreme Court shall be governed by the provisions which, immediately before the commencement of this Constitution, were applicable to the Judges of the Federal Court.

10. [1][(1). There shall be paid to the Judges of High Courts, in respect of time spent on actual service, salary at the following rates per mensem, that is to say ,-

The Chief Justice [2][9,000 rupees]

Any other Judge [3][8,000 rupees]:

Provided that if a Judge of a High Court at the time of his appointment is in receipt of a pension (other than a disability or wound pension) in respect of any previous service under the Government of India or any of its predecessor Governments or under the Government of a State or any of its predecessor Governments, his salary in respect of service in the High Court shall be reduced-

(a) by the amount of that pension, and

(b) if he has, before such appointment, received in lieu of a portion of the pension due to him in respect of such previous service the commuted value thereof, by the amount of that portion of the pension, and

(c) if he has, before such appointment, received a retirement gratuity in respect of such previous service, by the pension equivalent of that gratuity.]

(2) Every person who immediately before the commencement of this Constitution-

(a) was holding office as the Chief Justice of a High Court in any Province and has on such commencement become the Chief Justice of the High Court in the corresponding State under clause (1) of article 376, or

(b) was holding office as any other Judge of a High Court in any Province and has on such commencement become a Judge (other than the Chief Justice) of the High Court in the corresponding State under the said clause, shall, if he was immediately before such commencement drawing a salary at a rate higher than that specified in sub-paragraph (1) of this paragraph, be entitled to receive in respect of time spent on actual service as such Chief Justice or other Judge, as the case may be, in addition to the salary specified in the said sub-paragraph as special pay an amount equivalent to the difference between the salary so specified and the salary which he was drawing immediately before such commencement.

---

1 Subs. by the Constitution (Seventh Amendment) Act, 1956, sec. 25, for sub-paragraph (1).

2 Subs. by the Constitution (Fifty-fourth Amendment) Act, 1986 (34 of 1986), sec. 4, for "4,000 rupees" (w.e.f. 1-4-1986). Now Rs. 30,000 per mensem vide the High Court and Supreme Court Judges (Conditions of Service) Amendment Act, 1998 (18 of 1998), sec. 4 (w.r.e.f. 1-1-1996). Raised to Rs. 90,000 per mensem vide High Court and Supreme Court Judges (salaries and conditions of service) Amendment Act 2009.

3 Subs. by the Constitution (Fifty-fourth Amendment) Act, 1986 (34 of 1986), sec. 4, for "3,500 rupees" {w.e.f. 1-4-1986). Now Rs. 26,000 per mensem vide the High Court and Supreme Court Judges (Conditions of Service) Amendment Act, 1998 (18 of 1998), sec. 4 (w.r.e.f. 1-1-1996). Raised to Rs. 80,000 per mensem vide the High Court and Supreme Court Judges (Salaries and Conditions of Services) Amendment Act 2009.

[1][(3) Any person who, immediately before the commencement of the Constitution (Seventh Amendment) Act, 1956, was holding office as the Chief Justice of the High Court of a State specified in Part B of the First Schedule and has on such commencement become the Chief Justice of the High Court of a State specified in the said Schedule as amended by said Act, shall, if he was immediately before such commencement drawing any amount as allowance in addition to his salary, be entitled to receive in respect of time spent on actual service as such Chief Justice, the same amount as allowance in addition to the salary specified in sub-paragraph (1) of this paragraph.]

11. In this Part, unless the context otherwise requires- (a) the expression 'Chief Justice' includes an acting Chief Justice, and a 'Judge' includes an *ad hoc* Judge; (b) 'actual service' includes-

(i) time spent by a Judge on duty as a Judge or in the performance of such other functions as he may at the request of the President undertake to discharge;

(ii) vacations, excluding any time during which the Judge is absent on leave; and

(iii) joining time on transfer from a High Court to the Supreme Court or from one High Court to another .

PART E

PROVISIONS AS TO THE COMPTROLLER AND AUDITOR-GENERAL OF INDIA

12. (1) There shall be paid to the Comptroller and Auditor-General of India a salary at the rate of four thousand[2] rupees per mensem.

(2) The person who was holding office immediately before the commencement of this Constitution as Auditor-General of India and has become on such commencement the Comptroller and Auditor-General of India under article 377 shall in addition to the salary specified in sub-paragraph (1) of this paragraph be entitled to receive as special pay an amount equivalent to the difference between the salary so specified and the salary which he was drawing as Auditor-General of India immediately before such commencement.

(3) The rights in respect of leave of absence and pension and the other conditions of service of the Comptroller and Auditor-General of India shall be governed or shall continue to be governed, as the case may be, by the provisions which were applicable to the Auditor-General of India immediately before the commencement of this Constitution and all references in those provisions to the Governor-General shall be construed as references to the President.

1 Subs. by the Constitution (Seventh Amendment) Act, 1956, sec. 25, for sub-paragraphs (3) and (4).

2 The Comptroller and Auditor-General of India shall be paid a salary equal to the salary of the Judges of Supreme Court vide section 3 of Act 56 of 1971. The salary of Judges of the Supreme Court has been raised to Rs. 9,000 per mensem by the Constitution (Fifty-fourth Amendment) Act, 1986 and further raised to Rs. 30,000 p.m. by the High Court and Supreme Court Judges (Conditions of Service) Amendment Act, 1998 (18 of 1998), sec. 7 (w.r.e.f. 1-1-1996).

THIRD SCHEDULE

[ARTICLES 75(4), 99, 124(6), 148(2), 164(3), 188 AND 219][1]

FORMS OF OATHS OR AFFIRMATIONS

I

Form of oath of office for a Minister for the Union:

'I, A.B., do $\frac{\text{swear in the name of God}}{\text{solemnly affirm}}$ that I will bear true faith and allegiance to the Constitution of India as by law established, [2][that I will uphold the sovereignty and integrity of India] that I will faithfully and conscientiously discharge my duties as a Minister for the Union and that I will do right to all manner of people in accordance with the Constitution and the law, without fear or favour, affection or ill-will.'

II

Form of oath of secrecy for a Minister for the Union:

'I, A.B., do $\frac{\text{swear in the name of God}}{\text{solemnly affirm}}$ that I will not directly or indirectly solemnly affirm communicate or reveal to any person or persons any matter which shall be brought under my consideration or shall become known to me as a Minister for the Union except as may be required for the due discharge of my duties as such Minister.'

[3][III

A

Form of oath or affirmation to be made by a candidate for election to Parliament:

1, A.B., having been nominated as a candidate to fill a seat in the Council of States (or the House of the People) $\frac{\text{swear in the name of God}}{\text{solemnly affirm}}$ that I will bear true faith and allegiance to the Constitution of India as by law established and that I will uphold the sovereignty and 'integrity of India.'

B

Form of oath or affirmation to be made by. a member of Parliament:

'I, A.B., having been elected (or nominated) a member of the Council of States (or the House of the People) do that I will bear true faith and allegiance to the Constitution of India as by law established, that 1 will uphold the sovereignty and integrity of India and that I will faithfully discharge the duty upon which I am about to enter.'

---

1 See also articles 84(a) and 173(a).

2 Ins. by the Constitution (Sixteenth Amendment) Act, 1963, sec. 5.

3 Subs. by the Constitution (Sixteenth Amendment) Act, 1963, sec. 5, for Form III.

IV

Form of oath or affirmation to be made by the Judges of the Supreme Court and the Comptroller and Auditor-General of India:

'I, A.B., having been appointed Chief Justice (or a Judge) of the Supreme Court of India (or Comptroller and Auditor-General of India) do $\frac{\text{swear in the name of God}}{\text{solemnly affirm}}$ that I will bear true faith and allegiance to the Constitution of India as by law established, [1][that I will uphold the sovereignty and integrity of India,] that I will duly and faithfully and to the best of my ability, knowledge and judgment perform the duties of my office without fear or favour, affection or ill-will and that I will uphold the Constitution and the laws.'

V

Form of oath of office for a Minister for a State:

I, A.B., do $\frac{\text{swear in the name of God}}{\text{solemnly affirm}}$ that I will bear true faith and allegiance to the Constitution of India as by law established, [1][that I will uphold the sovereignty and integrity of India,] that I will faithfully and conscientiously discharge my duties as a Minister for the State of.." " and that I will do right to all manner of people in accordance with the Constitution and the law without fear or favour, affection or ill-will:

VI

Form of oath of secrecy for a Minister for a State:

1, A.B., do $\frac{\text{swear in the name of God}}{\text{solemnly affirm}}$ that I will not directly or indirectly communicate or reveal to any person or persons any matter which shall be brought under my consideration or shall become known to me as a Minister for the State of " "... except as may be required for the due discharge of my duties as such Minister:

[2]VII

A

Form of oath or affirmation to be made by a candidate for election to the Legislature of a State:

1, A.B., having been nominated as a candidate to fill a seat in Legislative Assembly (or Legislative Council), do $\frac{\text{swear in the name of God}}{\text{solemnly affirm}}$ that I will bear true faith and allegiance to the Constitution of India as by law established and that I will uphold the sovereignty and 'integrity of India'.

B

Form of oath or affirmation to be made by a member of the Legislature of a State:

'I, A.B., having been elected (or nominated) a member of the Legislative Assembly (or Legislative Council), do $\frac{\text{swear in the name of God}}{\text{solemnly affirm}}$ that I will bear true faith and allegiance to the Constitution of India as by law established, that I will uphold the sovereignty and integrity of India and that I will faithfully discharge the duty upon which I am about to enter.']

---

1 Ins. by the Constitution (Sixteenth Amendment) Act, 1963, sec. 5.

2 Subs. by the Constitution (Sixteenth Amendment) Act, 1963, sec. 5, for Form VII.

VIII

Form of oath or affirmation to be made by the Judges of a High Court:

I, A.B., having been appointed Chief Justice (or a Judge) of the High Court at (or of).......... do

swear in the name of God / solemnly affirm that I will bear true faith and allegiance to the Constitution of India

as by law established, [2][that I will uphold the sovereignty and integrity of India,] that I will duly and faithfully and to the best of my ability, knowledge, and judgment perform the duties of my office without fear or favour, affection or ill-will and that I will uphold the Constitution and the laws.

[2][FOURTH SCHEDULE

[ARTICLES 4(1) *AND* 80(2)]

ALLOCATION OF SEATS IN THE COUNCIL OF STATES

For each State or Union territory specified in the first column of the following table, there shall be allotted the number of seats specified in the second column thereof opposite to that State or that Union territory, as the case may be.

1.	Andhra Pradesh	18	2.	Assam	7
3.	Bihar	[3][16]	[4][4.	Jharkhand	6]
[5][*[5.]	Goa	1]	[6][*[6.]	Gujarat	11]
[7][*[7.]	Haryana	5]	*[8.]	Kerala	9]
*[9.]	Madhya Pradesh	[8][11]	[9][10.	Chhatisgarh	5]
[10][*[11.]	Tamil Nadu]	[11][18]	[12][*[12.]	Maharashtra	19]
[13][*[13.]	Karnataka]	12	*[14.]	Odisha	10
*[15.]	Punjab	[14][7]	*[16.]	Rajasthan	10
*[17.]	Uttar Pradesh	[15][31]	[16][18.	Uttarakhand	3]
*[19.]	West Bengal	16	*[20.]	Jammu & Kashmir	4

1 Ins. by the Constitution (Sixteenth Amendment) Act, 1963, sec.5.

2 Subs. by the Constitution (Seventh Amendment) Act, 1956, sec. 3, for the Fourth Schedule.

3 Subs. by the Bihar Reorganisation Act, 2000 (30 of 2000), sec. 7, for "22" (w.e.f. 15-11-2000).

4 Ins. by the Bihar Reorganisation Act, 2000 (30 of 2000), sec. 7 (w.e.f. 15-11-2000).

5 Ins. by Goa, Daman and Diu Reorganisation Act, 1987 (18 of 1987), sec. 6 (w.e.f. 30-5-1987).

6 Subs. by the Bombay Reorganisation Act, 1960 (11 of 1960), sec. 6 (w.e.f. 1-5-1960).

7 Ins. by the Punjab Reorganisation Act, 1966 (31 of 1966), sec. 9 (w.e.f. 1-11-1966).

8 Subs. by the Madhya Pradesh Reorganisation Act, 2000 (28 of 2000), sec. 7, for "16".

9 Ins. by Madhya. Pradesh Reorganisation Act, 2000 (28 of 2000), sec. 7.

10 Subs. by the Madras State (Alteration of Name) Act, 1968 (53 of 1968), sec. 5, for "Madras" (w.e.f. 14-1-1969).

11 Subs. by the Andhra Pradesh and Madras (Alteration of Boundaries) Act, 1959 (56 of 1959), sec. 8, for "17" (w.e.f. 1-4-1960).

12 Ins. by the Bombay Reorganisation Act, 1960 (11 of 1960), sec. 6 (w.e.f. 1-5-1960).

13 Subs. by the Mysore State (Alteration of Name) Act, 1973 (31 of 1973), sec. 5, for "Mysore" (w.e.f. 1-11-1973).

*Entry numbers have been renumbered by (i) the North Eastern Areas (Reorganisation) Act, 1971 (81 of 1971); (ii) the State of Mizoram Act, 1986 (34 of 1986); (iii) the Goa, Daman and Diu Reorganisation Act, 1987 (18 of 1987); (iv) the Madhya Pradesh Reorganisation Act, 2000 (28 of 2000) (w.e.f. 1-11-2000); (v) the Uttar Pradesh Reorganisation Act, 2000 (29 of 2000) (w.e.f. 9-11-2000); (vi) the Bihar Reorganisation Act, 2000 (30 of 2000) (w.e.f. 15-11-2000).

14 Subs. by the Punjab Reorganisation Act, 1966 (31 of 1966), sec. 9, for "11" (w.e.f. 1-11-1966).

15 Subs. by Orissa (Alteration of name) Act, 2011.

16 Subs. by Uttaranchal (Alteration of Name) Act, 2006.

[1][*[21.]	Nagaland	1]	[2][*[22.]	Himachal Pradesh	3]
[3][*[23.]	Manipur	1]	*[24.]	Tripura	1
*[25.]	Meghalaya	1	[4][*[26.]	Sikkim	1]
*[27.]	Mizoram	1	*[28.]	Arunachal Pradesh	1
*[29.]	Delhi	3	[6][*30.]	Puducherry	1
Total [5][233]]					

FIFTH SCHEDULE

[ARTICLE 244(1)]

PROVISIONS AS TO THE ADMINISTRATION AND CONTROL OF SCHEDULED AREAS AND SCHEDULED TRIBES

PART A

GENERAL

1. **Interpretation.**-In this Schedule, unless the context otherwise requires, the expression 'State' [7][***] does not include the [8][States of Assam] [9][[4][, Meghalaya, Tripura and Mizoram]].
2. **Executive power of a State in Scheduled Areas**.-Subject to the provisions of this Schedule, the executive power of a State extends to the Scheduled Areas therein.
3. **Report by the Governor [10][***] to the President regarding the administration of Scheduled Areas**.-The Governor [11][***] of each State having Scheduled Areas therein shall annually, or whenever so required by the President, make a report to the President regarding the administration of the Scheduled Areas in that State and the executive power of the Union shall extend to the giving of directions to the State as to the administration of the said areas.

---

1 Ins.. by the State of Nagaland Act, 1962 (27 of 1962), sec. 6 (w.e.f. 1-12-1963).

2 Ins. by the State of Himachal Pradesh Act, 1970 (53 of 1970), sec. 5 (w.e.f. 25-1-1971).

3 Subs. by the North Eastern Areas (Reorganisation) Act, 1971 (81 of .1971), sec. 10.

4 Ins. by the Constitution (Thirty-sixth Amendment) Act, 1975, sec. 4 (w.e.f. 26-1-1975).

5 Subs. by the Goa, Daman and Diu Reorganisation Act, 1987, sec. 6, for "232" (w.e.f 30-5-1987).

Entry numbers have been renumbered by (i) the North Eastern Areas (Reorganisation) Act, 1971 (81 of 1971); (ii) the State of Mizoram Act, 1986 (34 of 1986); (iii) the Goa, Daman and Diu Reorganisation Act, 1987 (18 of 1987); (iv) the Madhya Pradesh Reorganisation Act, 2000 (28 of 2000) (w.e.f. 1-11-2000); (v) the Uttar Pradesh Reorganisation Act, 2000 (29 of 2000) (w.e.f. 9-11-2000). (vi) The Bihar Reorganisation Act, 2000 (30 of 2000) (w.e.f. 15-11-2000).

6. Subs. by the Pondicherry (Alteration of name) Act. 2006.

7 The words and letters "means a State specified in Part A or Part B of the First Schedule but" omitted by the Constitution (Seventh Amendment) Act, 1956, sec. 29 and Sch.

8 Subs. by the North-Eastern Areas (Reorganisation) Act, 1971 (81 of 1971), sec. 71, for "State of Assam" (w.e.f. 21-1-1972).

9 Subs. by the State of Mizoram Act, 1986 (34 of 1986), sec. 39, for "Meghalaya and Tripura" (w.e.f. 20-2-1987).

10 Subs. by the Constitution (Forty-ninth Amendment) Act, 1984, sec. 3, for "and Meghalaya" (w.e.f. 1-4-1985).

11 The words "or the Rajpramukh" omitted by the Constitution (Seventh Amendment) Act, 1956, sec. 29 and Sch.

PART B

ADMINISTRATION AND CONTROL OF SCHEDULED AREAS AND SCHEDULED TRIBES

4. **Tribes Advisory Council.-**

(1) There shall be established in each State having Scheduled Areas therein and, if the President so directs, also in any State having Scheduled Tribes but not Scheduled Areas therein, a Tribes Advisory Council consisting of not more than twenty members of whom, as nearly as may be, three-fourths shall be the representatives of the Scheduled Tribes in the Legislative Assembly of the State:

Provided that if the number of representatives of the Scheduled Tribes in the Legislative Assembly of the State is less than the number of seats in the Tribes Advisory Council to be filled by such representatives, the remaining seats shall be filled by other members of those tribes.

(2) It shall be the duty of the Tribes Advisory Council to advise on such matters pertaining to the welfare and advancement of the Scheduled Tribes in the State as may be referred to them by the Governor [1][***]

(3) The Governor [2][***] may make rules prescribing or regulating, as the case may be,

(a) the number of members of the Council, the mode of their appointment and the appointment of the Chairman of the Council and of the officers and servants thereof,

(b) the conduct of its meetings and its procedure in general; and

(c) all other incidental matters.

5. **Law applicable to Scheduled Areas.-**

(1) Notwithstanding anything in this Constitution, the Governor [3][***] may by public notification direct that any particular Act of Parliament or of the Legislature of the State shall not apply to a Scheduled Area or any part thereof in the State or shall apply to a Scheduled Area or any part thereof in the State subject to such exceptions and modifications as he may specify in the notification and any direction given under this sub-paragraph may be given so as to have retrospective effect.

(2) The Governor [2][***] may make regulations for the peace and good government of any area in a State which is for the time being a Scheduled Area.

In particular and without prejudice to the generality of the foregoing power, such regulations may-

(a) prohibit or restrict the transfer of land by or among members of the Scheduled Tribes in such area;

(b) regulate the allotment of land to members of the Scheduled Tribes in such area;

(c) regulate the carrying on of business as money-lender by persons who lend money to members of the Scheduled Tribes in such area.

(3) In making any such regulation as is referred to in sub-paragraph (2) of this paragraph, the Governor I[ ] may repeal or amend any Act of Parliament or of the Legislature of the State or any existing law which is for the time being applicable to the area in question.

---

1 The words "or the Rajpramukh, as the case may be" omitted by the Constitution (Seventh Amendment) Act, 1956, sec. 29 and Sch.

2 The words "or the Rajpramukh" omitted by the Constitution (Seventh Amendment) Act, 1956, sec. 29 and Sch.

3 The words "or the Rajpramukh, as the case may be" omitted by the Constitution (Seventh Amendment) Act, 1956, sec. 29 and Sch.

(4) All regulations made under this paragraph shall be submitted forthwith to the President and, until assented to by him, shall have no effect.

(5) No regulation shall be made under this paragraph unless the Governor I[ ] making the regulation has, in the case where there is a Tribes Advisory Council for the State, consulted such Council.

PART C

SCHEDULED AREAS

6. **Scheduled Areas.-**

(I) In this Constitution, the expression 'Scheduled Areas' means such areas as the President may by order[1] declare to be Scheduled Areas.

(2) The President may at any time by order[2]-

(a) direct that the whole or any specified part of a Scheduled Area shall cease to be a Scheduled Area or a part of such an area;

[3][(aa) increase the area of any Scheduled Area in a State after consultation with the Governor of that State;]

(b) alter, but only by way of rectification of boundaries, any Scheduled Area;

(c) on any alteration of the boundaries of a State or on the admission into the Union or the establishment of a new State, declare any territory not previously included in any State to be, or to form part of, a Scheduled Area;

[3][(d) rescind, in relation to any State or States, any order or orders made under this paragraph, and in consultation with the Governor of the State concerned, make fresh orders redefining the areas which are as to be Scheduled Areas,] and any such order may contain such incidental and consequential provisions as appear to the President to be necessary and proper, but save as aforesaid, the order made under sub-paragraph (1) of this paragraph shall not be varied by any subsequent order.

PART D

AMENDMENT OF THE SCHEDULE

7. **Amendment of the Schedule.-**

(I) Parliament may from time to time by law amend by way of addition, variation or repeal any of the provisions of this Schedule and, when the Schedule is so amended, any reference to this Schedule in this Constitution shall be construed as a reference to such Schedule as so amended.

(2) No such law as is mentioned in sub-paragraph (1) of this paragraph shall be deemed to be an amendment of this Constitution for the purposes of article 368.

1 *See* the Scheduled Areas (Part A States) Order, 1950 (C.O. 9), the Scheduled Areas (Part B States) Order, 1950 (C.O. 26), the Scheduled Areas (Himachal Pradesh) Order, 1975 (C.O. 102) and the Scheduled Areas (States of Bihar, Gujarat, Madhya Pradesh and Orissa) Order, 1977 (C.O. 109).

2 *See* the Madras Scheduled Area (Cesser) Order, 1951 (C.O. 30) and the Andhra Scheduled Areas (Cesser) Order, 1955 (C.O. 50).

3 Ins. by the Fifth Schedule to the Constitution (Amendment) Act, 1976 (101 of 1976), sec.2.

SIXTH SCHEDULE

[ARTICLES 244(2) AND 275(1)]

PROVISIONS AS TO THE ADMINISTRATION OF TRIBAL AREAS IN [1][[2][THE STATES OF ASSAM [3][,MEGHALAYA, TRIPURA] AND MIZORAM]]

1. **Autonomous districts and autonomous regions.-**

(I) Subject to the provisions of this paragraph, the tribal areas in each item of [4][[5][Parts 1, II and IIA] and in Part III] of the table appended to paragraph 20 of this Schedule shall be an autonomous district.

(2) If there are different Scheduled Tribes in an autonomous district, the Governor may, by public notification, divide the area or areas inhabited by them into autonomous regions.[6]

(3) The Governor may, by public notification,-

(a) include any area in [4][any of the Parts] of the said table,

(b) exclude any area from [4][any of the Parts] of the said table,

(c) create a new autonomous district,

(d) increase the area of any autonomous district,

(e) diminish the area of any autonomous district,

(f) unite two or more autonomous districts or parts thereof so as to form one autonomous district,

[7][(ff) alter the name of any autonomous district,]

(g) define the boundaries of any autonomous district:

Provided that no order shall be made by the Governor under clauses (c), (d), (e) and (f) of this sub-paragraph except after consideration of the report of a Commission appointed under sub-paragraph (1) of paragraph 14 of this Schedule:

[8][Provided further that any order made by the Governor under this sub- paragraph may contain such incidental and consequential provisions (including any amendment of paragraph 20 and of any item in any of the Parts of the said table) as appear to the Governor to be necessary for giving effect to the provisions of the order.]

---

1 Subs. by the State of Mizoram Act, 1986 (34 of 1986), sec. 39(f), for "the State of Assam, Meghalaya and Tripura and in the Union Territory of Mizoram" (w.e.f. 20-2-1987).

2 Subs. by the North-Eastern Areas (Reorganisation) Act, 1971 (81 of 1971), sec. 71(i) and Eighth Sch., for" Assam" (w.e.f. 21-1-1972).

3 Subs. by the Constitution (Forty-ninth Amendment) Act, 1984, sec. 4, for "and Meghalaya" (w.e.f. 1-4-1985).

4 Subs. by the North-Eastern Areas (Reorganisation) Act, 1971 (81 of 1971), sec. 71(i) and Eighth Sch., for "Part A " (w.e.f. 21-1-1972).

5 Subs. by the Constitution (Forty-ninth Amendment) Act, 1984, sec. 4, for "Parts I and II" (w.e.f. 1-4-1985).

6 Paragraph 1 has been amended in its application to the State of Assam by the Sixth Schedule to the Constitution (Amendment) Act, 2003 (44 of 2003), sec. 2 (w.e.f. 7-9-2003) so as to insert after sub-paragraph (2) the following proviso; namely:- "Provided that nothing in this sub-paragraph shall apply to the Bodoland Territorial Areas District."

7 Ins. by the Assam Reorganisation (Meghalaya) Act, 1969 (55 of 1969), sec. 74 and Fourth Sch. (w.e.f. 2-4-1970).

8 Ins. by the North-Eastern Areas (Reorganisation) Act, 1971 (81 of 1971), sec. 71(i) and Eighth Sch. (w.e.f. 21-2-1972).

2. Constitution of District Councils and Regional Councils.-

[1][(1) There shall be a District Council for each autonomous district consisting of not more than thirty members, of whom not more than four persons shall be nominated by the Governor and the rest shall be elected on the basis of adult suffrage.][2]

(2) There shall be a separate Regional Council for each area constituted as an autonomous region under sub-paragraph (2) of paragraph 1 of this Schedule.

(3) Each District Council and each Regional Council shall be a body corporate by the name respectively of 'the District Council of *(name of district)*' and 'the Regional Council of *(name of region)*', shall have perpetual succession and a common seal and shall by the said name sue and be sued.[3]

(4) Subject to the provisions of this Schedule, the administration of an autonomous district shall, in so far as it is not vested under this Schedule in any Regional Council within such district, be vested in the District Council for such district and the administration of an autonomous region shall be vested in the Regional Council for such region.

(5) In an autonomous district with Regional Councils, the District Council shall have only such powers with respect to the areas under the authority of the Regional Council as may be delegated to it by the Regional Council in addition to the powers conferred on it by this Schedule with respect to such areas.

(6) The Governor shall make rules for the first constitution of District Councils and Regional Councils in consultation with the existing tribal Councils or other representative tribal organisations within the autonomous districts or regions concerned, and such rules shall provide for-

(a) the composition of the District Councils and Regional Councils and the allocation of seats therein;

(b) the delimitation of territorial constituencies for the purpose of elections to those Councils;

(c) the qualifications for voting at such elections and the preparation of electoral rolls therefor;

(d) the qualifications for being elected at such elections as members of such Councils;

---

1 Subs. by the Assam Reorganisation (Meghalaya) Act, 1969 (55 of 1969), sec. 74 and Fourth Sch., for paragraph (1) (w.e.f. 2-4-1970).

2 Paragraph 2 has been amended in its application to the State of Assam by the Sixth Schedule to the Constitution (Amendment) Act, 2003 (44 of 2003), sec. 2 (w.e..f. 7-9-2003), so as to insert after sub-paragraph (1), the following proviso, namely:- "Provided that the Bodoland Territorial Council shall consist of not more than forty-six members of whom forty shall be elected on the basis of adult suffrage, of whom thirty shall be reserved for the Scheduled Tribes, five for non-tribal communities, five open for all communities and the remaining six shall be nominated by the Governor having same rights' and privileges as other members, including voting rights, from amongst the un-represented communities of the Bodoland Territorial Areas District, of which at least two shall be women."

3 Paragraph 2 has been amended in its application to the State of Assam by the Sixth Schedule to the Constitution (Amendment) Act, 1995 (42 of 1995), sec. 2 (w.e.f. 12-9-1995), so as to insert in sub-paragraph (3), the following proviso, namely:-

* Provided that the District Council constituted for the North Cachar Hills District shall be called as the North Cachar Hills Autonomous Council and the District Council constituted for the Karbi Anglong District shall be called as the Karbi Anglong Autonomus Council." " Paragraph 2 has been amended in its application to the State of Assam by the Sixth Schedule to the Constitution (Amendment) Act, 2003 (44 of 2003), sec. 2 (w.e.f. 7-9-2003), so as to insert in sub-paragraph (3), after the proviso, the following proviso, namely:- "Provided further that the District Council constituted for the Bodoland Territorial Areas District shall be called the Bodoland Territorial Council."

(e) the term of office of members of [1][Regional Councils];

(f) any other matter relating to or connected with elections or nominations to such Councils;

(g) the procedure and the conduct of business [2][including the power to act notwithstanding any vacancy] in the District and Regional Councils;

(h) the appointment of officers and staff of the District and Regional Councils.

2[(6A) The elected members of the District Council shall hold office for a term of five years from the date appointed for the first meeting of the Council after the general elections to the Council, unless the District Council is sooner dissolved under paragraph 16 and a nominated member shall hold office at the pleasure of the Governor:

Provided that the said .period of five years my, while a Proclamation of Emergency is in operation or if circumstances exist which, in the opinion of the Governor, render the holding of elections impracticable, be extended by the Governor for a period not exceeding one year at a time and in any case where a Proclamation of Emergency is in operation not extending beyond a period of six months after the Proclamation has ceased to operate:

Provided further that a member elected to fill a casual vacancy shall hold office only for the remainder of the term of office of the member whom he replaces.]

(7) The District or the Regional Council may after its first constitution make rules [2][with the approval of the Governor] with regard to the matters specified in sub- paragraph (6) of this paragraph and may also make rules [2][with like approval] regulating-

(a) the formation of subordinate local Councils or Boards and their procedure and the conduct of their business; and

(b) generally all matters relating to the transaction of business pertaining to the administration of the district or region, as the case may be:

Provided that until rules are made by the District or the Regional Council under this sub-paragraph the rules made by the Governor under sub-paragraph (6) of this paragraph shall have effect in respect of elections to, the officers and staff of, and the procedure and the conduct of business in, each such Council.

[4][***] 3. **Powers of the District Councils and Regional Councils to make laws.-**

(1) The Regional Council for an autonomous region in respect of all areas within such region and the District Council for an autonomous district in respect of all areas within the district except those which are under the authority of Regional Councils, if any, within the district shall have power to make laws with respect to-

(a) the allotment, occupation or use, or the setting apart, of land, other than any land which is a reserved forest for the purposes of agriculture or grazing or for residential or other non-agricultural purposes or for any other purpose likely to promote the interests of the inhabitants of any village or town:

Provided that nothing in such laws shall prevent the compulsory acquisition of any land whether occupied or unoccupied, for public purposes [5][by the Government of the State concerned] in accordance with the law for the time being in force authorising such acquisition;

---

1 Ins. by the Assam Reorganisation (Meghalaya) Act, 1969 (55 of 1969), sec. 74 and Fourth Sch., for "such Councils" (w.e.f. 2-4-1970).

2 Ins. by the Assam Reorganisation (Meghalaya) Act, 1969 (55 of 1969), sec. 74 and Fourth Sch. (w.e.f. 2-4-1970).

3 Subs. by the Assam Reorganisation (Meghalaya) Act, 1969 (55 of 1969), sec. 74 and Fourth Sch., for certain words (w.e.f. 2-4-1970).

4 Second proviso omitted by the Assam Reorganisation (Meghalaya) Act, 1969 (55 of 1969), sec. 74 and Fourth Sch. (w.e.f. 2-4-1970).

5 Subs. by the North-Eastern Areas (Reorganisation) Act, 1971 (81 of 1971), sec. 71(i) and Eighth Sch., for certain words (w.e.f. 21-1-1972).

(b) the management of any forest not being a reserved forest;

(c) the use of any canal or water-course for the purpose of agriculture;

(d) the regulation of the practice of *jhum* or other forms of shifting cultivation;

(e) the establishment of village or town committees or councils and their powers;

(f) any other matter relating to village or town administration, including village or town police and public health and sanitation;

(g) the appointment or succession of Chiefs or Headmen;

(h) the inheritance of property;

(i) [1][marriage and divorce;]

(j) social customs.

(2) In this paragraph, a 'reserved forest' means any area which is a reserved forest under the Assam Forest Regulation, 1891, or under any other law for the time being in force in the area in question.

(3) All laws made under this paragraph shall be submitted forthwith to the Governor and, until assented to by him, shall have no effect.[2]

---

1 Subs. by the Assam Reorganisation (Meghalaya) Act, 1969 (55 of 1969), sec. 74 and Fourth Sch., for clause (i) (w.e.f. 2-4-1970).

2 Paragraph 3 has been amended in its application to the State of Assam by the Sixth Schedule to the Constitution (Amendment) Act, 2003 (44 of 2003), sec. 2 (w.e.f. 7-9-2003), so as to substitute for sub-paragraph (3), the following sub-paragraph, namely:- "(3) Save as otherwise provided in sub-paragraph (2) of paragraph 3A or sub-paragraph (2) of paragraph 3B, all laws made under this paragraph or sub-paragraph (1) of paragraph 3A or sub-paragraph (1) of paragraph 3B shall be submitted forthwith to the Governor and, until assented to by him, shall have no effect." Earlier sub-paragraph (3) was subs. by the Sixth Schedule to the Constitution (Amendment) Act, 1995 (42 of 1995), sec. 2 (w.e.f. 12-9-1995), so as to read as under: "(3) Save as otherwise provided in sub-paragraph (2) of paragraph 3A, all laws made under this paragraph or sub-paragraph (1) of paragraph 3A shall be submitted forthwith to the Governor and, until assented to by him, shall have no effect." ..After paragraph 3, the following paragraph has been inserted in its application to the State of Assam by the Sixth Schedule to the Constitution (Amendment) Act, 1995 (42 of 1995), sec. 2 (w.e.f. 12-9-1995), namely:- *"3A. Additional powers of the North Cachar Hills Autonomous Council and the Karbi Anglong Autonomous Council to make law.-(l)* Without prejudice to the provisions of paragraph 3, the North Cachar Hills Autonomous Council and the Karbi Anglong Autonomous Council within their respective districts, shall have power to make laws with respect to-

(a) industries, subject to the provisions of entries 7 and 52 of List I of the Seventh Schedule;

(b) communications, that is to say, roads, bridges, ferries and other means of communication not specified in List I of the Seventh Schedule; municipal tramways, ropeways, inland waterways and traffic thereon subject to the provisions of List I and List III of the Seventh Schedule with regard to such waterways; vehicles other than mechanically propelled vehicles;

(c) preservation, protection and improvement of stock and prevention of animal diseases; veterinary training and practice; cattle pounds;

(d) primary and secondary education;

(e) agriculture, including agricultural education and research, protection against pests and prevention of plant diseases;

(f) fisheries;

(g) water, that is; to say, water supplies, irrigation and canals, drainage and embankments, water storage and water power subject to the provisions of entry 56 of List I of the Seventh Schedule;

(h) social security and social insurance; employment and unemployment;

(i) flood control schemes for protection of villages, paddy fields, markets, towns, etc. (not of technical nature);

(j) theatre and dramatic performances, cinemas subject to the provisions of entry 60 of List 1 of the Seventh Schedule; sports entertainments and amusements;

(k) public health and sanitation, hospitals and dispensaries;

(l) minor irrigation;

(m) trade and commerce in, and the production, supply and distribution of, food stuffs, cattle fodder, raw cotton and raw jute;

(n) Libraries, museums and other similar institutions controlled or financed by the State; ancient and historical monuments and records other than those declared by or under any law made by Parliament to be of national importance; and

(o) alienation of land.

(2) All laws made by the North Cachar Hills Autonomous Council and the Karbi Anglong Autonomous Council under paragraph 3 or under this paragraph shall, in so far as they relate to matters specified in List III of the Seventh Schedule, be submitted forthwith to the Governor who shall reserve the same for the consideration of the President.

(3) When a law is reserved for the consideration of the President, the President shall declare either that he assents to the said law or that he withholds assent therefrom:

Provided that the President may direct the Governor to return the law to the North Cachar Hills Autonomous Council or the Karbi Anglong Autonomous Council, as the case may be, together with a message requesting that the said Council will reconsider the law or any specified provisions thereof and, in particular, will, consider the desirability of introducing any such amendments as he may recommend in his message and, when the law is so returned, the said Council shall consider the law accordingly within a period of six months from the date of receipt of such message and, if the law is again passed by the said Council with or without amendment it shall be presented again to the President for his consideration."

.After paragraph *3A,* the following paragraph has been inserted in its application to the State of Assam by the Sixth Schedule to the Constitution (Amendment) Act, 2003 (44 of 2003), sec. 2 (w.e.f. 7-9-2003), namely:-

"3B. *Additional powers to the Bodoland Territorial Council to make laws.-(l)* Without prejudice to the provisions of paragraph 3, the Bodoland Territorial Council within its areas shall have power to make laws with respect to-(i) Agriculture, including agricultural education and research, protection against pests and prevention of plant diseases; (ii) Animal husbandry and veterinary, that is to say, preservation, protection and improvement of stock and prevention of animal diseases, veterinary training and practice, cattle pounds; (iii) Co-operation; (iv) Cultural affairs; (v) Education, that is to say, primary education, higher secondary including vocational training, adult education, college education (general); (vi) Fisheries; (vii) Flood control for protection of village, paddy fields, markets and towns (not of technical nature); (viii) Food and civil supply; (ix) Forests (other than reserved forests); (x) Handloom and textile; (xi) Health and family welfare; (xii) Intoxicating liquors, opium and derivatives, subject to the provisions of entry 84 of List l of the Seventh Schedule; (xiii) Irrigation; (xiv) Labour and employment; (xv) Land and Revenue; (xvi) Library services (financed and controlled by the State Government); (xvii) Lotteries (subject to the provisions of entry 40 of List I of the Seventh Schedule), theatres, dramatic performances and cinemas (subject to the provisions of entry 60 of List I of the Seventh Schedule); (xviii) Markets and fairs; (xix) Municipal corporation, improvement trust, district boards and other local authorities; (xx) Museum and archaeology institutions controlled or financed by the State, ancient and historical monuments and records other than those declared by or under any law made by Parliament to be of national importance; (xxi) Panchayat and rural development; (xxii) Planning and development; (xxiii) Printing and stationery; (xxiv) Public health engineering; (xxv) Public works department; (xxvi) Publicity and public relations; (xxvii) Registration of births and deaths; (xxviii) Relief and rehabilitation; (xxix) Sericulture; (xxx) Small, cottage and rural industry subject to the provisions of entries 7 and 52 of List I of the Seventh Schedule; (xxxi) Social welfare; (xxxii) Soil conservation; (xxxiii) Sports and youth welfare; (xxxiv) Statistics; (xxxv) Tourism; (xxxvi) Transport (roads, bridges, ferries and other means of communications not specified in List I of the Seventh Schedule, municipal tramways, ropeways, inland waterways and traffic thereon subject to the provision of List I and List III of the Seventh Schedule with regard to such waterways, vehicles other than mechanically propelled vehicles); (xxxvii) Tribal research institute controlled and financed by the State Government; (xxxviii) Urban development-town and country planning; (xxxix) Weights and measures subject to the provisions of entry 50 of List I of the Seventh Schedule; and (xi) Welfare of plain tribes and backward classes:

Provided that nothing in such laws shall-

(a) extinguish or modify the existing rights and privileges of any citizen in respect of his land at the date of commencement of this Act; and

(b) disallow any citizen from acquiring land either by way of inheritance, allotment, settlement or by any other way of transfer if such citizen is otherwise eligible for such acquisition of land within the Bodoland Territorial Areas District.

4. **Administration of justice in autonomous districts and autonomous regions.-**

(l) The Regional Council for an autonomous region in respect of areas within such region and the District Council for an autonomous district in respect of areas within the district other than those which are under the authority of the Regional Councils, if any, within the district may constitute village councils or courts for the trial of suits and cases between the parties all of whom belong to Scheduled Tribes within such areas, other than suits and cases to which the provisions of subparagraph (1) of paragraph 5 of this Schedule apply, .to the exclusion of any court in the State, and may appoint suitable persons to be member of such village councils or presiding officers of such courts, and may also appoint such officers as may be necessary for the administration of the laws made under paragraph 3 of this Schedule.

(2) Notwithstanding anything in this Constitution, the Regional Council for an autonomous region or any court constituted in that behalf by the Regional Council or, if in respect of any area within an autonomous district there is no Regional Council, the District Council for such district, or any court constituted in that behalf by the District Council, shall exercise the powers of a court of appeal in respect of all suits and cases triable by a village council or court constituted under sub-paragraph (1) of this paragraph within such region or area, as the case may be, other than those to which the provisions of sub-paragraph (1) of paragraph 5 of this Schedule apply, and no other court except the High Court and the Supreme Court shall have jurisdiction over such suits or cases.

(3) The High Court [1][***] shall have and exercise such jurisdiction over the suits and cases to which the provisions of sub-paragraph (2) of this paragraph apply as the Governor may from time to time by order specify.

(4) A Regional Council or District Council, as the case may be, may with the previous approval of the Governor make rules regulating-

(a) the constitution of village councils and courts and the powers to be exercised by them under this paragraph;

(b) the procedure to be followed by village councils or courts in the trial of suits and cases under sub-paragraph (1) of this paragraph;

(c) the procedure to be followed by the Regional or District Council or any court constituted by such Council in appeals and other proceedings under sub- paragraph (2) of this paragraph;

(d) the enforcement of decisions and orders of such Councils and courts;

(e) all other ancillary matters for the carrying out of the provisions of sub-paragraphs (1) and (2) of this paragraph.

---

(2) All laws made under paragraph 3 or under this paragraph shall in so far as they relate to matters specified in List III of the Seventh Schedule, be submitted forthwith to the Governor who shall reserve the same for the consideration of the President.

(3) When a law is reserved for the consideration of the President, the President shall declare either that he assents to the said law or that he withholds assent therefrom:

Provided that the President may direct the Governor to return the law to the Bodoland Territorial Council, together with the message requesting that the said Council will reconsider the law or any specified provisions thereof and, in particular, will consider the desirability of introducing any such amendments as he may recommend in his message and, when the law is so returned, the said Council shall consider the law accordingly within a period of six months from the date of receipt of such message and, if the law is again passed by the said Council with or without amendment it shall be presented again to the President for his consideration."

1 The words "of Assam" omitted by the North-Eastern Areas (Reorganisation) Act, 1971 (81 of 1971), sec. 71(i) and Eighth Sch. (w.e.f. 21-1-1972).

[1][(5) On and from such date as the President may, [2][after consulting the Government of the State concerned], by notification appoint in this behalf, this paragraph shall have effect in relation to such autonomous district or region as may be specified in the notification, as if-

(i) in sub-paragraph (1), for the words "between the parties all of whom belong to Scheduled Tribes within such areas, other than suits and cases to which the provisions of sub-paragraph (1) of paragraph 5 of this Schedule apply,", the words "not being suits and cases of the nature referred to in sub- paragraph (1) of paragraph (5) of this Schedule, which the Governor may specify in this behalf," had been substituted;

(ii) sub-paragraphs (2) and (3) had been omitted; (iii) in sub-paragraph (4)- -

(a) for the words "A Regional Council or District Council, as the case may be, may with the previous approval of the Governor make rules regulating', the words "the Governor may make rules regulating' had been substituted; and

(b) for clause (a), the following clause had been substituted, namely:- (a) the constitution of village councils and courts, the powers to be exercised by them under this paragraph and the courts to which appeals from the decisions of village councils and courts shall lie;"

(c) for clause (c), the following clause had been substituted, namely:- "(c) the transfer of appeals and other proceedings pending before the Regional or District Council or any court constituted by such Council immediately before the date appointed by the President under sub-paragraph (5);" and

(d) in clause (e), for the words, brackets and figures "sub-paragraphs (1) and (2), the word, brackets and figures, sub-paragraph (1) had been substituted.][3]

5. **Conferment of powers under the Code of Civil Procedure, 1908, and the Code of Criminal Procedure, 1898; on the Regional and District Councils and on certain courts and officers for the trial of certain suits, cases and offences.-**

(l) The Governor may, for the trial of suits or cases arising out of any law in force in any autonomous district or region being a law specified in that behalf by the Governor, or for the trial of offences punishable with death, transportation for life, or imprisonment for a term of not less than five years under the Indian Penal Code or under any other law for the time being applicable to such district or region, confer on the District Council or the Regional Council having authority over such district or region or on courts constituted by such District Council or on any officer appointed in that behalf by the Governor, such powers under the Code of Civil Procedure, 1908, or, as the case may be, the Code of Criminal Procedure, 1898[4], as he deems appropriate, and thereupon the said Council, court or officer shall try the suits, cases or offences in exercise of the powers so conferred.

(2) The Governor may withdraw or modify any of the powers conferred on a District Council, Regional Council, court or officer under sub-paragraph (1) of this paragraph.

---

1 Ins. by the Assam Reorganisation (Meghalaya) Act, 1969 (55 of 1969), sec. 74 and Fourth Sch. (w.e.f. 24-4-1970).

2 Subs. by the North-Eastern Areas (Reorganisation) Act, 1971 (81 of 1971), sec. 71(i) and Eighth Sch., for certain words (w.e.f. 21-1-1972).

3 Paragraph 4 has been amended in its application to the State of Assam by the Sixth Schedule' to the Constitution (Amendment) Act, 2003 (44 of 2003), sec. 2 (w.e.f. 7-9-2003), so as to insert after sub-paragraph (5), the following sub-paragraph, namely:- "(6) Nothing in this paragraph shall apply to the Bodoland Territorial Council constituted under the proviso to sub-paragraph (3) of paragraph 2 of this Schedule."

(3) Save as expressly provided in this paragraph, the Code of Civil Procedure, 1908, and the Code of Criminal Procedure, 1898[1], shall not apply to the trial of any suits, cases or offences in an autonomous district or in any autonomous region to which the provisions of this paragraph apply.

[2](4) On and from the date appointed by the President under sub-paragraph (5) of paragraph 4 in relation to any autonomous district or autonomous region, nothing contained in this paragraph shall! in its application to that district or region, be deemed to authorise the Governor to confer on the District Council or Regional Council or on courts constituted by the District Council any of the powers referred to in sub-paragraph (1) of this paragraph.]

[3][6. **Powers of the District Council to establish primary schools, etc.-**

(1) The District Council for an autonomous district may establish, construct, or manage primary schools, dispensaries, markets, [4](cattle pounds], ferries, fisheries, roads, road transport and waterways in the district and may, with the previous approval of the Governor, make regulations for the regulation and control thereof and, in particular, may prescribe the language and the manner in which primary education shall be imparted in the primary schools in the district.

(2) The Governor may, with the consent of any District Council, entrust either conditionally or unconditionally to that Council or to its officers functions in relation to agriculture, animal husbandry, community projects, co-operative societies, social welfare, village planning or any other matter to which the executive power of the State [5][***] extends.]

7. **District and Regional Funds.-**

(1) There shall be constituted for each autonomous district, a District Fund for each autonomous region, a Regional Fund to which shall be credited all moneys received respectively by the District Council for that district and the Regional Council for that region in the course of the administration of such district or region, as the case may be, in accordance with the provisions of this Constitution.

[6][(2) The Governor may make rules for the management of the District Fund, or, as the case may be, the Regional Fund and for the procedure to be followed in respect of payment of money into the said Fund, the withdrawal of moneys therefrom, the custody of moneys therein and any other matter connected with or ancillary to the matters aforesaid.

(3) The accounts of the District Council or, as the case may be, the Regional Council shall be kept in such form as the Comptroller and Auditor-General of India may, with the approval of the President, prescribe.

(4) The Comptroller and Auditor-General shall cause the accounts of the District and Regional Councils to be audited in such manner as he may think fit, and the reports of the Comptroller and Auditor General relating to such accounts shall be submitted to the Governor who shall cause them to be laid before the Council.]

---

1 *See* now the Code of Criminal Procedure, 1973 (2 of 1974).

2 Ins. by the Assam Reorganisation (Meghalaya) Act, 1969 (55 of 1969), sec. 74 and Fourth Sch. (w.e.f. 2-4-1970).

3 Subs. by the Assam Reorganisation (Meghalaya) Act, 1969 (55 of 1969), sec. 74 and Forth Sch., for paragraph 6 (w.e.f. 2-4-1970).

4 Subs. by the Repealing and Amending Act, 1974 (56 of 1974), sec. 4 , for "cattle ponds'.

5 The words "of Assam or Meghalaya, as the case may be," omitted by the North-Eastern Areas (Reorganisation) Act, 1971 (81 of 1971), sec. 71(i) and Eighth Sch. (w.e.f. 21-1-1972).

6 Subs. by the Assam Reorganisation (Meghalaya) Act, 1969 (55 of 1969), sec. 74 and Fourth Sch., for sub-paragraph (2) (w.e.f. 2-4-1970).

8. **Powers to assess and collect land revenue and to impose taxes.-**

(1) The Regional Council for an autonomous region in respect of all lands within such region and the District Council for an autonomous district in respect of all lands within the district except those which are in the areas under the authority of Regional Councils, if any, within the district, shall have the power to assess and collect revenue in respect of such lands in accordance with the principles for the time being followed [1][by the Government of the State in assessing lands for the purpose of land revenue in the State generally].

(2) The Regional Council for an autonomous region in respect of areas within such region and the District Council for an autonomous district in respect of all areas in the district except those which are under the authority of Regional Councils, if any, within the district, shall have power to levy and collect taxes on lands and buildings, and tolls on persons, resident within such areas.

(3) The District Council for an autonomous district shall have the power to levy and collect all or any of the following taxes within such district, that is to say-

(a) taxes on professions, trades, callings and employments;

(b) taxes on animals, vehicles and boats;

(c) taxes on the entry of goods into a market for sale therein, and tolls on passengers and goods carried in ferries; and

(d) taxes for the maintenance of schools, dispensaries or roads.

(4) A Regional Council or District Council, as the case may be, may make regulations to provide for levy and collection of any of the taxes specified in sub-paragraphs (2) and (3) of this paragraph [2][and every such regulation shall be submitted forthwith to the Governor and, until assented to by him, shall have no effect].

9. **Licences or leases for the purpose of prospecting for, or extraction of, minerals.-**

(1) Such share of the royalties accruing each year from licences or leases for the purpose of prospecting for, or the extraction of, minerals granted by [3][the Government of the State] in respect of any area within an autonomous district as may be agreed upon between [2][the Government of the State] and the District Court of such district shall be made over to that District Council.

(2) If any dispute arises as to the share of such royalties to be made over to a district Council, it shall be referred to the Governor for determination and the amount determined by the Governor in his discretion shall be deemed to be the amount payable under sub-paragraph (1) of this paragraph to the District Council and the decision of the Governor shall be final.[4]

---

1 Subs. by the North-Eastern Areas (Reorganisation) Act, 1971 (81 of 1971), sec. 71(i) and Eighth Sch., for certain words (w.e.f. 21-1-1972).

2 Ins. by the Assam Reorganisation (Meghalaya) Act, 1969 (55 of 1969) sec. 74 and Fourth Sch. (w.e.f. 2-4-1970).

3 Subs. by the North-Eastern Areas (Reorganisation) Act, 1971 (81 of 1971), sec. 71(i) and Eighth Sch., for "the Government of Assam" (w.e.f. 21-1-1972).

4 Paragraph 9 has been amended in its application to the States of Tripura and Mizoram by the Sixth Schedule to the Constitution (Amendment) Act, 1988 (67 of 1988), sec. 2 (w.e.f. 16-12- 1988), so as to insert after sub-paragraph (2), the following sub-paragraph namely:- "(3) The Governor may, by order, direct that the share of royalties to be made over to a District Council under this paragraph shall be made over to that Council within a period of one year from the date of any agreement under sub-paragraph (1) or, as the case may be, of any determination under sub-paragraph (2)."

[1]10. **Power of District Council to make regulations for the control of money-lending and trading by non-tribals.**-

(I) The District Council of an autonomous district may make regulations for the regulation and control of money-lending or trading within the district by persons other than Scheduled Tribes resident in the district.

(2) In particular and without prejudice to the generality of the foregoing power, such regulations may-

(a) prescribe that no one except the holder of a licence issued in that behalf shall carry on the business of money-lending;

(b) prescribe the maximum rate of interest which may be charged or be recovered by a money-lender;

(c) provide for the maintenance of accounts by money-lenders and for the inspection of such accounts by officers appointed in that behalf by the District Council;

(d) prescribe that no person who is not a member of the Scheduled Tribes resident in the district shall carry on wholesale or retail business in any commodity except under a licence issued in that behalf by the District Council:

Provided that no regulations may be made under this paragraph unless they are passed by a majority of not less than three-fourths of the total membership of the District Council:

Provided further that it shall not be competent under any such regulations to refuse the grant of a licence to a money-lender or a trader who has been carrying on business within the district since before the time of making of such regulations.

(3) All regulations made under this paragraph shall be submitted forthwith to the Governor and, until assented to by him, shall have no effect.[2]

11. **Publication of laws, rules and regulations made under the Schedule.**-All laws, rules and regulations made under this Schedule by a District Council or a Regional Council shall be published forthwith in the Official Gazette of the State and shall on such publication have the force of law.

[3]12. [4]**[Application of Acts of Parliament and of the Legislature of the State of Assam to autonomous districts and autonomous regions in the State of Assam]**.-

(I) Notwithstanding anything in this Constitution-

---

1 Paragraph 10 has been amended in its application to the States of Tripura and Mizoram by the Sixth Schedule to the Constitution (Amendment) Act, 1988 (67 of 1988), sec. 2 (w.e.f. 16- 12-1988), as under:

(a) in the heading, the words "by non-tribals" shall be omitted;

(b) in sub-paragraph (1), the words "other than Scheduled Tribes" shall be omitted;

(c) in sub-paragraph (2), for clause (d), the following clause shall be substituted, namely:- "(d) prescribe that no person resident in the district shall carry on any trade, whether wholesale or retail, except under a licence issued in that behalf by the District Council."

2 Paragraph 10 has been amended in its application to the State of Assam by the Sixth Schedule to the Constitution (Amendment) Act, 2003 (44 of 2003), sec. 2 (w.e.f. 7-9-2003), so as to insert after sub-paragraph (3), the following sub-paragraph, namely:- "(4) Nothing in this paragraph shall apply to the Bodoland Territorial Council constituted under the proviso to sub-paragraph (3) of paragraph 2 of this Schedule."

3 Paragraph 12 has been amended in its application to the State of Assam by the Sixth Schedule to the Constitution (Amendment) Act, 1995 (42 of 1995), sec. 2 (w.e.f. 12-9-1995), so as to substitute in sub-paragraph (1), for the words and figure "matters specified in paragraph 3 of this Schedule", the words, figures and letter "matters specified in paragraph 3 or paragraph3A of this Schedule". .

4 Subs. by the North-Eastern Areas (Reorganisation) Act, 1971 (81 of 1971), sec. 71(i) and Eighth Sch., for the heading (w.e.f. 21-1-1972).

(a) no Act of the [1][Legislature of the State of Assam] in respect of any of the matters specified in paragraph 3 of this Schedule as matters with respect to which a District Council or a Regional Council may make laws, and no Act of the [4][Legislature of the State of Assam] prohibiting or restricting the consumption of any non-distilled alcoholic liquor shall apply to any autonomous district or autonomous region [2][in the State] unless in either case the District Council for such district or having jurisdiction over such region by public notification so directs, and the District Council in giving such direction with respect to any Act may direct that the Act shall in its application to such district or region or any part thereof have effect subject to such exceptions or modifications as it thinks fit;[3]

(b) the Governor may, by public notification, direct that any Act of Parliament or of the [4][Legislature of the State of Assam] to which the provisions of clause (a) of this sub-paragraph do not apply shall not apply to an autonomous district or an autonomous region [5][in that State], or shall apply to such district or region or any part thereof subject to such exceptions or modifications as he may specify in the notification.

(2) Any direction given under sub-paragraph (1) of this paragraph may be given so as to have retrospective effect.

[4][12A. **Application of Acts of Parliament and of the Legislature of the State of Meghalaya to autonomous districts and autonomous regions in the State of Meghalaya.**-Notwithstanding anything in this Constitution,-

(a) if any provision of a law made by a District or Regional Council in the State of Meghalaya with respect to any matter specified in sub-paragraph (1) of paragraph 3 of this Schedule or if any provision of any regulation made by a District Council or a Regional Council in that State under paragraph 8 or paragraph 10 of this Schedule, is repugnant to any provision of a law made by the Legislature of the State of Meghalaya with respect to that matter, then, the law or regulation made by the District Council or, as the case may be, the Regional Council whether made before or after the law made by the Legislature of the State of Meghalaya, shall, to the extent of repugnancy, be void and the law made by the Legislature of the State of Meghalaya shall prevail;

(b) the President may, with respect to any Act of Parliament, by notification, direct .that it shall not apply to an autonomous district or an autonomous region in the State of Meghalaya, or shall apply to such district or region or any part thereof subject to such exceptions or modifications as he may specify in the notification and any such direction may be given so as to have retrospective effect.]

[5][12AA. **Application of Acts of Parliament and of the Legislature of the State of Tripura to the autonomous district and autonomous regions in the State of Tripura.**- Notwithstanding anything in this Constitution-

1 Subs. by the North-Eastern Areas (Reorganisation) Act, 1971 (81 of 1971), sec. 71(i) and Eighth Sch., for "Legislature of the State" (w.e.f. 21-1-1972).

2 Ins. by the North-Eastern Areas (Reorganisation) Act, 1971 (81 of 1971), sec. 71(i) and Eighth Sch. (w.e.f. 21-1-1972).

3 Paragraph 12 has been amended in its application to the State of Assam by the Sixth Schedule to the Constitution (Amendment) Act, 2003 (44 of 2003), sec. 2 (w.e.f. 7-9-2003), so as to substitute in sub-paragraph (1), in clause (a), for the words, figures and letters "matters specified in paragraph 3 or paragraph 3A of this Schedule "the words, figures and letters "matters specified in paragraph 3 or paragraph 3A or paragraph 3B of this Schedule".

4 Paragraph 12A ins. by the Assam Reorganisation (Meghalaya) Act, 1969 (55 of 1969), sec. 74 and Fourth sch. (w.e.f. 2-4-1970) and subs. by the North-Eastern Areas (Reorganisation) Act, 1971 (81 of 1971), sec. 71(i) and Eighth Sch. (w.e.f. 21-1-1972).

5 Subs. by the Sixth Schedule to the Constitution (Amendment) Act, 1988 (67 of 1988), sec. 2 (w.e.f. 16-12-1988), for paragraphs 12AA and 12B. Earlier paragraph 12AA was inserted by the Constitution (Forty-ninth Amendment) Act, 1984, sec. 4 (w.e.f. 1-4-1985).

(a) no Act of the Legislature of the State of Tripura in respect of any of the matters specified in paragraph 3 of this Schedule as matters with respect to which a District Council or a Regional Council may make laws, and no Act of the Legislature of the State of Tripura prohibiting or restricting the consumption of any non-distilled alcoholic liquor shall apply to the autonomous district or an autonomous region in that State unless, in either case, the District Council for that district or having jurisdiction over such region by public notification so directs, and the District Council in giving such direction with respect to any Act direct that the Act shall, in its application to that district or such region or any part thereof, have effect subject to such exceptions or modifications as it thinks fit;

(b) the Governor may, by public notification, direct that any Act of the Legislature of the State of Tripura to which the provisions of clause (a) of the sub-paragraph do not apply, shall not apply to the autonomous district or an autonomous region in that State, or shall apply to that district or such region, or any part thereof, subject to such exceptions or modifications, as he may specify in the notification;

(c) the President may, with respect to any Act of Parliament, by notification, direct that it shall not apply to the autonomous district or an autonomous region in the State of Tripura, or shall apply to such district or region or any part thereof, subject to such exceptions or modifications as he may specify in the notification and any such direction may be given so as to have retrospective effect.]

[1][12B. **Application of Acts of Parliament and of the Legislature of the State of Mizoram to autonomous districts and autonomous regions in the State of Mizoram.-** Notwithstanding anything in this Constitution,-

(a) no Act of the Legislature of the State of Mizoram in respect of any of the matters specified in paragraph 3 of this Schedule as matters with respect to which a District Council or a Regional Council may make laws, and no Act of Legislature of the State of Mizoram prohibiting or restricting the consumption of any non- distilled alcoholic liquor shall apply to any autonomous district or autonomous region in that State unless, in either case, the District Council for such district or having jurisdiction over such region, by public notification, so directs, and the District Council, in giving such direction with respect to any Act, may direct that the Act shall, in its application to such district or region or any part thereof, have effect subject to such exceptions or modifications as it thinks fit;

(b) the Governor may, by public notification, direct that any Act of the Legislature of the State of Mizoram to which the provisions of clause (a) of this sub-paragraph do not apply, shall not apply to an autonomous district or an autonomous region in that State, or shall apply to such district or region, or any part thereof, subject to such exceptions or modifications, as he may specify in the notification;

(c) the President may, with respect to any Act of Parliament, by notification, direct that it shall not apply to an autonomous district or an autonomous region in the State of Mizoram, or shall apply to such district or region or any part thereof, subject to such exceptions or modifications as he may specify in the notification and any such direction may be given so as to have retrospective effect.]

13. **Estimated receipts and expenditure pertaining to autonomous districts to be shown separately in the annual financial statement.–** The estimated receipts and expenditure

1 Paragraph 12B subs. by the North-Eastern (Reorganisation) Act, 1971 (81 of 1971), sec. 71(i) and Eighth Sch., for paragraph 12A (w.e.f. 21-1-1972) and again subs. by the Government of Union Territories (Amendment) Act, 1971 (83 of 1971), sec. 13 (w.e.f. 29-4-1972) and further subs. by the Sixth Schedule to the Constitution (Amendment) Act, 1988 (67 of 1988), sec. 2 (w.e.f. 16-12-1988).

pertaining to an autonomous district which are to be credited to, or is to be made from, the Consolidated Fund of the State [1][***] shall be first placed before the District Council for discussion and then after such discussion be shown separately in the annual financial statement of the State to be laid before the Legislature of the State under article 202.

14. **Appointment of Commission to inquire into and report on the administration of autonomous districts and autonomous regions.-**

(l) The Governor may at any time appoint a Commission to examine and report on any matter specified by him relating to the administration of the autonomous districts and autonomous regions in the State, including matters specified in clauses (c), (d), (e) and (f) of sub- paragraph (3) of paragraph 1 of this Schedule, or may appoint a Commission to inquire into and report from time to time on the administration of autonomous districts and autonomous regions in the State generally and in particular on-

(a) the provision of educational and medical facilities and communications in such districts and regions;

(b) the need for any new or special legislation in respect of such districts and regions; and

(c) the administration of the laws, rules and regulations made by the District and Regional Councils and define the procedure to be followed by such Commission.

(2) The report of every such Commission with the recommendations of the Governor with respect thereto shall be laid before the Legislature of the State by the Minister concerned together with an explanatory memorandum regarding the action proposed to be taken thereon by [2][the Government of the state].[3]

(3) In allocating the business of the Government of the State among his Ministers the Governor may place one of his Ministers specially in charge of the welfare of the autonomous districts and autonomous regions in the State.

[4]15. **Annulment or suspension of acts and resolutions of District and Regional Councils.-**

(I) If at any time the Governor is satisfied that an act or resolution of a District or a Regional Council is likely to endanger the safety of India [5][or is likely to be prejudicial to public order], he may annul or suspend such act or resolution and take such steps as he may consider necessary (including the suspension of the Council and the assumption to himself of all or any of the powers vested in or exercisable by the Council) to prevent the commission or continuance of such act, or the giving of effect to such resolution.

(2) Any order made by the Governor under sub-paragraph (1) of this paragraph together with the reasons therefor shall be laid before the Legislature of the State as soon as possible and the order shall, unless revoked by the Legislature of the State, continue in force for a period of twelve months from the date on which it was so made:

---

1 The words "of Assam" omitted by the North-Eastern Areas (Reorganisation) Act, 1971 (81 of 1971), sec. 71(i) and Eighth Sch. (w.e.f. 21-1-1972).

2 Subs. by the North-Eastern Areas (Reorganisation) Act, 1971 (81 of 1971), sec. 71(i) and Eighth Sch., for "the Government of Assam" (w.e.f. 21-1-1972).

3 Paragraph 14 has been amended in its application to the State of Assam by the sixth Schedule to the Constitution (Amendment) Act, 1995 (42 of 1995), sec. 2 (w.e.f. 12-9-1995), so as to omit in sub-paragraph (2), the words "with the recommendations of the Governor with respect thereto".

4 Paragraph 15 has been amended in its application to the States of Tripura and Mizoram by the Sixth Schedule to the Constitution (Amendment) Act, 1988 (67 of 1988), sec. 2 (w.e.f. 16- 12-1988), so as to-

(a) in sub-paragraph (2), substitute for the words "by the Legislature of the State", the words "by him".

(b) the proviso shall be omitted.

5 Ins. by the Assam Reorganisation (Meghalaya) Act, 1969 (55 of 1969), sec. 74 and Fourth Sch. (w.e.f: 2-4-1970).

Provided that if and so often as a resolution approving the continuance in force of such order is passed by the Legislature of the State, the order shall unless cancelled by the Governor continue in force for a further period of twelve months from the date on which under this paragraph it would otherwise have ceased to operate.

[1]16. **Dissolution of a District or a Regional Council.-**

[2][(I)] The Governor may on the recommendation of a Commission appointed under paragraph 14 of this Schedule by public notification order the dissolution of a District or a Regional Council, and-

(a) direct that a fresh general election shall be held immediately for the reconstitution of the Council, or

(b) subject to the previous approval of the Legislature of the State assume the administration of the area under the authority of such Council himself or place the administration of such area under the Commission appointed under the said paragraph or any other body considered suitable by him for a period not exceeding twelve months:

Provided that when an order under clause (a) of this paragraph has been made, the Governor may take the action referred to in clause (b) of this paragraph with regard to the administration of the area in question pending the reconstitution of the Council on fresh general election:

Provided further that no action shall be taken under clause (b) of this paragraph without giving the District or the Regional Council, as the case may be, an opportunity of placing its views before the Legislature of the State.

[3][(2) If at any time the Governor is satisfied that a situation has arisen in which the administration of an autonomous district or region cannot be carried on in accordance with the provisions of this Schedule, he may, by public notification assume to himself all or any of the functions or powers vested in or exercisable by the District Council or, as the case may be, the Regional Council and declare that such functions or powers shall be exercisable by such person or authority as he may specify in this behalf, for a period not exceeding six months:

Provided that the Governor may by a further order or orders extend the operation of the initial order by a period not exceeding six months on each occasion.

(3) Every order made under sub-paragraph (2) of this paragraph with the reasons therefor shall be laid before the Legislature of the State and shall cease to operate at the expiration of thirty days from the date on which the State Legislature first sits after the issue of the orders, unless, before the expiry of that period it has been approved by the State Legislature.]

---

1 Paragraph 16 has been amended in its application to the States of Tripura and Mizoram by the Sixth Schedule to the Constitution (Amendment) Act, 1988 (67 of 1988), sec. 2 (w.e.f. 16- 12-1988), as under:

(a) in sub-paragraph (1), the words "subject to the previous approval of the Legislature of the State" occurring in clause (b), and the second proviso shall be omitted;

(b) for sub-paragraph (3), the following sub-paragraph shall be substituted, namely:- "(3) Every order made under sub-paragraph (1) or sub-paragraph (2) of this paragraph, along with the reasons therefor shall be laid before the Legislature of the State."

2 Paragraph 16 renumbered as sub-paragraph (1) thereof by the Assam Reorganisation (Meghalaya) Act, 1969 (55 of 1969), sec. 74 and Fourth Sch. (w.e.f. 2-4-1970).

3 Ins. by the Assam Reorganisation (Meghalaya) Act, 1969 (55 of 1969), sec. 74 and Fourth Sch. (w.e.f. 2-4-1970).

17. **Exclusion of areas from autonomous districts in forming constituencies in such districts.**-For the purposes of elections to [1][the Legislative Assembly of Assam or Meghalaya] [2][or Tripura] [3][or Mizoraml the Governor may by order declare that any area within an autonomous district [4][in the State of Assam or Meghalaya [5][or Tripura] [4][or Mizoraml as the case may be,] shall not form part of any constituency to fill a seat or seats in the Assembly reserved for any such district but shall form part of a constituency to fill a seat or seats in the Assembly not so reserved to be specified in the order.[5]

[6][***]

19. **Transitional provisions.**-

(l) As soon as possible after the commencement of this Constitution the Governor shall take steps for the constitution of a District Council for each autonomous district in the State under this Schedule and, until a District Council is so constituted for an autonomous district, the administration of such district shall be vested in the Governor and the following provisions shall apply to the administration of the areas within such district instead of the foregoing provisions of this Schedule, namely:-

(a) no Act of Parliament or of the Legislature of the State shall apply to any such area unless the Governor by public notification so directs; and the Governor in giving such a direction with respect to any Act may direct that the Act shall, in its application to the area or to any specified part thereof, have effect subject to such exceptions or modifications as he thinks fit;

(b) the Governor may make regulations for the peace and good government of any such area and any regulations so made may repeal or amend any Act of Parliament or of the Legislature of the State or any existing law which is for the time being applicable to such area.

(2) Any direction given by the Governor under clause (a) of sub-paragraph (1) of this paragraph may be given so as to have retrospective effect.

(3) All regulations made under clause (b) of sub-paragraph (1) of this paragraph shall be submitted forthwith to the President and, until assented to by him, shall have no effect.[7]

---

1 Subs. by the North-Eastern Areas (Reorganisation) Act, 1971 (81 of 1971), sec. 71(i) and Eighth Sch., for "the Legislative Assembly of Assam" (w.e.f. 21-1-1972).

2 Ins. by the Constitution (Forty-ninth Amendment) Act, 1984, sec. 4 (w.e.f. 1-4-1985).

3 Ins. by the State of Mizoram Act, 1986 (34 of 1986), sec. 39(f) (w.e.f. 20-2-1987).

4 Ins. by the North-Eastern Areas (Reorganisation) Act, 1971 (81 of 1971), sec. 71(i) and Eighth Sch. (w.e.f. 21-1-1972).

5 Paragraph 17 has been amended in its application to the Sate of Assam by the Sixth Schedule to the Constitution (Amendment) Act, 2003 (44 of 2003), sec. 2 (w.e.f. 7-9-2003), so as to insert the following proviso, namely:- "Provided that nothing in this paragraph shall apply to the Bodoland Territorial Areas District."

6 Paragraph 18 omitted by the North-Eastern Areas (Reorganisation) Act, 1971 (81 of 1971), sec. 71(i) and Eighth Sch. (w.e.f. 21-1-1972).

7 Paragraph 19 has been amended in its application" to the Sate of Assam by the Sixth Schedule to the Constitution (Amendment) Act, 2003 (44 of 2003), sec. 2 (w.e.f. 7-9-2003), so as to insert after sub-paragraph (3), the following sub-paragraph, namely:- "(4) As soon as possible after the commencement of this Act, an Interim Executive Council for Bodoland Territorial Areas District in Assam shall be formed by the Governor from amongst leaders of the Bodo movement, including the signatories to the Memorandum of Settlement, and shall provide adequate representation to the non-tribal communities in that area: Provided that the Interim Council shall for a period of six months during which endeavour to hold the election to the Council shall be made.

Explanation.-For the purposes of this sub-paragraph, the expression "Memorandum of Settlement" means the Memorandum signed on the 10th day of February, 2003 between Government of India, Government of Assam and Bodo Liberation Tigers."

[1][20. **Tribal areas.-**

(I) The areas specified in Parts I, II [2][,IIA] and III of the table below shall respectively be the tribal areas within the State of Assam, the State of Meghalaya [3][,the State of Tripura] and the [3][State] of Mizoram.

(2) [4][Any reference in Part I, Part II or Part III of the table below] to any district shall be construed as a reference to the territories comprised within the autonomous district of that name existing immediately before the day appointed under clause (b) of section 2 of the North-Eastern Areas (Reorganisation) Act, 1971:

Provided that for the purposes of clauses (e) and (f) of sub-paragraph (1) of paragraph 3, paragraph 4, paragraph 5, paragraph 6, sub-paragraph (2), clauses (a), (b), and (d) of sub-paragraph (3) and sub-paragraph (4) of paragraph 8 and clause (d) of sub-paragraph (2) of paragraph 10 of this Schedule, no part of the area comprised within the municipality of Shillong shall be deemed to be within the [5][Khasi Hills District].]

[3][(3) The reference in Part IIA in the table below to the 'Tripura Tribal Areas District' shall be construed as a reference to the territory comprising the tribal areas specified in the First Schedule to the Tripura Tribal Areas Autonomous District Council Act, 1979.]

TABLE

PART I

1. The North Cachar Hills District.

2. [6][The Karbi Anglong District.][7]

PART II

[8][1. Khasi Hills District.

2. Jaintia Hills District.]

3. The Garo Hills District.]]

[9][PART IIA

Tripura Tribal Areas District.]

PART III

[10][***]

[11][1. The Chakma District.

[12][2. The Mara District.

3. The Lai District.]]

1 Subs. by the North-Eastern Areas (Reorganisation) Act, 1971 (81 of 1971), sec. 71(i) and Eighth Sch., for paragraphs 20 and 20A .(w.e.f. 21-1-1972). Earlier paragraph 20A was inserted by the Assam Reorganisation (Meghalaya) Act, 1969 (55 of 1969), sec. 74 and Eighth Sch. (w.e.f. 2- 4-1970).

2 Ins. by the Constitution (Forty-ninth Amendment) Act, 1984, sec. 4 (w.e.f. 1-4-1985).

3 Subs. by the State of Mizoram Act, 1986 (34 of 1986), sec. 39(f), for "Union territory" (w.e.f. 20-2-1987).

4 Subs. by the Constitution (Forty-ninth Amendment) Act, 1984, sec. 4, for" Any reference in the table below" (w.e.f. 1-4-1985).

5 Subs. by the Government of Meghalaya Notification DCA 31/72/11, dated the 14th June, 1973, published in the Gazette of Meghalaya, Pt. VA, dated 23rd June, 1973, p. 200.

6 Subs. by the Government of Assam Notification T-A D/R/115/74/47, dated 14th October, 1976, for "The Mikir Hills District".

7 Paragraph 20 has been amended in its application to the State of Assam by the Sixth Schedule to the Constitution (Amendment) Act, 2003 (44 of 2003), sec. 2, so as to insert in Part I of the Table, after entry 3, the following, namely:- "3. The Bodoland Territorial Areas District.".

8 Subs. by the Government of Meghalaya Notification DCA 31/72/11, dated 14th June, 1973, published in the Gazette of Meghalaya, Pt. V A, dated 23rd June, 1973, p. 200.

9 Ins. by the Constitution (Forty-ninth Amendment) Act, 1984, sec. 4 (w.e.f. 1-4-1985).

10 The words "The Mizo District" omitted by the Government of Union Territories (Amendment) Act, 1971 (83 of 1971), sec. 13 (w.e.f. 29-4-1972).

11 Ins. by the Mizoram District Councils (Miscellaneous Provisions} Order 1972, published in the Mizoram Gazette, 1972, dated the 5th May, 1972, Vol. 1, Pt. II, p. 17 (w.e.f. 29-4-1972}.

12 Subs. by the Sixth Schedule to the Constitution (Amendment) Act, 1988 (67 of 1988), sec. 2 (w.e.f. 16-12-1988), for serial numbers 2 and 3 and the entries relating thereto.

[1][20A. **Dissolution of the Mizo District Council.-**

(I) Notwithstanding anything in this Schedule, the District Council of the Mizo District existing immediately before the prescribed date (hereinafter referred to as the Mizo District Council) shall stand dissolved and cease to exist.

(2) The Administrator of the Union territory of Mizoram may, by one or more orders, provide for all or any of the following matters, namely:-

(a) the transfer, in whole or in part, of the assets, rights and liabilities of the Mizo District Council (including the rights and liabilities under any contract made by it) to the Union or to any other authority;

(b) the substitution of the Union or any other authority for the Mizo District Council, or the addition of the Union or any other authority, as a party to any legal proceedings to which the Mizo District Council is a party;

(c) the transfer or re-employment of any employees of the Mizo District Council to or by the Union or any other authority, the terms and conditions of service applicable to such employees after such transfer or re-employment;

(d) the continuance of any laws, made by the Mizo District Council and in force immediately before its dissolution, subject to such adaptations and modifications, whether by way of repeal or amendment, as the Administrator may make in this behalf, until such laws are altered, repealed or amended by a competent Legislature or other competent authority;

(e) such incidental, consequential and supplementary matters as the Administrator considers necessary.

Explanation.-In this paragraph and in paragraph 20B of this Schedule, the expression 'prescribed date' means the date on which the Legislative Assembly of the Union territory of Mizoram is duly constituted under and in accordance with the provisions of the Government of Union Territories Act, 1963.

[2][20B. **Autonomous regions in the Union territory of Mizoram to be autonomous districts and transitory provisions consequent thereto.-**

(l) Notwithstanding anything in this Schedule,-

(a) every autonomous region existing immediately before the prescribed date in the Union territory of Mizoram shall, on and from that date, be an autonomous district in that Union territory (hereafter referred to as the corresponding new district) and the Administrator thereof may, by one or more orders,. direct that such consequential amendments as are necessary to give effect to the provisions of this clause shall be made in paragraph 20 of this Schedule (including Part III of the table appended to that paragraph) and thereupon the said paragraph and the said Part III shall be deemed to have been amended accordingly;

(b) every Regional Council of an autonomous region in the Union territory of Mizoram existing immediately before the prescribed date (hereafter referred to as the existing Regional Council) shall, on and from that date and until a District Council is duly constituted for the corresponding new district, be deemed to be the District Council of that district (hereafter referred to as the corresponding new District Council).

---

1 Paragraph 20A ins. by the Assam Reorganisation (Meghalaya) Act, 1969 (55 of 1969), sec. 74 and Fourth Sch. (w.e.f. 2-4-1970) and subs. by the Government of Union Territories (Amendment) Act, 1971 (83 of 1971), sec. 13 (w.e.f. 29-4-1972).

2 Paragraph 20B subs. by the Government of Union Territories (Amendment) Act, 1971 (83 of 1971), sec. 13, for paragraph 20A (w.e.f. 29-4-1972).

(2) Every member whether elected or nominated of an existing Regional Council shall be deemed to have been elected or, as the case may be, nominated to the corresponding new District Council and shall hold office until a District Council is duly constituted for the corresponding new district under this Schedule.

(3) paragraph 4 of this Schedule by the corresponding new District Council, the rules made under the said provisions by the existing Regional Council and in force immediately before the prescribed date shall have effect in relation to the corresponding new District Council subject to such adaptations and modifications as may be made therein by the Administrator of the Union territory of Mizoram.

(4) The Administrator of the Union territory of Mizoram may, by one or more orders, provide for all or any of the following matters, namely:-

(a) the transfer in whole or in part of the assets, rights and liabilities of the existing Regional Council (including the rights and liabilities under any contract made by it) to the corresponding new District Council;

(b) the substitution of the corresponding new District Council for the existing Regional Council as a party to the legal proceedings to which the existing Regional Council is a party;

(c) the transfer or re-employment of any employees of the existing Regional Council to or by the corresponding new District Council, the terms and conditions of service applicable to such employees after such transfer or re-employment;

(d) the continuance of any laws made by the existing Regional Council and in force immediately before the prescribed date, subject to such adaptations and modifications, whether by way of repeal or amendment, as the Administrator may make in this behalf until such laws are altered, repealed or amended by a competent Legislature or other competent authority;

(e) such incidental, consequential and supplementary matters as the Administrator considers necessary.[1]

[2][20C. **Interpretation.**-Subject to any provision made in this behalf, the provisions of this Schedule shall, in their application to the Union territory of Mizoram, have effect-

1 After paragraph 20B, the following paragraph has been inserted in its application to the State of Assam by the Sixth Schedule to the Constitution (Amendment) Act, 1995 (42 of 1995), sec. 2 (w.e.f. 12-9-1995), namely:- *"20BA. Exercise of discretionary powers by the Governor in the discharge of his functions.-* The Governor in the discharge of his functions under sub-paragraphs (2) and (3) of paragraph 1, sub-paragraphs (1), (6), sub-paragraph *(6A)* excluding the first two proviso and sub- paragraph (7) of paragraph 2, sub-paragraph (3) of paragraph 3, sub-paragraph (4) of paragraph 4, paragraph 5, sub-paragraph (1) of paragraph 6, sub-paragraph (2) of paragraph 7, sub-paragraph (4) of paragraph 8, sub-paragraph (3) of paragraph 9, sub-paragraph (3) of paragraph 10, sub-paragraph (1) of paragraph 14, sub-paragraph (1) of paragraph 15 and sub- paragraphs (1) and (2) of paragraph 16 of this Schedule, shall, after consulting the Council of Ministers and the North Cachar Hills Autonomous Council or the Karbi Anglong Autonomous Council, as the case may be, take such action as he considers necessary in his discretion."

After paragraph 20B, *the* following paragraph has been inserted in its application to the State of Tripura and Mizoram, by the sixth Schedule to the Constitution (Amendment) Act, 1988 (67 of 1988), sec. 2, namely:- *"20BB. Exercise of discretionary powers by the Governor in the discharge of his functions.-* The Governor in the discharge of his functions under sub-paragraphs (2) and (3) of paragraph 1, sub-paragraphs (1) and (7) of paragraph 2, sub-paragraph (3) of paragraph 3, sub-paragraph (4) of paragraph 4, paragraph 5, sub-paragraph (1) of paragraph 6, sub-paragraph (2) of paragraph 7, sub-paragraph (3) of paragraph 9, sub-paragraphs (1) of paragraph 14, sub- paragraph (1) of paragraph 15 and sub-paragraphs (1) and (2) of paragraph 16 of this Schedule shall, after consulting the Council of Ministers, and if he thinks it necessary, the District Council or the Regional Council concerned, take such action as he considers necessary in his discretion."

2 Paragraph 20C subs. by the Government of Union Territories (Amendment) Act, 1971 (83 of 1971), sec. 13, for paragraph *20A* (w.e.f. 29-4-1972).

(1) as if references to the Governor and Government of the State were references to the Administrator of the Union territory appointed under article 239, references to State (except in the expression 'Government of the State') were references to the Union territory of Mizoram and references to the State Legislature were references to the Legislative Assembly of the Union territory of Mizoram;

(2) as if-

(a) in sub-paragraph (5) of paragraph 4, the provision for consultation with the Government of the State concerned had been omitted;

(b) in sub-paragraph (2) of paragraph 6, for the words 'to which the executive power of the State extends', the words 'with respect to which the Legislative Assembly of the Union territory of Mizoram has power to make laws' had been substituted;

(c) in paragraph 13, the words and figures 'under article 202' had been omitted.]

21. **Amendment of the Schedule.-**

(I) Parliament may from time to time by law amend by way of addition, variation or repeal any of the provisions of this Schedule and, when the Schedule is so amended, any reference to this Schedule in this Constitution shall be construed as a reference to such Schedule as so amended.

(2) No such law as is mentioned in sub-paragraph (1) of this paragraph shall be deemed to be an amendment of this Constitution for the purposes of article 368.

SEVENTH SCHEDULE

[ARTICLE 246]

List I-Union List

1. Defence of India and every part thereof including preparation for defence and all such acts as may be conducive in times of war to its prosecution and after its termination of effective demobilisation. ,

2. Naval, military and air forces; any other armed forces of the Union.

[1][2A. Deployment of any armed force of the Union or any other force subject to the control of the Union or any contingent or unit thereof in any State in aid of the civil power; powers, jurisdiction, privileges and liabilities of the members of such forces while on such deployment.]

3. Delimitation of cantonment areas, local self-government in such areas, the constitution and powers within such areas of cantonment authorities and the regulation of house accommodation (including the control of rents) in such areas.

4. Naval, military and air force works.

5. Arms, firearms, ammunition and explosives.

6. Atomic energy and mineral resources necessary for its production.

7. Industries declared by Parliament by law to be necessary for the purpose of defence or for the prosecution of war.

8. Central Bureau of Intelligence and Investigation.

9. Preventive detention for reasons connected with Defence, Foreign Affairs, or the security of India; persons subjected to such detention.

1 Ins. by the Constitution (Forty-second Amendment) Act, 1976, Sec. 57. (w.e.f.3-1-1977)

10. Foreign affairs; all matters which bring the Union into relation with any foreign country.
11. Diplomatic, consular and trade representation.
12. United Nations Organisation.
13. Participation in international conferences, associations and other bodies and implementing of decisions made thereat.
14. Entering into treaties and agreements with foreign countries and implementing of treaties, agreements and conventions with foreign countries.
15. War and peace.
16. Foreign jurisdiction.
17. Citizenship, naturalisation and aliens.
18. Extradition.
19. Admission into, and emigration and expulsion from, India; passports and visas.
20. Pilgrimages to places outside India.
21. Piracies and crimes committed on the high seas or in the air; offences against the law of nations committed on land or the high seas or in the air.
22. Railways.
23. Highways declared by or under law made by Parliament to be national highways.
24. Shipping and navigation on inland waterways, declared by Parliament by law to be national waterways, as regards mechanically propelled vessels; the rule of the road on such waterways.
25. Maritime shipping and navigation, including shipping and navigation on tidal waters; provision of education and training for the mercantile marine and regulation of such education and training provided by States and other agencies.
26. Lighthouses, including lightships, beacons and other provisions for the safety of shipping and aircraft.
27. Ports declared by or under law made by Parliament or existing law to be major ports, including their delimitation and the constitution and powers of port authorities therein.
28. Port quarantine, including hospitals connected therewith; seamen's and marine hospitals.
29. Airways; aircraft and air navigation; provision of aerodromes; regulation and organisation of air traffic and of aerodromes; provision for aeronautical education and training and regulation of such education and training provided by States and other agencies.
30. Carriage of passengers and goods by railway, sea or air, or by national waterways in mechanically propelled vessels.
31. Posts and telegraphs; telephones, wireless, broadcasting and other like forms of communication.
32. Property of the Union and the revenue therefrom, but as regards property situated in a State [1][***] subject to legislation by the State, save in so far as Parliament by law otherwise provides.

[2][***]

34. Courts of wards for the estates of Rulers of Indian States.
35. Public debt of the Union.
36. Currency, coinage and legal tender; foreign exchange.

---

1 The words and letters "specified in Part A or Part B of the First Schedule" omitted by Constitution (Seventh Amendment) Act, 1956, sec. 29 and Sch.

2 Entry 33 omitted by the Constitution (Seventh Amendment) Act, 1956, sec. 26.

37. Foreign loans.
38. Reserve Bank of India.
39. Post Office Savings Bank.
40. Lotteries organised by the Government of India or the Government of a State.
41. Trade and commerce with foreign countries; import and export across custom frontiers; definition of customs frontiers.
42. Inter-State trade and commerce.
43. Incorporation, regulation and winding up of trading corporation banking, insurance and financial corporations but not including cooperatives societies.
44. Incorporation, regulation and winding up of corporations, whether trading or not, with objects not confined to one State, but not including universities.
45. Banking.
46. Bills of exchange, cheques, promissory notes and other like instruments.
47. Insurance.
48. Stock exchanges and futures markets.
49. Patents, inventions and designs; copyright; trade-marks and merchandise marks.
50. Establishment of standards of weight and measure.
51. Establishment of standards of quality for goods to be exported out of India or transported from one State to another.
52. Industries, the control of which by the Union is declared by Parliament by law to be expedient in the public interest.
53. Regulation and development of oil fields and mineral oil resources; petroleum and petroleum products; other liquids and substances declared by Parliament by law to be dangerously inflammable.
54. Regulation of mines and mineral development to the extent to which such regulation and development under the control of the Union is declared by Parliarnent by law to be expedient in the public interest.
55. Regulation of labour and safety in mines and oilfields.
56. Regulation and development of inter-State rivers and river valleys to the extent to which such regulation and development under the control of the Union is declared by Parliament by law to be expedient in the public interest.
57. Fishing and fisheries beyond territorial waters.
58. Manufacture, supply and distribution of salt by Union agencies, regulation and control of manufacture, supply and distribution of salt by other agencies.
59. Cultivation, manufacture, and sale for export, of opium.
60. Sanctioning of cinematograph films for exhibition.
61. Industrial disputes concerning Union employees.
62. The institutions known at the commencement of this Constitution as the National Library, the Indian Museum, the Imperial War Museum, the Victoria Memorial and the Indian War Memorial, and any other like institution financed by the Government of India wholly or in part and declared by Parliament by law to be an institution of national importance.
63. The institutions known at the commencement of this Constitution as the Banaras Hindu University, the Aligarh Muslim University and the [1][Delhi University; the University established in pursuance of article 371E;] any other institution declared by Parliament by law to be an institution of national importance.

---

1 Subs. by the Constitution (Thirty-second Amendment) Act, 1973, sec. 4, for "Delhi University and" (w.e.f. 1-7-1974).

64. Institutions for scientific or technical education financed by the Government of India wholly or in part and declared by Parliament by law to be institutions of national importance.

65. Union agencies and institutions for-

(a) professional, vocational or technical training, including the training of police officers; or

(b)the promotion of special studies or research; or

(c) scientific or technical assistance in the investigation or detection of crime.

66. Co-ordination and determination of standards in institutions for higher education or research and scientific and technical institutions.

67. Ancient and historical monuments and records, and archaeological sites and remains, [1][declared by or under law made by Parliament] to be of national importance.

68. The Survey of India, the Geological, Botanical, Zoological and Anthropological Surveys of India; Meteorological organisations.

69. Census.

70. Union Public Services; All-India Services; Union Public Service Commission.

71. Union pensions, that is to say, pensions payable by the Government of India or out of the Consolidated Fund of India.

72. Elections to Parliament, to the Legislatures of States and to the offices of President and Vice-President; the Election Commission.

73. Salaries and allowances of members of Parliament, the Chairman and Deputy Chairman of the Council of States and the Speaker and Deputy Speaker of the House of the People.

74. Powers, privileges and immunities of each House of Parliament and of the members and the Committees of each House; enforcement of attendance of persons for giving evidence or producing documents before committees of Parliament or commissions appointed by Parliament.

75. Emoluments, allowances, privileges, and rights in respect of leave of absence, of the President and Governors; salaries and allowances of the Ministers for the Union; the salaries, allowances, and rights in respect of leave of absence and other conditions of service of the Comptroller and Auditor-General.

76. Audit of the accounts of the Union and of the States.

77. Constitution, organisation, jurisdiction and powers of the Supreme Court (including contempt of such Court), and the fees taken therein; persons entitled to practise before the Supreme Court.

78. Constitution and Organisation [2][(including vacations)] .of the High Courts except provisions as to officers and servants of High Courts; persons entitled to practise before the High Courts.

[3][79. Extension of the jurisdiction of a High Court to, and exclusion of the jurisdiction of a High Court from, any Union territory.]

80. Extension of the powers and jurisdiction of members of a police force belonging to any State to any area outside that State, but not so as to enable the police of one State to exercise powers and jurisdiction in any area outside that State without the consent of the Government of the State in which such area is situated; extension of the powers and jurisdiction of members of a police force belonging to any State to railway areas outside that State.

---

1 Subs. by the Constitution (Seventh Amendment) Act, 1956, sec. 27, for "declared by Parliament by law".

2 Ins. by the Constitution (Fifteenth Amendment) Act, 1963, sec. 12 (with retrospective effect).

3 Subs. by the Constitution (Seventh Amendment) Act, 1956, sec. 29 and Sch., for entry 79.

81. Inter-State migration; inter-State quarantine.

82. Taxes on income other than agricultural income.

83. Duties of customs including export duties.

84. Duties of excise on tobacco and other goods manufactured or produced in India except-

    (a) alcoholic liquors for human consumption.

    (b) opium, Indian hemp and other narcotic drugs and narcotics, but including medicinal and toilet preparations containing alcohol or any substance included in sub-paragraph(b) of this entry.

85. Corporation tax.

86. Taxes on the capital value of the assets, exclusive of agricultural land, of individuals and companies; taxes on the capital of companies..

87. Estate duty in respect of property other than agricultural land.

88. Duties in respect of succession to property other than agricultural land.

89. Terminal taxes on goods or passengers, carried by railway, sea or air; taxes on railway fares and freights.

90. Taxes other than stamp duties on transactions in stock exchanges and futures markets.

91. Rates of stamp duty in respect of bills of exchange, cheques, promissory notes, bills of lading, letters of credit, policies of insurance, transfer of shares, debentures, proxies and receipts.

92. Taxes on the sale or purchase of newspapers and on advertisements published therein.

[1][92A. Taxes on the sale or purchase of goods other than newspapers, where such sale or purchase takes place in the course of inter-State trade or commerce.]

[2][92B. Taxes on the consignment of goods (whether the consignment is to the person making it or to any other person), where such consignment takes place in the course of inter-State trade or commerce.]

93. Offences against laws with respect to any of the matters in this List.

94. Inquiries, surveys and statistics for the purpose of any of the matters in this List.

95. Jurisdiction and powers of all courts, except the Supreme Court, with respect to any of the matters in this List; admiralty jurisdiction.

96. Fees in respect of any of the matters in this List, but not including fees taken in any court..

97. Any other matter not enumerated in List II or List III including any tax not mentioned in either of those Lists.

List II-State List

1. Public order (but not including [3][the use of any naval, military or Air force or any other armed force of the Union or of any other force subject to the control of the Union or of any contingent or unit thereof] in aid of the civil power).

[4][2. Police (including railway and village police) subject to the provisions of entry 2A of List I.]

3. [5][***] Officers and servants of the High Court; procedure in rent and revenue courts; fees taken in all courts except the Supreme Court.

---

1 Ins. by the Constitution (Sixth Amendment) Act, 1956, sec. 2 (w.e.f. 11-6-1956).

2 Ins. by the Constitution (Forty-sixth Amendment) Act, 1982, sec. 5 (w.e.f. 2-2-1983).

3 Subs. by the Constitution (Forty-second Amendment) Act, 1976, sec.. 57, for certain words (w.e.f. 3-7-1977). ;"

4 Subs. by the Constitution (Forty-second Amendment) Act, 1976, sec. 57, for entry 2 (w.e.f. 3-1-1977).

5 Certain words omitted by the Constitution (Forty-second (Amendment) Act, 1976, Sec. 57 (w.e.f. 3-1-1977).

4. Prisons, reformatories, Borstal institutions and other institutions of a like nature, and persons detained therein; arrangements with other States for the use of prisons and other institutions.

5. Local government, that is to say, the constitution and/powers of municipal corporations, improvement trusts, district boards, mining settlement authorities and other local authorities for the purpose of local self-government or village administration.

6. Public health and sanitation; hospitals and dispensaries.

7. Pilgrimages, other than pilgrimages to places outside India.

8. Intoxicating liquors, that is to say, the production, manufacture, possession, transport, purchase and sale of intoxicating liquors.

9. Relief of the disabled and unemployable.

10. Burials and burial grounds; cremations and cremation grounds.[1][***]

12. Libraries, museums and other similar institutions controlled or financed by the State; ancient and historical monuments and records other than those [2][declared by or under law made by Parliament] to be of national importance.

13. Communications, that is to say, roads, bridges, ferries, and other means of communication not specified in List I; municipal tramways; ropeways; inland waterways and traffic thereon subject to the provisions of List land List III with regard to such waterways; vehicles other than mechanically propelled vehicles.

14. Agriculture, including agricultural education: and research, protection against pests and prevention of plant diseases.

15. Preservation, protection and improvement of stock and prevention of animal diseases; veterinary training and practice. ;

16. Pounds and the prevention of cattle trespass.

17. Water, that is to say, water supplies, irrigation and canals, drainage and embankments, water storage and water power subject to the provisions of entry 56 of List I.

18. Land, that is to say, right in or over land, land tenures including the relation of landlord and tenant, and the collection of rents; transfer and alienation of agricultural land; land improvement and agricultural loans; colonization.

[3][***]

21. Fisheries.

22. Courts of wards subject to the provisions of entry 34 of List I; encumbered and attached estates.

23. Regulation of mines and mineral development. subject to the provisions of List I with respect to regulation and development under the control of the Union.

24. Industries subject to the provisions of [4][entries 7 and 52] of List I.

25. Gas and gas-works.

26. Trade and commerce within the State subject to the provisions of entry 33 of List III.

27. Production, supply and distribution of goods subject to the provisions of entry 33 of List III.

28. Markets and fairs. [5][***]

30. Money-lending and money-lenders; relief of agricultural indebtedness.

---

1 Entry 11 omitted by the Constitution (Forty-second Amendment) Act, 1976, sec- 57 (w.e.f. 3-1-1977).

2 Subs. by the Constitution (Seventh Amendment) Act, 1956, sec. 27, for "declared by Parliament by law"

3 Entries 19 and 20 omitted by the Constitution (Forty-second Amendment) Act, 1976, . sec. 57 (w.e.f. 3-1-1977).

4 Subs. by the Constitution (Seventh Amendment) Act, 1956, sec. 28, for "entry 52".

5 Entry 29 omitted by the Constitution (Forty-second Amendment) Act, 1976, sec. 57 (w.e.f. 3- 1-1977).

31. Inns and inn-keepers.

Incorporation, regulation and winding up of corporation, other than those specified in List I, and universities; unincorporated trading, literary, scientific, religious and other societies and associations; co-operative societies.

33. Theatres and dramatic performances; cinemas subject to the provisions of entry 60 of List 1; sports, entertainments and amusements.

34. Betting and gambling.

35. Works, lands and buildings vested in or in the possession of the State. [1][***]

37. Elections to the Legislature of the State subject to the provisions of any law made by Parliament.

38. Salaries and allowances of members of the Legislature of the State, of the Speaker and Deputy Speaker of the Legislative Assembly and, if there is a Legislative Council, of the Chairman and Deputy Chairman thereof.

39. Powers, privileges and immunities of the Legislative Assembly and of the members and the committees thereof, and, if there is a Legislative Council, of that Council and of the members and the committees thereof; enforcement of attendance of persons for giving evidence or producing documents before committees of the Legislature of the State.

40. Salaries and allowances of Ministers for the State.

41. State public services; State Public Service Commission.

42. State pensions, that is to say, pensions payable by the State or out of the Consolidated Fund of the State.

43. Public debt of the State.

44. Treasure trove.

45. Land revenue, including the assessment and collection of revenue, the maintenance of land records, survey for revenue purposes and records of rights, and alienation of revenues.

46. Taxes on agricultural income.

47. Duties in respect of succession to agricultural land.

48. Estate duty in respect of agricultural land.

49. Taxes on lands and buildings.

50. Taxes on mineral rights subject to any limitations imposed by Parliament by law relating to mineral development.

51. Duties of excise on the following goods manufactured or produced in the State and countervailing duties at the same or lower rates on similar goods manufactured or produced elsewhere in India:-

(a) alcoholic liquors for human consumption;

(b) opium, Indian hemp and other narcotic drugs and narcotics, but not including medicinal and toilet preparations containing alcohol or any substance included in sub-paragraph (b) of this entry.

52. Taxes on the entry of goods into a local area for consumption, use or sale therein.

53. Taxes on the consumption or sale of electricity.

[2][54. Taxes on the sale or purchase of goods other than newspapers, subject to the provisions of entry 92A of List I.]

55. Taxes on advertisements other than advertisements published in the newspapers [3][and advertisements broadcast by radio or television].

---

1 Entry 36 omitted by the Constitution (Seventh Amendment) Act, 1956, sec. 26.

2 Subs. by the Constitution (Sixth Amendment) Act, 1956, sec. 2, for entry 54.

3 Ins. by the Constitution (Forty-second Amendment) Act, 1976, sec. 57 (w.e.f. 3-1-1977).

56. Taxes on goods and passengers carried by road or on inland waterways.
57. Taxes on vehicles, whether mechanically propelled or not, suitable for use on roads, including tramcars subject to the provisions of entry 35 of List III.
58. Taxes on animals and boats.
59. Tolls.
60. Taxes on professions, trades, callings and employments.
61. Capitation taxes.
62. Taxes on luxuries, including taxes on entertainments, amusements, betting and gambling.
63. Rates of stamp duty in respect of documents other than those specified in the provisions of List I with regard to rates of stamp duty.
64. Offences against laws with respect to any of the matters in this List.
65. Jurisdiction and powers of all courts, except the Supreme Court, with respect to any of the matters in this List.
66. Fees in respect of any of the matters in this List, but not including fees taken in any court.

List III-Concurrent List

1. Criminal law, including all matters included in the Indian Penal Code at the commencement of this Constitution but excluding offences against laws with respect to any of the matters specified in List I or List II and excluding the use of naval, military or air forces or any other armed forces of the Union in aid of the civil power.
2. Criminal procedure, including all matters included in the Code of Criminal Procedure at the commencement of this Constitution.
3. Preventive detention for reasons connected with the security of a State, the maintenance of public order, or the maintenance of supplies and services essential to the community; persons subjected to such detention.
4. Removal from one State to another State of prisoners, accused persons and persons subjected to preventive detention for reasons specified in entry 3 of this List.
5. Marriage and divorce; infants and minors; adoption; wills, intestacy and succession; joint family and partition; all matters in respect of which parties in judicial proceedings were immediately before the commencement of this Constitution subject to their personal law.
6. Transfer of property other than agricultural land; registration of deeds and documents.
7. Contracts, including partnership, agency, contracts of carriage, and other special forms of contracts, but not including contracts relating to agricultural land.
8. Actionable wrongs.
9. Bankruptcy and insolvency.
10. Trust and Trustees.
11. Administrators-general and official trustees.

[1][11A. Administration of justice; constitution and organisation of all courts, except the Supreme Court and the High Courts.)

12. Evidence and oaths; recognition of laws, public acts and records, and judicial proceedings.
13. Civil procedure, including all matters included in the Code of Civil Procedure at the commencement of this Constitution, limitation and arbitration.
14. Contempt of court, but not including contempt of the Supreme Court.
15. Vagrancy; nomadic and migratory tribes.

---

1 Ins. by the Constitution (Forty-second Amendment) Act, 1976, sec. 57 (w.e.f. 3-1-1977).

16. Lunacy and mental deficiency, including places for the reception or treatment of lunatics and mental deficients.

17. Prevention of cruelty to animals.

[17A. Forests.

17B. Protection of wild animals and birds.]

18. Adulteration of foodstuffs and other goods.

19. Drugs and poisons, subject to the provisions of entry 59 of List I with respect to opium.

20. Economic and social planning.

[1][20A. Population control and family planning.]

21. Commercial and industrial monopolies, combines and trusts.

22. Trade unions; industrial and labour disputes.

23. Social security and social insurance; employment and unemployment.

24. Welfare of labour including conditions of work, provident funds, employers' liability, workmen's compensation, invalidity and old age pensions and maternity benefits.

[2][25. Education, including technical education, medical education and universities, subject to the provisions of entries 63, 64, 65 and 66 of List I; vocational and technical training of labour.]

26. Legal, medical and other professions.

27. Relief and rehabilitation of persons displaced from their original place of residence by reason of the setting up of the Dominions of India and Pakistan.

28. Charities and charitable institutions, charitable and religious endowments and religious institutions.

29. Prevention of the extension from one State to another of infectious or contagious diseases or pests affecting men, animals or plants.

30. Vital statistics including registration of births and deaths.

31. Ports other than those declared by or under law made by Parliament or existing law to be major ports.

Shipping and navigation on inland waterways as regards mechanically propelled vessels, and the rule of the road on such waterways, and the carriage of passengers and goods on inland waterways subject to the provisions of List I with respect to national waterways.

[3][33. Trade and commerce in, and the production, supply and distribution of,-

(a) the products of any industry where the control of such industry by the Union is declared by Parliament by law to be expedient in the public interest, and imported goods of the same kind as such products;

(b) foodstuffs, including edible oilseeds and oils;

(c) cattle fodder, including oilcakes and other concentrates;

(d) raw cotton, whether ginned or unginned, and cotton seed; and

(e) raw jute.]

[4][33A. Weights and measures except establishment of standards.]

34. Price control.

35. Mechanically propelled vehicles including the principles on which taxes on such vehicles are to be levied.

36. Factories.

---

1 Ins.. by the Constitution (Forty-second Amendment) Act, 1976, sec. 57 (w.e-.f. 3-1-1977).

2 Subs. by the Constitution (Forty-second Amendment) Act, 1976, sec. 57, for entry 25 (w.e.f. 3-1-1977).

3 Subs. by the Constitution (Third Amendment) Act, 1954, sec. 2, for entry 33.

4 Ins. by the Constitution (Forty-second Amendment) Act, 1976, sec. 57 (w.e.f. 3-1-1977).

37. Boilers.
38. Electricity.
39. Newspapers, books and printing presses.
40. Archaeological sites and remains other than those [1][declared by or under law made by Parliament] to be of national importance.
41. Custody, management and disposal of property (including agricultural land) declared by law to be evacuee property.

[2][42. Acquisition and requisitioning of property.]

43. Recovery in a State of claims in respect of taxes and other public demands, including arrears of land-revenue and sums recoverable as such arrears, arising outside that State.
44. Stamp duties other than duties or fees collected by means of judicial stamps, but not including rates of stamp duty.
45. Inquiries and statistics for the purposes of any of the matters specified in List II or List III.
46. Jurisdiction and powers of all courts, except the Supreme Court, with respect to any of the matters in this List.
47. Fees in respect of any of the matters in this List, but not including fees taken in any court.

EIGHTH SCHEDULE

[ARTICLES 344(1) AND 151]

Languages

1.	Assamese.	2.	Bengali.	[3][3.	Bodo.
4.	Dogri.]	[4][5.]	Gujarati.	[5][6.]	Hindi.
[3][7.]	Kannada.	[3][8.]	Kashmiri.	[6][[3][9.	Konkani.]
[7][10.	Maithili.]	[8][[9][11.]]	Malayalam.	[10][[11][12.	Manipuri.]
[12][[9][13.]]	Marathi.	[13][[9][14.]	Nepali.]	[14][[9][15.]]*	Odia
[12][[9][16.]]	Punjabi.	[12][[9][17.]]	Sanskrit.	[15][18.	Santhali.]
[12][[16][19.]	Sindhi.]	[12][[17][20.]]	Tamil.	[12][[15][21.]]	Telugu
[12][[15][22.]]	Urdu				

1 Subs. by the Constitution (Seventh Amendment) Act, 1956, sec. 27, for "declared by the Parliament by law"(w.e.f. 1.11.1956).

2 Subs. by the Constitution (Seventh Amendment) Act, 1956, sec. 26, for entry 42 (w.e.f. 1.11.1956).

3 Ins. by the Constitution (Ninety Second Amendment) Act, 2003, sec.2(a) (w.e.f. 7.1.2004).

4 Entry 3 renumbered as entry 5 by the Constitution (Ninety Second Amendment) Act, 2003, sec. 2(a).

5 Entry 4 to 7 renumbered as entry 6 to 9 by the Constitution (Ninety Second Amendment) Act, 2003, sec. 2(b).

6 Ins. by the Constitution (Seventy-first Amendment) Act, 1992, sec. 2(a)

7 Ins. by the Constitution (Ninety Second Amendment) Act, 2003, sec. 2(c)

8 Entry 7 renumbered as entry 8 by the Constitution (Seventy-first Amendment) Act, 1992, sec. 2(a).

9 Entry 8 renumbered as entry 11 by the Constitution (Ninety Second Amendment) Act, 2003, sec. 2(c).

10 Ins. by the Constitution (Seventy-first Amendment) Act, 1992, sec. 2(b).

11 Entry 9 to 14 renumbered as entry 12 to 17 by the Constitution (Ninety Second Amendment) Act, 2003, sec. 2(d).

12 Entry 8 renumbered as entry 10 by the Constitution (Seventy First Amendment) Act, 1992, sec. 2(b).

13 Ins. by the Constitution (Seventy-first Amendment) Act, 1992, sec. 2(c).

14 Entries 9 to 15 renumbered as entries 12 to 18 and entry 15 added by the Constitution (Twenty-first Amendment) Act, 1967, sec. 2(c).
* Subs. by constitution ninety sixth amendment Act 2011.

15 Ins. by the Constitution (Ninety Second Amendment) Act, 2003, sec.2(e).

16 Entry 15 renumbered as entry 9 by the Constitution (Ninety Second Amendment) Act, 2003, sec. 2(e).

17 Entry 16 to 18renumbered as entry 20 to 22 by the Constitution (Ninety Second Amendment) Act, 2003, sec. 2(f).

[1][NINTH SCHEDULE

[ARTICLE 31B]

1. The Bihar Land Reforms Act, 1950 (Bihar Act XXX of 1950).
2 The Bombay Tenancy and Agricultural Lands Act, 1948 (Bombay Act LXVII of 1948).
3. The Bombay Maleki Tenure Abolition Act, 1949 (Bombay Act LXI of 1949).
4. The Bombay Taluqdari Tenure Abolition Act, 1949 (Bombay Act LXII of 1949).
5. The Panch Mahals, Mehwassi Tenure Abolition Act, 1949 (Bombay Act LXIII of 1949).
6. The Bombay Khoti Abolition Act, 1950 (Bombay Act VI of 1950).
7. The Bombay Paragana and Kulkarni Watan Abolition Act, 1950 (Bombay Act LX of 1950).
8. The Madhya Pradesh Abolition of Proprietary Rights (Estates, Mahals, Alienated Lands) Act, 1950 (Madhya Pradesh Act 1 of 1951).
9. The Madras Estates (Abolition and Conversion into Ryotwari) Act, 1948 (Madras Act XXVI of 1948).
10. The Madras Estates (Abolition and Conversion into Ryotwari) Amendment Act, 1950 (Madras Act 1 of 1950).
11. The Uttar Pradesh Zamindari Abolition and Land Reforms Act, 1950 (Uttar Pradesh Act 1 of 1951).
12. The Hyderabad (Abolition of Jagirs) Regulation, 1358FC (No. LXIX of 1358, Fasli).
13. The Hyderabad Jagirs (Commutation) Regulation, 1359FC (No. XXV of 1359, Fasli).

[2][14. The Bihar Displaced Persons Rehabilitation (Acquisition of Land) Act, 1950 (Bihar Act XXXVIII of 1950).

15. The United Provinces Land Acquisition (Rehabilitation of Refugees) Act, 1948 (Act XXVI of 1948).
16. The Resettlement of Displaced Persons (Land Acquisition) Act, 1948 (Act LX of 1948).
17. Sections 52A to 52G of the Insurance Act, 1938 (Act IV of 1938), as inserted by section 42 of the Insurance (Amendment) Act, 1950 (Act XLVII of 1950).
18. The Railway Companies (Emergency Provisions) Act, 1951 (Act LI of 1951).
19. Chapter IIIA of the Industries (Development and Regulation) Act, 1951 (Act LXV of 1951), as inserted by section 13 of the Industries (Development and Regulation) Amendment Act, 1953 (Act XXVI of 1953).
20. The West Bengal Land Development and Planning Act, 1948 (West Bengal Act XXI of 1948), as amended by West Bengal Act XXIX of 1951.]

[3][21. The Andhra Pradesh Ceiling on Agricultural Holdings Act, 1961 (Andhra Pradesh Act X of 1961).]

22. The Andhra Pradesh (Telangana Area) Tenancy and Agricultural Lands (Validation) Act, 1961 (Andhra Pradesh Act XXI of 1961).
23. The Andhra Pradesh (Telangana Area) Ijara and Kowli Land Cancellation of Irregular Pattas and Abolition of Concessional Assessment Act, 1961 (Andhra Pradesh Act XXXVI of 1961).

---

1 Added by the Constitution (First Amendment) Act, 1951, sec. 14.

2 Added by the Constitution (Fourth Amendment) Act, 1955, sec. 5.

3 *Added by the Constitution (Seventeenth Amendment) Act, 1964, sec. 3.*

24. The Assam State Acquisition of Lands belonging to Religious or Charitable Institution of Public Nature Act, 1959 (Assam Act IX of 1961).
25. The Bihar Land Reforms (Amendment) Act, 1953 (Bihar Act XX of 1954).
26. The Bihar Land Reforms (Fixation of Ceiling Area and Acquisition of Surplus Land) Act, 1961 (Bihar Act XII of 1962), (except section 28 of this Act).
27. The Bombay Taluqdari Tenure Abolition (Amendment) Act, 1954 (Bombay Act 1 of 1955).
28. The Bombay Taluqdari Tenure Abolition (Amendment) Act, 1957 (Bombay Act XVIII of 1958).
29. The Bombay Inarns (Kutch Area) Abolition Act, 1958 (Bombay Act XCVIII of 1958).
30. The Bombay Tenancy and Agricultural Lands (Gujarat Amendment) Act, 1960 (Gujarat Act XVI of 1960).
31. The Gujarat Agricultural Lands Ceiling Act, 1960 (Gujarat Act XXVI of 1961).

The Sagbara and Meshwassi Estates (Proprietary Rights Abolition, *etc.)* Regulation, 1962 (Gujarat Regulation 1 of 1962).

33. The Gujarat Surviving Alienations Abolition Act, 1963 (Gujarat Act XXXIII of 1963), except in so far as this Act relates to an alienation referred to in sub-clause (d) of clause (3) of section 2 thereof.
34. The Maharashtra Agricultural Lands (Ceiling on Holdings) Act, 1961 (Maharashtra Act XXVII of 1961).
35. The Hyderabad Tenancy and Agricultural Lands (Re-enactment, Validation and Further Amendment) Act, 1961 (Maharashtra Act XLV of 1961).
36. The Hyderabad Tenancy and Agricultural Lands Act, 1950 (Hyderabad Act XXI of 1950).
37. The Jenmikaram Payment (Abolition) Act, 1960 (Kerala Act III of 1961).
38. The Kerala Land Tax Act, 1961 (Kerala Act XIII of 1961). ‘
39. The Kerala Land Reforms Act, 1963 (Kerala Act 1 of 1964).
40. The Madhya Pradesh Land Revenue Code, 1959 (Madhya Pradesh Act XX of 1959).
41. The Madhya Pradesh Ceiling on Agricultural Holdings Act, 1960 (Madhya Pradesh Act XX of 1960).
42. The Madras Cultivating Tenants Protection Act, 1955 (Madras Act XXV of 1955).
43. The Madras Cultivating Tenants (Payment of Fair Rent) Act, 1956 (Madras Act XXIV of 1956).
44. The Madras Occupants of Kudiyiruppu (Protection from Eviction) Act, .1961 (Madras Act XXXVIII of 1961).
45. The Madras Public Trust (Regulation of Administration of Agricultural Lands) Act, 1961 (Madras Act LVII of 1961).
46. The Madras Land Reforms (Fixation of Ceiling on Land) Act, 1961 (Madras Act LVIII of 1961).
47. The Mysore Tenancy Act, 1952 (Mysore Act XIII of 1952).
48. The Coorg Tenants Act, 1957 (Mysore Act XIV of 1957).
49. The Mysore Village Offices Abolition Act, 1961 (Mysore Act XIV of 1961).
50. The Hyderabad Tenancy and Agricultural Lands (Validation) Act, 1961 (Mysore Act XXXVI of 1961). “
51. The Mysore Land Reforms Act, 1961 (Mysore Act X of 1962).
52. The Orissa Land Reforms Act, 1960 (Orissa Act XVI of 1960).
53. The Orissa Merged Territories (Village Offices Abolition) Act, 1963 (Orissa Act X of 1963).

54. The Punjab Security of Land Tenures Act, 1953 (Punjab Act X of 1953).
55. The Rajasthan Tenancy Act, 1955 (Rajasthan Act III of 1955).
56. The Rajasthan Zamindari and Biswedari Abolition Act, 1959 (Rajasthan Act VIII of 1959).
57. The Kumaun and Uttarakhand Zamindari Abolition and Land Reforms Act, 1960 (Uttar Pradesh Act XVII of 1960).
58. The Uttar Pradesh Imposition of Ceiling on Land Holdings Act, 1960 (Uttar Pradesh Act I of 1961).
59. The West Bengal Estates Acquisition Act, 1953 (West Bengal Act 1 of 1954).
60. The West Bengal Land Reforms Act, 1955 (West Bengal Act X of 1956).
61. The Delhi Land Reforms Act, 1954 (Delhi Act VIII of 1954).
62. The Delhi Land Holdings (Ceiling) Act, 1960 (Central Act 24 of 1960).
63. The Manipur Land Revenue and Land Reforms Act, 1960 (Central Act 33 of 1960).
64. The Tripura Land Revenue and Land Reforms Act, 1960 (Central Act 43 of 1960).]

[1][65. The Kerala Land Reforms (Amendment) Act, 1969 (Kerala Act 35 of 1969).

66. The Kerala Land Reforms (Amendment) Act, 1971 (Kerala Act 25 of 1971).]

[2][67. The Andhra Pradesh Land Reforms (Ceiling on Agricultural Holdings) Act, 1973 (Andhra Pradesh Act I of 1973).]

68. The Bihar Land Reforms (Fixation of Ceiling Area and Acquisition of Surplus Land) (Amendment) Act, 1972 (Bihar Act I of 1973).
69. The Bihar Land Reforms (Fixation *of* Ceiling Area and Acquisition of Surplus - Land) (Amendment) Act, 1973 (Bihar Act IX of 1973).
70. The Bihar Land Reforms (Amendment) Act, 1972 (Bihar Act V of 1972).
71. The Gujarat Agricultural Lands Ceiling (Amendment) Act, 1972 (Gujarat Act 2 of 1974).
72. The Haryana Ceiling on Land Holdings Act, 1972 (Haryana Act 26 of 1972).
73. The Himachal Pradesh Ceiling on Land Holdings Act, 1972 (Himachal Pradesh Act 19 of 1973).
74. The Kerala Land Reforms (Amendment) Act, 1972 (Kerala Act 17 of 1972).
75. The Madhya Pradesh Ceiling on Agricultural Holdings (Amendment) Act, 1972 (Madhya Pradesh Act 12 of 1974).
76. The Madhya Pradesh Ceiling on Agricultural Holdings (Second Amendment) Act, 1972 (Madhya Pradesh Act 13 of 1974).
77. The Mysore Land Reforms (Amendment) Act, 1973 (Karnataka Act I of 1974).
78. The Punjab Land Reforms Act, 1972 (Punjab Act 10 of 1973).
79. The Rajasthan Imposition of Ceiling on Agricultural Holdings Act, 1973 (Rajasthan Act II of 1973).
80. The Gudalur Janmam Estates (Abolition and Conversion into Ryotwari) Act, 1969 (Tamil Nadu Act 24 of 1969).
81. The West Bengal Land Reforms (Amendment) Act, 1972 (West Bengal Act XXII of 1972).
82. The West Bengal Estates Acquisition (Amendment) Act, 1964 (West Bengal Act XXII of 1964).

---

1 Ins. by the Constitution (Twenty-ninth Amendment) Act, 1972, sec. 2.

2 Ins. by the Constitution (Thirty-fourt11 Amendment) Act, 1974, sec. 2.

83. The West Bengal Estates Acquisition (Second Amendment) Act, 1973 (West Bengal Act XXXIII of 1973).

84. The Bombay Tenancy and Agricultural Lands (Gujarat Amendment) Act, 1972 (Gujarat Act 5 of 1973).

85. The Orissa Land Reforms (Amendment) Act, 1974 (Orissa Act 9 of 1974).

86. The Tripura Land Revenue and Land Reforms (Second Amendment) Act, 1974 (Tripura Act 7 of 1974).

[1][[2][***]]

88. The Industries (Development and Regulation) Act, 1951 (Central Act 65 of 1951).

89. The Requisitioning and Acquisition of Immovable Property Act,. 1952 (Central Act 30 of 1952).

90. The Mines and Minerals (Regulations and Development) Act, 1957 (Central Act 67 of 1957).

91. The Monopolies and Restrictive Trade Practices Act, 1969 (Central Act 54 of 1969).

[2][***]

93. The Coking Coal Mines (Emergency Provisions) Act, 1971 (Central Act 64 of 1971).

94. The Coking Coal Mines (Nationalisation) Act, 1972 (Central Act 36 of. 1972).

95. The General Insurance Business (Nationalisation) Act, 1972 (Central Act 57 of 1972).

96. The Indian Copper Corporation (Acquisition of Undertaking) Act, 1972 (Central. Act 58 of 1972).

97. The Sick Textile Undertakings (Taking Over of Management) Act, 1972 (Central Act 72 of 1972).

98. The Coal Mines (Taking Over of Management) Act, 1973 (Central Act 15 of 1973).

99. The Coal Mines (Nationalisation) Act, 1973 (Central Act 26 of 1973).

100. The Foreign Exchange Regulation Act, 1973 (Central. Act 46 of 1973).

101. The Alcock Ashdown Company Limited (Acquisition of Undertakings) Act, 1973 (Central Act 56 of 1973).

102. The Coal Mines (Conservation and Development) Act, 1974 (Central Act 28 of 1974).

103. The Additional Emoluments (Compulsory Deposit) Act, 1974 (Central Act 37 of 1974).

104. The Conservation of Foreign Exchange and Prevention *of* Smuggling Activities Act, 1974 (Central Act 52 of 1974).

105. The Sick Textile Undertakings (Nationalisation) Act, 1974 (Central Act 57 of 1974).

106. The Maharashtra Agricultural Lands (Ceiling on Holdings) (Amendment) Act, 1964 (Maharashtra Act XVI of 1965).

107. The Maharashtra Agricultural Lands (Ceiling on Holdings) (Amendment) Act, 1965 (Maharashtra Act XXXII of 1965).

108. The Maharashtra Agricultural Lands (Ceiling on Holdings) (Amendment) Act, 1968 (Maharashtra Act XVI of 1968).

109. The Maharashtra Agricultural Lands (Ceiling on Holdings) (Second Amendment) Act, 1968 (Maharashtra Act XXXIII of 1968).

110. The Maharashtra Agricultural Lands (Ceiling on Holdings) Amendment) Act, 1969 (Maharashtra Act XXXVII of 1969).

---

1 Ins. by the Constitution (Thirty-ninth Amendment) Act, 1975, sec. 5.

2 Entry 87 and 92 omitted by the Constitution (Forty-fourth Amendment) Act, 1978, sec. 44 (w.e.f. 20-6-1979).

111. The Maharashtra Agricultural Lands (Ceiling on Holdings) (Second Amendment) Act, 1969 (Maharashtra Act XXXVI.II of 1969).
112. The Maharashtra Agricultural Lands (Ceiling on Holdings) (Amendment) Act, 1970 (Maharashtra Act XXVII of 1970).
113. The Maharashtra Agricultural Lands (Ceiling on Holdings) (Amendment) Act, 1972 (Maharashtra Act XIII of 1972).
114. The Maharashtra Agricultural Lands (Ceiling on Holdings) (Amendment) Act, 1973 (Maharashtra Act L of 1973).
115. The Orissa Land Reforms (Amendment) Act, 1965 (Orissa Act 13 of 1965).
116. The Orissa Land Reforms (Amendment) Act, 1966 (Orissa Act 8 of 1967).
117. The Orissa Land Reforms (Amendment) Act, 1967 (Orissa Act 13 of 1967).
118. The Orissa Land Reforms (Amendment) Act, 1969 (Orissa Act 13 *of* 1969).
119. The Orissa Land Reforms (Amendment) Act, 1970 (Orissa Act 18 of 1970).
120. The Uttar Pradesh Imposition of Ceiling on Land Holdings (Amendment) Act, 1972 (Uttar Pradesh Act 18 of 1973).
121. The Uttar Pradesh Imposition of Ceiling on Land Holdings (Amendment) Act, 1974 (Uttar Pradesh Act 2 of 1975).
122. The Tripura Land Revenue and Land Reforms (Third Amendment) Act, 1975 (Tripura Act 3 of 1975).
123. The Dadra and Nagar Haveli Land Reforms Regulation, 1971 (3 of 1971).
124. The Dadra and Nagar Haveli Land Reforms (Amendment) Regulation, 1973 (5 of 1973).

[1][125. Section 66A and Chapter IV A of the Motor Vehicles Act, 1939 (Central Act 4 of 1939).

126. The Essential Commodities Act, 1955 (Central Act 10 of 1955).
127. The Smugglers and Foreign Exchange Manipulators (Forfeiture of Property) Act, 1976 (Central Act 13 of 1976).
128. The Bonded Labour System (Abolition) Act, 1976 (Central Act 19 of 1976).
129. The Conservation of Foreign Exchange and Prevention of Smuggling Activities (Amendment) Act, 1976 (Central Act 20 of 1976). [2][***]
131. The Levy Sugar Price Equalisation Fund Act, 1976 (Central Act 31 of 1976).
132. The Urban Land (Ceiling and Regulation) Act, 1976 (Central Act 33 of 1976).
133. The Departmentalisation of Union Accounts (Transfer of Personnel) Act, 1976 (Central Act 59 of 1976).
134. The Assam Fixation of Ceiling on Land Holdings Act, 1956 (Assam Act 1 of 1957).
135. The Bombay Tenancy and Agricultural Lands (Vidarbha Region) Act, 1958 (Bombay Act XCIX of 1958).
136. The Gujarat Private Forests (Acquisition) Act, 1972 (Gujarat Act 14 of 1973).
137. The Haryana Ceiling on Land Holdings (Amendment) Act, 1976 (Haryana Act 17 of 1976).
138. The Himachal Pradesh Tenancy and Land Reforms Act, 1972 (Himachal Pradesh Act 8 of 1974).
139. The Himachal Pradesh Village Common Lands Vesting and Utilization Act, 1974 (Himachal Pradesh Act 18 of 1974).

1 Ins. by the Constitution (Fortieth Amendment) Act 1976, sec. 3.

2 Entry 130 omitted by the Constitution (Forty-fourth Amendment) Act, 1.978, sec. 44 (w.e.f. 20-6-1979).

140. The Karnataka Land Reforms (Second Amendment and Miscellaneous Provisions) Act, 1974 (Kamataka Act 31 of 1974).

142. The Karnataka Land Reforms (Second Amendment) Act, 1976 (Karnataka Act 27 of 1976).

142. The Kerala Prevention of Eviction Act, 1966 (Kerala Act 12 of 1966).

143. The Thiruppuvaram Payment (Abolition) Act, 1969 (Kerala Act 19 of 1969).

144. The Sreepadam Lands Enfranchisement Act, 1969 (Kerala Act 20 of 1969).

145. The Sree Pandaravaka Lands (Vesting and Enfranchisement) Act, 1971 (Kerala Act 20 of 1971).

146. The Kerala Private Forests (Vesting and Assignment) Act, 1971 (Kerala Act 26 of 1971).

147. The Kerala Agricultural Workers Act, 1974 (Kerala Act 18 of 1974).

148. The Kerala Cashew Factories (Acquisition) Act, 1974 (Kerala Act 29 of 1974).

149. The Kerala Chit ties Act, 1975 (Kerala Act 23 of 1975).

150. The Kerala Scheduled Tribes (Restriction on Transfer of Lands and Restoration of Alienated Lands) Act, 1975 (Kerala Act 31 of 1975). ,

151. The Kerala Land Reforms (Amendment) Act, 1976 (Kerala Act 15 of 1976).

152. The Kanam Tenancy Abolition Act, 1976 (Kerala Act 16 of 1976).

153. The Madhya Pradesh Ceiling on Agricultural Holdings (Amendment) Act, 1974 (Madhya Pradesh Act 20 of 1974).

154. The Madhya Pradesh Ceiling on Agricultural Holdings (Amendment) Act, 1975 (Madhya Pradesh Act 2 of 1976).

155. The West Khandesh Meshwari Estates (Proprietary Rights Abolition, *etc.)* Regulation, 1961 (Maharashtra Regulation 1 of 1962).

156. The Maharashtra Restoration of Lands to Scheduled Tribes Act, 1974 (Maharashtra Act XIV of 1975).

157. The Maharashtra Agricultural Lands (Lowering of Ceiling on Holdings) and (Amendment) Act, 1972 (Maharashtra Act XXI of 1975).

158. The Maharashtra Private Forests (Acquisition) Act, 1975 (Maharashtra Act XXIX of 1975).

159. The Maharashtra Agricultural Lands (Lowering of Ceiling on Holdings) and (Amendment) Act, 1975 (Maharashtra Act XL VII of 1975). .

160. The Maharashtra Agricultural Lands (Ceiling on Holdings) (Amendment) Act, 1975 (Maharashtra Act II of 1976).

161. The Orissa Estates Abolition Act, 1951 (Orissa Act I of 1952).

162. The Rajasthan Colonisation Act, 1954 (Rajasthan Act XXVII of 1954).

163. The Rajasthan Land Reforms and Acquisition of Landowners' Estates Act, 1963 (Rajasthan Act 11 of 1964).

164. The Rajasthan Imposition of Ceiling on Agricultural Holdings (Amendment) Act, 1976 (Rajasthan Act 8 of 1976).

165. The Rajasthan Tenancy (Amendment) Act, 1976 (Rajasthan Act 12 of 1976).

166. The Tamil Nadu Land Reforms (Reduction of Ceiling on Land) Act, 1970 (Tamil Nadu Act 17 of 1970).

167. The Tamil Nadu Land Reforms (Fixation of Ceiling on Land) Amendment Act, 1971 (Tamil Nadu Act 41 of 1971).

168. The Tamil Nadu Land Reforms (Fixation of Ceiling on Land) Amendment Act, 1972 (Tamil Nadu Act 10 of 1972).

169. The Tamil Nadu Land Reforms (Fixation of Ceiling on Land) Second Amendment Act, 1972 (Tamil Nadu Act 20 of 1972).

170. The Tamil Nadu Land Reforms (Fixation of Ceiling on Land) Third Amendment Act, 1972 (Tamil Nadu Act 37 of 1972).

171. The Tamil Nadu Land Reforms (Fixation of Ceiling on Land) Fourth Amendment Act, 1972 (Tamil Nadu Act 39 of 1972).

172. The Tamil Nadu Land Reforms (Fixation of Ceiling on Land) Sixth Amendment Act, 1972, (Tamil Nadu Act 7 of 1974).

173. The Tamil Nadu Land Reforms (Fixation of Ceiling on Land) Fifth Amendment Act, 1972 (Tamil Nadu Act 10 of 1974).

174. The Tamil Nadu Land Reforms (Fixation of Ceiling on Land) Amendment Act, 1974 (Tamil Nadu Act 15 of 1974).

175. The Tamil Nadu Land Reforms (Fixation of Ceiling on Land) Third Amendment Act, 1974 (Tamil Nadu Act 30 of 1974).

176. The Tamil Nadu Land Reforms (Fixation of Ceiling on Land) Second Amendment Act, 1974 (Tamil Nadu Act 32 of 1974).

177. The Tamil Nadu Land Reforms (Fixation of Ceiling on Land) Amendment Act, 1975 (Tamil Nadu Act 11 of 1975).

178. The Tamil Nadu Land Reforms (Fixation of Ceiling on Land) Second Amendment Act, 1975 (Tamil Nadu Act 21 of 1975).

179. Amendments made to the Uttar Pradesh Zamindari Abolition and Land Reforms Act, 1950 (Uttar Pradesh Act I of 1951) by the Uttar Pradesh Land Laws (Amendment) Act, 1971 (Uttar Pradesh Act 21 of 1971) and the Uttar Pradesh Land Laws (Amendment) Act, 1974 (Uttar Pradesh Act 34 of 1974).

180. The Uttar Pradesh Imposition of Ceiling on Land Holdings (Amendment) Act, 1976 (Uttar Pradesh Act 20 of 1976).

181. The West Bengal Land Reforms (Second Amendment) Act, 1972 (West Bengal Act XXVIII of 1972).

182. The West Bengal Restoration of Alienated Land Act, 1973 (West Bengal Act XXIII of 1973).

183. The West Bengal Land Reforms (Amendment) Act, 1974 (West Bengal Act XXXIII of 1974).

184. The West Bengal Land Reforms (Amendment) Act, 1975 (West Bengal Act XXIII of 1975).

185. The West Bengal Land Reforms (Amendment) Act, 1976 (West Bengal Act XII of 1976).

186. The Delhi Land Holdings (Ceiling) Amendment Act, 1976 (Central Act 15 of 1976).

187. The Goa, Daman and Diu Mundkars (Protection from Eviction) Act, 1975 (Goa, Daman and Diu Act I of 1976).

188. The Pondicherry Land Reforms (Fixation of Ceiling on Land) Act, 1973 (Pondicherry Act 9 of 1974).]

[1][189. The Assam (Temporarily Settled Areas) Tenancy Act, 1971 (Assam Act XXIII of 1971).

190. The Assam (Temporarily Settled Areas) Tenancy (Amendment) Act, 1974 (Assam Act XVIII of 1974).

191. The Bihar Land Reforms (Fixation of Ceiling Area and Acquisition of Surplus Land) (Amendment) Amending Act, 1974 (Bihar Act 31 of 1975).

192. The Bihar Land Reforms (Fixation of Ceiling Area and Acquisition of Surplus Land) (Amendment) Act, 1976 (Bihar Act 22 of 1976).

---

1 Ins. by the Constitution (Forty-seventh Amendment) Act, 1984, sec. 2 (w.e.f. 26-8-1984).

193. The Bihar Land Reforms (Fixation of Ceiling Area and Acquisition of Surplus Land) (Amendment) Act, 1978 (Bihar Act VII of 1978).

194. The Land Acquisition (Bihar Amendment) Act, 1979 (Bihar Act 2 of 1980).

195. The Haryana Ceiling on Land Holdings (Amendment) Act, 1977 (Haryana Act 14 of 1977).

196. The Tamil Nadu Land Reforms (Fixation of Ceiling on Land) Amendment Act, 1978 (Tamil Nadu Act 25 of 1978).

197. The Tamil Nadu Land Reforms (Fixation of Ceiling on Land) Amendment Act, 1979 (Tamil Nadu Act 11 of 1979).

198. The Uttar Pradesh Zamindari Abolition Laws (Amendment) Act, 1978 (Uttar Pradesh Act 15 of 1978).

199. The West Bengal Restoration of Alienated Land (Amendment) Act, 1978 (West Bengal Act XXIV of 1978).

200. The West Bengal Restoration of Alienated Land (Amendment) Act, 1980 (West Bengal Act LVI of 1980).

201. The Goa, Daman and Diu Agricultural Tenancy Act, 1964 (Goa, Daman and Diu Act 7 of 1964).

202. The Goa, Daman and Diu Agricultural Tenancy (Fifth Amendment) Act, 1976 (Goa, Daman and Diu Act 17 of 1976).]

[1][203. The Andhra Pradesh Scheduled Areas Land Transfer Regulation, 1959 (Andhra Pradesh Regulation I of 1959)

204. The Andhra Pradesh Scheduled Areas Laws (Extension and Amendment) Regulation, 1963 (Andhra Pradesh Regulation 2 of 1963).

205. The Andhra Pradesh Scheduled Areas Land Transfer (Amendment) Regulation, 1970 (Andhra Pradesh Regulation 1 of 1970).

206. The Andhra Pradesh Scheduled Areas Land Transfer (Amendment) Regulation, 1971 (Andhra Pradesh Regulation 1 of 1971).

207. The Andhra Pradesh Scheduled Areas Land Transfer (Amendment) Regulation, 1978 (Andhra Pradesh Regulation 1 of 1978).

208. The Bihar Tenancy Act, 1885 (Bihar Act 8 of 1885).

209. The Chhota Nagpur Tenancy Act, 1908 (Bengal Act 6 of 1908) (Chapter VIII- sections 46, 47, 48, 48A and 49; Chapter X-sections 71, 71A and 71B; and Chapter XVIII-sections 240, 241 and 242).

210. The Santhal Parganas Tenancy (Supplementary Provisions) Act, 1949 (Bihar Act 14 of 1949) except section 53.

211. The Bihar Scheduled Areas Regulation, 1969 (Bihar Regulation 1 of 1969).

212. The Bihar Land Reforms (Fixation of Ceiling Area and Acquisition of Surplus Land) (Amendment) Act, 1982 (Bihar Act 55 of 1982).

213. The Gujarat Devasthan Inams Abolition Act, 1969 (Gujarat Act 1& of 1969).

214. The Gujarat Tenancy Laws (Amendment) Act, 1976 (Gujarat Act 37 of 1976).

215. The Gujarat Agricultural Lands Ceiling (Amendment) Act, 1976 (President's Act 43 of 1976).

216. The Gujarat Devasthan Inams Abolition (Amendment) Act, 1977 (Gujarat Act 27 of 1977).

217. The Gujarat Tenancy Laws (Amendment) Act, 1977 (Gujarat Act 30 of 1977).

218. The Bombay Land Revenue (Gujarat second Amendment) Act, 1980 (Gujarat Act 37 of 1980).

219. The Bombay Land Revenue Code and Land Tenure Abolition taws (Gujarat Amendment) Act, 1982 (Gujarat Act 8 of 1982).

---

1 **Ins. by the Constitution** (Sixty-sixth Amendment) Act, 1990, sec. 2 (w.e.f. 7-6-1990).

220. The Himachal Pradesh Transfer of Land (Regulation) Act, 1968 (Himachal Pradesh Act 15 of 1969).
221. The Himachal Pradesh Transfer of Land (Regulation) (Amendment) Act, 1986 (Himachal Pradesh Act 16 of 1986).
222. The Kamataka Scheduled Castes and Scheduled Tribes (Prohibition of Transfer of certain Lands) Act, 1978 (Kamataka Act 2 of 1979).
223. The Kerala Land Reforms (Amendment) Act, 1978 (Kerala Act 13 of 1978)
224. The Kerala Land Reforms (Amendment) Act, 1981 (Kerala Act 19 of 1981).
225. The Madhya Pradesh Land Revenue Code (Third Amendment) Act, 1976 (Madhya Pradesh Act 61 of 1976).
226. The Madhya Pradesh Land Revenue Code (Amendment) Act, 1980 (Madhya Pradesh Act 15 of 1980).
227. The Madhya Pradesh Akrishik Jot Uchachatam Seema Adhiniyam, 1981 (Madhya Pradesh Act 11 of 1981).
228. The Madhya Pradesh Ceiling on Agricultural Holdings (Second Amendment) Act, 1976 (Madhya Pradesh Act I of 1984).
229. The Madhya Pradesh Ceiling on Agricultural Holdings (Amendment) Act, 1984 (Madhya Pradesh Act 14 of 1984).
230. The Madhya Pradesh Ceiling on Agricultural Holdings (Amendment) Act, 1989 (Madhya Pradesh Act 8 of 1989).
231. The Maharashtra Land Revenue Code, 1966 (Maharashtra Act 41 of 1966), sections 36, 36A and 36B.
232. The Maharashtra Land Revenue Code and the Maharashtra Restoration of Lands to Scheduled Tribes (Second Amendment) Act, 1976 (Maharashtra Act 30 of 1977).
233. The Maharashtra Abolition of Subsisting Proprietary Rights to Mines and Minerals in certain Lands Act, 1985 (Maharashtra Act 16 of 1985).
234. The Orissa Scheduled Areas Transfer of Immovable Property (By Scheduled Tribes) Regulation, 1956 (Orissa Regulation 2 of 1956).
235. The Orissa Land Reforms (Second Amendment) Act, 1975 (Orissa Act 29 of 1976).
236. The Orissa Land Reforms (Amendment) Act, 1976 (Orissa Act 30 of 1976).
237. The Orissa Land Reforms (Second Amendment) Act, 1976 (Orissa Act 44 of 1976).
238. The Rajasthan Colonisation (Amendment) Act, 1984 (Rajasthan Act 12 of 1984).
239. The Rajasthan Tenancy (Amendment) Act, 1984 (Rajasthan Act 13 of 1984).
240. The Rajasthan Tenancy (Amendment) Act, 1987 (Rajasthan Act 21 of 1987).
241. The Tamil Nadu Land Reforms (Fixation of Ceiling on Land) Second Amendment Act, 1979 (Tamil Nadu Act 8 of 1980).
242. The Tamil Nadu Land Reforms (Fixation of Ceiling on Land) Amendment Act, 1980 (Tamil Nadu Act 21 of 1980).
243. The Tamil Nadu Land Reforms (Fixation of Ceiling on Land) Amendment Act, 1981 (Tamil Nadu Act 59 of 1981).
244. The Tamil Nadu Land Reforms (Fixation of Ceiling on Land) Second Amendment Act, 1983 (Tamil Nadu Act 2 of 1984).
245. The Uttar Pradesh Land Laws (Amendment) Act, 1982 (Uttar Pradesh Act 20 of 1982).
246. The West Bengal Land Reforms (Amendment) Act, 1965 (West Bengal Act 18 of 1965).
247. The West Bengal Land Reforms (Amendment) Act, 1966 (West Bengal Act 11 of 1966).
248. The West Bengal Land Reforms (Second Amendment) Act, 1969 (West Bengal Act 23 of 1969).

249. The West Bengal Estate Acquisition (Amendment) Act, 1977 (West Bengal Act 36 of.1977).
250. The West Bengal Land Holding Revenue Act, 1979 (West Bengal Act 44 of 1979).
251. The West Bengal Land Reforms (Amendment) Act, 1980 (West Bengal Act 41 of 1980).
252. The West Bengal Land Holding Revenue (Amendment) Act, 1981 (West Bengal Act 33 of 1981).
253. The Calcutta Thikka Tenancy (Acquisition and Regulation) Act, 1981 (West Bengal Act 37 of 1981).
254. The West Bengal Land Holding Revenue (Amendment) Act, 1982 (West Bengal Act 23 of 1982).
255. The Calcutta Thikka Tenancy (Acquisition and Regulation) (Amendment) Act, 1984 (West Bengal Act 41 of 1984).
256. The Mahe Land Reforms Act, 1968 (Pondicherry Act 1 of 1968).
257. The Mahe Land Reforms (Amendment) Act, 1980 (Pondicherry Act 1 of 981).]

[1][257A The Tamil Nadu Backward Classes, Scheduled Castes and Scheduled Tribes (Reservation of Seats in Educational Institutions and of appointments or posts in the Services under the State) Act 1993 (Tamil Nadu Act 45 of 1994).]

[2][258. The Bihar Privileged persons Homestead Tenancy Act, 1947 (Bihar Act 4 of 1948).
259. The Bihar Consolidation of Holdings and Prevention of Fragmentation Act, 1956 (Bihar Act 22 of 1956).
260. The Bihar Consolidation of Holdings and Prevention of Fragmentation (Amendment) Act, 1970 (Bihar Act 7 of 1970).
261. The Bihar Privileged Persons Homestead Tenancy (Amendment) Act, 1970 (Bihar Act 9 of 1970).
262. The Bihar Consolidation of Holdings and Prevention of Fragmentation (Amendment) Act, 1973 (Bihar Act 27 of 1975).
263. The Bihar Consolidation of Holdings and Prevention of Fragmentation (Amendment) Act, 1981 (Bihar Act 35 of 1982).
264. The Bihar Land Reforms (Fixation of Ceiling Area and Acquisition of Surplus Land) (Amendment) Act, 1987 (Bihar Act 21 of 1987).
265. The Bihar Privileged Persons Homestead Tenancy (Amendment) Act, 1989 (Bihar Act 11 of 1989).
266. The Bihar Land Reforms (Amendment) Act, 1989 (Bihar Act 11 of 1990).
267. The Karnataka Scheduled Castes and Scheduled Tribes (Prohibition of Transfer of Certain Lands) (Amendment) Act, 1984 (Karnataka Act 3 of 1984).
268. The Kerala land Reforms (Amendment) Act, 1989 (Kerala Act 16 of 1989).
269. The Kerala land Reforms (Second Amendment) Act, 1989 (Kerala Act 2 of 1990).
270. The Orissa Land Reforms (Amendment Act, 1989 (Orissa Act 9 of 1990).
271. The Rajasthan Tenancy (Amendment) Act, 1979 (Rajasthan Act 16 of 1979).
272. The Rajasthan Colonisation (Amendment) Act, 1987 (Rajasthan Act 2 of 1987).
273. The Rajasthan Colonisation (Amendment) Act, 1989 (Rajasthan Act 12 of 1989).
274. The Tamil Nadu Land Reforms (Fixation of Ceiling on Land) Amendment Act, 1983 (Tamil Nadu Act 3 of 1984).
275. The Tamil Nadu Land Reforms (Fixation of Ceiling on Land) Amendment Act, 1986 (Tamil Nadu Act 57 of 1986).

---

1 Ins. by the Constitution (Seventy-sixth Amendment) Act, 1994, sec. 2 (w.e.f. 31-8-1994).

2 Ins. by the Constitution (Seventy-eighth Amendment) Act, 1995, sec. 2 (w.e.f. 30-8-1995).

276. The Tamil Nadu Land Reforms (Fixation of Ceiling on Land) Second Amendment Act, 1987 (Tamil Nadu Act 4 of 1988).

277. The Tamil Nadu Land Reforms (Fixation of Ceiling on Land) Amendment Act, 1989 (Tamil Nadu Act 30 of 1989).

278. The West Bengal Land Reforms (Amendment) Act, 1981 (West Bengal Act 50 of 1981).

279. The West Bengal Land Reforms (Amendment) Act, 1986 (West Bengal Act 5 of 1986).

280. The West Bengal Land Reforms (Second Amendment) Act, 1986 (West Bengal Act 19 of 1986).

281. The West Bengal Land Reforms (Third Amendment) Act, 1981 (West Bengal Act 35 of 1986).

282. The West Bengal Land Reforms (Amendment) Act, 1989 (West Bengal Act 23 of 1989).

283. The West Bengal Land Reforms (Amendment) Act, 1990 (West Bengal Act 24 of 1990).

284. The West Bengal Land Reforms (Tribunal Act, 1991 (West Bengal Act 12 of 1991).

Explanation.-Any acquisition made under the Rajasthan Tenancy Act, 1955 (Rajasthan Act III of 1955), in contravention of the second proviso to clause (1) of article 31 A shall, to the extent of the contravention, be void.]

[1][TENTH SCHEDULE

[ARTICLES 102(2) AND 191(2)]

PROVISIONS AS TO DISQUALIFICATION ON GROUND OF DEFECTION

1. **Interpretation**.-In this Schedule, unless the context otherwise requires,-

(a) 'House' means either House of Parliament or the Legislative Assembly or, as the case may be, either House of the Legislature of a State;

(b) 'legislature party', in relation to a member of a House belonging to any political party in accordance with the provisions of paragraph 2 or paragraph 3 or, as the case may be, paragraph 4, means the group consisting of all the members of that House for the time being belonging to that political party in accordance with the said provisions;

(c) 'original political party', in relation to a member of a House, means the political party to which he belongs for the purposes of sub-paragraph (1) of paragraph 2;

(d) 'paragraph' means a paragraph of this Schedule.

2. **Disqualification on ground of defection.**-(I) Subject to the provisions of paragraphs [2][paragraph 4 and 5], a member of a House belonging to any political party shall be disqualified for being a member of the House-

(a) if he has voluntarily given up his membership of such political party; or

(b) if he votes or abstains from voting in such House contrary to any direction issued by the political party to which he belongs .or by any person or authority authorised by it in this behalf, without obtaining, in either case, the prior permission of such political party,

1 Added by the Constitution (Fifty-second Amendment) Act, 1985, sec. 6 (w.e.f. 1-3-1985).

2 Subs. by Constitution (Ninety five Amendment) Act, 2003, sec. 5(b) for paragraph 3, 4 & 5 (w.e.f. 1-1-2004).

person or authority and such voting or abstention has not been condoned by such political party, person or authority" within fifteen days from the date of such voting or abstention.;

Explanation.-For the purposes of this sub-paragraph,-

(a) an elected member of a House shall be deemed to belong to the political party, if any by which he was set up as a candidate for election as such member;

(b) a nominated member of a House shall,-

(i) where he is a member of any political party on the date of his nomination as such member, be deemed to belong to such political party;

(ii) in any other case, be deemed to belong to the political party of which he becomes, or, as the case may be, first becomes, a member before the expiry of six months from the date on which he takes his seat after complying with the requirements of article 99 or, as the case may be, article 188.

(2) An elected member of a House who has been elected as such otherwise than as a candidate set up by any political party shall be disqualified for being a member of the-House if he joins any political party after such election.

(3) A nominated member of a House shall be disqualified for being a member of the House if he joins any political party after the expiry of six months from the date on which he takes his seat after complying with the requirements of article 99 or, as the case may be, article 188.

(4) Notwithstanding anything contained in the foregoing provisions of this paragraph, a person who, on the commencement of the Constitution (Fifty-second Amendment) Act, 1985, is a member of a House (whether elected or nominated as such) shall,-

(i) where he was a member of political party immediately before such commencement, be deemed, for the purposes of sub-paragraph (1) of this paragraph, to have been elected as a member of such House as a candidate set up by such political party;

(ii) in any other case, be deemed to be an elected member of the House who has been elected as such otherwise than as a candidate set up by any political party for the purposes of sub-paragraph (2) of this paragraph or, as the case may be, deemed to be a nominated member of the House for the purposes of sub-paragraph (3) of this paragraph.

[1][***]

4. **Disqualification on ground of defection not to apply in case of merger.-**

(I) A member of a House shall not be disqualified under sub-paragraph (1) of paragraph 2 where his original political party merges with another political party and he claims that he and any other members of his original political party.

(a) have become members of such other political party or, as the case may be, pf a new political party formed by such merger; or

(b) have not accepted the merger and opted to function as a separate group, and from the time of such merger, such other political party or new political party or group, as the case may be, shall be deemed to be the political party to which he belongs for the purposes of sub-paragraph (1) of paragraph 2 and to be his original political party for the purposes of this sub-paragraph.

(2) For the purposes of sub-paragraph (1) of this paragraph, the merger of the original political party of a member of a House shall be deemed to have taken place if, and only if, not less than two-thirds of the members of the legislature party concerned have

---

1 Paragraph 3 omitted by the Constitution (Ninety first Amendment) Act 2003, Sec. 5(c) (w.e.f. 1.1.2004)

agreed to such merger .

5. **Exemption.**-Notwithstanding anything contained in this Schedule, a person who has been elected to the office of the Speaker or the Deputy Speaker of the House of the People or the Deputy Chairman of the Council of States or the Chairman or the Deputy Chairman of the Legislative Council of a State or the Speaker or the Deputy Speaker of the Legislative Assembly of a State, shall not be disqualified under this Schedule,-

   (a) if he, by reason of his election to such office, voluntarily gives up the membership of the political party to which he belonged immediately before such election and does not, so long as he continues to hold such office thereafter, rejoin that political party or become a member of another political party; or

   (b) if he, having given up by reason of his election to such office his membership of the political party to which he belonged immediately before such election, rejoins such political party after he ceases to hold such office.

6. **Decision on questions as to disqualification on ground of defection.**-

   (I) If any question arises as to whether a member of a House has become subject to disqualification under this Schedule, the question shall be referred for the decision of the Chairman or, as the case may be, the Speaker of such House and his decision shall be final:

   Provided that where the question which has arisen is as to whether the Chairman or the Speaker of a House has become subject to such disqualification, the question shall be referred for the decision of such member of the House as the House may elect in this behalf and his decision shall be final.

   (2) All proceedings under sub-paragraph (1) of this paragraph in relation to any question as to disqualification of a member of a House under this Schedule shall be deemed to be proceedings in Parliament within the meaning of article 122 or, as the case may be, proceedings in the Legislature of a State within the meaning of article 212.

*7. **Bar of jurisdiction of courts**.-Notwithstanding anything in this Constitution, no court shall have any jurisdiction in respect of any matter connected with the disqualification of a member of a House under this Schedule.

8. **Rules.**-

   (I) Subject to the provisions of sub-paragraph (2) of this paragraph, the Chairman or the Speaker of a House may make rules for giving effect to the provisions of this Schedule, and in particular, and without prejudice to the generality of the foregoing, such rules may provide for-

      (a) the maintenance of registers or other records as to the political parties if any, to which different members of the House belong;

      (b) the report which the leader of a legislature party in relation to a member of a House shall furnish with regard to any condonation of the nature referred to in clause (b) of sub-paragraph (1) of paragraph 2 in respect of such member, the time within which and the authority to whom such report shall be furnished;

      (c) the reports which a political party shall furnish with regard to admission to such political party of any members of the House and the officer of the House to whom such reports shall be furnished; and

      (d) the procedure for deciding any question referred to in sub-paragraph (1) of paragraph 6 including the procedure for any inquiry which may be made for the purpose of deciding such question.

   (2) The rules made by the Chairman or the Speaker of a House under sub-paragraph (1) of this paragraph shall be laid as soon as may be after they are made before the House for a total period of thirty days which may be comprised in one session or in two or more successive sessions and shall take effect upon the expiry of the said period of thirty

* Paragraph 7 declared invalid in Kihoto Hollohon v. Zachilhu (1992) 1 SCC 309.

days unless they are sooner approved with or without modifications or disapproved by the House and where they are so approved, they shall take effect on such approval in the form in which they were laid or in such modified form, as the case may be, and where they are so disapproved, they shall be of no effect.

(3) The Chairman or the Speaker of a .House may, without prejudice to the, provisions of article 105 or, as the case may be, article 194, and to any other power which he may have under this Constitution direct that any wilful contravention by any person of the rules made under this paragraph may be dealt with in the same manner as a breach of privilege of the House.]

[1][ELEVENTH SCHEDULE

[ARTICLE 243G]

1. Agriculture, including agricultural extension.
2. Land improvement, implementation of land reforms, land consolidation and soil conservation.
3. Minor irrigation, water management and watershed development.
4. Animal husbandry, dairying and poultry.
5. Fisheries.
6. Social forestry and farm forestry.
7. Minor forest produce.
8. Small scale industries, including food processing industries.
9. Khadi, village and cottage industries.
10. Rural housing.
11. Drinking water.
12. Fuel and fodder .
13. Roads, culverts, bridges, ferries, waterways and other means of communication.
14. Rural electrification, including distribution of electricity.
15. Non-conventional energy sources.
16. Poverty alleviation programme.
17. Education, including primary and secondary schools.
18. Technical training and vocational education.
19. Adult and non-formal education.
20. Libraries.
21. Cultural activities.
22. Markets and fairs.
23. Health and sanitation, including hospitals, primary health centres and dispensaries.
24. Family welfare.
25. Women and child development.
26. Social welfare, including welfare of the handicapped and mentally retarded.
27. Welfare of the weaker sections, and in particular, of the Scheduled Castes and the Scheduled

1 Added by the Constitution (Seventy-third Amendment) Act, 1992, sec. 4 (w.e.f. 24-4-1993).

Tribes.

28. Public distribution system.
29. Maintenance of community assets.]

[1][TWELFTH SCHEDULE

[ARTICLE 243W]

1. Urban planning including town planning.
2. Regulation of land-use and construction of buildings.
3. Planning for economic and social development.
4. Roads and bridges.
5. Water supply for domestic, industrial and, commercial purposes.
6. Public health, sanitation conservancy and solid waste management.
7. Fire services.
8. Urban forestry, protection of the environment and promotion of ecological aspects.
9. Safeguarding the interests of weaker sections of society, including the handicapped and mentally retarded.
10. Slum improvement and upgradation.
11. Urban poverty alleviation.
12. Provision of urban amenities and facilities such as parks, gardens, play-grounds.
13. Promotion of cultural, educational and aesthetic aspects.
14. Burials and burial grounds; cremations, cremation grounds and electric crematoriums.
15. Cattle ponds; prevention of cruelty to animals.
16. Vital statistics including registration of births and deaths.
17. Public amenities including street lighting, parking lots, bus stops and public conveniences.
18. Regulation of slaughter houses and tanneries.]

1 Ins. by the Constitution (Seventy-fourth Amendment) Act, 1992, sec. 4 (w.e.f. 1-6-1993).

APPENDIX I

Additions to Specific Topics in This Book

Page No. 28

(Below matter is an update to Article 21A dealing with Right to Education)

Right to Privacy

- In the landmark case *K.S. Puttaswamy V. Union of India* which was passed in the year 2017, Right to Privacy was recognised as Fundamental Right and was then enshrined in Article 21 as a Right to life and personal liberty.
- The court said that, "the right to privacy is protected as an intrinsic part of the right to life and personal liberty under Article 21 and as a part of the freedoms guaranteed by Part III of the Constitution".

Interpretation of Article 21

- The scope of Article 21 has been widening by several landmark judgements.
- Some important cases concerned with Article 21

AK Gopalan Case (1950)

- The SC held that the expression 'procedure established by law', the Constitution has embodied the British concept of personal liberty rather than the American 'due process'.
- SC took a narrow view of Article 21.

Maneka Gandhi vs. Union of India Case (1978)

- Overturned the Gopalan case judgement
- The idea of personal liberty in Article 21 has a wide scope
- Article 21 must satisfy the requirements under Article 19 as well.
- Any procedure under law for the deprivation of life or liberty of a person must not be unfair, unreasonable or arbitrary.

Francis Coralie Mullin vs. Union Territory of Delhi (1981)

- Any procedure for the deprivation of life or liberty of a person must be reasonable, fair and just and not arbitrary or whimsical

Unni Krishnan vs. State of Andhra Pradesh (1993)

- SC upheld the expanded interpretation of the right to life.

The Court gave a list of rights that Article 21 covers based on earlier judgments.

Some of them are:

1. Right to privacy
2. Right to go abroad
3. Right to shelter
4. Right against solitary confinement
5. Right to social justice and economic empowerment
6. Right against handcuffing

7. Right against custodial death
8. Right against delayed execution
9. Doctors' assistance
10. Right against public hanging
11. Protection of cultural heritage
12. Right to pollution-free water and air
13. Right of every child to a full development
14. Right to health and medical aid
15. Right to education
16. Protection of undertrials

Page No. 201

(Below matter is an update to Article 370 regarding the special status of Jammu and Kashmir)

The abrogation of Article 370 to end the special status of Jammu and Kashmir

- With a resolution and a bill, the Central government scripted a historical change in the status of Jammu and Kashmir
- On August 5, 2019, Union Home Minister Amit Shah introduced a proposal in Parliament for ending the special status of Jammu and Kashmir and its bifurcation into two Union Territories.
- Jammu and Kashmir had a special status granted under Article 370 and Article 35A (created through a Presidential Order) of the Constitution

What is the present status of Article 370 ?

- Article 370 is an enabling provision.
- The Presidential order signed by the President of India has not scrapped Article 370.
- The special status of Jammu & Kashmir has been withdrawn by invoking article 370
- Article 370 is still on the statute book.
- Article 370 explains which parts of the Indian Constitution have jurisdiction over Jammu and Kashmir, which adopted a separate state constitution for itself during 1950s.
- Clause 3 of Article 370 empowers the President to decide the limit of the jurisdiction of the Indian Constitution over the state.
- Article 370 is still a part of the Indian Constitution and cannot be repealed or abrogated without a constitutional amendment (Article 368)
- The government has used Article 370 to announce that special status granted under this Article to Jammu and Kashmir has ended.
- This was done through a Presidential Order, which in effect, will supercede previous Presidential Orders issued under Article 370.
- This move by the government gives full applicability of the Indian Constitution in Jammu and Kashmir and the separate constitution of Jammu and Kashmir ceases to be in operation in the state.
- Earlier, only a set of limited provisions such as foreign relations, communication and defence had jurisdiction over Jammu and Kashmir.
- With state constitution rendered inoperative and Articles 1-2 applicable to Jammu and Kashmir, the central government got the power to redraw the map of the state.
- The government, accordingly, moved another resolution for bifurcation of Jammu and Kashmir.
- The resolution, adopted by Parliament, turns the existing state of Jammu and Kashmir into two Union Territories of Jammu-Kashmir and Ladakh respectively.

- The Union Territory of Jammu-Kashmir will have a legislature.
- Its new status will be comparable with that of Delhi and Puducherry, only two other Union Territories to have legislatures of their own.
- The Governor of Jammu and Kashmir will now become Lieutenant Governor.

Jammu and Kashmir Reorganisation Act, 2019

- It is an act by the Indian Parliament where the State of Jammu and Kashmir was bifurcated into two union territories - Jammu & Kashmir and Ladakh.
- The Union Territory of Jammu and Kashmir has a legislative assembly
- The L-G will have the power to dissolve the Jammu and Kashmir Legislative Assembly.
- The Union Territory of Ladakh does not have a legislative assembly and is administered by the Lieutenant Governor alone.
- The Union Territory of Ladakh will include the districts Leh and Kargil
- Out of the six Lok Sabha seats in the state of Jammu and Kashmir, five remained with the Union Territory of Jammu and Kashmir and one went to the Union Territory of Ladakh.

Union Territories of India

- Earlier there were Seven UTs - Andaman and Nicobar Islands, Chandigarh, Dadra and Nagar Haveli, Daman and Diu, Lakshadweep, National Capital Territory of Delhi and Puducherry.
- These are specified under Part II of the First Schedule to the Constitution of India, viz.
- National Capital Territory of Delhi and Puducherry - UT with a legislature.
- The state of Jammu and Kashmir has also been added along with Delhi and Puducherry to be a UT with a legislature.
- Article 240 - the President of India has the power to make regulations for UTs not having their own legislature.

Page No. 217

(Below matter is an update to First Schedule)

Updates/Amendments in First Schedule

Andhra Pradesh Reorganisation Act of 2014,

- The new state of Telangana was formed on 2nd June 2014.
- The Andhra Pradesh Reorganisation Act of 2014, commonly known as the Telangana Act, is an Act of Indian Parliament that bifurcated the state of Andhra Pradesh into Telangana and the residuary Andhra Pradesh state

Jammu and Kashmir Reorganisation Act, 2019*

- The act re-constituted the former state of Jammu and Kashmir into two Union Territories, one being Jammu and Kashmir and the other being Ladakh, with effect from October 31, 2019.

Total number of States and Union Territories of India at present

- India is a federal union comprising 28 states and 8 Union Territories, with a total of 36 entities.

Page No. 218

(Below matter is an update on Union Territories of India)

Union Territories of India (Updated)

- On 31st October, 2019 Jammu and Kashmir was removed from its status as a state and converted into Union Territory. Ladakh was separated from Jammu and Kashmir and was created as a separate Union Territory.
- The Union Territories of Dadra and Nagar Haveli and Daman & Diu were combined as one single Union Territory on 26th January 2020

The 8 Union territories of India are given below :

1. Ladakh
2. Jammu & Kashmir
3. Puducherry
4. Lakshadweep
5. Delhi
6. Chandigarh
7. Dadra and Nagar Haveli and Daman & Diu
8. Andaman and Nicobar Islands

Page No. 226

(Below matter is an update on the Fourth Schedule)

Updates in Fourth Schedule

- The Fourth Schedule was amended every time when a new state is formed or any amendment is made to the existing Acts.
- The present strength of Rajya Sabha is 245 members, of whom 233 are representatives of the States and Union Territories, and 12 are nominated by the President.

Allocation of seats in Rajya Sabha to each State/Union Territory

- Nominated Members 12
- Andhra Pradesh 11
- Arunachal Pradesh 1
- Assam 7
- Bihar 16
- Chhattisgarh 5
- Goa 1
- Gujarat 11
- Haryana 5
- Himachal Pradesh 3
- Jharkhand 6
- Karnataka 12
- Kerala 9
- Madhya Pradesh 11
- Maharashtra 19
- Manipur 1
- Meghalaya 1
- Mizoram 1
- Nagaland 1
- Odisha 10
- Punjab 7
- Rajasthan 10
- Sikkim 1
- Tamil Nadu 18
- Telangana 7
- Tripura 1
- Uttar Pradesh 31
- Uttarakhand 3
- West Bengal 16
- National Capital Territory of Delhi 3
- Puducherry 1
- Jammu & Kashmir 4

Total [245]

APPENDIX II

About Constitution Amendment and Key Amendments

How to Amend the Constitution?

- Constitution of India is a combination of flexibility and Rigidity
- Constitution must be amended if so required, but it must be protected from unnecessary and frequent changes.
- Constitution to be 'flexible' and at the same time 'rigid'.
- Flexible means open to changes and rigid means resistant to changes.

Constitutional makers' thoughts of flexibility

- Aware that there may be some faults or mistakes in the Constitution
- Constitution could not be totally free of errors.
- Whenever such mistakes would come to light it can easily amended

Constitutional makers' thoughts on Rigidity

- Strong centre
- Constitution was framing a federal polity
- The rights and powers of the States could not be changed without the consent of the States.
- Tough process of amendment

Amending Article of the Constitution

1. By a simple law of the Parliament (Example : Article 2 and 3)
2. By applying provisions of Article 368
   - The procedure of amendment in the constitution is laid down in Part XX (Article 368) of the Constitution of India.
   - It was borrowed from the South African constitution

Article 368 of Part XX of Constitution of India provides for two types of amendments.

1. Amendment can be made by special majority of the two houses of the Parliament.
2. It requires special majority of the Parliament and consent of half of the State legislatures.

Types of Amendments:

1. Simple Majority
   - This refers to the majority of more than 50% of the members present and voting.
2. Special Majority
   - A bill is said to be passed, if it is supported by a majority of 2/3rd members present and voting supported by over 50% of the total strength of the House.

Special Majority of Parliament and Consent of States

- This type of majority is required when federal structures need to be amended
- Apart from special majority by both the houses of the parliament, it requires consent of half of the state legislature by a simple majority
- There is no time limit within which states should give their consent to the bill

Kesavananda Bharati judgment

- Parliament cannot amend those parts which are part of the 'Basic Structure' of the constitution.
- Article 368: "Parliament under Article 368 can amend any part of the Constitution including the Fundamental Rights but without affecting the 'basic structure' of the Constitution".

Important Amendments to Indian Constitution

1st Amendment, 1950

Amend Articles/Schedules

- 15, 19, 85, 87, 174, 176, 341, 342, 372 and 376.
- Insert articles 31A and 31B
- Insert schedule 9.

Provisions

- Three more reasons for restricting freedom of speech and expression have been added: public order, friendly relations with foreign states, and incitement to an offence.
- It also made the restrictions 'reasonable' and, therefore, in nature, justiciable.
- Right to practice any profession or to carry on any trade or business as contained in Article 19 of the Constitution
- The Ninth Schedule along with Articles 31A and 31B were inserted in the Constitution to protect laws, such as the land reform and other laws, from being challenged in the courts on the ground of violation of fundamental rights.

7th Amendment, 1956

Amend articles/schedules

- 1, 3, 49, 80, 81, 82, 131, 153, 158, 168, 170, 171, 216, 217, 220, 222, 224, 230, 231 and 232.
- Insert articles 258A, 290A, 298, 350A, 350B, 371, 372A and 378A.
- Amend part 8.
- Amend schedules 1, 2, 4 and 7.

Provisions

- Reorganisation of states on linguistic lines
- Abolition of Class A, B, C, D states
- Introduction of Union territories.
- States reorganized into 14 states and 6 federal territories.
- Establishment of new High Courts, High Court Judges etc.

10th Amendment, 1961

Amend Article/Schedule

- Amend article 240.
- Amend schedule 1.

Provisions

- Incorporation of Dadra and Nagar Haveli as a Union Territory, consequent to acquisition from Portugal.

11th Amendment, 1961

- Amend articles 66 and 71.
- Proposed that election of President or Vice President could not be challenged on the ground of any vacancy in the appropriate electoral college.

12th Amendment, 1962

- Amend article 240 and Amend schedule 1
- Included Goa, Daman and Diu as a Union Territory and to amend Article 240 for the purpose.

13th Amendment, 1962

- Amend article 170.
- Insert new article 371A.
- Nagaland was formed with an agreement between Government of India and Naga People's Convention.

14th Amendment, 1962

- Amend articles 81 and 240.
- Insert article 239A.
- Amend schedules 1 and 4
- Pondicherry was included in the First Schedule as a Union Territory
- Creation of Legislature by Parliamentary law for Himachal Pradesh, Manipur, Tripura, Goa, Daman and Diu and Pondicherry

22nd Amendment, 1969

- Amend article 275.
- Insert articles 244A and 371B
- New autonomous state of Meghalaya with in the state of Assam.

24th Amendment, 1971

- Amend articles 13 and 368.
- Removed all doubts regarding the power of Parliament to amend the Constitution including the Fundamental Rights.
- Enable parliament to dilute fundamental rights through amendments to the constitution
- The President's assent to Constitutional Amendment Bill was made compulsory

25th Amendment Act, 1971

- Fundamental Right to Property was curtailed

26th Amendment Act 1971

- Amend article 366.
- Insert article 363A.
- Remove articles 291 and 362.
- Abolition of privy purse paid to former rulers of princely states which were incorporated into the Indian Republic.

31st Amendment, 1973

- Amend articles 81, 330 and 332.
- Increase size of Parliament from 525 to 545 seats.
- Reduced the upper limit for the representation of union territories from 25 members to 20.

35th Amendment, 1974

- Amend articles 80 and 81.
- Insert article 2A.
- Insert schedule 10.
- Conferred Sikkim the status of an associate State of Indian Union.

36th Amendment, 1975

- Amend articles 80 and 81.
- Insert article 371F.
- Amend schedules 1 and 4.
- Made Sikkim a full-fledged State of Indian Union and to include it in the First Schedule to the Constitution

40th Amendment Act, 1976

- Parliament was empowered to specify from time to time the limits of the territorial waters, the continental shelf, the exclusive economic zone (EEZ) and the maritime zones of India.

42nd Amendment, 1976

- Amend articles 31, 31C, 39, 55, 74, 77, 81, 82, 83, 100, 102, 103, 105, 118, 145, 150, 166, 170, 172, 189, 191, 192, 194, 208, 217, 225, 226, 227, 228, 311, 312, 330, 352, 353, 356, 357, 358, 359, 366, 368 and 371F.
- Insert articles 31D, 32A, 39A, 43A, 48A, 131A, 139A, 144A, 226A, 228A and 257A.
- Insert parts 4A and 14A.
- Amend schedule 7.
- Amendment passed during internal emergency
- Provides for curtailment of fundamental rights, imposes fundamental duties and changes to the basic structure of the constitution by making India a "Sovereign Socialist Secular Democratic Republic".
- The Supreme Court, in Minerva Mills v. Union of India, quashed the amendments to Articles 31C and 368 as it was in contravention with the basic structure of the Constitution.
- Ideals of socialism, secularism and the integrity of the nation were adopted
- Directive Principles were given precedence over Fundamental Rights
- Inserted a new chapter on the Fundamental Duties of citizens

44th Amendment, 1978

- Amend articles 19, 22, 30, 31A, 31C, 38, 71, 74, 77, 83, 103, 105, 123, 132, 133, 134, 139A, 150, 166, 172, 192, 194, 213, 217, 225, 226, 227, 239B, 329, 352, 356, 358, 359, 360 and 371F.
- Insert articles 134A and 361A.
- Remove articles 31, 257A and 329A.
- Amend part 12.
- Amend schedule 9.
- Amendment passed after revocation of internal emergency in the Country.
- Right to property from the list of fundamental rights and made it a legal right
- Provided ·armed rebellion· as one of the circumstances for declaration of emergency

52nd Amendment, 1985

- Amend articles 101, 102, 190 and 191.
- Insert schedule 10.
- Suitable provisions were made with respect to splits in and merger of political parties.
- Anti Defection Law - Provide disqualification of members from parliament and assembly in case of defection from one party to other.

- However, parts of the 10th Schedule to the Constitution of India was struck down by the Supreme Court in the case of KihotoHollohan v. Zachillhu 1992 SCR (1) 686, for being in contravention with Article 368 of the Constitution.

53rd Amendment, 1986

- Insert article 371G.
- Mostly revolved around the state of Mizoram.

55th Amendment, 1986

- Insert article 371H
- Conferred statehood on the Union Territory of Arunachal Pradesh

56th Amendment, 1987

- Insert article 371I.
- Union Territory of Daman and Diu and the formation of the state of Goa.

61st Amendment, 1989

- Amend article 326
- Reduction of the voting age from 21 to 18 years by amending Article 326

65th Amendment, 1989

- Amend article 338.
- National Commission for Scheduled Castes and Scheduled Tribes formed and its statutory powers specified in The Constitution.

66th Amendment, 1990

- Amend schedule 9
- Place land reform acts and amendments to these act under Schedule 9 of the constitution
- Andhra Pradesh, Bihar, Gujarat, Himachal Pradesh, Karnataka, Kerala, Madhya Pradesh, Maharashtra, Orissa, Rajasthan, Tamil Nadu, Uttar Pradesh, West Bengal and administration of the Union Territory of Puducherry were added to the Ninth Schedule
- Relating to land reforms and ceiling on agricultural land holdings)

69th Amendment, 1991

- Insert articles 239AA and 239AB.
- Union territory of Delhi was renamed as the National Capital Territory of Delhi

70th Amendment, 1992

- Amend articles 54 and 239AA.
- Included the elected members of the legislative assemblies of union territories (National Capital Territory of Delhi and Union Territory of Pondicherry)in the electoral college for the election of the President under Article 54 of the Constitution.

71st Amendment, 1992

- Amend schedule 8
- Included Konkani, Manipuri and Nepali languages in the Eighth Schedule to the Constitution.

73rd Amendment, 1993

- Insert part 9. Insert schedule 11.
- A new Part-IX and 11th Schedule were added in the Indian Constitution to recognize Panchayati Raj Institutions and provisions related to them
- Gave constitutional status to the Panchayati Raj Institutions

74th Amendment, 1993

- Insert part 9A, insert schedule 12, amend article 280.
- A new Part IX-A and 12th Schedule were added to the Indian Constitution
- Provisions for local administrative bodies in urban areas such as towns and cities were added.

86th Amendment, 2002

- Amend articles 45 and 51A.
- Insert article 21A.
- Article 21A deals with Right to Education that "the State shall provide free and compulsory education to all children of the age of six to fourteen years"
- A new Fundamental Duty under Article 51 A was added - "It shall be the duty of every citizen of India who is a parent or guardian to provide opportunities for education to his child or ward between the age of six and fourteen years"

87th Amendment, 2003

- Amend articles 81, 82, 170 and 330.
- 2001 national census population figures were to be used for state-wise distribution of parliamentary seats.

89th Amendment, 2003

- Amend article 338.
- Insert article 338A.
- The National Commission for Scheduled Castes and Scheduled Tribes was bifurcated into The National Commission for Scheduled Castes and The National Commission for Scheduled Tribes.

91st Amendment, 2003

- Amend articles 75 and 164.
- Insert article 361B.
- Amend schedule 10.
- Restricts the size of the Council of Ministers in the Union Government and in a State Government to fifteen percent of the total number of legislative members.

92st Amendment, 2003

- Amend schedule 8.
- Bodo, Dogri, Santali and Maithali were added as official languages to the 8th Schedule
- Total official languages were increased from 18 to 22

94th Amendment, 2006

- Amend article 164.
- To provide for a Minister of Tribal Welfare in newly created Jharkhand and Chhattisgarh States including Madhya Pradesh and Orissa.

97th Amendment, 2012

- Amend Art 19 and added Art 43B and Part IXB
- Co-operative Societies were granted constitutional status
- Right to form cooperative societies made a fundamental right (Article 19)
- A new Directive Principle of State Policy (Article 43-B) to promote cooperative societies

- A new part IX-B was added in the constitution for cooperative societies
- Added the words "or co-operative societies" after the word "or unions" in Article 19(l)(c) and insertion of article 43B i.e., Promotion of Co-operative Societies and added Part-IXB i.e., The Co-operative Societies.
- In July 2021 Supreme Court Struck Part of the amendment as it was not ratified by the states.

99th Amendment, 2012

- Insertion of new articles 124A, 124B and 124C. Amendments to Articles 127, 128, 217, 222, 224A, 231.
- Formation of a National Judicial Appointments Commission.
- The amendment was struck down by the Supreme Court on 16 October 2015.

100th Amendment, 2015

- Amendment of First Schedule to Constitution
- Exchange of certain enclave territories with Bangladesh and conferment of citizenship rights to residents of enclaves conseq uent to signing of Land Boundary Agreement (LBA) Treaty between India and Bangladcsh.

101st Amendment, 2017

- Introduction of "The Goods and Services Tax (GST)" and provision of compensation to states for loss of revenue on account of introduction of goods and services tax. Addition of articles 246A, 269A, 279A. Deletion of Article 268A.
- Amendment of articles 248, 249, 250, 268, 269, 270, 271, 286, 366, 368, Sixth Schedule, Seventh Schedule.

102nd Amendment, 2018

- Constitutional status to National Commission for Backward Classes.
- Addition of articles 338B, 342A, and Added Clause 26C. Modification of articles 338, 366

103rd Amendment, 2019

- A maximum of 10% Reservation for Economically Weaker Sections (EWSs) of citizens of classes other than the classes mentioned in clauses (4) and (5) of Article 15, i.e. Classes other than socially and educationally backward classes of citizens or the Scheduled Castes and the Scheduled Tribes.
- Inserted Clause [6] under Article 15 as well as Inserted Clause [6] under Article 16.

104th Amendment, 2020

- To extend the reservation of seats for SCs and STs in the Lok Sabha and states assemblies from Seventy years to Eighty years. Removed the reserved seats for the Anglo-Indian community in the Lok Sabha and state assemblies.
- Amend article 334.

105th Amendment, 2021

- Amended Article 338B, 342A and 366
- To designed to clarify that the states can maintain the "state list" of OBCs.
- To restore the power of the state governments to identify Other Backward Classes (OBCs) that are socially and educationally backward.
- This amendment annulled the Supreme Court judgement of 11 May 2021, which had empowered only the Central government for such identification

SUBJECT INDEX